*He called her
his little Zahareña—
a woman of forbidding
and inaccessible virtue. . . .*

"Can you never leave me alone?" Livia hissed. "Do you never tire of taking a woman who doesn't want you?"

"In time, it is possible you will learn to love me," Tariq said.

"Nothing is possible with us!"

"I will show you what is possible with us!" he roared, and lunged across the bed and caught her shoulder in a viselike grip.

She stared at the dark figure silhouetted against a brilliant shaft of moonlight. "He's trapped me!" she thought furiously. "Here I lie, naked as a statue carved from marble— and as cold and lifeless as a statue I will be!"

His lips trailed down the curve of her neck, seeking the soft fullness of her breasts. His hands, warm and sure, stroked the long lithe curves of her body, and she squeezed her eyes shut, determined to resist his tender caresses. Gooseflesh rose on her skin and, in a length of time too brief to measure, the alabaster statue became like clay in his hands.

Also published by Pocket Books/Richard Gallen

This Perilous Ecstasy
  by
Jeanne Sommers

Pillars of Heaven
  by
Leila Lyons

WINGS OF MORNING
Dee Stuart

PUBLISHED BY POCKET BOOKS NEW YORK

A POCKET BOOKS/RICHARD GALLEN *Original* publication

POCKET BOOKS, a Simon & Schuster division of
GULF & WESTERN CORPORATION
1230 Avenue of the Americas, New York, N.Y. 10020

ISBN: 0-671-41294-9

First Pocket Books printing September, 1980

10 9 8 7 6 5 4 3 2 1

POCKET and colophon are trademarks of Simon & Schuster.

Printed in the U.S.A.

For my mother

Chapter 1

Thunder rumbling across the snow-crested peaks of the lofty Serrania de Ronda woke her. Closer now, it erupted upon the town of Zahara perched on the crest of the mountain frontier between Ronda and Medina Sidonia. The tempest had raged for three days and nights, ever since the Feast of the Most Blessed Nativity.

Safe and warm in her bed, Olivia smiled to herself. The old year was not dying without a protest. Or was the storm heralding the arrival of 1481?

She snuggled under the warm covers and closed her eyes, willing sleep, to dream of Don Alonzo de Aguilar. Conjuring up his image, her heart beat faster. Aguilar, tall, lithe, yet muscular, sitting like a man of steel on his powerful war-horse. A captain in King Ferdinand's army, he was among the flower of Christian chivalry and one of the most valiant of the zealous knights driven to wipe out the infidels who desecrated the sacred soil of Andalusia. In fact, he was renowned throughout Spain for the very qualities his name, Aguilar—eagle—implied. The strength, skill and bravery with which he swooped down upon the enemy like a magnificent bird of prey, caused all to call him Aguilar—family, friends, and enemies alike.

Aguilar! Her fearless, gallant cavalier! She smiled in anticipation of when Ferdinand's campaign to rid the Moors from the Kingdom of Granada would end and her dream of happiness would be fulfilled. That day she, Olivia Larreta, would become Aguilar's bride.

1

Secure in the cragged fortress of Zahara, Livia no longer suffered her childhood terrors of the Moors. The town was guarded by a strong castle on a cliff so high that it was said to be above the drift of clouds. The impregnable security of Zahara had become so proverbial throughout Spain that a woman of forbidding and inaccessible virtue was called a Zahareña.

A crash of thunder, a brilliant flash of light, brought her to her feet. She dashed to the window and peered out through the driving snow—then drew in her breath sharply. In the glare of smoking torches, she saw the great wooden gate of the fortress swing open and the shining helmets and scarlet cloaks of soldiers galloping into Zahara. She let out a relieved sigh. The troops were returning from a foray. As the cavaliers drew nearer and the torches lighted their bronzed, bearded features, a strangled scream burst from her lips. These were not Ferdinand's men, but Moors who had adopted the Spanish mode of dress!

Livia's terrified gaze swept over the towers and bulwarks. The infidels had set scaling ladders against the walls and, swords in hand, were mounting the battlements. Urged on by the roll of drums and the blast of trumpets, they swarmed over the ramparts.

Townspeople flung open their doors and soldiers, buckling on their cuirasses, bolted into the street, shouting alarm to the sleeping citizens. Livia watched paralyzed with horror; as the soldiers rushed from their quarters, most were intercepted and cut down. Those who escaped wheeled about in confusion, not knowing where to strike.

Livia whirled from the window and sped across the tiled floor, down the dark hallway to her brother's room.

"Julian, Julian!" she shrieked. "Wake up!" She spun about and pounded on the door of the room where her father and stepmother lay sleeping. "Father! Margareta! Wake up! Hurry! The infidels are upon us!"

Julian's door was flung open, and a vigorous,

square-built youth stood frowning in irritation, his eyes
heavy-lidded with sleep.

"Olivia! *Madre de Dios!* Have you gone mad?"

Her parents' door burst open, and Inigo Larreta,
clad in a heavy brown wool robe stood on the threshold. He held a lamp whose glow illuminated a lined face
above a gray beard. Age had not borne him down. He
still evoked great dignity. At his elbow appeared
Margareta's squat figure; her black hair shot with
silver, her flashing eyes undimmed by time and trouble.
They stared at Livia, mouths agape in dazed stupefac-
tion.

"The Moors! The Moors are upon us, attacking the
town!"

Julian let out an incredulous oath and darted back
into his room. Moments later he emerged, garbed in a
sheepskin jacket and leather breeches, his sword in
hand. Murder flashed in his eyes. "Stay inside, all of
you!" he shouted. He bolted past them and was gone.

As though galvanized into action by Julian's departure, Inigo Larreta raced down the stairs, snatched up
his sword and dashed through the doorway into the
pelting snow.

Livia turned toward her dazed stepmother and
tugged on her arm. "Quickly, Margareta. We must lock
the door and shove the chest against it—"

She halted abruptly as Margareta fell to her knees
and buried her face in her hands. "Julian, Inigo!"
Margareta wailed. "Come back!"

Livia gripped her elbows and jerked her to her feet.
"They've gone. Quickly now. Help me!"

Like a blind woman, hands outstretched imploringly,
Margareta stumbled down the stairs after Livia, crying
at the top of her voice, "Julian, Inigo! Come back!"

Livia ran to the open door and seized the handle. In
the instant before she slammed it shut, Margareta
dashed into the street, shouting, "Julian, Inigo! Come
back, come back!"

Livia, unmindful that she wore only a linen shift,

darted after her into the winter storm. The narrow street teemed with terrified inhabitants running about like crazed animals, their grotesque shadows thrown against the ancient ochre walls.

The clash of weapons and shouts resounded through the streets. People fled their homes. Mothers dragged small children by the hand. Others desperately tried to load their possessions into carts, hoping to escape.

Fighting down the panic that threatened to paralyze her, Livia pushed through the throng. "Margareta!" she shouted. "Margareta!" In an effort to keep sight of her crazed stepmother, she stood on tiptoe to see above the heads of the crowd. The gilt helmets and turbaned heads of the Moors, their silken banners fluttering aloft as they charged through the streets shouting the war cry, struck terror in Livia's heart.

At the head of the powerful force rode King Muley Abdul Hassan, fierce sultan of Granada. The slashing scimitars of his men glinted in the light of burning houses as they rode through the town, maiming, killing all who barred their way.

Foot soldiers commandeered carts which they heaped with booty: rugs, chests, jewelry and money they had plundered. Margareta's gray-haired figure had disappeared from sight. Panic constricted Livia's throat. Frantically she tried to push through the mob that had closed in around her. Her dark hair, wet with drifting snowflakes, straggled over her shoulders. Her shift clung to her body like an icy sheath and her bare feet were numbed by the frozen ground. She shivered uncontrollably. Metal against metal rang in her ears as the Moors and Spaniards fought to the death.

Suddenly Livia felt a hand clutch her arm in an iron grip. She spun about and looked up into the leering, sweating face of a Moor. His thick lips were slack with lust and his evil eyes gleamed as they traveled down the soft curves of her body revealed by the sodden shift. A scream rose in her throat, ending in a strangled cry.

Her knee came up and she kicked viciously, aiming

at his groin. Her bare foot struck his boot and a searing pain shot up her leg. As she lunged backward and twisted to one side, the man's sweaty palm slipped from her waist. She broke into a run. She had gained only a few lengths when she was hemmed in by a wall of swarming citizens and soldiers.

She looked around desperately, searching for an opening in the crowd. The next instant, she felt a hand grasp the back of her shift, yanking her backward. The thin fabric gave way, ripping to the waist. She stumbled and fell to her knees. Half-blinded by snow and tears streaking down her face, she crawled toward the side of the street. Rough hands jerked her to her feet. "A prize!" the Moor yelled.

Livia opened her mouth to cry out, but no sound came out. She had been taught Arabic and understood only too clearly what was being said. Another Moor grasped Livia and clutched her tightly to his chest. "I'll take this one!" he shouted exultantly. "She is too much for you!"

At that moment, her first captor descended upon them, his face contorted in fury. "The woman is mine!" With a bellow, he swung his scimitar with demonic rage, dealt his comrade a stunning blow to the head, then tossed Livia upon a cart loaded with rugs. His furious companions bore down on him.

Brandishing his scimitar, he roared, "Hold! The woman is yours after I'm done with her!"

Livia struggled to her knees and had gained the far side of the cart when her assailant sprang upon her. With a jubilant laugh, he rolled her onto her back and straddled her legs, pinning her down. The sound of her own screams deafened her. He clutched the hem of her gown, whipped it up about her hips and with one hand, began to explore the soft curves of her body. With the other, he fumbled at his waist, loosening his belt.

Livia's hands flew up and her nails scraped down the leering face that hovered above her, leaving a red-seamed trail in the swarthy flesh.

His head jerked back. Once again her clawing fingers found their mark. Her nails raked his face and sank into his eyes. The man exploded in a howl of pain and struck her violently across the cheek. Her head twisted savagely to one side, her eyes squeezed shut, her mouth tightened in a grimace of pain. Through waves of terror, she heard a wild shout and the terrible hiss of a blade slicing the air in a death-dealing arc.

A heavy weight collapsed upon her, knocking the breath from her lungs. The weight slid abruptly from her body. Livia's eyelids flew open and she gazed up into the darkest, most penetrating eyes she had ever beheld, fierce as the eyes of a desert hawk. Petrified, she gazed at the Moorish commander mounted on an ebony war-horse. His gilt helmet gleamed in the torchlight and his crimson cloak swirled about him. Broad-shouldered, his very carriage bespoke power. A full beard, black as his eyes, framed an oval face seemingly tanned by the desert. His features were expressionless.

Never taking his eyes from hers, he wiped his scimitar clean of blood and slid it into a richly enameled sheath. He leaned down and, with one swift motion of his powerful arm, swept her from the cart and set her sideways before him on his charger. An uncontrollable trembling seized her; whether from the freezing snow stinging her bare flesh, or from fright, she could not have said.

Once again the Moor leaned down from his mount, swept a green and gold tapestry from the heap in the cart and flung it about her shoulders. He wheeled his horse about and urged him into a trot down the street cluttered with the bodies of the vanquished.

Speechless with fear, Livia tightly clutched the tapestry, trying to draw some warmth from its heavy folds. The struggle within the fortress appeared to be over. The men of Zahara had fought gallantly to save their homes and families, only to lose life themselves, she thought morosely. Those who were not slain were scurrying to take refuge in secret places. Others surrendered.

The storm continued its howling. Above it she heard the blast of a trumpet echoing through the streets, summoning all the citizens to assemble, unarmed, in the public square.

The Moorish commander drew rein beside his king and sat silent and unmoving, watching. Tears stung Livia's eyes at the sight of her friends and neighbors, crowded together, half-naked, surrounded by guards. Her heart contracted at the sound of their pitiful pleas shredding the winter night.

The fiery Muley Abul Hassan, seated on his white horse, turned a deaf ear to their cries. His hooded eyes met those of her captor and he raised a hand in a gesture of dismissal. "Return to our fortress and advise the council to prepare a victory celebration!"

Chapter 2

The terse order of the Moorish king struck fresh terror into Livia's heart. What would become of her now?

Her captor turned his stallion about, issued a sharp command to his band of soldiers, then urged his steed into a trot toward the great western gate which led from the fortress. An icy fear coursed through her. Surely he would not carry her away from Zahara!

"Unhand me, you brigand!" Livia demanded, struggling to slide from the horse's back.

Ignoring her, the Moor flung an arm about her, imprisoning Livia against his chest. She could read no expression in the bronzed face, nor in the burning eyes that regarded her impassively from under straight thick brows.

Rage and indignation drove out her fear. "You must let me go!" she shouted.

His visage remained impassive. As though she had not spoken, he spurred his mount onward, down the street strewn with the dead and dying. Livia's heart quailed at the sounds of their moans. As they neared the gate, her gaze fell upon a pale lined face with a head of iron-gray locks among the sprawled bodies.

"Father!" she screamed, clawing at the arm that held her. "Let me go! At once!"

The Moor made no reply, but stared straight ahead, his eyes unyielding as he urged his steed down a steep trail lighted only by the flickering torches held aloft by the advance guard.

Enraged, Livia twisted to face him and pounded on

his chest with clenched fists. "You must let me go! I must see to my family!"

His arm tightened about her slender waist. His mouth stretched in a grim line, but he made no reply.

"Listen to me!" cried Livia. "My father and stepmother may be wounded—dying! They will surely freeze to death lying in the street among the fallen. And if by chance they have lived through your vile attack, they are too old, too feeble to survive the march with your prisoners to . . . to wherever you came from."

"Granada."

"Granada!" she breathed in a voice barely above a whisper. Her hands tightened on the tapestry she clutched under her chin. From Aguilar she had heard tales of how the Moors treated their prisoners there. After herding them like cattle on an interminable march through the mountains, they were imprisoned in the bowels of the Alhambra, put in chains and forgotten; or they were thrust into deep caves on the hillsides where they were locked up at night and rented out by day to be exploited for manual labor. Only the unlucky lived. The hope of being rescued in a year or two, or three, by one of the armies of Isabella and Ferdinand could not sustain them, especially elderly people like her own parents.

Her blood seemed to freeze. Fear mixed with anger coursed through her. In a voice that shook, she asked, "Are we to be cast into one of your filthy pestholes and left to rot? Or is it your intention to use us ill, as your heathen cutthroats attempted to use me?"

The commander's cold, appraising gaze swept over her dark hair flowing from her high rounded forehead, the alabaster perfection of her skin, the wide-set brown eyes that gave her an appealing air of innocence, the generous mouth whose full lips promised delight, and down her body whose rounded breasts and long slender thighs were molded by the fabric she clung to. Implacable, his expression gave away nothing.

"I know not of your parents' fate. *You* shall be a prize for Prince Boabdil, son of King Muley. Boabdil searches for a suitable bride. You are the fairest of the jewels taken in Zahara. In you he will be well pleased."

Livia drew herself stiffly erect and turned to stare directly into his piercing eyes. With haughty contempt she replied, "I shall be a bride—the bride of Don Alonzo de Aguilar, captain in King Ferdinand's army, to whom I am betrothed."

He gazed at her unmoved. "You shall do as I say."

She regarded him for a long moment. Desperately she searched her mind for a way to reach this stone-hearted infidel. If she could not save herself, perhaps she could still save her family. Her lips pressed together in a determined line.

"Order your guards to release my parents and my brother Julian, and I will go with you to Granada."

His straight brows rose in wonder. "You would give up your own freedom in exchange for that of your family?"

Livia nodded. "I am willing to make a pact with you." It was not as great a sacrifice as the Moor imagined, for Aguilar had told her that all Andalusia, and Granada in particular, was a thorn in the flesh of their sovereigns; one which was to be pulled without delay. Surely Aguilar would rescue her before a marriage could take place.

The Moor's brow furrowed in anger. "You dare to offer to make a pact with me, Tariq Ibn Ziyah, commander-in-chief of King Muley's army?"

Her Spanish pride piqued, Livia's eyes flashed fire. "And I am Señorita Olivia Larreta. The House of Larreta is an old and noble one. If you destroy us, it will go hard with you when Ferdinand takes Granada!"

The man let out a shout of mirthless laughter. "We Arabs have held domination over Andalusia for seven hundred years. We've no intention of giving up the paradise for which our ancestors fought and died! As King Muley told your sovereign when he ceased paying tribute, the mints of Granada no longer coin gold, but steel." His expression turned solemn. "In any case, I do not make pacts with captives." There was an ominous note of finality in his voice.

Livia stared at him, breathing defiance, "Then put me to the sword!"

"That I shall not do!"

A sudden flare of torchlight illuminated the harsh lines of his face, deep-set eyes, aquiline nose and his mouth set in a remorseless line above his full beard. In that instant she knew she could never persuade this man to do her bidding against his will.

Tears of rage sprang to her eyes. "I would prefer death to being your prisoner!"

His voice, quiet and deadly, sent a shiver down her spine.

"A prisoner does not strike bargains with her captors. You would do well to remember it. You will become the bride of Prince Boabdil."

"That *I* shall not do!" Livia said scornfully.

"You will do as I say!" replied Tariq in a tone as hard and implacable as the rocky terrain of Zahara. And yet, Livia reminded herself, the great walled cliffs of Zahara had been scaled; she would find a way to break the will of this man. She would make him rue the day he had ever set eyes upon her!

She turned from him then, straining to see through the darkness. And as they proceeded ever-downward along the steep, narrow trail, she fought the panic that threatened to rob her of her last strength as well as the grief that would have brought her to submission.

At length, lulled by the swaying movement of Tariq's mount and warmed by his powerful body as he held her securely in his arms, her eyelids grew heavy and exhaustion overcame her.

What seemed like hours later, she was awakened by the cessation of motion and the mutters of soldiers stirring about. Strong arms lifted her gently down and set her on her feet.

"Here we make camp until daylight," Tariq said brusquely.

Wide awake and rested, Livia glanced quickly about her. The snowfall had stopped, and the troops had halted beneath a lone stand of pines. The men had tethered their horses to nearby saplings and set about erecting tents for the use of their officers. Tariq gestured toward a white tent set a short distance apart from the others which Livia surmised was reserved for their commander-in-chief.

Livia shook her head defiantly.

When she did not move, Tariq grasped her elbow, propelled her through the doorway and motioned toward a thick bed of carpets. "You will sleep there."

Once again Livia stood unmoving, her chin raised stubbornly. "Where do the prisoners rest for the night?" she demanded. "I wish to search for my family. I shall stay the night with them."

"We are the advance guard. The prisoners march well to the rear of us. You will stay the night with me."

Indignation brought color flooding to Livia's cheeks. She said icily, "I've no intention of sharing my bed with you!"

"It is *my* bed," Tariq said coldly.

Livia whirled about and broke into a run. Before she had taken three strides, Tariq reached out, caught her shoulder and spun her about. He scooped her up in his arms, crossed the room and flung her down upon the pile of carpets, then whipped his crimson cloak from his shoulders and dropped it on the foot of the temporary bed. She had lost hold of the tapestry which had slipped down about her waist along with her torn shift. Suddenly she was aware of Tariq's jet eyes roving down her nude body as he divested himself of the heavy suit of chain mail he wore over a black and gold tunic. A slow smile spread across his face; whether in approval or amusement at her discomfiture, she had no way of knowing. Frantically, she pulled the material about her and sat back on her heels, her black hair tumbled about her shoulders, her dark eyes flashing. "Barbarian!"

"Enough!" roared Tariq. "Lie down and be silent." Never taking his penetrating gaze from her, he continued to disrobe.

She opened her mouth to protest; then, thinking it wise not to anger him further, she cast him a scornful glance and eased down upon the soft bedding where she lay rigid as one dead. Her mind churned with but one thought: escape.

If only she could get to the horses. She was an expert rider. She knew the trails surrounding Zahara as well as the byways of Seville, where she had been born. Somehow she would find her way to Cordoba, to Aguilar. And if she did not find her way to Cordoba, any fate was better than being forced to marry Boabdil. A bitter smile twisted Livia's lips. How ironic that she and her family had fled to Zahara for safety; and where were they now? Her customary optimism asserted itself. Perhaps it was not her father lying among the fallen. Perhaps tomorrow she would find him and Margareta among the prisoners. And handsome, irrepressible Julian—always with an eye to the main chance. How many girlish hearts would be broken if he were to pass from their lives! But then he had been in many a scrape from which he'd managed to extricate himself. Maybe his luck would hold. She smothered a deep sigh and turned her attention to Tariq.

Through slitted lids, Livia watched him silhouetted in the gleam of moonlight that slanted through the tent flap. He had discarded his cloak and armor and held in his hand a heavy belt of golden filigree studded with precious gems. She closed her eyes against the sight of him clad only in a white *galabia,* or shirt, and trousers. Moments later, she felt the weight of his body beside her as he stretched out on the rugs, pulled up his heavy cloak and spread it over them. Every nerve in her tensed and she readied herself for flight.

As Tariq's strong hand gripped her wrist, she started up, crying out in protest. She felt his breath warm on her neck as his deep voice sliced through the night.

"You need have no fear for your virtue. And I'll have no fear for your safety, should you try to depart." Suddenly she felt cold metal encircle her wrist and a tug as he fastened the other end of the gold belt securely to his own wrist. "This way we shall both sleep well."

He remained still for a few seconds. Then Livia felt a gentle pull on the belt as he drew her down so that they lay facing each other side by side. She watched him, mesmerized.

He reached out and traced the outline of her nose with a single finger, passing it over her lips and chin. Breathless and tembling, she felt that they were merging, his warmth flowing around her, into her, their separateness dissolving. He raised his head and with a hungry, searching tenderness, kissed her and then withdrew his mouth to brush her breasts with his lips. Aroused by the lightness of his touch, she burned with expectation, with desire mingled with fear. Livia was filled with an agonizing and humiliating sense of her vulnerability.

She turned away from him, raising clenched fists to her eyes, knowing she was helpless to resist him. The golden chain stretched taut between them. She heard him sigh, and once again felt the chain bite into her wrist. But when she lay back, she saw Tariq gazing at her with eyes full of amusement, as though satisfied with the knowledge that had he wished, he could have conquered her aristocratic pride.

The deep murmur of his voice, tinged with fear, came through the darkness. "Do you imagine I'd offer our prince a gift of tarnished gold?"

Her heart beat violently and then slowed with the understanding that he was not going to take her. Tears of relief stung her eyelids, mixed with anger at him and at herself that he had so easily brought her to the verge of submitting to him. He spoke no more, and soon his deep even breathing told her he slept.

Memories of Zahara flashed through her mind: The horror of the Moors galloping down upon the sleeping fortress—and townspeople running, screaming in terror, cut down mercilessly—her family scattered. The lean, gray-haired form she had seen lying among the bodies could not have been her father—could not be!

Livia was paralyzed by a merciful numbness, a feeling of such desolation that she felt no more pain or grief. She started up at an eerie sound, listening. It was only the mournful hoot of an owl.

Chapter 3

The touch of a hand clasping her shoulder woke Livia. Startled, her eyes flew open, and she gazed up into the unfathomable face of the Moor who knelt at her side, garbed for battle. For a moment he regarded her intently and she thought she saw a look of misgiving in his dark eyes that quickly vanished under veiled lids.

He spoke in a low voice, used to command. "Dawn is upon us. Rouse yourself at once. We make ready to depart."

Livia's gaze traveled upward. The white tent, translucent in the gray early morning light, was dappled with shadows of pine branches overhead. She felt a chill and was suddenly aware that the tapestry had slipped from her shoulders and, at the same time, that the Moor had unfastened the golden chain that had bound them together. Her eyes blazed defiance and she lay unmoving.

Tariq's hand shot out. He gripped her arm and, rising to his feet, jerked her up to face him. His piercing eyes challenged hers. "March!"

A shiver shook Livia's slender body. Gooseflesh rose on her skin and tautened the nipples on her high, firm breasts. He bent down swiftly, picked up the rumpled tapestry and draped it awkwardly about her. Her chin lifted and with stately grace she swept through the doorway.

They broke camp and moved on, more swiftly now. Livia, seated before Tariq astride his great black charger, bore herself with a proud air. In the glare of the rising sun, she discerned that Tariq had about him a look of commanding brutality. There could be no mistake. He was accustomed to power. He had earned it and he expected to be obeyed. She steeled herself against him, and her soft, full lips curved in a determined smile. The Moor could conquer all of Spain, but he would never conquer her!

Although she was well aware that the ancient kingdom of Granada was one of the most mountainous regions of Spain, her gaze traveled over the vast sierras—the chains of mountains—in awestruck wonder. Destitute of shrub or trees, and mottled with variegated marbles and granites, the mountains raised their sunburnt summits against a deep blue sky. Yet, far below in their rugged bosoms, Livia beheld fertile valleys where in summer the desert and the garden vied for mastery and the very rocks seemed to yield the fig, the orange and the citron and to blossom with myrtle and rose.

Now and again in the wild passes, Livia caught sight of walled towns and villages built like eagle eyries among the cliffs and surrounded by Moorish battlements. Often they were obliged to alight and lead their mounts up and down steep paths that resembled the broken steps of a staircase. At times the road wound along dizzy precipices, without parapets to guard them from the gulfs below. Other times they struggled through ravines, worn by water torrents.

They halted only to sleep and eat. The Moors had taken care to have their *alforjas*—the saddlebags of coarse cloth—well stocked with provisions and their *betas*—the leather bottles—filled with choice Valdepeñas wine for a supply across the barren mountains. As Tariq tilted his *beta* to his lips, Livia studied him covertly. His muscular form evidenced strength; his complexion, dark and sunburnt, spoke of much time in the saddle; his eyes were resolute, but his expression was quiet, except when kindled by sudden emotion. Though she found his demeanor frank, manly and courteous, Livia remained on guard; when she faced him, it was with calm defiance. If he thought she would grovel at his feet, pleading for mercy, he would soon see how wrong he was. She would show him she possessed a strength of will that few *men* possessed.

As their animals wound slowly along the crags, Livia stiffened her spine, pushing down her fear as they descended precipitous cliffs, silhouetted in full relief against the sky. Later she toiled up the deep, arid chasms below them.

Day blended into night, night into day, until at last the snow-clad mountains gave way to the *vega*, a broad barren plain that stretched as far as the eye could see. As her gaze swept over the sere winter landscape, she glimpsed scattered villas or a straggling herd of cattle attended by a lonely herdsman, motionless as a statue, with his long pike rising into the air.

At sunset, after a day of hard riding, they emerged from a grove of olive trees now shorn of leaves. Livia drew in her breath sharply. In the distance rose the Moorish capital of Granada dominated by the ruddy towers of the fortress of the Alhambra, while far above it the snowy summits of the Sierra Nevada shone like silver. The day was without a cloud, and the heat of the sun warmed them despite the cool breezes from the mountains. Livia's fears returned in full measure, and she clutched the tapestry more tightly about her. As they galloped across the *vega*, her heart seemed to thunder in time to the pounding of the horse's hooves.

As they drew nearer, she saw that the walls of the fortress stretched irregularly around the crest of a lofty hill that overlooked the city. Now, in the rays of the setting sun, they glowed crimson. It came to her that the Arabic name—*al Qal' Al-Hamra*—the Red Citadel, had been corrupted by the Spaniards to the Alhambra. Aguilar had once told her that the entire kingdom of Granada with its encircling mountains and forts was one vast fortress, and the Alhambra in its midst was a

citadel in itself, one of the strongest in the whole of
Spain. Hidden at its center lay the king's palace.

Livia stared up at the walls studded with watchtowers
and battlements, the crescent banner fluttering in the
breeze, and a shiver shook her from head to toe. An
overwhelming premonition surged through her that
once inside, she would never escape. She had never
been wanting in courage and now with a sinking feeling
inside her breast, she sensed she would need every bit
she possessed.

Chapter 4

Livia squared her shoulders, bracing herself for whatever was to come, determined not to let this heathen see the alarm that engulfed her. They galloped on between hedges of aloes and Indian figs, through a wilderness of orchards and vines. As they paraded through the gates of the city, news of their victory spread. Throngs of people awaiting their return, greeted them with cheers.

Livia clenched her jaw and closed her ears against the roaring crowd as they crossed Vivarambla Square and passed the main street of the great bazaar, a maze of narrow alleys and small shops. Her apprehension rose, and she could not still the tremors that shook her. If Tariq noticed, he gave no sign of it.

The sun was setting when they ascended a steep, narrow ravine alongside the ramparts of the fortress and came to a halt before a stone gateway at the foot of a huge square tower. A guard motioned them on, and they passed through the massive gate under an arch half the height of the tower bearing an engraved hand on the keystone.

As if to distract her, Tariq murmured close to her ear, "The hand symbolizes the five precepts of the Koran. We pass through the Gate of Justice."

"Justice!" blurted Livia. "From the Moors! Surely you jest!"

Tariq made no reply, but as the horse trotted on through another gate surmounted by a small loft with a double window he said, "And the Wine Gate, where untaxed wine is sold to the inhabitants."

"Wine!" exclaimed Livia. "To Moslems! You mock me!"

Once again he made no reply, but guided his mount through an open passageway into a large plaza and along a steep ravine.

"The place of the cisterns," said Tariq. "We have cut great reservoirs from the rock to supply us with water."

She compressed her lips in a tight line. Whether the Moor took pride in his fortress and wished to boast of its marvels, or whether he thought to alleviate her anxiety by distracting her, she didn't know. Whichever it was, she thought venomously, he was not succeeding. She shuddered as the great black stallion cantered through the crowded *medina*—or town—lying in the shadow of the palace, scattering the populace before them.

Tariq drew up abruptly, leaped from his horse and flung the reins to an attendant. Wordlessly, he lifted Livia down and led her past porters' lodges and guardhouses, past patios graced by gardens and pools, through a simple portal into the interior of the palace.

Her apprehensions were forgotten as she stood surveying the scene before her. A sense of unreality gripped her and Livia felt as though she had been transported into another time. A vast rectangular court paved with white marble stretched before her dazzled eyes. At each end a row of slender columns supported a gallery of lacy fretwork. Dominating the court, bordered by a hedge of myrtles, lay an immense pool in which gleaming goldfish darted.

Tariq strode briskly forward, dragging Livia along at his side, unmindful of her frantic clutching at the tapestry.

They proceeded into an oblong anteroom whose lower walls were adorned with colorful mosaic tiles above which intricate geometric designs were carved in plaster. Sounds of music and revelry seemed to echo from the ceiling. Glancing upward, Livia saw an elaborately carved dome of cedarwood. Her gaze traveled downward. Beneath an archway on the far side of the hall were massive wooden doors from behind which the sounds of the festivity issued.

"It appears that word of your victory has preceded your arrival," Livia noted disdainfully. Drawing herself up to her full height she said, "Surely you would not subject your prisoner—this jewel you have captured for your prince—to the ridicule of his court. Take me away at once!"

As though she had not spoken, Tariq, still gripping her wrist, strode swiftly across the hall and threw open the doors that gave onto a huge square room. Livia gasped in astonishment. In the golden light of the setting sun that streamed in through tall, deeply recessed windows, she saw a scene of revelry which defied any she had witnessed in the most frivolous courts of Spain.

Voices and laughter echoed under the lofty ceiling while men and women wearing vividly colored silks, brocades and velvets adorned with precious gems reclined on furs, carpets and bright cushions strewn about the floor. They helped themselves from brass trays laden with stuffed lamb, veal and chicken, and fine ceramic plates heaped with grapes, figs and nuts, candies and pastries. Others drank from silver goblets filled by slaves from pitchers flowing with wine. Smoke from charcoal braziers and oil lamps mingled with the spicy aroma of sandalwood and curled upward to the domed ceiling.

Someone was singing a plaintive tune in a high-pitched minor key. A bevy of bright-eyed slave girls in colorful gauzy tunics and trousers writhed and whirled seductively to the accompaniment of lutes, violins and tambourines.

Livia's gaze was drawn to the far side of the room where, in a central recess, a man garbed in red velvet robes embroidered in gold sprawled upon the royal throne. In his white turban gleamed a ruby encircled by diamonds. Was this Prince Boabdil? To her astonishment, his complexion was fair, his hair and beard flaxen. He was somewhat short of handsome and appeared mild-mannered. At his side, resting within the curve of his arm, sat a woman whom Livia judged to be a year or two older than herself and beside whose beauty every other woman in the room paled. Crowning a doll-like face, her glossy black hair coiled high on her head was entwined with emeralds and pearls. Over trousers of rich green brocade, she wore a tunic of embroidered gold cloth which accentuated her voluptuous figure. Around her neck sparkled a magnificent necklace wrought of gold filigree inlaid with emeralds and diamonds. The prince was smiling down upon the woman who gazed fatuously up into his face.

Suddenly aware of her own appearance, her hair straggling over her shoulders, the soiled makeshift cloak, her tattered shift, Livia looked up at Tariq. She opened her mouth to protest at being put on display like a prize mare, but at the sight of the expression of rage that contorted his features, the words died on her lips. Doubtless the victorious commander was fuming because in the frenzy of their celebration his entrance had gone unmarked.

Suddenly Livia's eye was caught by those of a man reclining among a circle of laughing and drinking courtiers on her right. With an expression of astonished admiration, he stared straight into her eyes. Their gaze locked and held. The man's sleek black hair, dark, appraising gaze, thin, smiling lips under a thick moustache, his spade-shaped beard and swarthy coloring gave him a worldly air that she instinctively distrusted.

Abruptly, he leaned toward a petite girl clad in layers of sheer pink gauze, and whispered in her ear. She glanced toward the doorway, let out an astonished cry, then jumped to her feet, ran to Tariq and threw her arms about his neck.

"Tariq!" she cried in excited tones. "You've returned at last—what a marvelous surprise! The guards did not herald your approach!"

Livia surveyed the girl with lively interest. Her gleaming hair caught up in a circlet of rubies at the nape of her neck came to a striking widow's peak above a face so clear and luminous that it could have been carved from alabaster. The round face, with its prominent cheekbones and wide brow, was alert and expressive, and there was a hint of resolution in her chin. But her almond-shaped eyes were her most spectacular feature: large and intelligent, and of the depth and richness of black velvet.

Tariq's stern features softened in a semblance of a smile as he bent down to bestow a perfunctory kiss on the girl's brow and gently disengaged her arms from about his neck. "It appears they had more interesting activities to occupy their time," he said stiffly. "And since you've received no word of our arrival and cannot know whether our king is victor or vanquished, what is the occasion for this joyful celebration?"

The girl lowered her gaze and moistened her lips with the tip of her tongue. "I am not the one to tell you, Tariq."

His expression hardened and Livia's sympathy went out to the girl as he towered over her, formidable in gleaming gilt helmet and scarlet cloak.

"Nizam! Speak—at once!"

She lifted her chin and bleakly gazed up into his face. "We celebrate a marriage—" she halted abruptly, as though loath to go on.

A flash of mingled shock and surprise lighted his solemn face. "A marriage! It must be that of some noble personage to warrant such a feast."

"Yes, yes it is that," Nizam murmured.

Tariq's hard gaze seemed to bore into the girl. "Well?"

"Prince Boabdil," Nizam said apologetically.

Tariq's thick brows furrowed in a fierce scowl. "And our prince's bride?"

Again the girl lowered her head and murmured almost inaudibly, "Khadija."

"Khadija!" Tariq exploded.

"I fear he could not resist the lady's charms," Nizam said softly.

Livia studied the girl's pale face in an effort to discern whether the girl's expression bore out the note of sarcasm Livia imagined she'd heard in Nizam's voice.

Tariq's angry gaze swept the noisy crowd of revelers and came to rest upon the throne across the room. Whether the prince and his bride had heard his startled exclamation, or whether they had sensed an alien presence, Livia could not fathom; but at that moment their absorption in each other broke. They drew apart, their astonished gaze fixed upon Tariq. The woman's face paled, as though she had seen an apparition. Then, as if shot from a crossbow, she leaped to her feet and ran joyfully across the crowded chamber toward Tariq.

Tariq stood motionless, silent and unsmiling, watching until she stood before him, hands outstretched beseechingly. Before she could speak, he said coldly, "I'm told congratulations are in order for our prince . . ." He paused for a fraction of a second, regarding her with a hard, critical stare, ". . . and for you also. You have married well."

Khadija cast a withering look upon Nizam. "I regret that you've heard the news from someone else. I myself wished to tell you of my marriage."

Tariq's powerful shoulders lifted in an indifferent shrug. Then, as if a curtain had been drawn, his features set in the impenetrable mask Livia knew so well by now. "Who bears the news is of no importance. I wish you great happiness."

Tariq's harsh tone belied his words, and Livia surmised that Khadija, at least, had the power to penetrate his granite heart.

Color flooded Khadija's neck and face and, turning her head as if to avoid Tariq's critical eyes, her gaze fell upon Livia. A brittle smile brightened her features.

"Ah, Tariq, I see you've brought me a gift from Zahara!" Her glittering black eyes swept Livia from head to toe in swift appraisal.

Her pride roused, Livia drew herself erect and with all the dignity she could summon, stared disdainfully down upon Khadija.

"How well I shall like a slave to attend me," Khadija trilled. "She is ungainly tall, but comely under all that filth. I believe she will do. I will have her as my personal handmaiden."

Livia's cheeks burned and her bosom swelled with animosity; but before she could speak, Tariq snapped, "I delivered the prisoner from the ravages of our lecherous foot soldiers. She is not a gift for you, Khadija, but for Nizam."

Nizam's delicate brows lifted in astonishment. "I am most grateful, Tariq, but whatever shall I do with her?"

"Do with her as you like!" Tariq roared. He spun on his heel and strode from the hall.

Livia's lips curved in a small, exultant smile. Now she would not be forced to marry Prince Boabdil!

Chapter 5

It was clear that Nizam was as displeased with having fallen heir to Livia as Khadija would have been pleased to possess her. The girl's manner was courteous, yet at the same time, distant. Though Nizam was smaller than she, Livia found the girl's air of self-composure unnerving. And now her erect carriage and aloof demeanor made Livia apprehensive. Still, she reassured herself, she was far better off with the aloof Nizam than she could have been. So great was her relief at having escaped marriage to Prince Boabdil, and having escaped servitude under Khadija as well, that she willingly followed Nizam from the lofty throne room, down dimly lighted passageways whose twistings and turnings seemed to have no end.

At least she was not to be cast into one of the wretched prisons in the caves to be hired out to do manual labor, or to molder under the floors of the palace. For this, too, she was thankful. She took a deep breath and told herself sternly that she could endure being a slave to this slender girl—until Aguilar should come and rescue her.

At the end of one of the labyrinthine corridors, they stepped through a curtained doorway into Nizam's apartment. Livia had a swift impression of an airy room, a blue velvet divan strewn with green and yellow silk cushions, a glowing brass brazier, colorful wall hangings and low-silled arched windows that looked out upon distant mountain peaks. A doorway in the far

wall led to a room beyond in which Livia saw a bed
mounted in an alcove draped with soft blue hangings.

Nizam crossed to a carved oak chest in one corner
and drew out a long-sleeved tunic of blue and gold
striped silk, bright blue trousers and white cotton
undergarments which she thrust into Livia's hands.
Eyeing her coldly, as though Livia were a stray cat she
had been forced to take in, Nizam said, "I'll order a
servant to bring a tub of hot water. Bathe and put on
these garments. Then I'll decide what's to be done with
you."

The tub was brought, filled with steaming water, and
Livia was left alone. She eased down into the tub,
reveling in the feel of the hot water on her skin,
splashing it over her slender body as if to wash away the
horror of the past few days.

At length she emerged from the tub and rubbed her
body briskly with a linen towel until her skin glowed.
She smiled to herself, feeling ridiculous as she donned
the strange garments, then returned to the sitting room.
Nizam was seated on a cushion before the double
window, and Livia sank down upon a cushion across
from her. Nizam's fine, arched brows rose in surprise.

"You appear much more presentable than I had
imagined possible. I am relieved, to say the least."
Nizam's voice, gentle when she had spoken with Tariq,
took on the sharpness of a dagger. "Nevertheless, I've
no wish to keep you, even as a slave. I abhor all
Spaniards." Glaring at Livia, she went on. "When I
was but a child, the Spanish dogs, cut down my parents
and my sisters before my very eyes during one of their
murderous attacks. My brother and I alone escaped."
Tears welled in Nizam's luminous eyes. Despite her
loathing for the Moors, Livia felt a swift pang of
sympathy for the girl, drawn to her by the kinship of
their common tragedy.

Livia said softly, "I fear my own family has perished
at the hands of your soldiers."

Nizam's eyes widened and a soft rush of air escaped

her lips. Then, as though wary of her emotions betraying her into sympathizing with the enemy, she shrugged and replied harshly, "The fortunes of war. Still, I cannot abide your presence . . . much as I dislike refusing the gift of my brother."

"Brother!" Livia echoed, dismayed.

Nizam nodded. "My brother Tariq saved me from death—and worse—at the hands of the unbelievers," she said quietly.

"That . . . that barbarian!" Livia exclaimed. It seemed incredible that this fierce warrior who organized the pillaging and killing of Zahara could have a family.

"My brother is far from a barbarian," Nizam said coldly. "He can be as tender as he is warlike."

Despite herself, Livia was intrigued. She had thought of Tariq Ibn Ziyah as an anonymous character, confident of his own nature and caring for no one.

"Tariq is loyal to his people and his faith," Nizam continued, devotion shining in her eyes. "He is determined to drive the Christian army from the Kingdom of Granada and will dare any risk in the pursuit of his goal. Be warned. His strength of purpose knows no bounds. He does not accept defeat. Further, may I remind you that he rescued *you* from rape!"

Though disconcerted, Livia did not abandon her previous conviction that he was a savage, ill-natured heathen. She gazed straight into Nizam's eyes and in a low voice replied, "There is nothing very surprising about Tariq's defending his sister; and that he rescued *me* is outweighed by the fact that he wanted me only as a prize for Prince Boabdil. That he could imperviously watch the suffering of the hapless inhabitants of Zahara, confirms my low opinion of him."

"You are naïve," said Nizam with a pitying shake of her shining head.

Livia felt a warm flush suffuse her cheeks as Nizam went on.

"Doubtless you have grown up sheltered in the

bosom of your aristocratic family," Nizam observed, "teething on frightful tales of the horrors inflicted by us. Yet your own countrymen are no less guilty of the same offenses. If Tariq appears indifferent to suffering, it is because he abhors the carnage of war and must brace himself against it."

Livia felt a slight stab of shock pass through her. She had thought the man callous. It had not occurred to her that his heartless demeanor was just a defense against the inevitable tragedy of war.

"And, after all," Nizam continued, "Tariq brought you to safety here in the Alhambra."

Though Livia fought against it, a needling doubt entered her mind, but not sufficiently strong to make her change her opinion of Moslems, or Tariq Ibn Ziyah. But there was no use arguing with the girl. She lowered her gaze and made no reply.

As Nizam continued to extol Tariq's virtues, Livia covertly studied Nizam's features. Livia could see a resemblance to Tariq in the sensuous curve of her lips, the serious, burning eyes, the clean line of her jaw that had not hardened into the unyielding lines of her brother's. Now, as Nizam spoke of Tariq, a smile graced her lips and a dimple appeared in her chin. Livia idly wondered whether a similar dimple was concealed under Tariq's luxuriant beard. Nizam possessed the same air of calmness as Tariq; both detached and confident in equal measure in their statements, though their calmness did not preclude the swift, knife-edged reply in word and deed. She turned her attention to what Nizam was saying.

"You are fortunate that, though you are a Spaniard, you possess a rare beauty. There is a place for you in the Alhambra. I shall arrange with the Sultana Ayxa for you to join the harem."

An anguished cry burst from Livia's lips. "You cannot send me there! I am betrothed to a captain in King Ferdinand's army!" Her voice rose rebelliously. "I will not go to the harem!"

Nizam's cheeks flushed crimson. "You are my property. I may do with you as I wish."

"Please, I beseech you! I would sooner be a slave—washing the king's feet—than be in his harem."

Nizam shrugged. "There is little difference between washing Muley's feet and sharing his bed." A secretive smile touched her lips, deepening the dimple in her chin. "Less will be required of you in his bed."

"No!" cried Livia. "I'll not submit to him. Never!"

"Come now," said Nizam with an impatient wave of her hand. "There are a score of beauties from which he can choose. It's said he soon tires of new maidens, finding all the same in the darkness. You will not often be called upon to please him. And, if you are clever, you can learn to evade the apple."

"Apple?"

Nizam smiled. "It is Muley's habit to bathe with his wives and the houris, after which he presents an apple to the one he desires." At the sight of Livia's stricken face, her expression softened. "If it eases your mind, it is rumored that he takes his pleasure more in the *looking* upon his beauties than in the *performing* with them."

Livia shook her head vehemently. "No! I will not go!"

"Perhaps, if you incur the favor of Ayxa, you may be spared Muley's attentions. She may decide to keep you as a handmaiden."

"Ayxa?"

"Ayxa la Horra, the chaste." Once again Nizam allowed herself a slight smile. "So called because she is of such immaculate and inaccessible virtue. Ayxa is the first wife of King Muley—the bride of his youth and the mother of Boabdil." A flicker of compassion crossed her delicate features. "Ayxa long maintained undisputed sway over the harem until, as her youth passed away and her beauty declined, a formidable rival arose. Zoraya. Rather than a haven of shelter and safety for the women of the household, as a harem is meant to be, it became the scene of inveterate jealousies and intrigues. Moslems may take four wives, you see."

"Oh? I've heard your sultans took many wives."

Nizam shook her head. "It is possible for the wealthy to enjoy the favors of regiments of women, for two reasons. Divorce is easy for men. Our ancient kings married scores of women, for tribal alliances, and divorced them honorably after one night.

"Also, our men are allowed concubines, whose children are regarded as legitimate. The Sultana Zoraya, once Muley's concubine, is as ambitious as she is beautiful, and some years ago she persuaded Muley to marry her. She bore him two sons, Cad and Nazar." A rueful smile touched Nizam's lips. "A constant and bitter battle rages between Ayxa and Zoraya as to which of Muley's sons will inherit the throne." Nizam rose to her feet. "But enough talk. I will take you to meet the Sultana Ayxa, who will arrange for your chambers."

Livia suppressed a sigh. Plainly there was nothing further to be gained by pleading with Nizam. She would have to throw herself upon the mercy of the Sultana Ayxa la Horra.

Once again Livia followed Nizam along narrow halls that turned abruptly at right angles, a rectangular maze of patios and chambers. Over her shoulder Nizam explained, "The palace is divided into three sections. The first, which you entered from the Court of the Cisterns, is devoted to justice and administration. On Monday and Thursday mornings King Muley appears before his people. After a recitation from the Koran, citizens put their pleas before him or his vizier."

Livia's hopes surged anew. Perhaps she, too, could plead her case.

They emerged upon the Court of Myrtles where, in the gathering dusk, long shadows fell upon the white marble paving and the mirror surface of the pool gleamed darkly, lending the courtyard an air of mystery and enchantment. A shiver ran down Livia's spine.

Suddenly it was easy to believe that this splendid palace was the scene of grim deeds and bloody retribution.

Nizam paused and raised her hand in a sweeping gesture. "Adjoining this area is the Serai—the king's official residence—where he receives more distinguished visitors. The courtyard opens upon the loftiest tower in the Alhambra, the Comares Tower. The Hall of the Comares—the ambassadors—is the center of the political and diplomatic life."

Nizam moved on, leading the way down another labyrinth. "Linked to the Serai is the harem. Here the king lives his private life with his family."

"In the harem!" exclaimed Livia.

"It is the Spaniards who have corrupted our word *hamman* to mean an orgiastic debauch," Nizam snapped. "In Arabic, the word is linked to the concept of the sacred, or taboo." Abruptly she turned down an elbow-shaped passage. "We are now in the Hall of the Ajimeces where rooms are reserved for the sultana." She paused before a doorway hung with heavy gold brocade curtains and after announcing their presence to a dark-skinned slave girl, they were granted admittance to Ayxa's apartment.

The antechamber was spacious and airy, though much more elegant than Nizam's. Brass lamps, which hung from slipper holders on the walls, shed a soft radiance over the room. Livia's eyes were drawn to an exquisite wall tapestry designed in squares depicting an oasis where trees sheltering nightingales spread over beds of stylized flowers. A vivid red, blue and gold medallion carpet with arabesque motifs graced the floor.

A divan covered with animal skins smoothed to softness extended along three sides of the room and in its center sat a small, compact woman clad in a long tunic of saffron yellow embroidered in bright colors. Her glossy hair was drawn into a knot entwined with pearls. Her olive complexion appeared as soft as doeskin. Heavy jeweled earrings sparkled from elongated earlobes, as though weighing them down. Rings flashed on fingers thickened with the years as the sultana gathered up cards spread out on a small brass table before her.

At their approach, the woman glanced up, and Livia stifled a gasp. From her eyes emanated a look so discerning and at the same time so proud-spirited, that Livia halted mid-stride. She did not envy Zoraya her contest of wills with this indomitable woman.

After dispensing with the amenities, Nizam put forth her request. Ayxa's thin brows rose and as her gaze swept Livia, she nodded in approval.

Livia's heart pounded in her ears. The sultana liked her. Surely she would not countenance her being given to Muley, but would, as Nizam had suggested, keep her for her own handmaiden. To Livia's consternation, a sly smile curved Ayxa's lips and a spark of malice gleamed in her dark eyes. "The girl will indeed be a welcome addition to the king's bevy of houris."

Shaken, Livia burst out, "But Nizam thought you may prefer to keep me for your own handmaiden!"

"On the contrary. I would much prefer to see you divert the king's mind from that interloper Zoraya . . . and perhaps the high-and-mighty woman will learn that she is not the only star in Muley's firmament."

"But you cannot send me to the harem!" cried Livia.

Without looking up from her cards, Ayxa retorted, "You would do well to heed an old Arab proverb: Sorrow endureth for the night, but joy ariseth in the morning."

Livia's heart seemed to cease its beating. Her chin rose disdainfully. Clearly it would be futile to protest the sultana's decision. But it would be even more futile for King Muley to try to bed her!

An exultant gleam shone from Ayxa's eyes as she riffled the pack of cards in her hands. Glancing up at Nizam, she said, "Find the girl a chamber in the harem quarters." With a brief nod of dismissal, she turned back to her game, laying the cards, one by one, on the table before her.

Telling herself sternly that she must not give in to despair, Livia followed Nizam from the room.

Nizam laughed softly. "As you see, Ayxa is an inveterate gambler."

Livia made no reply, thinking that much as she loathed these people, she was forced to accord a grudging admiration to Ayxa.

Livia's chamber in the harem was small and sparsely furnished with the usual divan and colorful floor cushions, carpets, oil lamps and an ornate brass-studded oak chest for her belongings. Eager for the release of sleep, she undressed quickly, crawled into her bed in the alcove and drew the curtains. But when sleep came, it was invaded by dreams of warriors wielding scimitars and the enraged visage of Tariq Ibn Ziyah.

The following morning Livia was awakened by Amina, a smiling, sloe-eyed houri who entered her chamber bearing an armload of clothing, a colorful array of silks, brocades and gauzy chiffon fabrics, for her to wear.

"You will come with me now, to meet the king's maidens," Amina said pleasantly.

"No," Livia said coldly. "I do not care to join the—"

Amina laughed, shaking her head. "If you do not come, the eunuch will come to fetch you!"

Livia bit her lip to keep from snapping at Amina who only meant to be kind. She wished she didn't know Arabic. Then, perhaps, she wouldn't understand with such glaring certainty what was happening to her. She donned a pair of full red silk trousers gathered about the ankles, and an embroidered Persian blue tunic, then fastened a golden girdle about her narrow waist. Seething at being subjected to this indignity, she followed Amina to a sunny sitting room where the houris gathered in the mornings.

Apparently vying with one another in lavish displays of attire and other alluring finery, they wore garments of rich fabrics patterned with stripes or stylized flowers and were adorned with fine pearls and precious stones all about their necks, ears and arms. They were lovely, Livia was loath to admit; moderately plump, with voluptuous curves and long, sleek hair. She noted they were given to wearing fresh-scented perfumes and to her surprise, Livia found herself thinking they were quite lively, moved with grace and spoke with charm and wit.

Several maidens were occupied at a loom. Others embroidered or strummed romantic ballads on their lutes. When Amina presented her, Livia summoned a feeble smile then strolled to a window where she stood staring in gloomy silence at the forbidding mountains that ringed the city. One thought occupied her mind: how to escape her splendid prison. She sighed deeply. There must be a way. And she would find it.

Chapter 6

That afternoon Livia kept to her room and enjoyed a respite from the excited chatter of the houris. Her thoughts were interrupted by the sound of a gentle voice calling her name. She looked up in surprise as the hangings over the doorway parted and Amina hurried into her chamber.

"Come, Livia," said the girl, smiling. "We go now to the royal baths."

"I do not choose to go," Livia said, hoping that she could defy Amina's summons by sheer audacity.

Amina's tinkling laughter rippled through the room. "My innocent, you have no choice! Once again. If you do not appear, the eunuch will escort you."

Vexed, Livia set her lips grimly and rose to follow Amina. She was familiar with the infidels' practice of bathing; in the cities occupied by the Moors, all Moslems, as well as assimilated Christians and Jews, bathed regularly. Cordoba alone boasted more than nine hundred *hammans*—the public baths. During the mornings and evenings, adolescent boys scrubbed and soaped the male Cordobans. In the afternoons, the women would gather at the baths to meet their friends and exchange gossip. Skilled artists in makeup would remove their body hair and perfume their tresses with civet oil. Livia preferred to bathe in private.

Apprehensive, she walked stiffly beside Amina along the corridors and down a flight of stone steps to the baths.

When she stepped through the entrance, her anxiety was momentarily forgotten as she looked in wonder at the grace of the chamber. Four pillars supported arcades in the center of which hung a lantern that shed a soothing light upon walls adorned with black, gold, green and white tiles above which wooden latticework was gilded and polychromed in shades of gold, blue, sea-green and red. A small fountain bubbled in the center of the room.

"This is the resting room where we disrobe," Amina said.

Livia surveyed the stone couches recessed in the walls that were strewn with rugs and discarded garments. Feeling her face grow warm with embarrassment, Livia shed her clothes. Suddenly aware that she stood almost a head taller than her Moorish companions, that her skin glowed with the satin luster of ivory, shades paler than the olive-toned flesh of the houris, she felt horribly conspicuous. She tried to ignore the covert glances, the open stares of the girls whose curious eyes traveled over her long slender legs, narrow waist and full breasts so unlike their own softly rounded figures and small peaked mounds.

Amina and Livia moved on to a room paved with white marble where channels down the center served to carry away the water, and pale light streamed down through star-shaped openings in the roof. Livia plunged into a hot bath, then into water so cold that her teeth chattered. They proceeded to the vapor baths where the steamy atmosphere made her gasp for breath. As they emerged, attendants dashed cold water on them. Livia bit her lips to keep from crying out. Meekly, she submitted to the ministrations of an attendant who, with a prickly piece of sacking in her hand, scoured her raw, then massaged her skin with oil and sprinkled her with rosewater.

Holding her head high, and with the dignity of one clothed in her finest raiment for an appearance at the Spanish court, Livia moved on with the houris to the chamber of repose. In the doorway, she stopped short. Reclining among the cushions in an alcove, King Muley clad in a gold robe and turban, surveyed his beauties with undisguised pleasure. Livia stiffened as a slave approached him bearing a silver salver laden with dried figs, grapes and apples. In a gallery overhead musicians struck up a ballad on lutes, tambourines and fiddles. Muley's lascivious gaze traveled about the room where Livia stood, as though transfixed.

Did she only imagine that his roving eyes singled her out—a new face? Quickly, she sank down on a cushion on the floor amid a bevy of maidens, hoping to escape his notice. She watched him from the corner of her eye. He was a stringy man, his brown cheeks crisscrossed with deep wrinkles. His icy brown eyes, glimmering out from behind a curious filminess, were quick and decisive.

All at once the low hum of conversation, the ripples of laughter subsided as King Muley reached out a mottled hand and lifted an apple from the salver. He held it up before him, turning it this way and that so that its polished red surface gleamed in the light. Deliberately, he rose from his couch and strolled about the room, bestowing an indulgent smile first upon one, then another of his maidens. Every bright, sparkling eye was fixed upon him, and lips curved enticingly.

Slowly, irrevocably, he drew near Livia. A tremor of fear ran down her spine and she swayed backward so that her face was hidden behind the heads of Amina and the maiden seated beside her. The king paused, smiling down upon the upturned faces. Livia held her breath, thinking he must surely hear her heart hammering in her breast. He reached out and with the sweeping gesture of one bestowing a precious gift, thrust the shining apple into Amina's eager hands.

Small cries, exclamations of approval, rippled throughout the room. To Livia's dismay, winning Muley's favor was apparently a coveted honor. Amina gathered a flowing pink robe about her and rose. King

Muley made a slight bow, took her hand, and in a courtly manner escorted her from the room.

"Ah!" exclaimed the girl beside Livia, her lips drawn down in a pout. "He has chosen Amina for the second time this month. It is not fair!"

Livia uttered a silent prayer of thanksgiving.

The moment the king and Amina disappeared through the doorway, Livia jumped up, drew on her tunic and trousers and slipped from the room unnoticed. Swiftly she made her way up the stone stairs, across the arcade at one end of the Court of Myrtles and sped along the length of the pool, searching frantically for the entrance to the palace. Somehow she would find a way to Cordoba.

She darted down a passageway and stopped short, face to face with a blank wall as the hall came to an abrupt end. A pox on these people and their constantly bending corridors that never led anywhere directly, Livia thought furiously. Unexpectedly, she heard the sound of voices coming from the right. She veered left.

She had gone only a few yards when she heard footsteps behind her. She quickened her pace. The footsteps quickened. Not daring to look around, she broke into a run.

"Livia!"

Her name echoed down the shadowy hall. Her mouth grew dry and her legs shook. She ran faster, but her pursuer was gaining on her.

"Livia, hold!"

Another blank wall loomed ahead. Panic rose in her throat. Which way? Decide, quickly! Confused, she paused and the next instant a strong hand gripped her elbow and twisted her about. Breathless, panting with fright, she gazed up into the eyes of the swarthy, too-handsome man who had stared at her in such open admiration last night in the throne room.

The man's thin lips curved in a smile like that of a jackal.

"Why in such a rush, my pigeon? Here in the

Alhambra we lead a serene existence. There is no need for such haste . . . unless you were thinking of taking flight."

Livia felt her face burn with color. "I . . . I'm lost. I cannot find the way back to my chamber."

He offered her his arm. "Then allow me to escort you."

A gigantic diamond ring winking on his index finger gave his talonlike hand a sinister look that sent a chill down her spine. Reluctantly, she placed her hand in the crook of his arm. She forced her voice to be calm.

"How do you know my name, and the location of my chamber?"

His smile was too broad, too indulgent. "The moment I saw you standing in the doorway with Tariq, I knew you were the woman for whom I've been searching all of my life."

Livia sighed inwardly. Even the Arabs, imaginative as they were said to be, masters of poetry without peer, employed the same words to approach a woman as other men—words that she had heard many times before.

"And so, I lost no time in learning who you are and where you reside. I am like Malik Manshard Majlauk, one of the king's viziers." His smile stretched to an insinuating leer. "You are most fortunate that I have taken an interest in you—in your welfare—for I have the ear of the king and can be of inestimable aid in making all of your days . . . and nights . : . most enjoyable."

Livia recognized the name as one of Kurdish origin. The very thought of the Kurds, noted for their cruelty, made her quiver inside. With effort, she kept her voice level and controlled. "Thank you. You are most kind, but I've no intention of spending all my days or nights at the court of Granada."

He grasped one of her hands tightly in his own sinewy fingers. "I—personally—will see to your pleasure. Our days will be filled with joy and sunshine, I

promise you. And our nights . . ." His voice trailed off
as he halted before an archway hung with black velvet
draperies. He thrust them aside and ushered her
through.

Livia's startled gaze swept over a room whose
furnishings, from tapestries to divan, cushions and
carpets, were all in hues of scarlet, black and white.
Stunned, she cried out, "This is not the entrance to the
harem!"

An expansive smile crossed Malik's sharp features
and he raised his arm in a sweeping gesture. "Welcome
to my chambers!" To Livia, the huge diamond on his
finger seemed to flash a warning. She turned to flee, but
Malik stood feet apart, his hands gripping the doorway, blocking her path. "Stay, my pigeon."

He took her arm and led her across the room to the
divan spread with fur pelts. "I wish only to show you
where to find me if you should need my help." He
gestured to a low table which held a ceramic jug
embellished with black and rust designs and two
goblets. "Allow me to pour you some wine before I
escort you to your room."

Thinking it wise not to arouse the man's ire by
refusing his hospitality, Livia sank down upon the
divan. She would sip the wine quickly, then take her
leave.

Malik eased down beside her, took up the jug and
filled their goblets.

"I had not thought to see a Moslem partaking of
wine," Livia said lightly. "I'm told that partaking of
alcoholic beverages is against the tenets of the Koran."

"Alas," Malik said, throwing up his hands in a
helpless gesture, "even the most devout sometimes lack
constancy in following the precepts of the Prophet
Mohammed. One cannot expect those who live in a
country where the grape thrives and the citizens raise it
for sale, not to partake of its fruits. We must make
certain the product is of the high quality we wish to
attain."

Livia's lips curved in an amused smile. "The Moors have an answer for everything."

While Malik rambled on, speaking of the delights of life at the Alhambra, Livia sipped her drink and helped herself from a great bowl of nuts and candies on the table.

"But Rabi ben Zaid describes our land so much better than I," Malik said. He took up a thick volume from the table and began to read aloud:

"The month of January: the water in the rivers feels tepid and vapors rise from the earth. The sap rises in the wood of the trees . . ."

He paused, lifting his eyes to hers, smiling in an intimate fashion. His fingers tugged at his beard. Livia began to feel uneasy.

The falcons of Valencia build their nests and begin to mate. Horses feed on young shoots. Cows calve. The young of ducks and geese are hatched. Now is the time to plant grain and the mallow and to put in stakes for the olive, pomegranate and similar fruit trees. The early narcissi bloom. Trellises are put up for the early vines and other climbing plants. Purslane should be planted and sugarcane harvested, beets preserved and *sherāb*—syrup, prepared from bitter lemons.

Livia suspected that Malik had his reasons for holding her a captive audience, but she had no wish to stay to discover what they were. She set her goblet down and stood. "Your almanac is most fascinating, Malik, but I must go."

He reached up, grasped her arm, and pulled her down on the divan beside him. "Do you not understand, my pigeon?"

"No!" Livia said sharply. "I don't know what you're talking about."

Malik's lascivious smile broadened. "This is the season when all Granada comes to life. The time for planting, the time for mating."

Livia could only stare at him in stunned silence. He leaned toward her, his mouth close to hers. "I wish only to taste the wine of your sweet lips." His arm encircled her waist.

She glared at him, her dark eyes flashing with scorn. "Let me go!"

His eyes returned her challenge, and a slow sneering smile crept across his thin lips, mocking her defiance. Her stare grew more contemptuous and unwavering. His smile faded.

"Do not delude yourself that you belong to Tariq, that you are his slave merely because he took you captive." His lips twisted. "Tariq should have married long since. In accordance with our custom he should have taken a wife at the age of twenty. But he needs no woman!"

Livia's eyes blazed. "That is good news indeed. I've no intention of marrying him!"

Something akin to hatred kindled in Malik's eyes. "It is well," he said in a voice fraught with jealousy, "for though he is commander-in-chief, and because his valor has been awarded property that should have been mine, the pendulum will swing. The day will come when I will wield the greatest power in Granada. Vengeance will be mine. I will see that Tariq receives his due."

Without warning, he lunged toward her. His arms enveloped Livia, crushing her to his chest, squeezing the air from her lungs and his mouth clamped down upon hers. His moustache prickled her lip and his alcohol-laden breath seared her cheeks. She gasped for breath and tried to cry out, but his darting tongue ran over her lips, exploring her mouth so that she choked on the scream that rose in her throat.

She hammered on his back and kicked at him savagely. Malik threw the weight of his body upon her, forcing her down upon the thick fur covering the divan. She ceased beating on his back and, in an effort to wrench free of him, twisted her body from side to side, her arms flailing the air. But her struggles only served to inflame him further. Her right hand grazed the wine jug. She reached out, groping air, until her fingertips touched the handle. She gripped it tightly, swung her arm upward in an arc and brought the jug crashing down upon the back of Malik's head.

"Ei-yee!" he shouted. In the same instant, the brittle pottery shattered, and blood-red rivulets cascaded over his brow into his eyes and dripped down his chin, spattering his tunic. He leaped up and wiped his face on his sleeve, cursing.

Livia sprang to her feet and dashed from the room. She plunged blindly down one corridor then another until at last she emerged onto a small patio where a slave was bent over a rosebush, turning the soil. Startled, he glanced up. The stunned look on his face warned Livia how disheveled she must appear.

She crossed to the fountain bubbling in the center of the patio, bathed her face and arms and wiped them on the hem of her tunic. Then she bade the young man to escort her to the harem. As they proceeded, she heard a high-pitched voice resounding over the towers—the muezzin calling Moslems to prayer. Though she did not share their faith, the lingering music of the words was strangely compelling. They hung over the palace and seemed to follow her inside her prison of lonely grandeur.

Chapter 7

Livia lived in torment that the king would choose her for his favor. During the daily baths, his milky gaze would travel casually over her body, lingering on her full, young breasts and the gentle swell of her thighs. Then she would freeze, certain her day of doom had come. At last she resolved to endure her anguish no longer. She squared her shoulders, strode to Nizam's chamber and without waiting to be announced, burst in.

Nizam was seated cross-legged on the floor, her head bent over a small table strewn with papers, pens and a brass inkpot. She looked up, her brows raised in astonishment as Livia bore down upon her like an avenging fury.

Without preamble, Livia said, "Muley has not chosen to present me with his ridiculous token. Clearly I do not please him, as you and the sultana predicted. Therefore, I demand to be released from the harem."

Nizam set down her pen and regarded Livia with a level gaze. "Do not fret. King Muley is noted for his cruel nature. He enjoys the game of cat-and-mouse. Just when you have despaired, thinking he will never grant you his favor, he will choose you."

Livia clenched her fists at her sides in an effort to control her temper. "You misunderstand me, Nizam. I am most thankful that that evil old man has chosen to ignore me! And should he ever choose me, I shall leap from a window of the highest tower in the Alhambra. I would sooner be dashed upon the rocks than to lie in the softest bed with him!''

Nizam shook her head in the unruffled manner that so infuriated Livia. "It is the will of Allah."

"What is the will of Allah?" demanded a harsh voice.

Livia turned about. In the doorway stood Tariq, his thick brows raised in question. Apparently he had just returned from tending to some business outside the palace, for he wore a red and white checked *keffiyah* round his head and shoulders and a brown tunic lined with fur, under which Livia glimpsed a red and gold striped ankle-length *galabia* belted at the waist.

Striding into the room, he repeated, "What is the will of Allah?"

"That King Muley should single me out for his favor," Livia said icily.

Tariq shed his *keffiyah* and fur-lined tunic, dropped down on the divan, stretched out his long legs before him and regarded Livia with casual unconcern. "Do not trouble yourself. All you need do is keep from his sight."

"That is not easy for one in the harem," Livia snapped.

Tariq paused in the act of stroking his soft, full beard. *"You* in the harem? What nonsense!"

Nizam rose and crossed to stand before her brother. "Forgive me, Tariq. I'd no use for a handmaiden. I did not mean to cast aside your gift, but I didn't know what else to do with her. In the harem she'll be well cared for—"

"You sent her to the harem?" An angry red suffused Tariq's face as he stared incredulously at Nizam.

Nizam nodded and sounded genuinely contrite. "I'm sorry, Tariq. I thought it would be best."

"It is not best!" His voice took on the flat, hard tone Livia knew so well. "I did not bring the jewel of Zahara to be so used. To the victor goes the spoils. If you have no use for her, I have."

Livia felt a chill go through her, raising the hair on the nape of her neck.

"I fear it is too late," retorted Nizam. "Muley has already marked her presence. He will never permit you to take one of his houris."

Tariq's jaw hardened and his eyes burned with unholy fire. "The king owes his commander-in-chief a greater debt than he can ever repay. He'll not cavil when I make clear to him that the girl was sent to the harem by mistake, that I mean to take her for my bride."

"Bride!" Livia erupted. "Not so long as there is a breath left in my body, will you take me as your bride!"

Tariq turned a furious glare upon her. "Be still, woman. You have nothing to say in the matter."

Livia bore down upon him, her hands planted on her hips. "I have much to say, and I will!" she stormed. "Do you never listen to any voice but your own? I have told you before, I am betrothed. I cannot marry you. But even if I were *not*, I would not marry you!"

Tariq stared up at her, pinpoints of light shining from his dark eyes. In a steely voice, he said, "And as I have told you on earlier occasions, you will do as I order."

"No!" Livia shrieked, stamping her foot. "I will not marry you—you murderer, plunderer, despoiler of women!"

In one swift motion, Tariq rose from the divan and his hand shot out, catching both of Livia's wrists in a cruel grip. His eyes looked deeply into hers. "Enough of this unseemly behavior. I will settle a generous dowry upon you. That should please you."

"I don't want your filthy money, I want my freedom!"

"Silence!" Tariq thundered. "I will hear no more of your childish protests."

Seeing that her defiance served only to irritate him further, she took a deep breath and with great effort gained control of her anger.

"Tariq, I beseech you. Do not force this marriage

upon me. I . . . I—" She paused, choking upon the words she was about to utter. "I will be your slave, but not your wife."

"Enough!" Tariq shouted, thrusting her roughly from him. She reeled backward and fell to her knees among the pillows on the divan. Quickly, she righted herself and sat rubbing her chafed wrists. "Infidel!"

As though she had not spoken, Tariq turned to Nizam. "The *adalides* have brought word that our soldiers will arrive in the city with the prisoners within two days. The victory celebration will provide a suitable occasion for the wedding ceremony. See that my bride is prepared." Without a backward glance, Tariq strode from the chamber.

Tears of rage and frustration coursed down Livia's cheeks. She was unable to speak. Nizam eased down beside her and patted her shoulder consolingly.

"I am truly sorry, Livia. Though I harbor much hatred toward your countrymen, I had no wish for things to turn out so. But you must see that Tariq expects to be obeyed. My brother has a reputation for decisiveness. He knows what he wants and takes it." Nizam let out a deep sigh and her voice grew husky. "I understand how you feel. I, too, suffer the misfortune to love the wrong man."

"It is right and fitting that I should wed Aguilar!"

"As is Raduan for me," said Nizam sorrowfully. "But Tariq has refused to give his consent. I, too, am forbidden to marry the man I love." She bestowed a rueful smile upon Livia. "Once again you and I share a common plight."

Livia's head jerked up in dismay and she dabbed at her tear-streaked face with the hem of her tunic. "By what right does he forbid you to marry whomever you please?"

"Now that our father is dead, Tariq is the head of our family."

"But Tariq seems deeply devoted to you. Why should he deny you your heart's desire?"

Nizam shook her head hopelessly, "A devoted brother he is, and as such, he will choose a proper husband for me. Raduan Venegas is the last man he would choose." She paused as if it were hard for her to go on. Then, regaining her composure, she said softly, "All is not as it seems here in our earthly paradise. The men surrounding the king are driven by lust for power and wealth. His enemies look forward to the day Muley dies so they can seize the throne. There are many factions in the city—in the court itself—all scheming one against the other."

Livia's smooth brow creased in a perplexed frown. "Will not Babdil reign upon his father's death? Is he not the rightful heir to the throne?"

Nizam nodded. "So it would seem. But on the day of Boabdil's birth, in accordance with our custom, the court astrologers cast his horoscope. Their prophecy is legend. They said that Boabdil would one day sit on the throne, but that the downfall of the kingdom would be accomplished during his reign. From that time, the prince has been regarded with aversion by his father and subjected to all manner of persecutions, so that he has been cursed with the name of *El Zogoybi*,—The Unfortunate. In truth, he has survived till now only under the protection of his mother Ayxa."

"Could not Boabdil seize the throne if the people wish it?"

Nizam nodded. "It is possible. But you reason without the influence of Muley's second wife, Zoraya. The woman can charm an asp, and her ambition knows no bounds. She is Muley's favorite sultana. She has been his favorite ever since she first came to Granada. She was captured as a child from the Christians and raised in Granada as a Moslem. As she grew up, her surpassing beauty gained her the name of Zoraya—the Morning Star. After becoming Muley's wife, she acquired complete ascendancy over his mind. Zoroya wants to elevate her children over Boabdil. So the two factions headed by Axya and Zoroya cause constant intrigues. Raduan is the son of a vizier who supports Zoroya."

"Venegas sounds Castilian," Livia said, smiling wryly.

Nizam had the grace to blush. "Raduan's grandfather was a Spaniard, but he and his children, and their children, were all brought up as Moslems. Their tie to Zoraya is inspired by their kindred ancestry. Raduan supports Zoraya. Tariq supports Ayxa and Boabdil."

Sighing deeply, Nizam rose from the divan. "I must accept my fate, just as you must accept yours."

"No!" Livia cried passionately.

"You will be wiser and much happier if you do," Nizam went on calmly. "You must marry my brother. It is the will of Allah!"

"It may be the will of Allah," snapped Livia, tossing her head, "but I am not subject to Allah's will, and I shall do as I wish."

Nizam's slight figure stiffened and she stared coldly down at Livia. "My brother is an excellent match. There are many women in the court who would give all they possess for a smile from Tariq, but he has found none who please him. You are fortunate. There are worse fates than marrying my brother." Her ebony eyes seemed to bore into Livia's soul. "You will do his bidding."

As Livia returned Nizam's icy stare, she permitted herself an arch smile. "We shall see."

Chapter 8

Two days later, on a crisp sunny afternoon, Livia sat in her room in the harem, mending the hem of her blue brocade tunic. A brisk wind swept across the plain, stirring the frosty air within the palace halls and she shivered. She set her mending aside and crossed to pull the hangings over the embrasure when her attention was caught by the sounds of shouts from the sentries of the fortress. She darted to the window which overlooked the town and far below she saw the inhabitants spilling into the streets from their red-tiled dwellings. Her gaze traveled to the *vega* stretching beyond the city, and her hand flew to her mouth stifling a startled cry. A baggage train was crawling across the broad plain like a monstrous snake.

"Livia! Livia!" a voice shouted from the doorway.

She whirled about as Tariq, clad in his fur-lined tunic against the chill winter winds, strode into her chamber, his black eyes burning with excitement.

"Livia, hurry and put on your cloak. The army returns from Zahara. King Muley will ride out to meet the troops and has ordered my squadron to escort them into the city. I wish you to observe their entry from the belvedere in the Comares Tower." He reached out a hand toward her. "Quickly!"

Livia felt a hot flood of anger surge through her and stood as though rooted to the floor. "How dare you!" she burst out. "How dare you subject me to the humiliation of viewing a victory which celebrates a Castilian defeat—to watch my people driven into the city like cattle! Have you not a wit of compassion in your body?"

Tariq's dark, bearded face flushed scarlet, but his voice remained controlled. "You wrong me, Livia."

For an instant, she imagined she saw a fleeting expression of hurt under his veiled lids, then quickly dismissed the idea. The man was incapable of feeling any emotion, particularly for her.

"It was my thought that you might wish to view the prisoners in the hope of seeing your family. Would it not be better to know that they are alive than to believe them dead?"

Taken aback, Livia stood silent for a moment. Her heart beat wildly. It was possible that her father, Margareta and Julian had not died at Zahara. It was even possible that they had survived the march to Granada; but the chance was so remote, she dared not allow herself to hope. Seething with resentment, she crossed to face Tariq.

"The last thing I wish to do is watch the Moors' triumphant procession!" she said, making no effort to conceal the bitterness in her voice. "And I am not at all certain that it would be better for my family to be Muley's captives than to be lying dead in Zahara!"

Tariq regarded her for a moment in silence. His black eyes hardened and he gave an indifferent shrug. "As you wish," he murmured and left.

Agitated, Livia paced the floor and pressed the palms of her hands over her ears to shut out the sounds of the victorious cries, the commotion rising from the town. After a while, her anger subsided. However remote, there was still the possibility that she would see her family. Hope flared anew, spurring her into action.

She snatched up her black woolen mantle, flung the hood over her head and hastened through the zigzagging corridors and out to a rampart that overlooked the town. She threaded her way through the spectators thronging the battlements to where she could see the vanguard of the Moorish soldiery urging their steeds up the steep avenue of trees and fountains. Down in the square, preparations were being made for jousts and other festivities. Her breath caught in her throat. Beyond, through the arched stone gates of the town, rode Tariq, mounted on his shining black stallion, escorting King Muley at the head of his troops laden with spoil. His guards proudly bore the banners and pennons taken at Zahara which fluttered in the chill February wind.

Livia's heart gave a sickening lurch. Behind them, labored a wretched line of men, women and children worn out with fatigue, haggard with despair.

An awesome silence fell over the citizens as they beheld the wavering parade of prisoners, as though they were overcome with sudden realization of this cruel scene. Mothers clasped their infants to their breasts as the hapless females of Zahara trudged past carrying their dying children in their arms.

To Livia's amazement, a low growl of discontent rose from the populace and steadily grew louder. On every side murmurs of pity for the sufferers were mingled with curses at the barbarity of the king. Old men who had experienced the calamities of warfare voiced dire warnings of further troubles. Wordlessly, those of the court gathered on the rampart turned their backs and withdrew into the sanctuary of the palace. At length Livia became aware of Nizam's small, straight-backed figure standing beside her, grim and silent.

Nizam touched Livia's arm. "Come, this is not good for you to look at," she said gently. "We will ask Tariq to consult the lists for members of your family."

Livia stood dazed, as though unable to drag her eyes from the ragged skeletons that passed before her. Taking Livia's elbow firmly, Nizam led her from the rampart, inside to her chamber.

"I'm sorry," Nizam said quietly.

A feeling of desolation such as Livia had never known swept over her and she sank down on a cushion, making no reply. She would not have recognized her father and Margareta if she had seen them among the wretched captives; nor had she seen anyone who resembled Julian of roguish eye, swaggering along with his somewhat bold and daring air. She did not hear Nizam depart, nor, moments later, did she hear Tariq enter. His hand on her shoulder startled her from her melancholy thoughts. She jerked from his grasp.

He regarded her solemnly, a question in his eyes. At last he said softly, "Did you see your parents? Your brother?"

She turned her head away and stared out the window.

"Did you see them?" he demanded sharply.

Slowly she shook her head, unable to fathom whether he hoped she had found them. "I would prefer to see them dead," she said, fearing for their state of health.

Tariq bent over her and put an arm about her slender shoulders. His voice was unbelievably gentle. "Livia, I would not wish this upon you—upon anyone—but I have examined the list. The name Larreta does not appear. I had hoped there was some mistake, that in the confusion . . ." He broke off.

She knew what he was trying to say, but she would not let herself believe it. She thrust his arm from her shoulders and leaped to her feet shrieking, "You and your war! Is war, too, the will of Allah?" She stopped short, taken aback by the expression of genuine sorrow in his eyes.

"The people do not always observe the teachings of the Prophet. Yet, the preparations for festivity have ceased, and the food which was to have feasted the conquerors has been distributed among the captives."

"That changes nothing!" Livia cried, flinging up her arms in a sweeping gesture. "Will a little food restore their bodies, their homes—"

She halted abruptly as a voice from the courtyard, where nobles and *alfaquis,* or holy men, had gathered to congratulate the king, burst like thunder upon her ears.

Livia and Tariq ran to the window and leaned out to look upon the scene below.

"Woe! Woe! Woe to Granada!" exclaimed a voice. The ruins of Zahara will fall upon our heads. My spirit tells me that the end of our empire is at hand!"

People shrank back aghast and left the man standing alone in the center of the square. He was an ancient man in the rude woolen sacking of a dervish. Age had withered his form without quenching the fire of his spirit, which glared in baleful luster from his eyes.

"He is a holy man," explained Tariq, "one of the *santons* who pass their lives in hermitages, in fasting, meditation and prayer until they attain the purity of saints and the foresight of prophets."

Privately, Livia branded him a fanatic possessed by the devil.

"They are sometimes permitted to predict the truth to their followers," Tariq went on, "but with the proviso that their predictions shall be of no avail."

The voice of the *santon* resounded through the lofty halls of the Alhambra and struck silence into the crowd of courtly sycophants. Livia's gaze flew to King Muley. He alone stood unmoved, eyeing the hoary anchorite with scorn as though his predictions were the ravings of a maniac.

The *santon* rushed from the royal presence, and descending into the city, hurried through its streets. His voice echoed throughout the town in awesome denunciation.

As Livia watched, she saw terror break out upon the faces of those who clearly considered these ravings as a prophecy. Many fled the scene, dashing into their homes to hide. Others gathered together in knots in the streets and squares, alarming each other with dismal forebodings and cursing the rashness and cruelty of the king.

Livia felt only relief. There would be no victory celebration. Tariq would not marry her now, in light of this catastrophe. He would delay the ceremony. Before it could take place, she would be gone.

She watched Muley intently. The only indication that he had been affected was the ashen pallor of his complexion.

"Let the music and the feasting begin!" he shouted.

Livia was distracted by Tariq, who raised a hand as if in signal to three of his comrades who stood talking under an archway, then nodded to a priest, a huge rotund man wearing a brown cassock and a towering turban on his head. The priest detached himself from the courtiers and hurried from the square.

Tariq turned to Livia and tucked her hand in the crook of his arm. "Come, our presence is required in the throne room."

At the feel of his muscular arm and the strength of his body so close to hers, a strange tingling sensation flowed through Livia. Unaccountably, she felt secure. But how could she feel this way on the arm of a man who was determined to possess her? Reason asserted itself. Tariq protected her against Muley and would, if she asked, protect her against the lecherous Malik. Tariq was her protector, that was all.

In the throne room, the nobles and Muley's adherents drank and dined with a pretense of abandon as if to celebrate as the king commanded. But it seemed to Livia that a pall hung over the room. She stood at Tariq's side, stiff and unsmiling, as he presented her to various members of the court. She loathed them all, and wished the festivities would end.

At length Tariq glanced down at her and said softly, "The night grows cold and the fires burn low. We've wasted enough time catering to the King's vanity. Now we must go." He grasped her hand and led her through the crowd.

As she hurried along at Tariq's side, she asked, "Where? Where are we going?"

"To Nizam's apartment. It is there the ceremony will take place."

"Ceremony!" cried Livia in a voice that almost failed her.

"This should come as no surprise to you," said Tariq harshly. "I told you we would be married today."

"No!" She came to a sudden halt and stood bracing her back against a wall. In the dim light of the brass lamp overhead, she saw his jaw harden and his eyes, fierce as a desert hawk's, seemed to pierce her soul.

"You will speak your vows, or return to the harem where you will remain to delight the old king whenever he takes a fancy to you."

Livia swallowed hard, unable to speak. Tears stung her eyelids. A terrifying vision of Muley bestowing the apple upon her rose to her mind, quickly supplanted by a more terrifying image of Malik clutching her to him, his hands and lips violating her body.

Tariq's hand tightened on her arm, bruising the tender flesh. "Shall we proceed?"

Livia bit her lip to keep from crying out in protest. Mutely, she nodded.

Tariq strode on and as she struggled to keep abreast of him, one thought surfaced from her frenzied mind. One measure of hope. Malik had implied that Tariq should have married long ago. Nizam had said that her brother had never found a woman to please him. Perhaps he was marrying her only to comply with an edict in the Koran. If so, she would be his wife in name only. She clung to this thought as though she were drowning in flood waters.

When they entered Nizam's apartment, a hush fell over the room. The brown-robed priest was seated on the divan with a huge book open on his knees. Seated also, in a circle around him, were the three men Tariq had summoned from the courtyard.

Livia looked up at Tariq, her eyes wide with panic. "Nizam!" she said breathlessly. There was still time; the wild idea had come to her that she could flee while he sought out his sister. "Where is Nizam? I wish her to be present,"

Wordlessly, Tariq ushered her across the room, thrust her through the dark blue velvet curtains that divided Nizam's sitting room from her bedchamber, leaving Livia alone with his sister.

Nizam stood waiting, pale and nervous, sympathy shining from her almond-shaped eyes. As if knowing that nothing she could say would alleviate Livia's anguish, she silently draped a white silk mantle about Livia's shoulders and fastened a circlet of rubies and pearls atop her dark hair then gestured toward a gold silk cushion upon the floor.

"Be seated," Nizam said softly. "I will tell you when to speak."

Livia sank down on her knees, her hands clasped in her lap. Her palms were moist and she felt her mind go blank so that she could not think. Surely God would strike her dead before she could be joined to an infidel!

The priest began in a singsong tone, words whose meaning did not penetrate Livia's dazed mind, then stopped abruptly on a note of questioning.

"Say no," Nizam hissed.

"No," Livia said flatly, unable to comprehend a word in her shock.

There was a long silence, then the priest and one of the men began conversing in low tones. Tariq joined in.

"They are talking about your dowry," said Nizam.

After another silence, the priest addressed another question to Livia.

"He asked if you were being forced into the marriage," Nizam whispered. "Say no."

Livia opened her mouth to speak, but no sound came forth. She sat frozen, dazed by an overwhelming sense of unreality. Nizam leaned forward. Her slender hand shot out, and she pinched Livia's wrist.

"No," whispered Livia over the strangling sensation in her throat.

She heard the priest ask Tariq several questions. Then it was her turn again.

"Say yes." Nizam urged.

"Yes," said Livia barely above a whisper.

It was not until Nizam leaned forward and kissed her, that she realized the ceremony was over. She sat stunned, feeling nothing. Nizam took her by the hand and drew her to her feet. As Nizam pushed back the door hangings, Livia gasped in surprise. The sitting room was deserted. Wordlessly, Nizam led her from the apartment, through the halls to Tariq's chambers.

In the sitting room, the first thing that met her frightened gaze was a large square mirror in a silver filigree frame propped up on a low table before the divan. Before it lay a small shawl stiff with embroidered birds, flowers and leafy boughs. On either side stood a silver candlestick, and in the center, a blue-velvet-bound copy of the Koran. A samovar stood on the floor. On a tray beside it were a single tea glass, a cone of sugar, and a silver plate piled high with lozenge-shaped cakes.

Nizam placed her hands on Livia's shoulders, forcing her down upon a cushion before the table so that she looked straight into the mirror in which the door of the room was reflected.

"Wait here for your bridegroom," Nizam said, then gave her an affectionate hug and ran from the chamber.

Livia's nervous gaze swept over the room lighted by the glow of brass oil lamps. The walls were hung with colorful silken tapestries. Wall niches held books, a chess set, a bronze ewer with a spout in the shape of a crowing rooster and a basin used to wash before and after meals, and an ivory box intricately carved with script and foliage. The divan, covered in gold brocade, was strewn with bright pillows. The floor boasted rush mats overlaid with deep red pile carpets. A rosy glow emanated from a shining brass brazier that sent out a feeble warmth.

Livia sat with her hands clasped tightly at her waist, trying to still her trembling when, reflected in the depth of the mirror, she saw Tariq walk through the doorway.

His expression was grave as he approached her. She

watched him warily. Without speaking, he lifted the glass from the table and filled it with tea, then sprinkled a little sugar upon the embroidered shawl and spread it over her hair. "Don't move, or the sugar will sift down your neck." He lifted the shawl by its four corners and sifted the sugar into the glass of tea. Then he stirred it and offered her a sip.

"To drink tea from the same glass, sweetened just this way, is the first act of man and wife," Tariq said softly.

With shaking fingers, Livia raised the glass to her lips, sipped the sweet liquid, then handed the glass to Tariq.

When they had finished, Tariq said solemnly, "You understand, by virtue of this ceremony, that you are now converted from Christianity to Islam. You will take the name I have chosen: Aisha."

Something inside her snapped, plunging her back into reality. She stared up into his face, her eyes kindling with indignation and outrage. "My name is Olivia, Olivia I shall remain. I shall answer to no other."

Their gazes locked and held and a dangerous light flashed from Tariq's eyes. "You are Aisha."

She glared at him, set her lips in a thin determined line, and made no reply.

He looked at her kneeling before him, her eyes bright with defiance, defenseless as a frightened bird, and a smile tugged at the corners of his mouth. He gestured toward the bedchamber. "Your wedding chest with your bridal garments is in there. Go and don your nightrobe, Aisha."

She glanced toward the room and glimpsed a sleeping alcove hung with gold brocade curtains. On the floor beside it was an oak chest studded with an intricate design of brass nailheads. She felt a sinking sensation within her, as though the blood were being drawn from her body. She was to share Tariq's apartment . . . and his bed. Her heart pounded in her breast. Her fingers felt frozen and she clasped them more tightly together, too terrified to move. At last she found her voice.

"I do not answer to Aisha!"

Tariq let out an amused chuckle. "We shall see. Perhaps all you can manage is one command at a time." Suddenly he scowled and roared, "Go and put on your nightrobe!"

Livia leaped to her feet and fled into the bedchamber. She flung the curtains closed and with shaking hands lifted the lid of her wedding chest. In the center was a tray that held a tooled leather pouch with a thong drawstring, along with other small objects encased in blue velvet which she surmised must be jewels. My dowry, thought Livia with a bitter smile. She slid the tray to one side and drew out a garment that lay on top of the well-laden chest: a long white sleeveless robe of double layers of chiffon.

She tried to block from her mind the unthinkable thought of what was about to happen. Hurriedly, Livia took off her garments lest Tariq should grow impatient and burst in upon her. In desperation, she seized upon one last hope. If Tariq had married her only on a whim, from some perverse motive of satisfying his vanity, or the court, or the Koran, perhaps he would allow her to sleep apart from him. But even as she thought it, she knew that this proud and arrogant Moor was the sort of man who would take what was his right.

Chapter 9

Livia's heart hammered like a fist in her breast, and she felt a tight, choking sensation in ther throat. Suddenly her only thought was to make haste, to leave this room before he forced her upon the bed. Her back stiffened in determination. He would have to chain her to the wall to keep her there. She would insist upon sleeping on the divan.

"Aisha!" roared Tariq from the sitting room.

Gripped by a paralyzing spasm of panic, she stood frozen, unable to move.

There was a long, intense silence. Then Tariq's voice erupted again. "Come here!"

Fearing that he would charge into the bedchamber to fetch her, Livia stepped forward and parted the curtains. She stifled a gasp. Tariq had snuffed out the lamps and drawn back the heavy draperies from the window embrasure.

The moon shone with a clear, brilliant light that flooded the room. Her gaze flew to Tariq. He had shed his tunic and was clad in a long white linen *galabia* and trousers. He stood at the low table before the divan, pouring wine from a ewer into two silver goblets.

Without looking up, he said, "Come here, Livia."

Reluctantly she crossed to his side. His dark eyes flicked over her from the top of her luxuriant hair, flowing loosely over her shoulders, down the length of her slender erect figure to her toes, then traveled slowly upward to linger on the diaphanous layers of snowy chiffon that barely concealed her nudity, whose soft folds accentuated the enticing curves of her breasts and hips.

A warm flush crept up her neck, into her cheeks. She could read neither approval nor disapproval in his gaze, and unaccountably a small stab of disappointment swept through her. Sternly she told herself that at least he had not appraised her as though she were a prize lamb going to the slaughter. As he bent over the table, the fabric of his shirt strained across the breadth of his muscular shoulders and the thought of being trapped in the embrace of his arms terrified her.

Solemn and unsmiling, he took up the goblets and offered one to Livia. "We shall drink a toast to eternal happiness in our marriage."

Ignoring the proffered goblet, she stepped back. It did not appear to her that Tariq was at all happy over their marriage, but he could be no less happy than she! "Our marriage is the last thing I will toast!"

Tariq's dark brows rose and a cynical smile touched his lips. "And what of eternal happiness?"

"Happiness is not possible, married to you!"

He smiled down at her as though amused, a knowing, patronizing smile that infuriated her. If only there were some way she could reach him! But he remained imperturable, always in control. In her fury, she made a silent vow: One day I will penetrate that cold self-assurance, and I will destroy you!

He set her goblet on the table and said calmly, "You should drink it anyway. It will warm you."

If this man thought to do away with her resistance by plying her with wine, he was wrong! Her mounting rage warmed her more than any wine could have done.

"I am quite warm enough!"

"Good!" He drained the wine from his goblet and set it down on the table. "Come with me to the window. There is something I wish to show you."

Willing to do anything to delay the encounter she feared, Livia quickly crossed to the three-sided balcony. She stood staring out a double arched window, acutely aware of Tariq's presence behind her; the heat of his body, his head close to hers, his bearded chin grazing the top of her hair. Every nerve in her body was drawn fine, tingling with apprehension lest he touch her.

Her gaze swept the hillsides pockmarked with caves where the prisoners were. A shudder went through her and she was thankful that her family's name had not appeared on the lists. She glanced downward, then drew in her breath sharply at the sight of the sheer drop from the walls of the fortress to the rocky ground below. Her eyes followed along the valley where moonlight gilded a winding river like a silver ribbon.

"The Darro," murmured Tariq, "the lifeblood of the Alhambra. When Muhammad Ibn Ahmar took Granada more than two centuries ago, only the old Ziridian fortress—*the alcazaba*—stood on the outer spur of the hill. Ibn Ahmar erected the high walls and towers, fencing in the broader ridge of the hill. The building of the palace was made possible after he diverted the water of the Darro, bringing it to the top of the mountain and along the slopes down to the *Sabika*, the spur of the Alhambra. It is a garden flowing with streams—the Koran's description of paradise."

Suddenly Livia understood why the kingdom of Granada was of such great importance to the Moors, and a cold tremor ran down her spine: They would never surrender. Then, thinking of the graceful arcades supported by slender columns, the lacework arches and stucco tracery, the soaring domes shedding their luminous light, and the splendor of the marbled halls, she turned to face Tariq.

"One would think your builders would have erected a structure that would endure rather than this crystalline palace of plaster and wood," she said tartly.

Tariq shook his head. "The *alcazaba* will endure forever, but the palace was not built to last." His lips curved in a condescending smile that infuriated her. "We Moslems are aware of the transitory nature of things. Islamic palaces are meant to house the man temporarily authorized to enforce the laws of our religion. His successor would efface or destroy what he has left and would wish to reside in a different place."

"That is well," Livia said venomously. The Christian army will soon wipe this stronghold from the face of the land!"

Tariq let out a shout of laughter. "The unbelievers have tried for centuries to drive us from Spain. They will never succeed. The entire kingdom of Granada is encircled by mountains, and the city is one vast fortress. The Alhambra itself is a citadel—one of the strongest in the whole of Spain." His voice took on an ominous tone. "Do not waste your time in foolish dreaming, thinking that you will be rescued."

Livia felt her face flame at his canny reading of her thoughts. Behind his phlegmatic exterior, he was more perceptive than she had imagined. He was an enemy to be reckoned with.

"In any case," Tariq continued, "if you could but read the inscriptions upon the walls of the palace, you would understand: *Wa lā ghāliba illa-Llāh*. There is no victor besides God."

"I have read your inscriptions!" Livia snapped. "Your conquerors were most thorough in assimilating our people. We learned not only to speak, but to read and write Arabic in Seville, before we fled for our lives to Zahara."

"Seville?" Tariq repeated, perplexed. "Seville is under Castilian domination. It could not have been the Moors who drove you from your home. Who, then?"

Livia's fine brows drew together in annoyance. She had no wish to speak of her past, but the longer they talked, the longer she could defer her doom.

"No," Livia admitted ruefully. "It was not the Moors. You see, Queen Isabella and King Ferdinand are as intent upon unifying their people as they are on pacifying them. Four years ago they became obsessed with purity of blood and established the royal Inquisition designed to insure a purely Catholic Spain.

"Father and I are of Castilian blood, so we were safe. However, after my mother's death, when I was but two, Father married Margareta, a Jew. A year later, Julian was born." Livia paused, as though it were painful for her to go on.

When Tariq said nothing, she continued. "Last year, I shall never forget the day—February 6, 1481—was held the first *auto-da-fé* of the Spanish Inquisition."

Tariq regarded her with grave eyes and said nothing.

"Six prisoners found guilty of heresy and unwilling to repent were turned over to the secular authorities and burned at the stake. No Jew was safe from the purge. Father feared for the lives of Margareta and Julian and fled with us to Zahara."

Tariq's strong hands tightened on her shoulders. "You need have no fear of the Moors. Should an enemy surrender, he must be given protection. If he is a heathen, he must convert to Islam or be killed. But if he belongs to the 'people of the holy book,' as does a Jew or Christian, he is free to continue to practice his own religion as long as he recognizes the sovereignty of Islam.

"Islam, you see, is the renewal, or restoration of the original religion of Abraham. It is as the root of a tree of which Judaism and Christianity are branches. If Jews and Christians are unfaithful to the heritage of Abraham, hostile to Islam, Moslems have the right to take up the sword against them. In fact, it is the duty of every Moslem to fight the holy war whenever our community is threatened. Those who are killed in the holy war die as a witness of the divine truth and are admitted to paradise. And so, you see, we shall win our battle with the Spaniards."

Livia's lips curved scornfully. She wanted to take him to task at the travesty of the Moors' "protection," but it would serve no purpose to arouse his anger. Instead, she moved away from him, across the embrasure to stare out the window at the ochre-tiled roofs of the town, and beyond to the gardenlike *vega* blanched white by moonlight. Tariq moved to her side.

"And what of your past?" Livia asked, feeling like Sheherezade, who staved off death at the hands of the sultan with tales for a thousand and one nights.

Tariq's dark brows rose in surprise. For a moment he said nothing, as though considering whether or not to speak of his past. At last he said, "I have been most fortunate to inherit the best of two worlds.

"My father was a Berber, a descendant of those who first landed in southern Spain in the spring of 711. They were noted for courage in war, hardihood in farming, honesty in personal dealings and a passionate attachment to saints.

"My mother was a Bedouin, daughter of a family whose ancestors roamed the deserts of Arabia and, sometime in the eleventh century, migrated to Africa. They consider themselves the only true Arabs."

Livia, studying his stalwart figure, his oval face framed by his thick beard, his fierce eyes and bronzed skin, could easily imagine him roaming the deserts with his nomadic ancestors. A new understanding came to her of this enigmatic Moor, confident of his own nature and dependent on no one.

He smiled wryly. "I was named after the Berber chieftan who lead the invasion of Spain. Tariq Ibn Ziyad, who bequeathed his name to the mountain of rock to the south: Jebal Tariq."

"I have read the history of the Moorish conquests," Livia said coldly.

Unperturbed by her barb, Tariq grinned down at her. "If you read Arabic, you will enjoy Nizam's poetry. She is our court poet."

His words evoked the memory of the day Livia had burst in upon Nizam bent over the table in her chamber, pen in hand. Perhaps, through the bond of the girl's poetry, they might become friends. Despite

Nizam's antipathy toward Spaniards, Livia felt a kinship with the girl and longed for her friendship in this
alien land. "I should like to read it." She turned from
Tariq, crossed to the opposite window and gazed high
up the mountain slope at a cluster of slender white
towers and arcades.

Tariq moved to her side. "You see before you the
summer palace of the king, the Generalife, the garden
of the architect, which we pronounce hener-al-eefy.
Below it lies the *Dar al Arusa*—the Bride's House—
and on the summit, the palace of the Alijares."

Livia's gaze wandered over the hilltops covered with
gardens, pergolas and small palaces, lingering on the
spires of pointed cypresses dark against the sky.

Tariq placed an arm lightly about her shoulders. She
stiffened and his arm tightened about her. "One day
when the sun grows warm, we shall go there, you and I.
The gardens are the most magnificent on earth. We'll
sit in the patio of the rose laurel and enjoy the perfume
of the jasmine, the murmur of the fountains, the song
of the nightingale. You shall play the lute for me and
sing romantic ballads, and I shall read you poetry."

Livia bit her lip to keep from uttering the protest that
sprang to her mind. It would not do to arouse his ire
now, but she knew that strolling through the romantic
gardens of the Generalife was the last thing she would
do with Tariq Ibn Ziyah.

Gently, his fingers caressed a tendril of hair that
curled about her temple, and trailed down the slender
curve of her neck. A tremor ran through her. He
placed a finger under her chin and turned her face up to
his. When he spoke, his voice was unbelievably gentle,
and a tenderness that she would not have believed
possible shone from his dark eyes.

"You have nothing to fear from me, little one."

Tears of relief sprang to her eyes and she breathed a
long thankful sigh. He was not going to take her.
Malik's spiteful accusation was true!

He bent his head to hers and his lips brushed her

eyelids, her cheeks, her lips. "If Granada is Islam's paradise on earth, her earthly goddess is a woman whose face is as round as the full moon, her hair darker than the night, her cheeks white and rosy, her eyes intensely black and large like those of a wild deer, her eyelids languid, her mouth small with teeth like pearls set in coral, her bosom like the pomegranate, her lips wide and her fingers tapering—like you, my Zahareña."

A rosy flush warmed her cheeks and she drew back and stood looking up into his face, her lips slightly parted in wonder, her eyes shining with gratitude.

He smiled down at her and his low, deep voice was like a caress. "You are like the poem:

> A laugh revealing pearls,
> A face, beautiful as the moon.
> Time is too narrow to contain it,
> But my heart does so.

Livia drew in her breath softly. She had been prepared to fight this infidel's advances tooth and nail, but how could she fight a man whose only weapon was poetry! She gazed deep into his eyes, eyes that burned with a look of such intensity that she knew she could never plumb their depths. She seemed caught up in a spell, unable to detach her gaze from his. Her heart beat frantically, like the wings of a caged bird, her breast rising and falling with her short, shallow breaths. At last she said, "You told me you wished to show me—"

A smile curved his lips. "Ah, yes. I'd forgotten. Come here." Sliding an arm about her waist, he led her to the center window in the embrasure and leaned over the low sill. "Look below, near the base of the wall."

Livia bent forward, acutely aware of Tariq's arm tightening about her waist as she peered down at a tangle of brambles and nettles.

"There, in the thicket. Do you see it?"

"A nest!" exclaimed Livia in surprise. "Nightin-gales?"

Tariq nodded. "The young birds have just hatched. I've been watching them since they were eggs. A miracle, do you not agree?"

Livia drew back and smiled up into his tanned, solemn face. "Yes, a miracle," she said softly, thinking that the miracle was that a commander in the most feared army on earth could be moved by the sight of a nightingale's nest. "I love the nightingale because it sings night and day, Livia said quietly."

Tariq's mouth curved in an amused smile. "If you want to know what it means to be driven to madness by that unfinished feeling, live in a garden that boasts a nightingale. Never was one known to complete its song. The best of them will stop right in the middle of a trill." His finger traced the line of her cheekbone down to her chin. "The nightingales are not the only miracle I've seen this day."

He bent his head to hers. Livia gazed up at him as though mesmerized, unable to move. Her eyes closed and all thought fled from her mind. She was aware of nothing but Tariq's lips on hers, warm and tender. His arms did not reach out to imprison her, nor did he press her to him as she had feared. There was no attacker to fend off.

Mindful of the window at her back, she swayed toward him, as though drawn by his strength, his warmth, in the chill night air wafting through the embrasure. Her lips lingered on his. Without volition, her hands crept up to his shoulders. His lips grew more demanding and, helpless to resist, her mouth clung to his. She felt light-headed and her knees trembled.

She was dimly aware of his hands on her back as they sank to their knees upon the thick carpet, and then she knew nothing except the excitement of his lips on her own.

A chill breeze eddied around them. She shivered and

instinctively her body curved to his. His arms tightened about her protectively, his lips moved from hers, kissing her eyes, her cheeks, her throat, the hollow between her breasts. Firm, gentle hands pressed against the small of her back and her body arched, thrusting upward with an urgency she was powerless to control. He buried his face between her breasts, nudging aside the thin fabric of her gown, exposing a full white breast to the moonlight, his mouth seeking, exploring.

A gasp of pleasure escaped her and an overpowering languor flowed through her as he eased her down upon the soft carpet. He covered her body with his and slid her gown from her shoulders. She was no longer cold, but warm with the heat of his desire kindling her own. Again his mouth sought hers. She clung to him as he slipped her gown down about her waist. His hands stroked her long slender legs as he drew the filmy garment along the length of her body and cast it aside.

A voice in her head cried out in protest, but the words would not form on her lips. She was lost, caught up in a rapture she was helpless to resist. She was unaware that he had taken off his own garments until she felt the thick, curly mat of hair that covered his chest and legs soft against her skin.

Coaxing, pressing, his strong, gentle fingers sought out hollows and angles, stirring her longing to the point of desperation. As his caresses grew more ardent, more demanding, her ardor rose, matching his, and her slender body molded to his shape. With passionate tenderness he raised his narrow hips and thrust into her. Feeling herself carried with him, almost before knowing they had begun, almost before her slight resistance to his entrance had ended, it was over, culminating in an ecstasy that left her weak and spent, and strangely, with a feeling of contentment such as she had never known.

Gently Tariq lifted her in his arms, carried her to the

gold divan and set her down among the pillows. He stretched out beside her and pulled a covering of furs over them, tucking the pelts about her shoulders. Drowsily Livia cast a sidelong glance at Tariq lying close to her side. Her lips curved in an ironic smile. She had sworn to sleep on the divan.

Chapter 10

Livia awoke at sunrise to the strains of the muezzin's chant. Brilliant shafts of light glanced through the windows, bathing the room in a golden glow. As her gaze fell upon the soft carpet in the embrasure, the memory of her passionate union with Tariq flooded her mind and she blushed deeply. What could have possessed her, that she had no more self-control than . . . than the most wanton houri in the harem? She turned to face Tariq. The place where he had lain beside her was empty. Unaccountably, she felt an odd sense of loss, of having been deserted.

She started at a noise in the bedchamber and the next instant Tariq strode through the doorway and crossed to her side. With a slight sense of shock it struck her that her phantom lover who had wooed her in darkness and moonlight now appeared as a stranger before her; handsome, robust, regal, a formidable figure clad in a vivid blue tunic and trousers under a short-sleeved, ankle-length scarlet robe belted at the waist with a wide gold sash. An immaculate white turban accentuated his ruddy complexion and full beard.

She could read no expression in his impenetrable countenance, but in his dark eyes smoldered an inner fire, a gleam which Livia interpreted as exultation at having triumphed over his captive. The thought filled her with rage.

He knelt on the edge of the divan and gently kissed her brow. Then, smiling down at her, he murmured,

"You are the wife of whom men dream. I fear your unbridled passion swept me off my feet."

She thought she heard a hint of mockery in his voice. "You Arabs lay claim to being the heirs of chivalry," Livia said contemptuously, "but your seduction of me was not the act of a chivalrous knight and was unworthy of you."

He regarded her solemnly, but amusement glinted in his eyes. "There is an Arab proverb: A soft tongue can take milk from a lioness!"

Livia sat bolt upright. Hot color flooded her neck, up into her face and she glared at him. "You! You defiler of women!" she erupted. "You knew all too well what you were about! Far from being overwhelmed with passion, you set out to seduce me as thoroughly, as cleverly as you would have planned an attack upon an impregnable fortress!"

A quirk of laughter tugged at the corners of his mouth and he held out his hands palms up, his brows raised in question. "How else was I to take my Zahareña?"

Livia snatched up a pillow and flung it at his head. Dodging the missile, he let out a shout of laughter which only inflamed her further. As he walked across the room she snatched up another pillow and yet another, and hurled them at him, one after the other. Tariq stepped swiftly through the doorway and was gone, his laughter echoing down the passageway after him.

Livia flung herself down upon the divan and beat the sofa with clenched fists. Her cheeks burned at the memory of Tariq's lips warm on hers, the touch of his gentle hands that turned her body to tallow. What a blackguard he was! To make matters worse, though she fought against it, she had exulted in the fulfillment of utter surrender. If only she could recapture the thrill, the glow of Aguilar's chaste and noble love. If only he would come for her soon!

At length, her ire exhausted, she leaped up from the divan, marched into the bedchamber and flung on her clothes. She would show this barbarian that she was not to be won by sweet murmurs of romantic poetry and soft caresses, that she was not to be his merely by virtue of words spoken by a Moslem priest!

She threw open the lid of her bridal chest, snatched up an armload of garments and fled from Tariq's apartment. After taking several wrong turns, she dashed through the harem quarters to her room. Here she would stay. Should Tariq come to claim her, he would have to drag her out kicking and screaming in a way that would bring the walls of this delicate plaster palace down about his ears!

She spent the day in her chamber, ordering a slave to bring her food and a tub in which to bathe. As she sank down into the warm, soothing water, unbidden there rose to her mind the memory of the touch of Tariq's knowledgeable hands caressing her. Quickly she banished the thought. With a vengeance, she scrubbed her body till her creamy skin reddened and stung. She stepped from the tub and after a brisk rubdown, splashed her skin liberally with the sweet scent of rosewater. She had soaped and rinsed her hair and now sat before the window, letting the sun warm her body, running her fingers through the silken strands of her long black tresses.

At last she felt cleansed of her ravishment by Tariq. She dressed in a yellow silk tunic and blue and white striped trousers, then took up a lute which Amina had given her. At the memory of Amina's suggestion that she learn to play prettily and thus make herself more appealing to add to the king's pleasure, the corners of Livia's mouth turned down. She had enjoyed playing the instrument in the days before her family had fled from Seville, and now she found the Arab lute responding to her touch. As she held it in her lap and plucked the yellow, red, white and black strings, she found solace in its soft mellow tones. She tried to strum the ballads she had heard the slave girls sing, improvising to the plaintive melodies in an outpouring of her longing for Aguilar.

Eventually darkness closed in upon her. She lighted the oil lamps and crossed the room to peruse the books standing in a wall niche. She took down a volume of Nizam's poems and curled up in a corner of the divan to read. But the poems of unrequited love and romance only made her feel lonely and restless. Her mind wandered. Where was Tariq?

As the evening wore on, her loneliness turned to apprehension. Surely he would burst through the doorway at any moment. She had girded herself to do battle with him and now she was eager for the battle to start. She could not prepare for bed until she had driven him away, for it would be folly to appear before him in the diaphanous white gown that had so inflamed his desire last night.

The muezzin's call, heralding the beginning of the night, sounded and still Tariq did not come. Her eyelids closed, the volume slid from her hand and sleep freed her from reality to dream of her cavalier Alonzo de Aguilar.

Tariq did not appear that night, nor the next. With each hour that passed, Livia's annoyance mounted. She paced the room like a caged panther, peering out the window a thousand times. How dare this arrogant soldier marry her and then cast her aside as he would a battle-scarred cuirass! The everyday sounds of life going on in the palace without her only increased her distress. The insidious, debasing suspicion that she had failed to delight him in their frantic lovemaking lurked in the recesses of her mind. Had he found her wanting? Or had he decided, after hearing her wild accusations the next morning, that he was well rid of her? No, she told herself sternly. She, Olivia Larreta, daughter of a proud and aristocratic Castilian family, would not accept this possibility.

When three days and nights had passed, she could

endure the waiting no longer. She squared her shoulders and marched from her chamber to seek out Nizam. True, Nizam had no sympathy for Spaniards, but on the day Livia had been forced to marry Tariq, Nizam's soft brown eyes had betrayed some feeling for Livia's plight. That Tariq had deserted her would add weight to her plea.

As Livia traversed the dimly lighted passageways of the Alhambra, her mind was in a turmoil, trying to decide upon the best approach. At last she resolved to prevail upon Nizam to speak to Tariq on her behalf. Surely Nizam would understand how it felt to be married to a man one loathes, subject to his demands, his desires, when all the while one's heart longed for another. Nizam must convince Tariq that an unwilling bride was worse than no bride at all.

As Livia hurried along, she paused, distracted from her thoughts by an odd sense of unease. To her surprise, the Hall of the Alberca was deserted, as was the adjoining Hall of Ambassadors. No one was about. An unnatural hush pervaded the palace. Beyond, in the Court of Myrtles, even the birds were silent. She shrugged and hastened on. When she arrived breathless before the doorway to Nizam's chamber, her way was barred by a young girl who insisted that her mistress did not wish to be disturbed.

Darting past her, Livia burst into the room. Nizam was seated near the window, a glazed expression on her delicate face, her shoulders slumped, her hands clasped tightly about a folio of paper lying in her lap. Her entire demeanor conveyed the air of one who had suffered a shock.

"Nizam, I must speak with you!" cried Livia, rushing to her side. "I regret to interrupt your writing, but it is a matter of the utmost importance."

Nizam turned to face her and regarded her with a remote stare. "You have not heard the news?"

"News! How would I have heard the news?"

Nizam uttered a hopeless sigh and in a voice of doom

said, "King Muley has confined Prince Boabdil and his mother Ayxa in the Tower of Comares. They are virtual prisoners there!"

Livia's eyes widened in shocked disbelief as she waited for Nizam to go on.

"It's said that Muley received information of a plan by Boabdil's adherents to depose the king and place Boabdil upon the throne." Nizam shook her head in foreboding. "The king sets the stars at defiance. You should have heard him ranting about, calling to everyone's mind the prediction of the astrologers that the youth would one day cause the ruin of Granada. He swore to have Boabdil executed."

Livia sank down on a cushion beside Nizam. "Surely they cannot put him to the sword with no reason . . ."

Nizam's soft dark eyes kindled with outrage. "He has reason. The viper Zoraya has seen to that. She will provide the proof, though nothing could be more untrue."

"Have you spoken of this to Raduan?"

Nizam nodded and her eyes filled with tears. "We . . . we argued about it until he dismissed me. He takes the king's part. He will not listen to me. There is nothing to be done."

"Tariq?"

Nizam said with asperity, "You forget that Tariq is commander-in-chief of the king's army. Though his sympathies lie with Boabdil, while the king lives, Boabdil has no right to the throne."

"Was not Tariq one who plotted to depose the king?"

Nizam tilted her head to one side and regarded Livia with a puzzled frown. "How could he? Tariq has been gone these past three days on forays." Livia's brows rose in astonishment as Nizam continued vexedly. "Even knowing that this exploit must draw upon him the wrath of the Christians, the king threw off all reserve and made attempts to surprise the enemy— without success. The people of the town mutter their discontent. It was this ill-timed action that fomented the conspiracies among the nobles. Of course, Zoraya was quick to take advantage of this turn of events and reported all to Muley."

Livia gazed at her in stunned silence as she considered the news that Tariq had been gone these past days. She asked quietly, "Has Tariq returned?"

"No," Nizam said shortly. He returns tomorrow." Deep in thought, Livia made no reply.

Nizam eyed her curiously. "Did you not know that Tariq had left?"

Livia shook her head wordlessly.

Nizam's voice was soft, almost apologetic. "The troops departed in the greatest secrecy, before dawn's light. Perhaps Tariq had no wish to wake you with the news that he was riding out to battle. Doubtless he left word with a servant who neglected to give you his message."

Apparently Nizam wished to soften the insult that Tariq had gone without a word; or was she merely defending her brother's actions? *Had* Tariq left word for her, Livia wondered. Or had he not cared whether or not she knew of his activities? She took a deep breath in an effort to steady her nerves.

"It was Tariq of whom I wished to speak, Nizam. I have left his chambers to return to the harem." Undaunted by Nizam's incredulous gasp, she plunged on, stating her case. When she had done, Nizam stared at her in disbelief.

"You do not intend to honor your vow of marriage?"

"Please understand," pleaded Livia. "My situation is impossible! Surely you must agree." She clasped Nizam's hands in entreaty. "Please, I beseech you, speak with Tariq on my behalf."

Nizam's face flamed and a hard light came into her eyes. "It is unthinkable that a woman would turn her back upon a marriage with a man of such virtue and chivalrous nature as my brother Tariq! I now speak to *you* upon *his* behalf. If you are wise, you will accept your marriage as the will of Allah!"

Livia stared into Nizam's eyes and saw not a glimmer of understanding. She felt a sinking sensation, as though she were drowning. There was no help to be had from Nizam. Choking down tears of disappointment, Livia jumped to her feet and fled from the chamber.

Chapter 11

Upon entering her own room, Livia stopped short.
Darkness had fallen and in the soft glow of the oil
lamps, the room appeared as she had left it. A sixth
sense warned her, however, that something was amiss.
She drew in her breath sharply and it came to her then
what was wrong. A spicy aroma lay heavily on the air.
Her gaze fell upon a small table on which stood an
incense burner in the shape of a bird. From the holes
pierced in its breast and head wafted the fumes of
sandalwood. Where the bird had come from, she had
no idea.

As she moved toward it, a tall figure garbed in a
black turban, tunic and trousers rose up from among
the pillows in the sleeping alcove and strode toward
her.

"Malik!"

His eyes flicked to the incense burner. "I see you
appreciate my gift." His mouth turned downward at
the corners, giving him an air of discontent even when
at peace with the world. "I've been waiting for you. I
thought you might be lonely with Tariq gone. The
messengers tell me he won't return until tomorrow."

Livia drew herself up to her full height. "I am not
lonely, Malik. I've things to do." In a tone of dismissal,
she added, "Please excuse me."

She strode to a chest in the corner, raised the lid and
lifted out the royal blue brocade tunic which she had

not finished hemming, then seated herself on a floor cushion and took up her needle and thread.

Malik stood motionless, watching her every move. "Of course I'll excuse you." His tone was deceptively amiable. "But you do owe me an apology."

Livia, head bent over her needlework, studied him from under lowered lids. His thick moustache furred his thin lips; his brows almost met over a large, long nose; his eyes were small and beady, set too close together. His manner, his gleaming obsidian eyes, reminded her of a snake. Without looking up, she replied, "I'm sorry, Malik, but you overstepped your bounds. Now please go."

He uttered a harsh, unpleasant laugh that grated on Livia's ears. "You do not appear sorry."

Livia looked up and fixed him with a stern glare. "You forget yourself. I am married to Tariq. He will not take lightly your forcing your attentions upon me."

Malik crossed the room and stood looking down at her, arms folded across his chest. The huge diamond on his index finger glinted ominously and his presence filled the room. Deliberately avoiding his eyes, Livia concentrated on her stitches, her needle flashing in and out of the fabric.

Malik's hand shot out. He grasped her chin firmly in his talonlike fingers, tilting her face upward. "Your vows mean nothing. You are married in name only. Tariq cares nothing for you. He and his sister both hate the Spanish dogs!"

Livia forced her voice to remain calm. "Since he has married me, he has obviously overcome his aversion to Spaniards. In any case, our marriage was not necessary. He could have forced himself upon me." She jerked her head sharply in an effort to slip from his grasp, but he held her chin in a grip of steel.

"Oh, but your marriage *was* necessary," said Malik with a sly smile. "Tariq had a score to settle with our pleasure-loving Prince Boabdil. And, when you were sent to the harem, he was forced to marry you to prevent our wily king from using you for his pleasure. Your fine cavalier could not countenance that."

"Nonsense!" said Livia sharply. "He brought me here for the purpose of marrying Boabdil."

"Exactly. And Boabdil spurned his gift because he had taken Khadija—"

In a violent motion, Livia struck his hand away and jumped to her feet clutching the tunic to her breast as though to defend herself against Malik's advances. "I wish to hear no more of your gossip, your petty court intrigues. Leave me. At once!"

Malik gripped her shoulders and drew her roughly to him. He pressed her close against his chest, crushing the garment she was mending between them. "Livia, please, you don't understand how I feel about you. Tariq cares nothing for you. I adore you. I worship the ground you walk on. I asked Muley to give you to me on the very day that Tariq snatched you from the harem and married you. It was a vile act on his part, a grave injustice to you. He didn't want you for himself, yet he didn't want anyone else to have you."

As she looked up at him, it struck Livia that though there was peace on his face, there was malice in his heart. He was jealous of Tariq's favor with Boabdil and envious of his military success. She turned her attention to what Malik was saying.

"I will give you everything you've always wanted. I am the king's right hand. He will grant me anything I ask. He will order Tariq to divorce you, if I request it. You have no love for Tariq—do not deny it!"

Confused and upset, Livia raised her hands and pushed hard against his chest, trying desperately to shove him away. "No! No, I do not love Tariq, but—"

Malik brought his mouth down on hers in a punishing kiss that bruised her lips and made her cry out in pain. She felt panic, as though she were being suffocated. Her arm flew up and with all the strength she could muster, she drove the needle into Malik's chest.

He drew back abruptly, then glanced down at the needle protruding from his chest. He threw back his head and emitted a scornful laugh. Thunderstruck, Livia stared at him as he plucked it from his tunic, held it at arm's length and let it fall upon the carpet.

His eyes narrowed to slits. "I like a woman with fire, my dove. All the more challenge in the taming. Next time, make certain you do not waste your weapon on a suitor who is armed against the winter's chill . . . and the thrust of pinpricks." He took her hands in his and pressed them hard against his chest. Through the wool fabric, she could feel the thick leather of the vest he wore underneath.

Fright made her voice tremble, shattering the tone of command she had intended. "Malik, you must go. Go this instant!"

Malik's expression turned to one of bafflement mixed with annoyance. He raised his hands in a helpless gesture. "You must not be afraid of me. I wish only to love you."

Livia stepped back abruptly and stumbled over the cushion on which she had been sitting. Swiftly Malik's arms encircled her. With a wrathful shriek, Livia came to her feet. Her eyes blazed with loathing as he squeezed her against his sinewy body. He covered her mouth with his own and forced her lips apart, his darting tongue stabbing. Bending her backward, his arm securely about her waist, his knee plunged between her thighs.

A feeling of revulsion swept through her and a suffocating sensation blocked the air from her throat. Frantically, she tried to swallow and could not. Abruptly Malik's mouth left hers, trailing moist kisses down her neck. Her breasts rose as she drew in a great gasp of air that exploded in a scream that seemed to echo throughout the halls and penetrate to the furthest corners of the palace.

Startled, Malik jerked upright. A furious scowl contorted his features. Livia closed her eyes and let out

another knife-edged scream, then another and another.
She heard him utter a stream of curses, felt his arms
drop from her sides. As though powerless to stop, her
screams went on and on as she sank to her knees upon
the floor.

Gradually, she became aware of an emptiness closing
in around her. Her screams subsided. Malik was gone.
She could have cried with relief. And then a strange
thought struck her: Malik had fled, yet no one had
come to her rescue.

It was not until the following afternoon that Livia
learned why no one had come to her aid. She was
seated with the harem maidens, her thoughts occupied
with Tariq. Had he returned? She tried to put down the
irritation that plagued her. If he had, why had he not
sought her out? If he should seek her out, of course,
she would not follow him to his apartments. Yet,
perversely, she seethed inside over his neglect.

Determined to put Tariq from her mind, she took up
her lute and was strumming a cheerful tune when
Amina rushed into the room, her eyes shining, her face
flushed, bursting with news. Excited cries rose from the
houris seated nearby. Amina's voice rose, the babble
ceased and Livia's hands dropped from her instrument
as she listened to Amina's incredible tale.

"Last night one of Ayxa's spies warned her of her
son's imminent danger of falling under Muley's sword.
She gathered her female attendants about her, then
bribed the guard to unlock her from the apartment in
which she was held so she could visit Boabdil in the
Comares Tower." Amina's bright eyes sparkled as she
rushed on. "Then she tied together her scarves and
those of her attendants and lowered him from a balcony
hillside which sweeps down to the Darro. Some of her
adherents met him and spirited him away to Guadix,
south of town. King Muley ordered a search for him,
but to no avail!"

Livia, though she held little sympathy for the infidels, was thankful that Boabdil had made good his escape. She could not help but admire the intrepid Ayxa for aiding him. At that moment her thoughts were interrupted by a black eunuch who appeared at the doorway to summon the women to the king's bath. She rose to her feet and followed the maidens, but instead of accompanying them to the baths, she made her way up a back stairway to a balcony that overlooked a small patio where it was unlikely anyone would find her. Sheltered from the wind, she sat, eyes closed, basking in the warmth of the afternoon sun. She breathed deeply of the fresh air, a pleasant relief from the heavy incense and perfumes of the harem.

She had no idea how long she had been sitting there when the sound of heated voices floated up to her from the garden below. She rose to her feet and peered over the wooden balustrade. Khadija, wearing a black woolen mantle, sat on a stone bench under an almond tree whose slender branches were budding fresh leaves. With an impatient gesture, she reached up and flung back her hood. Her heart-shaped face was flushed with color. Her eyes, darkened with kohl, flashed fire. Her hands, nails tipped with henna, gripped the bench. With an intuitive flash, Livia realized that she was the sort of woman who would make trouble for the pleasure of it.

Livia leaned forward in order to see the object of her ire. Scowling down at Khadija, hands clasped behind his back, stood Tariq. His raised voice sliced through the silent garden.

"Could you not have waited for my return?"

And Khadija's strident reply. "They told me you were dead—that you had died during the foray against Zahara."

"Who told you that?" Tariq demanded.

Khadija shrugged. "I don't recall." She jumped up from the bench and flung her arms about Tariq's neck. "Who told me matters not, my darling. What matters is that you are here now."

Tariq disengaged her arms roughly. "It matters to me! Would you accept the word of someone who would say anything, one who is eager to start rumors to discredit the king!"

Khadija gazed earnestly up into Tariq's face. "Oh, no. It was someone of import—someone who would know, should know!"

"Was it Malik?" Tariq grasped her shoulders and shook her hard. "Tell me: Was it Malik?"

"Yes, yes, it was! Surely the king's vizier should know if his commander-in-chief had fallen. You cannot blame me for thinking you dead!"

In quiet, icy tones Tariq replied, "You know very well that Malik never forgets a slight, real or imagined, and lives for the day when he can bring me down. Even if he had spoken the truth, I'd not have been cold in my grave before you leaped into the arms of Boabdil."

Khadija's voice turned pleading. "What else could I do? One does not refuse a prince."

"You could have told him you were betrothed to me!"

"I told him as much. A prince cares nothing for that. He . . . he commanded me to marry him."

Livia could endure to hear no more, and ran from the balcony back to her chamber. Malik was right. Tariq cared nothing for her. He had married her to even a score with Khadija. Livia's mouth turned down in a bitter smile. How clever of Tariq. In one stroke he had evened the score with Khadija for her faithlessness and at the same time had deprived Boabdil of his "jewel" of Zahara. Oh, thought Livia, close to despair, if only I could escape this place! She flung aside the draperies at the window, sank to her knees and leaned her arms on the sill. She gazed across the barren *vega* and upward to the peaks of the mountains. How she longed to fly over them, to Cordoba. Back to Alonzo de Aguilar. Tears formed in the corners of her eyes and streamed down her cheeks.

The sound of swishing silk and someone calling her

name aroused her from her melancholy musing. She turned to see Nizam hurrying into the room.

"What's this? Tears?" asked Nizam, not unkindly. "Well, you can stop crying, Livia. I've come to tell you that Tariq has come home. Repair the ravages to your face and prepare to greet your husband."

"Husband! Tariq wishes to be my husband no more than I wish to be his wife. Doubtless you think he married me from some sense of chivalry, to save me from the clutches of old Muley. Well, you're wrong! He married me to spite Khadija—and Boabdil as well!"

Nizam's face took on a waxen pallor. "Not Tariq. He would never stoop to—"

"Can I doubt the evidence of my own eyes?" Over a lump in her throat, Livia recounted the scene she had just witnessed. When she finished, Nizam's features softened. Sympathy shone from her eyes.

"I'm sorry, Livia. I would not have thought it. I was not aware that my brother had intended to marry Khadija."

Livia's face flushed scarlet with outrage. "I am but a pawn in this game of chess your people play. Why won't Tariq let me go, back to my own country, my own people, to Aguilar? At least you reside under the same roof as your lover!"

Nizam stared at her, silent for a moment, as though weighing her words. At last she sighed. "That is true, Livia. You must have patience. Time has a way of altering circumstances. We must submit to the will of Allah."

Livia threw up her hands in a helpless gesture and sank down onto the divan. "Whatever happens, you call it the will of Allah! If I should escape the Alhambra, is that, too, the will of Allah?"

Nizam nodded mutely, and her large eyes kindled with compassion. "We can only wait."

Livia dropped her gaze and thought: Yes, we must wait, but only until I can find a way to flee from Granada. It occurred to her then that one benefit had

resulted from her discovery of Tariq's perfidy. She had
found a friend in Nizam.

After Nizam took her leave, Livia bathed her face
and combed her hair, then donned scarlet trousers and
a tunic woven in a design of golden birds on silk. She
would make herself presentable for Tariq. Not for his
pleasure, as Nizam had suggested, but to bolster her
confidence when she confronted him and ordered him
to be gone. She had not long to wait.

She heard someone striding briskly down the corri-
dor and was surprised to discover that she recognized
Tariq's authoritative step. She took up a volume of
Nizam's poems and sat reading quietly on the divan.
Livia did not look up when he entered the room.

"What is the meaning of this?" demanded Tariq in a
low, tight voice.

She glanced up at him towering above her in his
fur-lined tunic and brown *keffiyah*, held in place by two
turns of a black rope. His dark eyes sparkled with rage.
He reminded her of a wild desert chieftain. Shrinking
inside at the formidable expression on his face, she
inclined her chin and raised her brows in haughty
disdain. "The meaning of what?"

"Do not play the innocent with me! Why are you
here in the harem? Why have you taken your possessions from my apartment? Why were you not there
waiting for me?"

"My life does not revolve around your comings and
goings. In truth, my life does not concern you at all. I
shall remain here."

His eyes narrowed and he studied her appraisingly,
as if to divine the reason for her behavior. "Do you
mean to say you did not enjoy our lovemaking—the
hours we shared on our wedding night?"

Livia leaped up from the divan, spilling the folio of
poems on the floor. "Enjoy bedding with you! You are
no better than an animal! You repel me!"

She saw the line of his jaw harden under his full

beard, and anger flamed in his face. "I see that the gentle approach was a mistake after all. Good women are obedient. You are my wife. You will share my apartment and my bed."

"I'm your wife in name only," hissed Livia. "And from this moment on, that is the way it will—"

Before she could finish speaking, Tariq bent down, swept her up in his arms and tossed her over his shoulder like a sheep which had strayed from the flock.

"Put me down!" "Put me down this instant!"

"I'll put you down, my Zahareña—right in my bed where you belong!" He strode from the room and down the long passageway.

"I won't go with you!" shouted Livia, hammering on his back with her fists and kicking her legs. One sandal, then the other flew from her feet. "I won't, do you hear!"

Ignoring her protests, he strode on, as though unaware of those who cast startled glances at them as he proceeded through the latticed halls to his own apartment.

Once inside, he flung Livia down upon the divan. Quivering with fury, she rose to her knees, her mass of shining black hair tumbled about her shoulders.

Arms akimbo, Tariq glared down at her. "Prepare for bed." He turned away and cast off his tunic. Livia watched him from the corner of her eye. When he pulled his shirt over his head, she sprang up and ran toward the door of the sitting room. As she plunged between the hangings, she was halted midstride by a violent jerk. She cried out in pain and staggered backward as Tariq's strong fingers, entwined in her thick hair, pulled her struggling to her feet.

He released his hold, but his powerful arms closed about her waist. She squirmed against him, trying to wrench free. He released her abruptly. Once again he twisted his fingers in her hair and, holding her at arm's length, like a puppet dangling from a shining silken skein, led her to the divan.

"I ordered you to disrobe. Do so."

Livia stood staring at him defiantly, every muscle in her body rigid. "Never! By your own actions, you have brought this upon yourself."

He let go of her hair. His hands came down upon the shoulders of her tunic. A ripping sound rent the air and the thin silk parted as he yanked the tunic from her shoulders then stripped her trousers down over her hips. A cloud of crimson silk floated to the floor. She wanted to dive into the divan pillows to hide her nakedness. Instead, she stood her ground, still as a column of marble, contempt shining from her eyes.

"Despoiler of women!"

Tariq's eyes narrowed and his lips curved in a caricature of a smile as his eyes caressed the soft creamy curves of her slender figure. "I shall not disappoint you!"

In one swift motion he flung an arm about her waist, slid the other under her knees and placed her on the sofa. She squeezed her eyes shut and bit her lips to keep from crying out. She lay stiff and unyielding, dimly aware that he was discarding the rest of his clothes. She shivered with an unexpected chill and then she felt his warm body pressed upon her own. His hands, strong yet tender, fondled her breasts and traveled downward over her hips.

"Oh, God," Livia prayed, "let this be over soon!"

With all the strength she could muster, she controlled the urge to fight him, for she knew it would be useless; that she would only prolong her agony and ultimately she would be forced to submit to his desire. She made her mind go blank, blocking out Tariq and his ardent caresses. During the timeless moments that followed, she began to relax, to feel languid. Without volition her body began to respond to his demands. An excruciating excitement that she had never known before surged through her and suddenly she was clinging to Tariq, seeking his lips with her own. His touch set her senses aflame and little cries of ecstasy escaped her. Her reason told her to resist, but passion overcame reason, demanding to be assuaged. As Tariq took his pleasure, it was matched by her own responses until one final surge that carried her floating, into another worldly place and left her limp and sated, to drift into the blessed oblivion of sleep.

Chapter 12

On Friday, as was their custom, all the Moslems of the palace assembled at the Great Mosque for noon prayer. Although there was an area at the back set aside for women, Livia did not attend. She refused to adopt Islam. Instead, she was dressing to go to a gathering at Ayxa's apartment after the service. She was attending to her own toilette, for the young slave girl Tariq had given her had complained of a queasy stomach and Livia had dismissed her for the afternoon.

Livia donned pink trousers and a tunic of pale pink and rose layers of chiffon, then wound her hair in a gleaming coil atop her head. Thinking to set off her raiment to better advantage, she opened the lid of her bridal chest and scanned the tray which contained the dowry Tariq had bestowed upon her. From the sparkling array of jewels, she lifted a gold necklace with a pendant edged with stylized snakes, and a wide gold bracelet studded with cones of twisted wire, and clasped them about her neck and wrists. She took up the leather pouch of golden dinar to tie to the girdle of her tunic, then thought better of it. The pouch was heavy and cumbersome. She would not be gone long. She dropped it in the tray and slammed down the lid of the chest.

Upon entering Ayxa's apartment, her eyes widened in astonishment; among ten or twelve ladies of the court who moved about the chamber, she saw not only Boabdil's gentle first wife, Morayma, but Khadija as well. Livia bent over a table to select a sweetmeat. As

she straightened, her eyes met Khadija's lynx-eyed
stare. The woman's eyes raked Livia from head to toe,
her smoldering gaze filled with venom. Livia drew
herself erect and with a queenly air, surveyed Khadija
in cool appraisal, taking in her flowing purple tunic
overlaid with a sleeveless gold robe, and the array of
precious jewels which sparkled from her ears, neck,
wrists and ankles. Animosity flowed palpably between
them. With an insolent toss of her head, Khadija
turned her back to Livia. Without a word having been
spoken, Livia knew that the battle lines had been
drawn. She turned to join a circle of ladies chatting with
Ayxa and Morayma.

"How beautifully your hair is arranged," Morayma
said with a shy smile. "Perhaps I could borrow your
slave to dress my own stubborn locks."

"You flatter me," Livia replied, pleased. "My girl is
ill. I dismissed her and arranged it myself."

They continued to chat about the damp weather, and
about the bitter taste of the oranges this season. After a
short while, Livia saw Khadija slip unobtrusively
through the door hangings of the sitting room without
so much as a farewell to anyone. It was perhaps half an
hour later that Livia had an uncanny feeling of being
watched. Slowly she turned to face a pair of malevolent
eyes. Khadija had returned.

The afternoon passed quickly and Livia returned to
her chamber with a feeling of pleasure and exultation.
The ladies of the court had been surprisingly agreeable,
and Ayxa, too, had been especially cordial so that
despite Livia's antipathy toward her, Livia found
herself warming to the lionhearted sultana.

Livia removed her jewelry and opened her bridal
chest to replace it in the tray. As she did so, a gasp of
dismay escaped her. The tooled leather pouch was not
there. With mounting anxiety, she set the tray on the
floor, upended the chest and dumped the contents on
the carpet. Hastily, she shook out each garment. Her
dowry of golden dinar was gone.

Thinking someone was playing a cruel trick upon her, Livia ran to the sleeping alcove, searched the bed and peered behind her chest and Tariq's. She dashed into the sitting room and looked among the cushions behind the divan, and in the wall niches behind books and in bowls and ewers and vases, then to the embrasure to search behind the table and among the floor cushions. The pouch was nowhere to be found.

With a rising sense of panic, she raced to Nizam's chambers.

"Come quickly, Nizam. I'm afraid I've taken leave of my senses!"

Without question, Nizam leaped to her feet and hurried down the passageways at Livia's side while Livia, close to tears, recounted her actions of the afternoon.

Nizam made no reply, but in a calm, methodical manner, searched Livia's wedding chest and the apartment without success. When she was done, she turned to Livia, a grave expression on her face and something akin to pity shining from her eyes.

"I'll report your loss to the steward at once. Your dowry will be found."

"I don't like to think that one of the slaves has made off with it," said Livia miserably.

"One of them did *not* make off with it," Nizam said sharply. "They well know that if one article is missing from the palace, they will all lose not only a hand, but their heads!"

Nizam had hardly left the room when the curtains parted to reveal Khadija poised in the doorway, a sphinxlike smile curving her sensuous lips.

"Nizam almost knocked me off my feet just now. She murmured something about a thief ransacking your chambers." Khadija's black-winged brows rose in question. "I cannot believe I heard her correctly."

Distraught, Livia clasped her hands at her waist in an effort to control her agitation. "I fear it is so. My entire dowry is gone."

Khadija regarded her with a pitiful gaze. A smug smile spread across her face.

"Tariq could not have settled much upon you."

"To me it was a fortune," Livia said quietly.

In patronizing tones Khadija replied, "Surely you have scratched a mark upon your money to identify it."

"No . . . no," Livia stammered. "I had not thought of that." Shaking her head in disbelief, Khadija gave a hopeless shrug. Her voice was heavy with reproof. "I trust that not all your gold was in that one place."

"Yes," Livia murmured, feeling abominably stupid.

"How foolish," Khadija replied in a superior voice that set Livia's teeth on edge. "I never keep my gold all together. This should teach you always to set a little aside in a secret place."

Resentment churned inside Livia. She would not allow this woman to intimidate her. Livia could not endure to bandy words with her one moment longer.

"You must excuse me," Livia said coldly. "I must find Tariq."

A malicious glint sparkled from under Khadija's narrowed lids. "Ah, yes. You had best tell him at once. I well know how angry our commander-in-chief can become. And when he hears of your negligence, his wrath will know no bounds. I would not wish to be in your position."

"You need have no fear of that!" Livia snapped, glaring at Khadija. As the woman continued to block the doorway, an overpowering fury welled up inside Livia. With a lightning motion, she shoved Khadija aside and fled down the twisting corridor.

But Khadija's sharp words had struck their mark. Livia dared not think of what Tariq would do when he learned she had let her dowry be stolen. On impulse, she decided she would not tell him tonight, but pray it would be recovered before he discovered it was gone.

The next morning, moments after Tariq had left, Khadija, swathed in filmy layers of orange gauze, her thick black hair flowing round her shoulders, once again appeared in the doorway. Livia barely managed to conceal her annoyance.

Feigning a smile of concern, Khadija asked, "Have you found your dowry?" Without waiting for a reply, the woman sauntered inside and crossed to the divan. She stretched out on her back, her hands folded behind her head, and stared up at the ceiling. "Now tell me what happened."

With an effort, Livia pushed down her resentment at this intruder demanding to know the details of her misfortune. In an unemotional voice, she told Khadija exactly what had transpired. As she related these events, Livia studied Khadija's face intently. Khadija's expression was one of avid interest. Her eyes gleamed, her lips barely concealed a smile. Suddenly Livia knew that Khadija was enjoying this recital, taking pleasure in watching her agitation.

Several days passed, with no further news of Livia's tooled leather pouch. With a sigh of resignation, she faced the fact that it was gone forever. The time had come to confess the loss to Tariq. When at last she summoned the courage to confront him, she could not hide the misery in her eyes. He would chide her for her carelessness and tell her she should not have left the money unguarded, but should have taken it with her to Ayxa's chamber. She braced herself against his wrath, made all the more bitter by the knowledge that she deserved whatever abuse he heaped upon her.

When she had finished, Tariq stood silently, scowling down at her, his arms folded across his chest. Anger flared in the depths of his dark eyes. At last he spoke in a hard voice.

"I recall that you had several gems taken to a jeweler in the *medina* to see to having them set into a necklace. Are you certain the pouch is not in his shop?"

Livia swallowed hard and ran her tongue over dry

lips. "I have told you, Tariq. I saw it in my bridal chest when I took out the jewelry I wore to Ayxa's."

He was silent for a moment, as though deep in thought. Finally he sighed and said, "You reproach yourself far more than I would do. We will speak no more of the matter." He swung about and strode from the room.

Livia let out a long relieved sigh, but berating herself for her carelessness, did not cease with his leaving.

In an effort to distract Livia's mind from her misfortune, Nizam ordered a slave to bring to Livia's chamber a thick leather-bound copy of the Koran which was placed upon a folding wooden stand carved with the name of Allah and arabesques and flowers. Nizam herself brought fine paper from Samarkand, pens and a brass inkpot inlaid with silver, which she spread upon the table in the embrasure. She then set Livia to copying pages from the holy book that would be used by visitors to the mosque.

Loath to copy the Koran, Livia seated herself on a cushion before the table and became absorbed in the copying of the *suras* in the flowery cursive style known as "thuluth"; the task which had promised to be distasteful soon became a welcome diversion.

Early the next morning Livia was seated at the table, pen in hand, when Nizam burst into the room. "Livia!" she exclaimed. "Your dowry has been found!" She thrust the drawstring pouch into Livia's hands. "A priest found it in the mosque of the palace."

With trembling fingers, Livia loosened the thongs, upturned the pouch and a shower of gleaming coins scattered over the table.

"See if it is all there!"

Together they counted the dinar and when they were done, Livia looked up at Nizam, gaping in astonishment. "It is there! All the gold—intact!"

Nizam stood, hands on her hips. "If nothing is missing, your dowry must have been taken for spite—for meanness—to discomfit you."

Livia gave a rueful nod, loath to think that anyone would dislike her so.

"And by someone whose mind is twisted," Nizam added, her brows drawn in a perplexed frown.

Livia nodded mutely, stunned by the intensity of a hatred that would drive anyone to commit such a malicious act.

It was not until after Nizam had gone and Livia sat reflecting upon her words that a suspicion began to form in her mind. Who would know that her slave girl had been dismissed and was not guarding her apartment? Who would know that she herself was gone at that time? Malik? Tariq? Or someone who was present at Ayxa's gathering? Who wished her ill? Who would steal a treasure and not keep it? Whose mind was twisted by ambition and jealousy? Livia's mouth curved down in a grimace. All the residents of the palace answered to that charge. But why commit such a deed against *her*? *She* held no favor with the king. Who would envy her, a prisoner in the Alhambra? No one. She must be mistaken. Unbidden, one of Ayxa's maxims rose to her mind: Beware the fury of a woman scorned. Had not many women been scorned by Tariq?

That evening, when Livia told Tariq her dowry had been found, his surprise was as great as his pleasure. "Apparently the thief had a change of heart. Allah smiles upon you, my Zahareña."

Livia shook her head. "I am certain that the pouch was never meant to be found with the contents intact. I suspect that the person who stole it did not wish to be labeled a thief, and therefore cast it away, taking nothing—leaving it to the finder to keep or turn back to a steward—whichever his conscience dictated."

Tariq pursed his lips as though considering her words. "Where was it found?"

"In the mosque, here in the palace."

Tariq's eyes fixed upon her were intent, questioning.

"You believe you know who took your dowry, do you not?"

Livia nodded.

Tariq's brow furrowed in a scowl. "Who, then?"

Livia ignored his question. "Nizam believes it was stolen for spite, by someone who hates me. I do not like to think that anyone detests me to such an extent, but I fear she is right in her—"

"Who?" Tariq interrupted. "Tell me who?"

Livia shook her head. "No. It is one among those whom you hold in the highest regard. I cannot say."

Tariq reached out and grasped her shoulders. "You must tell me. I command you." His grip tightened cruelly and he shook her hard.

Without volition, the name "Khadija" burst from her lips.

"Khadija!" exclaimed Tariq. He paused, as though considering, then to Livia's surprise, he said, "It is possible." Abruptly he released his hold and turned as if to go. "We shall see."

Wishing she had not let Khadija's name slip, Livia caught hold of Tariq's arm and clung to him to prevent his leaving. She gazed up into his face, her eyes pleading. "Tariq, please. You must promise me that you will inflict no punishment upon her; after all, there is no proof of her guilt. Stay your hand. There will be time enough to act when the truth reveals itself, as it surely will."

The dowry theft was not mentioned again until two days later, when Livia and Tariq had retired for the night. Out of the darkness, as he lay close beside her, he remarked, "I think when you went to prayer on Friday, the thongs securing the pouch to your belt came loose; that you dropped it in the mosque where the priest later found it."

Livia lay in stunned silence. Tariq had not thought of this explanation earlier when they had discussed the

matter. Obviously he had discussed it with Khadija
. . . and she had provided him with a convenient
explanation. Tears stung Livia's eyelids. She could not
fault him for defending Khadija, but that he did it by
blaming Livia's own carelessness and stupidity, hurt
more than she could bear. Further, he chose to ignore
the fact that she had never once set foot inside the
Great Mosque of the Alhambra. She felt betrayed, cast
out from the closeness they had begun to share, lost
and alone.

Chapter 13

Despite Tariq's power to arouse her passions to heights she had not dreamed possible, Livia's heart remained untouched. It is lust and lust alone that the infidel satisfies by possessing my body, she told herself. She would never willingly submit to him, never! Livia believed that in his heart he longed for Khadija. That she was but a substitute for the sloe-eyed woman made Livia's blood boil. For that matter, she thought with some chagrin, her own heart yearned after Aguilar. Tariq was no substitute for Aguilar, but a ruthless man who had fought his way up to a position of power in the court and who violated the body and soul of a woman who belonged to another. If this is the will of Allah, thought Livia, it is a destiny I cannot accept. Her days and nights were plagued by but one desire: To escape the Alhambra and to reach Aguilar.

As the days wore on, she became familiar with every hall and passageway, every tower and every gate in her splendid prison. Secretly, she made preparations for her flight. When the opportunity presented itself, she would be ready.

One afternoon, late in February, Livia was seated on a small balcony on the western wall of the ramparts, basking in the sunshine when her attention was caught by a cloud of dust rolling across the *vega*. Shading her eyes with her hand, she discerned a Moorish horseman spurring across the plain. He did not rein in his panting animal until he alighted at the gate of the Alhambra.

She recognized him as one of Muley's scouts, and by

the look of him, he was bursting with news. Livia sprang to her feet and leaned over the balustrade to watch as the inhabitants of the palace rushed into the courtyard below.

The haggard *adalide*, flushed with terror and excitement, flung himself from his mount and shouted, "The Christians are in the land! Alhama is captured! They came upon us—we know not from where, or how—and scaled the walls of the castle in the night. There has been dreadful fighting, and when I spurred my horse from the gate of Alhama, the castle was in possession of the Spanish!"

Livia smiled inwardly as a feeling of exultation coursed through her. At last it had begun. Ferdinand's armies were marching upon this last kingdom of the infidels! Alhama, known as the "Key to Granada," was but eight leagues southwest and seemingly impregnable. It was also the richest town in all of Andalusia, for it was here that the riches of the royal treasury were stored. A prize indeed, thought Livia.

A short while later Tariq sought her out to bid her goodbye and her heart lurched at the sight of him garbed for battle in a gilt helmet and suit of chain mail, his scarlet cloak swirling about him. "The king is certain that retribution has come upon him for the horror he inflicted upon Zahara."

"As well he might!" Livia snapped. "And you, I surmise, are to drive out the Christians?"

"It is only some transient party of marauders intent upon plunder." His voice turned heavy with irony. "You need not fear for my safety, my love. The king assures us that a little succor thrown into the town will be sufficient to expel them from the castle and drive them away."

"Be assured that your safety is the least of my concerns," Livia said bitterly. But even as she spoke the words, her heart denied them. Fearful that he would read the truth in her eyes, she remained remote as he placed his hands on her shoulders and kissed her lightly on the lips. Wordlessly she watched him go, trying to tell herself she hoped he would never return.

After the departure of King Muley's troops, a silence pervaded the palace, as though holding all in readiness to celebrate the victory that was certain to come.

The following afternoon, drawn by the sound of Moorish horsemen clattering through the gates in tumultuous confusion, Livia and the courtiers rushed to the square.

"Alhama is fallen!" cried the horsemen. "The Christians garrison its walls. The key of Granada is in the hands of the enemy!"

Livia, observing from the shelter of an archway, could barely contain her excitement. Her heart swelled with a wild surge of jubilation, then immediately contracted with a mind-numbing dread. Had Tariq, too, fallen at Alhama? She stifled the thought and reminded herself sharply that soon she would leave the Alhambra forever, that she cared nothing for Tariq Ibn Ziyah.

Now, as the populace heard these words of defeat, they remembered the denunciation of the *santon*. His prediction echoed and reechoed throughout the city, and its fulfillment appeared to be at hand. Old men, who had taken refuge in Granada from fallen dominions, groaned in despair at the thought that war was to follow them into this last retreat, to lay waste to this pleasant land, and to bring sorrow upon their declining years.

The women were louder in their grief, for they foresaw evil befalling their children. Abruptly, as if on signal, they clutched their black cloaks up to their chins and like a flock of ravens stormed through the halls of the Alhambra into the presence of the king. Livia, who stood directly in their path, was caught up in the throng and swept along with them into the throne room. All at once, she felt a strong hand grip her arm. Startled, she stared up into the grinning face of Malik.

"It is dangerous for you to be among this mob, my pigeon. Stand here at my side and I'll protect you until the crowd disperses. She jerked her arm away and glanced frantically about her, but there was no escape through the press of women jammed into the hall. Ignoring Malik, Livia turned her attention to the hysterical women. They wept, tore their hair, blaming Muley for a war they did not want, for so cruelly devasting Zahara. Livia paled, a tremor ran down her spine and her euphoria ebbed away. Why did she not feel the happiness she had anticipated at the news that the Spaniards were poised on the threshold of Granada, and that Zahara had been avenged in full measure? Instead, she felt only pity for the panic-stricken women of the city.

Muley, seated upon his carpet-draped throne, regarded his distraught people with hard eyes, then clamped his chin in his hand, and froze there, his brown lips curved downward.

"Do not be deceived," Malik whispered close to Livia's ear. The king is a bold and fearless warrior. He thinks that he can win through blind violence. He will soon make this blow recoil upon the heads of the enemy.

"Muley has learned that the captors of Alhama are only a handful. Though they are in the center of his lands, they lack munitions and provisions for sustaining a siege. If he moves quickly, he can surround them, cut off all aid and entrap them in the fortress they have taken."

For Muley Hassan, to think was to act. Consequently, he was prone to act too precipitately. He left Granada with a huge force, but little preparation, confident of a quick victory. Hour after hour Livia paced the floor of her chamber, restless and out of sorts, awaiting news. As each day dragged past, scouts would bring reports of the campaign at Alhama, that proved far more difficult than anticipated. The Moors suffered immense losses. To compound the problem, the Spanish were able to send for reinforcements. According to one of the messengers, the daring Don Alonzo de Aguilar was riding to their aid.

Aguilar! Livia's heart leaped. His name resounded in her ears like a drumbeat. During the following weeks, she existed in torment, torn between relief that Aguilar was on his way and worry over his safety. The knowledge that he was one of the most distinguished of the Christian warriors did nothing to allay her fears.

At length, further tidings reached the eager populace of the Alhambra. When Muley discovered that Ferdinand himself was coming with additional troops, he decided no time could be lost. Alhama must be carried by one last attack or abandoned entirely. The desperate attempt failed. Fearing entrapment, Muley retreated.

It was shortly after noon when, Livia and Nizam, joined the other courtiers to greet the first arrivals as they galloped through the gates. "Alhama is lost!" cried the soldiers.

The prediction of the *santon* was on everyone's lips and appeared to be coming to pass. The outcome was as Livia had expected. Now, after the long tense days of waiting, a feeling of relief overwhelmed her and a tremor shook her from head to foot. Weakly she leaned her back against a sun-warmed wall, and her gaze swept over the bedraggled column of soldiers. She did not see Tariq. A strange sinking sensation settled in the pit of her stomach and Livia felt a sense of loss she could not fathom. Had she not wished with all her heart that Tariq would be killed? Now the thought of this brave man cut down, or lying wounded and left to die, filled her with sadness. Her legs trembled. She felt faint and clutched Nizam's arm for support. Nizam, dazed by the news of their defeat, stood like a slender reed, as though steeling herself against the sight of the bedraggled army. At that moment, one of Tariq's aides shoved through the throng and stopped before them.

Through parched lips, he murmured, "You need

have no fear for Tariq. He rides with the rear guard, escorting the wounded." Livia could only nod. Tears sprang to Nizam's eyes and a smile lighted her face. She thanked the soldier, then turned to make her way through the crowd, drawing Livia with her.

"Come. We will climb the Comares Tower to watch for Tariq's return."

Again Livia nodded. The sinking sensation lifted, and tears of relief stung her eyes. Her tears were for Nizam, she told herself. Tears of joy for Nizam at the news that her brother was safe.

"Did you hear?" asked Nizam. "It's said that King Muley is so baffled and disappointed that he has already gathered up Zoraya and fled to Alixares, his royal country palace!"

Livia's gaze flew upward toward the Mountain of the Sun where Alixares, with its gardens and fountains, looked down upon the city of Granada. In the back of her mind she thought: Boabdil hides at one palace and Muley at another. If only Aguilar would arrive, the plum of Granada was ripe for picking!

Livia felt she had been waiting for dreadful hours when at last Tariq strode into their chambers. At first sight of him, she drew in her breath sharply. His usually bronzed visage was gaunt and gray with fatigue. His helmet, which he carried under his arm, gleamed dully through dust, and his crimson cloak was spattered with splotches of dirt and the blood of his enemies. Then, with a slight sense of shock, she perceived that far from crushed and humbled by defeat as she had expected him to be, Tariq bore himself with the proud carriage of the unvanquished. His great, dark eyes burned with renewed determination to drive away the unbelievers.

With an effort, she greeted him with an air of calm detachment. Livia would not let him see her relief that he was unscathed. After divesting himself of his battle attire, he drew her down beside him on the divan. His features were set in harsh lines for, despite the fact that defeat only served to strengthen his purpose, his mood

was dour over the loss of the "Key to Granada."
Though she had no wish to hear it, he launched into an
account of the battle, as if to explain to himself how it
had been lost. Though she detested tales of violence
and death of Christians and Moors alike, Livia made a
pretense of listening. She said nothing, letting his words
flow in one ear and out the other, until the name of
Alonzo de Aguilar brought her to attention.

"He recognized it was madness to attempt to oppose
us with his handful of men, and that he would be
intercepted before reaching Alhama, and withdrew his
forces to Antiquera. We pursued him for a while, then
Muley gave up the chase." Tariq's expression hardened
and his voice was heavy with irony. "I'm sure you are
relieved to know that your gallant knight lives to fight
another day."

Livia's face radiated happiness. Aguilar! Safe!
"Therein lies an omen for you, Tariq. Aguilar lives to
take what is rightly his: his dominion and his lady." Her
hard gaze bored into him. "It is the will of Allah!"

Tariq's eyes kindled with quick anger and his lips
stretched into a taut line. "We shall see what is the will
of Allah!" He rose abruptly and walked from the room.

All the conflicting passions pent up within Livia
seemed to explode. Tariq's implacable manner, his
implied threat, and now his stalking from their chamber
as if her words were of little consequence, all combined
to rouse her to a fever pitch of fury. She had done with
biding her time.

Livia sprang to her feet, ran to the doorway and
peered down the corridor. When Tariq disappeared
from view, she hurried along the zigzaging passageways. Her heart pounded in her ears as she halted,
breathless, before a doorway.

"Malik, Malik!" she called softly.

Immediately, the curtains were flung aside and Malik
stood staring down at her. A pleased, surprised expression spread across his swarthy countenance.

"Ah, my little bird!" He executed a mock bow. "You

have come to me at last, as I knew one day you would! The great Tariq has been defeated, the idol toppled from his pedestal. It pleases me that you finally recognize that it is I who am worthy of your love and admiration."

He opened his arms as if to embrace her. Swiftly, she pushed past him and gained the far side of the room, behind a table. "Malik, you must help me!"

He halted midstride and eyed her with a puzzled expression. "Have I ever wished to do anything but to help you? I desire only your happiness."

"Yes, I know that, Malik." She gave him her most engaging smile. "That is the very reason I came to you for aid. I must have a horse—a stout steed capable of traveling a distance . . . and saddlebags stocked with provisions."

"But what is this? Surely you cannot be setting off on a journey—now of all times, when the castle is in an uproar and nobody knows from one day to the next who is king, who is a friend, who an enemy?"

Livia extended her hands in entreaty. "That is the point, Malik. Just now all is mad confusion. Now is the best time for me to flee from Granada."

Malik's brows drew together in a frown. He pursed his lips and stroked his small beard with a thumb, as though deep in thought. "Where will you go?"

"Antiquera," said Livia haltingly. "I . . . I have friends there. She had no wish to risk the chance for Malik's help by revealing that she planned to meet Aguilar.

His calculating gaze swept over her, as though he suspected she was not telling him something. "Is Tariq aware that you are leaving him?"

"Of course not!" said Livia, growing impatient.

A crafty light crept into his narrow eyes. "Surely you do not intend to ride alone."

"I must!" In her effort to convince him of this necessity, her tone was sharper than she had intended.

"I know the road well. I'm an expert horsewoman. I can travel faster by myself."

Malik shrugged, poured wine into two goblets and held one out to her. She shook her head. Malik sipped his wine thoughtfully, studying her over the rim of the goblet. In a dry voice, he asked, "Have you considered what Tariq will do when he finds his pigeon has flown?"

"I do not need you to remind me of what Tariq is capable of!"

His thin lips curved slyly. "What do you wish of me?"

When she had apprised him of her plan, he nodded agreeably. "You run a great risk, but you've nothing to lose—but your freedom, and perhaps your life."

"I do not have my freedom now, Malik, and my life is not worth living with Tariq!"

He inclined his head. In the red glow emanating from the brazier it seemed to Livia that his face took on a sinister expression. It occurred to her that Malik did not want her for himself, so much as he wished to wreak his vengeance upon Tariq. His voice came to her, full of guile. "I will free you from him."

That night, following the muezzin's call, Livia in a voice rife with concern, told Tariq, "You must be weary after the long days and nights of battle. Let us retire." Tonight, she thought, he would have no desire to possess her.

Tariq's eyes met hers and in them was a question mingled with surprise and pleasure at her eagerness. Without speaking, he slid into bed beside her and gathered her in his arms. "Come to me, my Zahareña!"

"No!" cried Livia. His brows drew together in bafflement. A tense, compelling expression flickered in the dark, unfathomable depths of his eyes. Abruptly he reached out and caught her to him. His mouth fastened upon hers hungrily. She jerked her head sharply to one side and, twisting from his grasp, she rolled away from him to the edge of the bed. In an instant, he rolled her back against his chest where he held her in a smothering embrace. He laughed triumphantly. A triumphant laugh burst from Livia, too; she knew this was a temporary surrender. She would soon have her way. He took her with a violent passion as though drawing solace from her body, seeking oblivion in her arms. Her lips burned from the searing pressure of his kiss and though she did not return his ardor, her senses reeled, responding to his touch. She braced her hands against his shoulders, fighting down the desire that flamed within her. She forced herself to lay passive in his arms, accepting the insistent pressure of his mouth, the stirring touch of his hands, determined she would give him no pleasure—the sooner to cool his ardor, the sooner to be free of him. She endured his love-making, strengthened by the knowledge that this would be the last time she would be forced to share his bed, to submit to his insatiable demands.

Long after Tariq's deep, even breathing assured her that he was sleeping soundly, Livia rose, flung her mantle about her shoulders and tiptoed into the sitting room. She parted the hangings, crossed to the window and leaned far over the sill, searching, waiting.

The night air seemed unusually chill and damp, the crescent moon, shedding its silvery light over the sleeping city, too bright. After what seemed an eternity, a shadow detached itself from the bushes growing at the base of the rampart far below. A figure raised an arm in signal. The way was clear.

Livia spun about and from beneath the floor cushions, drew lengths of shawls and scarves she had knotted together earlier in the day. Swiftly she tied one end to a window post and crept over the sill. Clinging tightly to the makeshift rope, she slid slowly down the rough brick wall. Her hands grew moist and her heart hammered in her breast.

Apprehension surged through her. She did not like Malik's plan, but he had overruled her protests, insisting that should the sentries on the watchtowers see the vizier skulking about the walls, his presence would be suspect, whereas slaves were always about. Despite her misgivings, Livia had agreed to allow his servant Bakhr to meet her. Bakhr would escort her to a secret place where Malik could meet her with a horse without arousing suspicion.

Sharp pains shot up her arms. Her fingers held desperately to a knot and refused to do her bidding. Dangling from the silken skein, she glanced down at Bakhr. Her heart skipped a beat. Her makeshift rope would not reach the ground. She would have to fall—and count on the slave to catch her. What if she should break a leg, sprain an ankle? Her head spun with a sudden dizziness. Livia must not look down at the distance she still had to go. She forced herself to look up, and a scream rose in her throat.

Far above her, peering from the window, loomed a bearded face whose features were contorted with rage. A strangled cry burst forth from her lips. Tariq's dark visage, his rumpled hair and beard, his staring eyes rimmed with white were those of a wild man. She heard a shouted command. A light flashed on in the chamber behind him. Her hands seemed fused to the embroidered shawl. Panic overwhelmed her.

"Jump!" shouted Bakhr. "Jump!"

Chapter 14

Livia's rump struck the rocky ground, knocking the breath from her body. She felt Bakhr's hands under her arms, raising her to her feet. She stood unsteadily on shaking legs, gasping with terror.

"Hurry!" Bakhr hissed. "Your horse is waiting. This way!" He led off at a brisk pace along the narrow dirt path encircling the battlements and Livia stumbled at his heels, trying to keep up with him.

As they approached the square base of the Comares Tower, Livia forced herself to run faster. If only they could gain the far side, they would be out of sight of anyone in pursuit.

They raced around the corner of the tower, keeping close under the wall which jutted out toward the River Darro. As they turned the corner, Livia let out a relieved breath. At that moment a metallic creaking split the night air raising gooseflesh on her skin.

On their left, concealed by scrubby hedges, a door in the wall was flung open and a turbaned figure bolted through the doorway and stood blocking their path. His giant form loomed before them. His beard bristled and his powerful shoulders were hunched like those of a lion poised for the kill.

"You dare to run from me!" roared Tariq.

Livia opened her mouth to speak, but no sound came forth. Terror-stricken, she could only stare at him.

"Who steals my wife will not see the dawn!"

Moonlight glinted on a silver blade clenched in Tariq's fist. With a lightning motion, he lunged forward and buried his dagger in Bakhr's neck. There was a strangled cry and blood spurted from the throat of the hapless slave. Livia let out a shriek and, covering her face with her hands, sank to the ground.

Tariq's great hands gripped her shoulders, yanking her to her feet. "Who is it you are meeting?" he bellowed.

She shook her head miserably. "No one."

"Do not lie to me!" Tariq thundered, shaking her until her teeth chattered. "Who is your lover?"

"I've no lover!" screamed Livia.

"We shall see!"

He caught her upper arm in a cruel grip and pulled her along the rough path. Nettles and weeds clutched at her clothes as they circled the irregular walls at breakneck speed. At length they drew near to a stand of young oaks growing on the banks of the Darro. As Tariq strode toward the cluster of trees, the soft whinny of a horse broke the stillness of the night air. Livia trembled uncontrollably. Tariq would find her horse saddled, provisioned, waiting. All hope was lost.

He dragged her staggering, stumbling at his side, into the shelter of the trees. As though he had struck her a blow, she jerked back in shock. Not one, but two horses stood tethered under the leafy canopy, pawing the ground as if impatiently awaiting their riders. Clearly, Malik had planned to flee with her. Angry color suffused her cheeks. She should have suspected as much when he agreed so readily to her plan.

"Do you still swear you have no lover?" Tariq demanded in a voice heavy with sarcasm.

She shook her head wildly as tears of frustration streaked down her cheeks.

Ignoring her denial, Tariq raged on. "Your lover has flown."

"I have no lover!" cried Livia. "I was going to—" Abruptly she broke off. Innate caution kept her from telling her plans. Let Tariq think I've a lover, she thought savagely. Let my phantom lover take the blame for trying to carry me away—and I will watch and wait—and escape to Aguilar. With a bitter smile, she murmured, "It is the will of Allah."

White-lipped, Tariq said no more, but led her in silence back inside the palace. His controlled fury was more frightening than if he had heaped curses upon her head, or ranted, giving vent to the wrath boiling within. What would happen to her now? What punishment would he inflict upon her? Would he cast her aside? Lock her in the filthy, pest-ridden prison beneath the floor of the Alhambra, nevermore to see the light of day, to rot in darkness?

Once inside their apartment, he flung her upon the bed and turned away. She dared not move or breathe. She heard the clink of metal and moments later Tariq returned to her side. He slid one end of his gold filigree belt about her wrist, linked the other end to his wrist and lay down beside her. In a low voice he said, "You are mine and always will be. Tell that to your lover—never forget it!"

Livia made no reply. In the darkness she smiled to herself, knowing that though she spent the rest of her life with Tariq Ibn Ziyah, she would never be his.

When she awoke her gaze fell upon a square of sunshine high on the colorful wall-hanging in the bedchamber. She had slept late. All at once the events of last night crowded her mind. But now, in the clear morning light, they took on an air of unreality, like a horrible nightmare. She determined resolutely to forget them. All that was past and done. She would see what today would bring. Without thinking, she raised her arms overhead in a languorous stretch. As her bruised muscles cried out in protest, she was suddenly aware that the manacle was gone. Her head snapped around. The space beside her in the bed was empty.

She rushed into the sitting room and glanced quickly about her. It too was deserted. She ran to the doorway and flung the draperies aside, then drew back in

dismay, snapping the curtains closed. In the passageway stood one of the huge eunuchs of King Muley's
harem.

Indignation rose like gorge in her throat. So this was
to be her fate. She was to be watched over, spied on,
every minute of the day and night. Seething, she paced
the floor. Had this eunuch been ordered to keep her
here, or would he dog her footsteps wherever she
went? Well, she would not leave this chamber. She
would make Tariq come to her, and when he came, she
would treat him with all the contempt she could
summon. She dressed in a chartreuse tunic and trousers
embroidered with gold thread, brushed her hair till it
gleamed blue-black, perfumed her long tresses with
rosewater, then brought out paper, pens and inkpot
and set to copying pages from the Koran. All the while
she worked, she kept one eye on the doorway, thinking
how much pleasure it would give her to toss the brass
inkpot and its contents straight into the face of Tariq
Ibn Ziyah!

After a time, she became engrossed in her task and
regained a measure of calm. Her serenity was short-
lived. As though divining her intention to remain in
seclusion, shortly after the noon call to prayer, a slave
girl entered bearing a tray of food which had been sent
by Tariq.

With effort, Livia controlled an impulse to sweep the
food to the floor and stood silently by while the girl
placed the tray on the table and left. She regarded the
steaming bowl of stew, the plate of dried plums, figs
and raisins, and nutmeats with disdain. She would
touch nothing.

As the day wore on and hunger gnawed at her vitals,
Livia decided that Tariq would be none the wiser if a
small portion were missing. She ate ravenously, careful
to leave enough food to convince Tariq that she had
refused his offering.

By late afternoon he had not returned and her anger
mounted. Was she to remain in seclusion forever?

Stiffening her spine, she resolved to leave the remainder of her food untouched. The moment Tariq appeared in the doorway, she would hurl it at his head!

She heard the muezzin call for the sunset prayer. She wiped her pens and put them away, then took up her lute and halfheartedly strummed several romantic ballads. It seemed that she struck one discordant note after another, and at length she cast the instrument aside with an impatient sigh. Music did not suit her mood today. She lighted the oil lamps, crossed to a wall niche and glanced over Tariq's collection of books: *The Fables of Bidpai*, *The Thousand and One Nights*, *Diwan*, and other volumes of poetry. She took down the *Rubaiyat* of Omar Kayyam and curled up on the divan to read.

Darkness had fallen. She raised her head from her reading, straining her ears, listening. A strange sound was rising from the city, like the gathering of a storm. She rose to her feet and started across the room. Before she had gained the embrasure, the hangings over the doorway parted and Tariq burst inside. Without warning, he swept her up in his arms and dashed from the apartment. All thoughts of the role she'd planned to play—the cold reception she'd planned to give him—fled from her mind.

"What is it?" she shrieked. "What's happening?"

Tariq's eyes gleamed with an unholy light and his voice was tense with excitement held in check. "Civil war has broken out. Boabdil has been brought back by the conspirators. He has entered the Albaycin in triumph and has been proclaimed king. Soon he will take the palace. I'm taking you to Malik. You and the other women will be under his protection. All are to be locked in the Tower of Comares for safekeeping."

A hysterical laugh escaped her at the incongruity of Tariq's turning her over to Malik. But Malik had all he could do to herd Ayxa, Nizam and the other ladies of the court, and their children and slaves as well, into the apartments of the massive tower. The hysterical women, not knowing what calamity had befallen them, fluttered about like birds. At length, under the iron command of Ayxa, they grew silent. In calm, decisive tones, the sultana, who had her own network of informants, told them what had transpired.

"When Boabdil heard that his father had retired to Alixares, he seized the opportunity to return to Granada with his supporters. When Boabdil entered the city, he was hailed as the new king because of the people's dissatisfaction with the way Muley lost Alhama. But there was such a din that Muley was able to hear it at his retreat. He sent some men to investigate and discovered that his vizier, Vanegas, had ordered the royal guards to attack the rebels. Muley hurried to the Alhambra, confident that once ensconced there he could put a quick end to the outbreak. But when he arrived"—here Axya paused, permitting herself a congratulatory smile—"he found the situation was far from being under control and ran back to his summer palace again."

No one could settle down to sleep. In a buzz of excitement, the women ran to the various windows, pushing each other aside in their eagerness, to view what was happening in the town.

The conflict lasted throughout the night with carnage on both sides. In the morning they learned from one of Ayxa's messengers that Muley had given up the throne in favor of Boabdil, acceding to the legendary prediction. Then Muley had made yet another hasty retreat along with Vanegas and some troops.

Livia realized that if the Moors were fighting among themselves, they would be an easy conquest for Ferdinand. She saw that Nizam was beside herself with worry. Her chin trembled and she wrung her hands nervously in her lap. When Livia tried to comfort her, she burst out, "You do not understand. Muley was joined by many powerful people. Raduan is with them. And, it's rumored that Muley was joined also by his brother El Zagal—The Valiant—who is popular in many parts of the kingdom. All of his supporters have offered to aid him in suppressing the rebellion. The battle within our own walls isn't over!"

The following day passed without incident. Thinking the danger past, the ladies of the court returned to their quarters. But as Livia and Nizam passed through the portal, the guard barred their way and ordered them back inside the tower.

"Tariq Ibn Ziyah has not given permission for you to depart. Until he does, you must remain here."

Livia bristled. "Why are we left to languish here?" she demanded. Send for Tariq Ibn Ziyah—at once!"

The guard gave an emphatic shake of his turbaned head. "It is impossible. Boabdil has sent him to inspect the defenses of the outlying fortresses. Your husband wishes to be assured of your safety in his absence.

"And when is he to return?"

The guard shrugged, "A week . . . or longer." Then he slammed the wooden door and locked it. Livia beat upon the door, shouting indignant protests and demanding to be released, all to no avail. Nizam, tearful and near despair over Raduan's having left the city, occupied herself until bedtime composing poetry dedicated to her lover.

Livia paced the floor until at length, her fury spent, she sank down on a divan. Sleep would refresh her. Tomorrow she would see to their release.

Sleep, however, would not come. She lay wakeful and alert to all the sounds of the palace. She heard a faint rumble thundering down from the hills. The sound had a familiar ring. A furrow creased her brow as she strove to remember. And then it struck her. She had heard the same noise the night the Moors attacked Zahara.

She leaped up from the divan, flew to the window and peered out. A fearful shriek filled the room. Far below, like eerie specters in the moonlight, she saw King Muley Hassan mounted on a white charger at the head of what could be no less than five hundred cavalrymen. He urged his men forward. Other men slammed ladders in place and were mounting the walls of the palace.

Her attention was distracted by a loud commotion at the door. Suddenly Aben Comixa—the *alcayde*, the mayor and supporter of Boabdil—accompanied by a number of the garrison and its inhabitants, burst inside their chambers. Ruddy-faced, his eyes bulging with fear, the *alcayde* gasped: "We seek asylum. Muley has attacked while people were sleeping. He spares neither age nor rank nor sex. The fountains run red with blood!"

Livia stood transfixed, regarding him with stunned disbelief while Nizam cried, "Next he will ascend the tower. We will all be slain!"

Aben Comixa shook his head. "He will not lose time in pursuing us. He is anxious to secure the city and to wreak his vengeance on its rebellious inhabitants."

Livia rushed back to the window and leaned far out over the sill. The defenseless citizens, startled from their sleep, rushed forth to learn the cause of the alarm. The city was soon completely roused. Lights blazed in every street revealing the scanty number of the band that had been dealing such fatal vengeance. It was soon apparent to Livia that Muley had been mistaken in his conjecture. The great mass of people, incensed by his tyranny, zealously favored his son. Many of King Muley's followers were slain, the rest driven from the city. The old monarch, with the remnant of his band, galloped to safety through the gates of the city and, it was rumored, was on his way to Malaga.

Livia turned to Nizam. Trying to keep the jubilant note from her voice, said, "It is true, is it not, that the Moors are now separated into two hostile factions?" Nizam shook her head and regarded Livia steadily. "Do not place your hope for deliverance upon the squabbles of our rulers, for though blood may spill between them, they will never fail to unite against the Christians."

"Then they shall go down together!" As soon as she had uttered the spiteful words she wished them back, for she was loath to hurt Nizam, already bereft that Raduan Venegas had fled with Muley's forces.

As the days passed Nizam continued to lament Raduan. She had soon tired of writing poetry and now fretful, vented her ill humor on Livia.

"Why doesn't my brother give permission for our release?" she said miserably. "Oh, Livia, I know how you feel, parted from your Aguilar. I am beside myself from missing Raduan." Distraught, she would ask again and again, "Do you think Muley will return to do battle at Granada? Do you think the Christians will attack Muley's camp at Malaga? Oh, if only I could fly to Malaga to be with Raduan!"

One sunny afternoon during one such scene, Livia was seated at the window watching the activity in the *medina*, when her gaze strayed to the *vega*. As Nizam ended her melancholy plaint with the wish that she could fly to Malaga, Livia whirled to face her.

"You *can* fly to Malaga, Nizam. Look!"

Nizam darted to Livia's side and peered out the window as Livia raised her arm in a sweeping gesture toward the plain. A long column of horses and mules whose heads drooped under their burdens wound toward the city.

"They will unload their wares at the caravansary, rest their animals, then pack them with goods to be transported south to Malaga." In low, urgent tones, she added, "You could join them."

"No, I could not!" exclaimed Nizam, aghast.

"But you can!" Livia insisted, her eyes sparkling with excitement. She eyed Nizam's necklace set with rubies and pearls, her gold bracelets and anklets, and a plan took shape in her mind. "You can bribe the guards with your jewels and—"

Nizam shook her head and threw up her hands, jangling the bracelets in a hopeless gesture. "Such a thing as traveling alone is not done by our women. Even were I to defy our traditions, we haven't jewels enough between us to purchase the lives of the guards. Should they set me free, their lives would be forfeit."

Her words recalled the memory of Tariq's quick dispatch of Bakhr. "Then let us bribe a slave to exchange garments with you. Disguised as a servant, surely you can slip past the guards."

Again Nizam shook her head. "It is of no use. The slave girls, too, wish to live."

Livia pressed her lips together and said no more.

Another night and a day passed, and as they watched the caravan unload goods, lead and iron were brought in to be packed for transport, Nizam grew more impatient.

On the morning of the third day, Nizam, preoccupied, confronted Livia across their breakfast tray. She toyed with her food while Livia devoured honey, barley bread, walnuts, and dried figs. At last Nizam let out a despondent sigh.

"I would depart with the caravan if you would agree to accompany me, but we cannot so much as find a way to escape this chamber!"

Livia suppressed a smile. It was the moment she had awaited. She had planned from the start to flee with the caravan. The only danger was that Tariq would return before they made good their escape. She would have to risk it. Livia leaned toward Nizam and whispered, "I have thought of a way."

In the late afternoon, one of the chamber servants pounded on the door and demanded the guard's attention. When he jerked open the door, she ordered him to carry out two carpets that were rolled up on the floor. They were infested with fleas and must be taken out to be beaten at once.

Shortly thereafter, under the guard's watchful eye,

two robust youths bore the carpets to the nether regions of the palace where they were dropped on the floor to await someone's attention.

When, at last, the muezzin's call signaled prayer, the servants hurried away to the fountains to wash. The carpets unrolled, as if by magic. Two slight figures arose from their midst, bent down and rolled them up again swiftly. Then while everyone else was praying toward Mecca, they fled through the empty halls of the Alhambra.

Once safe in Nizam's apartment, Nizam dispatched a servant to the town to learn where the caravan was bound and when it would depart. The girl returned with news that gladdened their hearts and, at the same time, vexed Livia and brought tears of disappointment to Nizam's eyes. As Livia had surmised, the caravan was bound for Malaga, but it would not depart for another three days. Livia was thankful that Tariq would be gone at least a week inspecting defenses.

It was agreed between them that in order to avoid suspicion, they would remain apart: Nizam in seclusion in her quarters and Livia hidden in Tariq's chambers, their whereabouts known only to Nizam's young slave girl who would bring them food and drink. They would meet on Thursday morning at the caravansary, the Corral del Carbon.

To Livia's consternation, another problem arose to plague her, but she forebore to mention it to Nizam now. In three days, the problem might have resolved itself.

Chapter 15

Shortly before daybreak on Thursday morning, Livia stared down at the colorful fringed carpet on which she had placed her meager belongings. Now that the time of departure was upon her, she was torn with indecision, for the problem which had plagued her these past days had not been resolved. Determined to look on the bright side of the matter, she reminded herself that there were still several hours before they would depart. There was still time. Perhaps the excitement, her nervousness over the dangerous course she and Nizam were about to undertake would bring on the indication she so anxiously awaited. She folded the carpet around her possessions, flung her black mantle about her shoulders, then hurried purposefully through the palace halls.

All went well until she entered the Court of the Myrtles. Her heart skipped a beat. A tall, turbaned figure, indistinguishable in the feeble gray light, was walking down the length of the pool. As he drew nearer, her pulse quickened. Malik! She had not laid eyes on him since the night of Muley's attack. He had not dared to approach her at the tower, Livia thought savagely. He would do well to keep his distance after the vile trick he had played on her. Even thinking of it made her blood boil. But she could not take him to task now.

She slipped behind a pillar of the arcade, hoping

Malik hadn't seen her and peered cautiously from behind it. He was craning his neck, squinting through the dim light.

"Livia! Livia, is that you?"

She took a deep breath, squared her shoulders, then stepped out, smiling. "I was not certain who was approaching. One cannot be too cautious when accosted by strangers."

Missing her barb, Malik frowned at the carpet clutched in her arms. "What have you there?"

"Oh, this?" she said lightly. "It is but Tariq's prayer rug." Nervously she fingered the tattered fringe. "The fringe needs mending. I'm taking it to a shop in the bazaar."

Malik's eyes narrowed as he studied her face in shrewd appraisal. "At this hour of the morning?"

"I wish to bring it early so it'll be finished today. I wish to surprise Tariq."

Malik scowled. "Ah, yes. The king expects him back before sunset."

Livia stifled a gasp of surprise and managed to keep her composure. "I'd best hurry, then."

"I'd best go with you," Malik said dryly. "It isn't safe for you to go into the city alone."

Livia shook her head vehemently. "No. No, that won't be necessary. I'm to meet Nizam, and then we will shop in the bazaar." Malik opened his mouth, but before he could protest, Livia said, "I must fly!" She brushed past him and fled down the Court of the Myrtles and through the portico. Without pausing to look back to see if Malik had followed her, she hurried across the Plaza of the Cisterns, out the gate and down the hill.

She threaded her way through the dirty, crowded streets and swept past the gatekeeper at the Corral del Carbon. As she entered the courtyard, the pungent odor of the stables assailed her nostrils. The place was crowded with travelers shrouded in burnooses, their hoods pulled over their heads. Men were shouting orders and tying bundles to the backs of mules. Others mounted horses draped in necklaces, bells and trappings of turquoise, their manes and faces glistening with henna stain to keep away evil.

Livia scanned the area for Nizam. Her gaze swept upward to the guest rooms on the floors above. Surely Nizam had not taken a chamber! A slight motion from a black-swathed figure seated on the edge of the fountain in the center of the courtyard drew her attention. Her apprehension mounted and her heart beat wildly as she joined Nizam on the rim of the pool. Nizam's oval face was flushed. Her enormous eyes sparkled with excitement.

"All is in readiness," Nizam said softly. "They have but to finish watering the horses." Noting the dour expression that came over Livia's face, she paused and then in a voice full of concern said, "Livia, are you not feeling well? What ails you?"

Livia's troubled gaze met Nizam's. "The worst has happened. I had hoped to the very last minute . . . till now—" Her voice broke.

Baffled, Nizam gazed at her mutely, waiting for her to go on.

"I fear I cannot accompany you after all!"

Nizam's hand rose to her mouth and she stared at Livia in shock. "But you must!"

"I cannot." A sob rose in her throat and she almost choked on the words: "I fear I carry Tariq's child." She looked down at her fingers nervously twisting the knotted fringe of the carpet.

Nizam's eyes widened. "No!" she gasped. "It cannot be! You must be mistaken!"

Livia shook her head. "It has been well over a month since—" Again her voice broke and her hand flew to her breast. "And now there are other signs . . ."

Nizam gazed at her for a moment in awestruck silence, then burst out, "You must come with me, regardless. You yourself have said that Tariq cares nothing for you. He has treated you shamefully. You owe him nothing!"

Livia let out a sigh of despair. "You must see that I cannot go to Aguilar bearing another man's child."

"Then come with me to Malaga," Nizam insisted. "I will care for you and your baby as well."

"No. I cannot foist my burdens upon you. And there is the infant to consider. One cannot bear a child in the camp of the enemy. The danger is too great." The call of the caravan leader resounded above the din of the courtyard, and Livia rose to her feet. "Come. I will see you off."

Nizam stood up reluctantly and regarded Livia with pleading eyes. "Is there no way I can convince you to come with me?"

"None."

They made their way to the end of the train of animals. Livia, her eyes brimming with tears, watched while a boy helped Nizam climb on the back of a fractious horse.

Nizam settled into the saddle and turned to Livia. Suddenly, her mouth opened in a silent cry, as she gazed past Livia's shoulder.

Livia whirled about and froze. Not ten feet away, thrusting startled citizens from his path, was Tariq, his features contorted in a fury more terrible than Livia could have imagined. In an effort to still the trembling that seized her, she took a deep breath and drew herself up to her full height. Her chin rose in defiance as Tariq bore down upon them. From his brilliant black eyes flashed shards of light that seemed to pierce her soul.

He caught Livia's forearm and yanked her to his chest. "What is the meaning of this?"

Stunned speechless, Livia could only stare up into his face. Swiftly he bent down, seized the carpet in her arms and shook it open. At the sight of Livia's garments, he thrust it aside, strewing the rug and its contents on the ground.

Nizam's voice slashed through his rage, bringing him up short. "I am going to Malaga to join Raduan."

"You are not going anywhere!" Gripping Livia's wrist with one hand, Tariq lunged toward Nizam. With a violent motion, she twisted away from him and cried out, "Unhand me, Tariq. Do not try to stop me, for I—"

Before she could finish, he swung upon Livia. "And you!" His tone of barely controlled fury was more frightening than if he had shouted at her. "You dare once again to leave me?"

She opened her mouth to speak but could not force the words out.

Tariq went on in a low voice. "If my sister is bent upon leaving, so be it. If she wishes to throw her life away and bring disgrace upon our house, I cannot stop her. But you, my Zahareña, are a different matter!"

At last Livia found her voice. "I . . . I had decided not to leave you. I am merely bidding Nizam farewell."

Tariq kicked at her bright blue tunic crumpled on the ground and his hand on her arm tightened cruelly. "Do not insult me further by lying to me, Livia! Do you know the fate that befalls those who lie?"

Defiantly, Livia stared straight into his eyes, her diamond-hard gaze clashing with his. "Though you cut out my tongue, it will not alter the truth!"

His thick brows furrowed and his lips turned down. "I shall see that you have no occasion to lie to me again, nor the opportunity to desert me in the future!"

He turned to Nizam and gazed at her for a moment without speaking. Livia thought she saw an expression of sorrow flash in his eyes and then disappear, so quickly that she was not sure she had seen it. Gravely, he raised an arm in salute. "Farewell. *As-salaam alaykum*. Peace be upon you!"

Abruptly he wheeled about and, dragging Livia along at his side, he elbowed his way through the throng. Livia jerked around, looked over her shoulder and raised a hand in a feeble wave toward Nizam. The lead horses were urged into a trot and the caravan began to wend slowly down the narrow street toward the gate of the city.

With an air of contempt, Livia struggled to match Tariq's pace as he pulled her with merciless speed through the square of the Vivarambla, past the mosque, and up the hill leading to the Alhambra.

It occurred to her that she might allay his wrath by telling him she was carrying his child, but she immediately thought better of it. This granite-hearted infidel would not be moved by such news. And if he were, she thought perversely, she had no reason to give him cause for joy.

Once inside the palace, he led her up the narrow stone stairs of the Comares Tower to a small room. He thrust her inside and slammed the door.

It was not until Livia heard the key grate in the lock that she allowed herself to give in to her feelings. Desolation such as she had never known swept through her. She flung herself down upon the divan and gave way to a fit of weeping. Then, not one to take pleasure in crying for long, she soon regained a measure of composure and rose to her feet to look about her prison.

The chamber was much like the one she had occupied earlier. It was sparsely furnished with a divan and two cushions. Rush mats covered the floors. The walls were decorated with colorful tiles and above them was a delicate tracery of calligraphy, vines and leaves. She strolled to the double window through which streamed pale spring sunlight. Then, clutching her mantle about her, she stepped out upon a small belvedere, or balcony. In the distance rose the snow-crested peaks of the Sierra Nevada and two floors below her spread a small courtyard enclosed by an arcade, similar to others which were scattered throughout the palace. Rose bushes, denuded of leaves, their thorny brown branches like claws, bordered a shell-shaped pool in which a fountain gurgled. A swallow swooped down, perched on the fluted rim, then flew up to the limb of an almond tree just beginning to bud.

Her attention was caught by a stalwart figure emerging from the arcade, and she thought her heart would stop beating. Tariq strode across the garden. In the next instant, another figure detached itself from the shadows of the colonnade on the far side of the patio. Her hooded cloak did not hide her sleek black hair or her voluptuous curves.

"Khadija!" Livia sputtered.

The woman ran to Tariq, flung her arms about his neck and kissed him with a fervor that made Livia clench her teeth. How dare that woman embrace her husband!

Tariq raised his head and glanced about, as though a sixth sense had warned him that watchful eyes were observing their tryst. Apparently reassured, he smiled down at Khadija, slid an arm about her shoulders and led her from the courtyard, down a flight of shallow stone stairs and out of sight among the tall cypresses that grew thickly about the palace.

Seething with indignation, Livia fled from the belvedere. Hurt surged through her. Suddenly she was glad she hadn't told Tariq of the advent of their child. In truth, she had longed to tell him, but had decided it would be wiser to wait for a more propitious moment—a time when he would be more receptive. Perhaps he would rejoice at the news that he was to have an heir. And, in sharing his delight, she hoped that she too could take pleasure in the baby. Thus far, the very thought of bearing the child of a man she despised filled her with loathing. But now—now that she saw with her own eyes that he was still enamored of the wanton Khadija, he did not deserve the pleasure of knowing he had sired a child.

"I'll never tell him!" she muttered wrathfully, clenching her fists in rage.

February wore into March, and Livia passed the days
in the tower taking pleasure from watching Granada
burst into bloom. The almond tree in the garden
exploded in a shower of parchment blossoms. The first
crimson roses came into flower and the white storks
returned to their homes among the crannies of the
ochre-tiled roofs of the city. Tariq did not come near
her. Memories of the nights they had lain together,
their bodies joined in a passionate embrace, rose
unbidden to her mind and time and again she made a
conscious effort to stamp them out. If he stubbornly
refused to believe she was not going to flee from
Granada with Nizam, she, just as stubbornly, refused
to reveal her secret to him. In time it would reveal
itself. At least he could not choose to disbelieve she was
with child!

She was permitted to roam at will throughout the
palace only in the company of Naja, the eunuch Tariq
had set to guard her. Frequently she would visit the
intrepid Ayxa. They would play cards or backgammon
in quiet relaxation while they chatted. One afternoon
when they fell into a discussion of the precepts of the
Koran, Ayxa fixed her penetrating eye upon Livia and
said, "Did you know that the knightly attitude toward
women is Islamic in origin—doubly rooted in Islam? It
dates back to the desert warriors of pre-Islamic Arabia
who were famous not only as expert horsemen and
swordsmen, but also as poets and often as great
lovers."

"Ha!" Livia said scornfully, snapping a card down on
the table.

Ayxa continued, "The knightly attitude is also a
result of the great worth attached by Islam to the
relationship between man and woman. 'Marriage is one
half of religion,' said the Prophet. Our alleged contempt for women is misunderstood. Islam does not
despise women, it simply makes a marked distinction
between the sexes and appoints each its separate role.

As a being with an immortal soul, woman, in the Islamic view, is man's equal; otherwise there would be no women venerated as saints in the world of Islam."

Ayxa paused and when Livia made no reply, she went on. "As a wife, she is subject to her husband. She must obey the man, not because he is necessarily a better person than she, but because the female nature finds its fulfillment in obedience, just as it is the man's duty to command."

Livia felt a hot flush of anger creep up her neck, into her cheeks. She said quietly, "I hold myself responsible for my own actions, and am subject only to the command of God and king!"

As though Livia had not spoken, Ayxa continued, "The home belongs to the woman, and the man is only a guest there."

• Livia's eyes widened in sudden understanding. This explained the despotic role exercised by women within the Moslem family. But it did not explain why Ayxa had chosen to lecture her. Unless—she glanced down at her flowing pink tunic—it revealed nothing. She had told no one but Nizam of the baby. Whether Livia's actions were an attempt to put from her mind the fact of her pregnancy which she deplored, or to avenge Tariq, she could not have said. In an effort to change the subject, Livia said, "I should like to see your summer palace, the Generalife."

Imperturbably Ayxa went on. "Courtly love, the chivalric concept, came into Christendom from Islam, where women are perceived as different beings from men—as remote and mysterious creatures however close a wife may be to her husband."

"I have never thought of myself as being remote and mysterious," Livia said wryly.

Ayxa nodded, as if she had thought as much. "This mystery engenders a cult of selfless devotion to a woman. In truth, jealousy, in the eyes of an Arab, is a virtue insofar as it concerns the family; for the family—and above all the women belonging to it—are a sanctuary." With an air of triumph, she placed three cards upon the table.

Livia looked her directly in the eyes. "I am not an Arab, or a Moslem."

Determined to have the last word, Ayxa replied, "The Prophet tells us to seek wisdom, even in China." And the subject was closed.

On other days Livia occupied herself with copying pages from the Koran and strumming new ballads on the lute. It began to seem that she would spend the rest of her days in limbo, one day flowing into the next like the never-ceasing murmur of the fountains and streams that graced the gardens of the Alhambra, when a new worry rose to plague her. Under the folds of her flowing tunic, her flat abdomen gave little evidence of the burden she carried. Guilt assailed her. Had her resentment at her unwanted pregnancy harmed the child; marked it to be stillborn?

Upset, she at last confided her fears to Ayxa.

The sultana's shrewd eyes sparkled in amusement. "Calm yourself. You are of tall and slender stature and carry the babe high. It may well not be until the seventh month that of a sudden, you will show."

Thus reassured, Livia's natural optimism reasserted itself. Then, at the end of June, tidings were brought that King Ferdinand had departed from Cordoba to march on Loxa, a city of great strength situated in a pass of the mountains between the kingdoms of Granada and Castile. The Moorish troops were called to arms. From her window, Livia watched Tariq mount his black stallion and ride through the gates of the Alhambra, his green and gold banners shining in the morning sunlight. It struck her then that Tariq had that same ravenous ambition to distinguish himself before all others and at any cost, to immortalize himself through word or deed, that lies deep in the hearts of the sons of the desert. Even knowing this, she knew she would never know him truly.

After he had gone, she felt only relief mixed with joy. Though he had disdained to visit her, the mere knowledge that he was in the palace and doubtless taking his pleasure with Khadija, was a constant thorn in her flesh. Now she felt happy to be rid of his disturbing presence. Her lighthearted mood was soon dispelled. To her rage, she discovered that Tariq had left orders with Naja, the eunuch, that she was not to leave her chambers until his return. As the days passed, her ill-humor mounted until she became obsessed with the desire to be free.

One soft summer morning, just before noon, as she sat reading on the belvedere, her attention was caught by the sight of Malik clad in a fine robe of striped red, white and green cotton, strolling through the garden below. She rose from her seat and leaned over the balustrade.

"Malik! What news have you of Loxa?"

Swiftly he crossed the courtyard and stood gazing up at her, an insinuating smile on his thin lips. "The battle is not yet joined, but let us speak of more interesting matters."

She smiled in return, thankful that she had donned a full flowing robe of Persian linen whose blue and yellow design concealed her distended waist, which had yet to fulfill Ayxa's prediction. She chatted of this and that, deliberately enticing him with flashing eyes and soft words. At length her lips curved in a wistful smile and she murmured, "Ah, how sweet it would be if I, too, could walk with you in the garden."

Malik's face brightened and he uttered the harsh laugh that grated on her nerves. "Perhaps I can arrange it. I've friends in high places, you know. The Lord of the Keys, for one."

"Oh, I doubt you could overcome Naja," retorted Livia with a deprecatory smile. "He is ever-vigilant, and his loyalty cannot be bought. Even you cannot corrupt Tariq's guard."

Challenged by the mention of Tariq's power, Malik's eyes narrowed and he sneered. "If Tariq's faithful guard is ordered away by a higher authority—"

"Impossible!" interrupted Livia. With a hopeless shrug of her shoulders she pulled out of his view.

Chapter 16

Sooner than Livia would have thought possible, the heavy door swung open and Malik stood leering at her from the threshold. He held out his arms and she ran toward him, quickly sidestepping him and dashed down the stairs.

Malik, close on her heels, let out a shout of laughter. "By Allah, you are a vixen, but the prize is well worth the chase!"

Gooseflesh prickled the back of her neck as she raced in the direction of the harem. Upset, and confused by the zigzagging corridors, she missed the one she sought. In desperation, she veered left and raced down the length of a narrow passage that ended in an elbowlike turn. She let out a gasp of astonishment as she emerged upon the Court of the Lions. Her gaze traveled swiftly about the lacy fretwork, the colonnades and pavilions at each end, the gardens blooming with jasmine and roses and the fountain in the center whose massive marble basin was supported on the backs of twelve stone lions spurting water from their mouths. No one was about. Too late she recalled that it was Friday noon, when all the faithful of the palace went to the mosque to pray.

She bolted toward the fountain, dropped to her knees and crouched between two lions whose grinning faces seemed to mock her. She strained her ears, listening for Malik's footsteps over the sound of gushing water. A jubilant burst of laughter erupted over her shoulder. She wheeled about. Malik stood

towering over her, a victorious expression on his lean
face. She was trapped on her knees. A tremor shook
her as Malik reached out, grasped her upper arms and
drew her to her feet.

With a lightning movement, she wrenched free and
ran around the bowl of the fountain. Suddenly she
stopped short and her breath caught in her throat.
Malik had circled in the opposite direction. She was
headed straight into his arms. She retraced her steps,
Malik hard on her heels. She felt his hand clutch her
shoulder and the next instant he spun her around to
face him.

His arms went around her waist in a bone-crushing
grip. She uttered a scream that ended in a choked cry
as his hot, moist lips pressed down upon her mouth as
though to devour her. She felt his hands on her
buttocks, clasping her body against his thighs. Her
heart hammered in her ears and she thrust her hands
hard against his shoulders in an effort to shove him
away.

A burst of laughter erupted deep in his throat and
the pressure of his lips increased, forcing her head
back, his chest pressed hard against her breasts.
Desperately, she fought to free herself, but her struggles were futile against his strength.

All at once she went limp in his arms. Choking down
an overwhelming sense of revulsion, she willed herself
to relax, to endure his embrace. Her arms went about
his neck in a pretense of succumbing to his ardent
caresses. Close to her ear, he whispered, "You see, my
dove? It is pleasant to be loved by Malik!"

She made no reply, but remained deathly still, every
nerve ending tingling as she forced herself to wait.
Again his mouth sought hers, and as their lips clung, he
relaxed his hold on her. His hands roamed her body,
fondling her breasts, and when she could endure it no
longer, she lunged to one side, eluding his outstretched
arms.

She sprinted toward the Hall of Kings under the east portico and as she drew near, her desperate gaze swept the tiled walls, searching for a door. There was none!

When Malik reached Livia, he threw back his head in a shout of laughter, as though enjoying the sport. "You temptress! Enchantress! Now you shall deliver what you promise!"

"I promised nothing!"

Malik's face darkened with anger. Unused to being thwarted, he did not take it well. His expression turned menacing. "I will have you, Livia!"

Driven by fear, she lunged to her right. Malik raced after her. Livia flew across the courtyard toward the Court of the Two Sisters. She heard Malik's enraged shout as she dashed across the pavement. The luminous honeyed light that shone from the vast beehive dome overhead revealed no hiding place, and the calligraphy adorning the walls blurred as she sped through the Court of the Two Sisters and garden of Daraxa, under another archway and down a long, dim corridor where a eunuch stood guarding the door to the harem.

With a gasp of relief, she flung herself through the doorway into the sitting room amid the startled houris gathered there. She collapsed and sat quaking at the sound of Malik's enraged voice demanding that the eunuch deliver her into his hands. For the first time, Livia was thankful for the sanctuary.

During the days that followed, Livia remained sequestered in the harem, not daring to risk Malik's revenge. Less than a week had passed when a hubbub from the town brought the houris rushing to the windows. "The army returns victorious!"

A shiver of anticipation surged through Livia. What would Tariq do when he discovered she had escaped? Of one thing she was certain. His wrath would know no bounds.

A short time later, when Tariq entered the harem, Livia could read nothing in his solemn mien. His features were inscrutable as he escorted outside. To her astonishment, he led her to his own apartment. He seated her on the gold divan, then stood, arms folded across his chest, head lowered, regarding her with a thoughtful gaze. Livia sat unmoving. Her anxiety mounted as she stared up into his face bronzed by the sun; his broad shoulders emanating power. A tremor of fear ran down her spine. When he spoke, his voice was stern and forbidding.

"Though it angers me to find that you escaped the tower, I am gratified that though you gained your freedom, you did not attempt to flee the palace."

All at once, the pent-up resentment she had held in check for so long erupted, and without intending to, she burst out, "Do not flatter yourself, Tariq! It is not for you that I remain here against my will, but for your child!"

Tariq's head jerked up as though she had struck him, and an expression of such joy spread over his countenance that she could not endure watching it. Quickly, she lowered her gaze. A sense of wonder stole over her; she had at last penetrated his granite heart. She should feel elated, but she did not—the victory was hollow and without meaning.

In one swift motion, Tariq dropped down beside her and clasped her slender hands in his. "Can this be so? Are you certain you are to give me an heir?"

She nodded mutely.

He released her hands and smoothed down the folds of her flowing pink tunic then cupped his palms over the fullness of her belly. He looked into her face with an expression of awe and reverence as though beholding a miracle, his eyes alight with happiness.

"You will present me with the gift of which every Arab dreams—a son!"

Bracing her hands on the divan, Livia drew away from him. Resentment welled up in her anew at having been forced to give this man such a gift at the sacrafice of her own virtue . . . and at the cost of her marriage to the only man in the world she truly loved. "Your heir may well be a daughter," she said waspishly.

He made no reply, but leaned forward and pressed his ear against the rounded curve of her belly. "In my mind I hear his voice," he said softly, smiling with pleasure.

His tenderness unnerved her. She squirmed uneasily, shifting her weight and at that moment the baby let loose a strong kick.

Tariq raised his head and chuckled delightedly. "Even now he displays the strength of a lion!"

Perversely, Livia wanted to hurl cruel words at him, words that would crush him, but she could not summon to mind anything to dim his rapture. She watched him as though mesmerized, unable to raise her voice against him.

"You shall bear me a son," pronounced Tariq happily. "*Inshallah.* It is the will of Allah!"

Livia suppressed a smile, thinking that her pregnancy was more the will of Tariq; but for a reason she could not fathom, she found herself wishing for a son.

That evening when she heard Tariq's footsteps echoing down the corridor, she paused, cocking her head to listen. She thought she had heard him whistling—most uncharacteristic of the somber Tariq. She glanced up as he entered and a cry of surprise escaped her.

He held aloft a golden cage whose fine wires formed an intricate design of curlicues and arabesques ending in a domelike minaret. Inside perched a bird that could fit in the palm of her hand, trilling an exquisite song.

Livia ran across the room and peered eagerly at the bird whose russet feathers ended in a reddish rump and tail. His plain appearance was enhanced by the beauty of his song, though now it seemed to Livia to have a plaintive quality. The bird fixed his bright gaze upon her and appeared to regard her shyly.

"Oh, how lovely!"

"A *bulbul*—a nightingale," Tariq said grinning. "To keep you company when I depart to fight."

A troubled frown creased Livia's smooth brow. "Must we always speak of war?"

As though sensing the tension in the air, the nightingale ceased his song in mid-trill.

Tariq sank down upon a cushion on the floor and, sighing deeply, he set his turban aside and ran his hands through his crisp black hair. "It is always with us. We were victorious at Loxa only because we held a strategic bridge and because Morayma's father tricked the Christians by attacking the Spanish encampment front and rear. Also, Muley mustered an army, though he wasn't successful in helping. If he had remained idle, it would have ruined him in the eyes of his people. So now he marches along the seacoast."

"And you will go to his aid?"

Tariq shook his head. "Boabdil will not hear of it."

Livia's heart swelled with gladness. She felt relieved that Boabdil's forces would not join old Muley's. The realization brought her up short. She must take care lest she be deterred from her vow to make this infidel rue the day he had taken her. She must harden her heart against Tariq.

Despite her resolve, she found that she enjoyed the sunny, lazy afternoons spent with Tariq strolling in the gardens sweet with the scent of jasmine and roses, and the soothing music of water splashing in the fountains. She would sit quietly, listening while Tariq spoke of love and chivalry and murmured romantic verses for which the Arabs were famous. She felt a never-ending sense of wonder that a man so powerful in the court, a hero on the battlefield, so violent in his passions, could at the same time woo her with gentle sentiments. And deep in her heart, Livia exulted that it was she who had the ability to charm this stony-hearted man to the heights of rapture.

On a sultry afternoon, early in July, a mass of billowing clouds hung over the city like smoke and the air was deathly still. Livia lighted the lamps against the early darkness, then taking up her lute she seated herself in the window. She was singing softly and plucking the strings, when Tariq stormed into their chamber, his face livid. He strode to the embrasure, wrenched the lute from her hands and flung it across the room.

"What have you done to me?" he bellowed. "Is it vengence you seek to wreak upon me, playing me for the fool?"

Stunned speechless, defenseless against the murderous expression in his eyes, Livia could only look up at him, her heart pounding.

"Did you think I would not learn of your perfidy?" He clenched his fists at his sides as though to keep from strangling her. "Were I not a follower of the Prophet, I would fling you and the bastard you carry to your death upon the rocks below!"

His rage served only to inflame her. "I know not what you're talking about! Explain yourself, at once!"

"*Puta!* It is not my child you carry, but Malik's!"

"That is not true!" Livia cried, stumbling to her feet.

"How would you know?" Tariq thundered. "Did you not invite your guards—every man in the palace—to share your bed in my absence?"

"No!" Tears of anger blinded her and trickled down her cheeks.

Tariq's lips curled in a sneer. "How pleased you must have been when I turned you over to Malik for safekeeping the night that fighting broke out in the palace!"

"No, no!" Livia cried, stretching out her arms in entreaty.

With a furious gesture, Tariq struck down her hands. "Do you deny that it was Malik with whom you planned to flee? Malik whose horse stood waiting with yours to carry you away from Granada? And who apprised me of your whereabouts when you tried to flee with Nizam? Your lover Malik! I had thought him to be concerned for your welfare, but at last the truth is revealed. He knew perfectly well that I would put a stop to his faithless mistress leaving him!"

"Stop, stop!" Livia screamed, covering her ears with her hands. "This is not true. None of it is true!"

"Who released you from the tower before you tried to flee with Nizam? And who released you when I was gone at the siege of Loxa? Tell me! Who?"

Unable to speak, Livia stared up at him with terrified eyes. Her knees trembled for she had not known the towering heights his rage could reach.

"You need not bother denying it!" In a voice heavy with sarcasm, he continued. "Malik released you, in return for favors given him in the past and favors he knew he could expect in the future!"

Livia took a deep breath. "You great camel-headed fool! Don't you know that Malik is your enemy? He fabricates these lies to destroy you. His jealousy of you knows no bounds. You can put no stock in his words. His accusations are lies, all of them! True, Malik's horse stood next to mine, and he once released me from the tower—but things are not as they appear. You cannot trust Malik's word!"

"I know that," said Tariq in low, ominous tones. But it is not Malik who has shed light upon your infidelity, who has apprised me of all that has transpired behind my back, but one whose word I can trust. I learn the truth from Khadija."

"Khadija!" Livia spat, her rage matching his. "That painted, lying daughter of a dog! You are even a greater fool than I imagined. If you choose to believe the word of such a woman, so be it. I will not waste one breath by dignifying the tales of such a wanton with a reply!"

Livia drew herself to her full height and glared up into his face with something akin to hatred shining from her eyes. "From this moment on, do not speak to me. Do not come near me. Do not even enter a room in which I am present, for I wish never to lay eyes upon you again, so long as I live!" She swept past him, her pink robe swirling in a cloud about her as she fled from the chamber.

Chapter 17

Shortly before dawn, on a morning late in September 1482, when the air was filled with wood smoke, the grapes were harvested and the lush green foliage of the *vega* had begun to fade, Livia was delivered of a son. Drowsy with sleep, she heard someone bend over the child and whisper the first words every Moslem child hears and the last words murmured at his grave: "There is no god but Allah, and Mohammed is his Prophet."

She opened her eyes and gazed about Nizam's room where she had stayed ever since the night of Tariq's accusations.

During the interminable days and nights of waiting, her only joy and companion had been Bulbul, the nightingale which she'd had brought to Nizam's apartment. From dawn till close of day, Livia had been comforted by the bird's rich musical song which never failed to dispel her own feelings of desolation.

As the days of her confinement passed, her anger toward Tariq had drained away and when she thought of him it was with a remote impassivity such as she would feel toward anyone who had shown himself to be no friend. He had not come to her, and she had assured herself repeatedly that this was exactly as she wished. But last night, at the onset of her labor, thinking that he should know, she had dispatched a slave to tell him of the impending birth of his child. He had not come.

At length it became evident that he had no intention of visiting his son. Apparently he continued to nurture his evil suspicions and now refused to acknowledge the child. Resentment built toward the infant whose advent had caused her so much grief.

Livia resolved to hand the boy over to an amah in the palace. She would then appeal to a *gadi*—a judge who arbitrated domestic disputes. If a *gadi*'s conciliation failed, as it surely would, a husband could divorce his wife simply by repeating three times: "I dismiss thee," and after three months the divorce would become final. Doubtless, Tariq would comply with her wishes, if indeed he himself had not already approached the *judge,* she thought bitterly. That decision made, she sighed deeply and lay back on the pillow and closed her eyes. Livia dozed throughout the day, barely conscious of Ayxa, Amina and others who tiptoed into her chamber to view the child, then tiptoed out again.

Toward evening she stirred and sat up, vaguely aware that something was amiss. She glanced about her. The apartment was unnaturally silent. The soft golden glow of the setting sun illuminated the child sleeping soundly in a wooden cradle beside her bed. She arose from the bed and strode barefoot across the soft carpet into the sitting room. All was quiet. No one was about. Her servant had probably gone to fetch her evening meal and would return shortly.

Quiet pressed around Livia like a shroud. She shivered and wrapped her arms about her. Her glance fell upon the golden cage standing near the window and then it came to her, Bulbul was silent. Now that she thought of it, she had not heard his song all afternoon. She ran to the cage and clutching the wires, stared at the bird huddled on the bottom, it's head down, as though pecking at a crumb beneath his wing.

"Bulbul, Bulbul?" called Livia, softly. The bird did not stir. Livia flung open the door, reached inside and seized the small feathered creature. A tremor of dread ran through her and her hand shook as she drew back. The bird's eyes were closed. With one finger she stroked the small head. He did not move. Gently, Livia turned him over in her hand. His head wobbled grotesquely as her trembling fingers found the broken bones in his neck.

With a strangled cry, she cradled the bird against her breast and sank to her knees on the floor, tears streaming down her cheeks. There her slave girl found her. In a choked voice Livia told her the cause of her grief.

The girl regarded her in startled dismay. "But who would do such a thing?"

Who, indeed, thought Livia miserably. Malik? Khadija? Or Tariq?

It was as if the last bit of compassion within her had died with Bulbul. Henceforth, she vowed she would not allow her spirit or her flesh to be conquered by the ruthless barbarian Tariq, nor the *puta* Khadija, nor the lascivious Malik.

The following day she asked her slave girl to find a wet nurse to whom she could hand over Tariq's child. But none was to be found in the palace. Determined to carry out her resolve, Livia sent the girl into the city to find one. The girl returned, her eyes worried, to face Livia with a helpless shrug. "No one wishes an extra mouth to feed."

"But I will pay!" exclaimed Livia. "Did you tell them that?"

The girl nodded. "No one will take the child." There was nothing for it, thought Livia, vexed, but to nurse the child, to care for him herself until an amah could be found. As she looked down upon his small, round, honey-skinned face, the thatch of dark hair above his brow, his trusting eyes, so like Tariq's, fringed with thick black lashes, a wave of pity swept through her for this child no one wanted. Unaware that she was smiling, Livia murmured, "Since you have nothing else, little one, I shall give you a noble name to carry with you into the world: Harun, along with an honorific title—al-Rashid, follower of the right path. May it serve you well!"

As the sun-filled days of September merged with the cold damp days of winter, Livia kept Rashid constantly at her side. December passed unremarked in this heathen land and filled her with longing to be present at the Feast of the Most Blessed Nativity which would be celebrated in every Christian city, village and hamlet of Spain. One day shortly after the new year, her slave girl appeared on the threshold with a woman-of-the-night who had been blessed with an infant. The woman's eyes gleamed with avarice as she offered to act as Rashid's wet nurse, for only a few dinar each week.

Livia, bristling at the very thought of giving him over to a *puta*, let loose a tirade and ordered the woman from the palace. Her young servant, taken aback protested, "I thought you wished a wet nurse."

"So I do," snapped Livia, "but the boy cannot go to live in a *kahn*. I must think of his future!"

As time passed, Livia began to take delight in Rashid. Only one shadow marred the smooth perfection of her days: Tariq had never come to see the baby. In fact, Livia was certain that he had gone out of his way to avoid them. Sternly she told herself that she was thankful that he kept his distance; that it was better for herself, and for Rashid as well. Her only regret was that Nizam was not here to see her adorable son and to watch him grow healthy and strong.

At length an amah was found. A plump, smiling girl named Hajai, daughter of an impoverished family in the Albaycin. No mention was made of taking Rashid to live with her family, and Hajai came to reside at the palace.

Winter lingered on, cold and gray and wet, until one day the almond trees again put forth white tissue blossoms, the sweet scent of jasmine pervaded the air, and the swallows swooped down from their nests in the palace. At last spring had come, and with it, a letter from Nizam brought by one of the fleet-footed members of the postal service.

Livia broke open the seal and her eyes flew down the page of fine, even script.

Nizam had married Raduan Venegas and taken a room with a family in Malaga, not too far from the citadel, where she could be near him. They had been deliriously happy until recently, when Ferdinand had decided that an invasion might be safely made into a mountainous region near Malaga.

Raduan feared that since Malaga was weakly garrisoned and had too few cavalry, the Spanish might even extend their ravages to their very gates.

A feeling of apprehension crept through Livia as she read on.

Though the Spaniards had intended to conduct their expedition with great speed and secrecy, word of the preparations reached the garrison at Malaga commanded by El Zagal, Muley's younger brother. At the head of the Christian vanguard laying waste the country rode Don Alonzo de Aguilar.

Aguilar! Livia's heart leaped up and her fingers tightened on the page as she read on.

The Moors intercepted them. The ambush lasted several nights. In the darkness and confusion, the bands of the Christian commanders became separated from one another. El Zagal attacked the rear guard. The enemy lost all presence of mind. Most fled and were then either slain or taken captive. Raduan distinguished himself by capturing some nobles.

Hundreds of prisoners were taken, some to be sold as slaves, other to be led captive to Granada.

I have prevailed upon Raduan to learn the whereabouts of Aguilar. He has determined that Aguilar is not held prisoner here in Malaga. Nor does he think he has fallen in battle, for it would be known, had so mighty a commander fallen. I regret that I cannot inform you more fully as to his fate.

I have included my address in the hope that you will write me news of yourself and the court.

Livia felt the color drain from her face. She must get

hold of herself. She could not—would not—believe that the eagle Aguilar had been struck down. She sighed deeply, folded the letter away, took pen and paper in hand and sat down to write to Nizam of the birth of her son.

A tumult in the streets of the town brought Livia to her feet. She did not need to be told the cause of the commotion. With heavy heart, she forced herself to go with the courtiers to watch in awestruck horror as the prisoners taken in the mountains of Malaga were paraded in triumph through the gates of the city. Spoils of splendid armor and weapons and many horses, magnificantly caparisoned, together with numerous standards, had been taken.

Livia's heart thudded against her breast and her knees shook as she raised a hand to shade her eyes against the burning afternoon sun and scanned the wretched train for the sight of Aguilar's banner.

The Moors were in a frenzy; they thought the victory a work of Allah. Sick at heart, Livia turned away from the sight. Aguilar's banner was not among those captured, nor could she distinguish Aguilar himself marching among the ragged band of captives. She leaned weakly against the wall, her mind in a turmoil. If Aguilar was not held prisoner at Malaga, and if he had not fallen in battle, he must be among these prisoners straggling into Granada—must be!

Chapter 18

Livia hastened back to her chamber where she paced the floor in a fury of impatience until sunset. When she heard the voice of the muezzin, she donned a mantle, took up a small lamp and swiftly made her way to the door leading to the dungeon. Golden dinar exchanged hands. The guard saw no harm in allowing this fragile young woman a brief visit. As she crept down the dank stairs to the bowels of the palace, the stench of excrement and rotting bodies choked her and she clutched the folds of her mantle tightly about her face. The lamplight cast eerie shadows upon the stone walls. Livia shuddered at the sound of moans and the clanking of chains that assaulted her ears. At the end of the passageway she raised the lamp high overhead and stopped short, gasping.

Bodies lay strewn about the dirt floor of a vast cavernlike chamber, limp, ragged bundles crawling with vermin that called to her mind paintings of those creatures struck down by the Black Death. Her stomach lurched and she choked down the bile that rose in her throat at the sight of the skeletal figures whose manacled wrists were chained to rings in the walls. The vaulted room echoed with low moans that resembled animal howlings, and stifled shrieks mingled with ravings. She took a deep breath and slowly picked her way through the human debris.

Livia searched each face, shrinking from the piteous pleas for food and water. As she moved on, hands reached out to clutch at her skirts, and an overwhelming feeling of pity for these poor wretches engulfed her. She wished with all her heart that she could minister to their entreaties.

Suddenly a burning-eyed, hollow-cheeked soldier rose to his feet and stood blocking her way. Noting his rich garb and armor streaked with dirt and blood, Livia judged him to be one of the Spanish nobles taken in the mountains of Malaga. His feverish eyes widened in incredulous disbelief as he gaped at Livia's pale features revealed in the halo of lamplight.

"What do I behold?" he cried. "A Spanish woman wearing the garb of a Moor!" He spat in disgust. "An apostate consorting with the enemy to save her skin!"

Quick anger flamed in her cheeks. "It was not by choice! I remain a Christian and a Spaniard to the death, though I was forced to wed the Moorish commander Tariq!"

A cynical smile spread over the man's haggard face. "Then you may use your influence on my behalf."

"I have no influence with . . ."

"I am no common soldier to be buried alive in this hole, but the Count de Cifuentes!" he bellowed. "I demand an audience with Boabdil, at once!"

With some difficulty, Livia calmed his rage and promised to intercede with King Boabdil on his behalf, then asked eagerly for news of Aguilar.

The count shook his head hopelessly. "Aguilar led the vanguard of our force, but in the confusion I don't know what happened to him." Livia bit her lip to keep from crying. A vision of Aguilar lying dead in a rock-strewn pass swam before her eyes, and she quickly put it down. Such thoughts were not to be borne. He was not dead. Could not be dead! Hope would sustain her. With weary steps, she forced herself to move on, hoping to find another person who might know of Aguilar. But as she proceeded she found no one who knew of him, her spirits flagged. Close to despair, she entered the last of the cavelike chambers. Here the prisoners lay quiet and unmoving and, judging by the nauseating stench of decaying bodies, there were many from whom the last breath of life had long since departed. With a hopeless sigh, she swung the lamp in one last arc. She turned to leave when from the corner of her eye she saw a captive raise a hand in a mockery of a wave as his lips formed a soundless cry.

As though transfixed, she stared at the emaciated specter slumped against a wall. His dark eyes glittering from his waxen countenance compelled her to go nearer. With faltering steps, she approached him and shone the light down upon his head. A choked cry burst from her lips. She sank to her knees and flung her arms about his neck, pressing her cheek against his grizzled face. Tears welled in her eyes.

"Julian! Julian!" she murmured again and again. "I had given you up for dead!"

Shock flickered in his eyes. He clutched a fold of her cloak, as if clinging to life itself. Through parched, cracked lips came a hoarse whisper, "Livia! Surely I have descended to hell, but why are *you* . . ." Exhausted with the effort to speak, his voice trailed off.

She drew back and gripped his shoulders hard, as if to force him into awareness. "Julian, do you hear me?"

He looked at her with a glazed expression and made no reply. She shook him gently. "Julian, I'm going to leave now, to see to your release. Do you hear me?"

She saw the light of understanding spread over his dazed countenance. He blinked in response. She leaned forward, kissed him lightly on the brow then rose to her feet and hastened back through the putrid dungeon and up the stairs into the halls of the palace.

Swiftly, she made her way to Ayxa la Horra. For the first time, Livia was grateful for the intrigues, the struggle for power that constantly occupied the woman's thoughts. Livia found her seated on the divan, her short squat body enveloped in a brilliant green brocade caftan embroidered with silver thread and encrusted with pearls. Around her neck was draped a silver filigree necklace, and matching triangles dangled from her ears. Her head was bent over a map of the kingdom of Granada on which her finger traced a route. At Livia's approach, her bejeweled finger paused between Loxa and Lucena, a town held by the Christians. Ayxa looked up and a pleased smile of recognition spread over her smooth olive features.

With breathless urgency, Livia explained that she wished to free her brother. Ayxa regarded her through narrowed eyes and nodded sympathetically. "Alas, I can do nothing. Boabdil has taken to the hills to engage in falconry, a sport of which he is passionately fond. No one is to be released—not even the Count de Cifuentes."

Livia took a deep breath. Somehow she would have to convince Ayxa of the importance of freeing Julian. Desperately, she searched her mind for a means to stir the sultana to help her. Ayxa's jealousy of Zoraya might suffice. Quickly, Livia explained that Julian had been taken captive at Zahara by the uxorious Muley, who even now languished with Zoraya at Malaga. Surely the release of one of Muley's prisoners would be a small but delicious revenge. She paused, awaiting Ayxa's reaction.

"Tell me something of your brother," Ayxa said softly.

"Julian is an artisan of the first rank," Livia said eagerly. "And so handsome he can charm the birds from trees—in Arabic, Spanish and Hebrew as well. He is bold, courageous and fearless—"

Ayxa raised a hand, stemming Livia's flow of compliments. A smile curved her lips and a calculating look came into her eyes as Ayxa sought a way in which she could use Julian to her advantage.

"My brother could be of great use to you," Livia said persuasively. "He knows the countryside like the colors of his palette and can travel anywhere unchallenged because he speaks several languages.

Ayxa pursed her lips, frowning in thought while Livia stood waiting, her hands folded tightly at her waist to still their shaking. After what seemed an eternity, Ayxa nodded curtly.

"Surely Boabdil will not notice the loss of an insignificant artisan. I will have the prisoner sent to your chambers. When he is fit to travel, bring him to me." She waved a hand in dismissal and bent to resume her study of the map.

As Livia hurried back to her quarters in Nizam's apartment, a small ironic smile lighted her features. It was only because of her dispute with Tariq over Rashid's parentage that she could remain in Nizam's apartment. There she could hide Julian without interference from anyone.

When Julian was brought to her, she ordered a slave to bathe him, clothe him in fresh garments and place him on a bed she had prepared on the divan. She then set about feeding him a thin broth and barley bread.

Late the following afternoon, Julian's strength had begun to return and he sat up braced upon the pillows, telling her of his escape from Zahara.

Seated beside him, Livia listened avidly, never taking her eyes from his face as he told her how he had struck the lid from a wine cask, let the wine flow into the street, then had hidden inside the great oaken barrel. When darkness had fallen, he had left his hiding place and taken refuge in a burned-out house.

Livia's dark eyes widened in astonishment. "Why did you not flee the town?"

Julian's pale features took on a set, pained look. "I had to stay—to find our mother and father—" He paused, as though it were difficult for him to go on.

Livia's heart seemed to stop beating. "And did you find them?"

Julian's eyes met hers, a shadow in their depths. "Yes, lying near the gate. If there is any solace to be taken, it is that their end was swift." He sighed deeply. "I placed them upon a cart . . . and took them to the cemetery. After that I joined the army." Livia's gaze fell. Tears ran down her cheeks.

Julian reached out and clasped her hands in his. "Try not to grieve, *niña*. They are together for all time, as they would have wished." He leaned toward her and his lips brushed her brow in a gentle comforting kiss.

The swish of the hangings over the doorway cut sharply through the silence and Livia sprang up. Her hand flew to her mouth, smothering a shriek.

Tariq, his face contorted with hideous rage, crossed the room in three paces and at the same time drew his scimitar from its jeweled sheath. With a bellow, he raised the weapon over his head. In the moment before it slashed downward, Livia flung herself against Julian's chest, shielding him with her body. She squeezed her eyes shut, bracing herself against the swift descent of Tariq's flashing steel blade.

Suddenly she felt strong fingers dig into the flesh of her arm and with a violent jerk, she was flung upon the floor. Tariq, formidable in black turban and tunic, his face a mask of fury, stood towering over her. Once again the scimitar arced upward. Livia leaped to her feet and reaching out with both hands, clung to Tariq's arm as it descended in a powerful swing, deflecting the blow.

"No, Tariq!" she screamed. "No! It is Julian! My brother Julian!"

Tariq shook off her hands, clutched his arm and stood staring first at Livia, then at Julian, in incredulous disbelief. When he spoke, his voice was hard, edged with suspicion. "I was told that you had a prisoner released. I was not told he was your brother!"

Her first impulse was to tell him that it was by Ayxa's order that Julian had been released, but she feared he would countermand the order—if only to prove that the commander-in-chief outranked the sultana. Instead, she cried out, "Who carried this tale? Khadija?" Noting the flush that spread quickly across Tariq's face from beard to brow, her anger overrode her fear. "Your informant is most unreliable, as usual," she went on, her eyes blazing. "Naturally, I do not expect you to

accept my word! Go and consult your lists—your
jailer—and you will find I speak the truth!"

Tariq fixed his penetrating gaze upon her, as though
assessing the truth of her words, then slowly slid his
scimitar into its sheath.

Sensing her advantage, Livia clasped Tariq's hands in
her cold ones. She looked up into his face, her eyes
pleading. "Tariq, let Julian stay—at least until he is
able to walk about. Surely you cannot be so inhuman as
to allow your wife's brother to lie starving, rotting in
the pesthole beneath the palace. It would bring evil
upon your house . . ." She paused, fumbling for words.
Then struck by an inspiration, she added, "Is this the
will of Allah?"

As she gazed earnestly at Tariq, she saw a flash of
indecision mixed with sympathy that quickly disappeared. His expression turned impassive. He was silent
for a moment, as though weighing his thoughts. At last
he said, "The man is a prisoner. He will remain a
prisoner."

"No!" cried Livia. "You cannot . . ."

Ignoring Livia's anguished cry, he continued. "He
must keep within the confines of the palace and set to
work repairing the plaster and tile adornments of the
walls." Turning his implacable gaze on Julian, he
added, "And should you take your leave, your sister's
life will be forfeit."

Before Livia could speak her gratitude, Tariq stalked
out.

Blustery March days blended into the soft golden
days of April. The fig, olive and pomegranate trees
leafed out and the *vega* grew green with crops of wheat,
barley and grapes, its fields and hillsides thick with
lemon, orange and mulberries. Each day Livia strolled
with Julian in the gardens, and under the healing sun
and clear, sweet air, Julian prospered and grew strong.
When she was not with Julian, she spent much of her
time with Rashid. She enjoyed most the hour before

sunset prayer when Hajai would bring him to her and she would play with him until Hajai returned.

Early one evening after Hajai had taken Rashid away, Livia and Julian strolled among the gardens in the shadow of the Great Mosque. They ambled on past a large square pool in whose green depths were mirrored the graceful arches and portico of the Tower of the Ladies, then mounted the stone stairs to a terrace and sat down on a bench beside a smaller pool in which a fountain bubbled.

Livia sat enraptured as the soft evening breeze caressed her hair, and cupolas and ancient towers glared redly in the magical light of the setting sun. Shadows lengthened languidly and the air was full of the sonorous flute sounds and the ocarina chirping of the birds. At dusk the silence surrounding the nightingales' singing and the tumble of waters was broken by the clear sound of a bell that sounded on the watchtower.

"It's said that on a still day, the bell can be heard as far as ten leagues away."

She didn't hear Julian's reply for just then two figures emerged from the Lady Tower and strolled under the shadow of the arcade. Livia could not mistake Tariq's massive frame, the powerful set of his shoulders, the easy grace of his stride. And there was no doubt as to the identity of his voluptuous companion adorned with sparkling jewels and clad in a filmy purple tunic that revealed every sensuous curve of her thighs and ripe breasts.

Livia stiffened and quick color reddened her cheeks, searing her senses. Anger, jealousy, envy, outrage—she could not name it. She assured herself quickly that she was unnerved only because Tariq was her husband, because he showed so little regard for their marriage bonds. Apparently, he and Khadija had managed to keep their affair a well-kept secret from the court, she thought bitterly. If word of it reached Boabdil's ears, they would meet with a swift and terrible end.

As though sensing her feelings, Julian's brows lifted in surprise. "Why the sudden ruffling of feathers, *niña*?

At that moment, Khadija paused and turned to face Tariq. She stood on her toes and tilted her face up to his. His arms went about her waist and their lips met and clung.

Livia wanted to shout, to cry out. Instead, she sat, unable to drag her gaze from the infuriating sight of their ardent embrace.

"Livia, what ails you?" Julian asked, alarmed.

"My husband's senses are addled by the charms of Khadija." Livia snapped. "He had intended to marry her, it seems, but upon his return from the assault upon Zahara, he found her wed to Boabdil. He married me to avenge her, and now he makes a mockery of our vows."

Tariq and Khadija drew apart and the woman's deep-throated laughter rippled across the gardens. Livia turned to Julian. Without thinking, she burst out, "Would that he had met his just fate at Zahara!"

She should have anticipated Julian's reaction, but she had forgotten his quick temper, his impulsiveness, his zeal for righting a wrong. Bold as he was boastful, he jumped to his feet, his youthful features hardened into those of a man afire with righteous indignation. In a low, tight voice, he exclaimed, "No man brings dishonor to my sister!"

Julian seemed eager not only to defend her honor, but to avenge their parents' death and his own imprisonment.

"He will meet his fate now!" Julian exploded. Muttering an oath, he swung about as if to descend upon Tariq and Khadija.

Livia lunged forward and clutched the hem of his shirt with both hands. "Julian! Wait!"

Julian whirled upon her, his eyes wild and staring. "Leave off, Livia. I will avenge your honor. The infidel will not live to dishonor you further."

A chilling fear swept through her. Her brother's

prowess would be no match for the expertise of the seasoned warrior Tariq. Her mind reeled as she sought desperately for a means to delay Julian's attack. "Please," she gasped, tugging on his shirt. "You must wait!"

"No!"

"Think!" Livia insisted sharply. "If you kill Tariq now, Khadija will remain as a witness. You will never escape. You will be put to death, and what would that avail either of us?"

Julian glared down at her, his handsome features twisted into a grimace. "When, then?"

"I will invent an excuse to lure him to my rooms, and you can do away with him there." A quick glance over Julian's shoulder assured her that Tariq and Khadija had moved out of sight. "In any case, they have gone now. Do not fly up like a headless rooster, Julian. Wait to challenge Tariq on your own ground, on your own terms."

With an exasperated sigh, Julian sank down on the bench beside her. "So be it. But we must act without delay."

Relieved that she had brought Julian to his senses and gained time—time for him to cool his rage—Livia nodded. "It will be done."

Chapter 19

Julian gave Livia no peace. Each day he grew more insistent, demanding to know when she would entice Tariq to her chamber. He raved against the Moor, deploring his brazen romance with Khadija; castigating him for believing she had had an affair with Malik; and, above all, denigrating him for his refusal to acknowledge his own son. The more Julian gave voice to his outraged sense of justice, heaping tinder on the flames of Livia's discontent, the more she was swept up in Julian's plan to rid herself of Tariq once and for all.

Julian cocked his head and his intense gaze bored into her as he thrust home his final argument: "You will then be free to marry Aguilar!"

All reason left her, and the day came when she convinced herself that even death was too good for Tariq, and no more than he deserved for his faithlessness.

Livia dispatched a servant to him with a message in which she insisted she must speak with him upon a matter of the utmost importance. She asked that he come to her an hour after sunset. Shortly, the servant returned bearing his reply. Tariq Ibn Ziyah was otherwise engaged—with Khadija, thought Livia venomously—but he would honor her with his presense the following evening.

Livia fought down a mounting sense of terror at the deed she was about to perpetrate. Her heart hammered in her breast and her hands were clammy as she arranged a blue lusterware decanter and glasses on a brass tray on the low table in the window embrasure. With hands that shook, she placed the cushions on the carpeted floor so that she would sit with her back to the windows and Tariq would be forced to sit facing the view of the landscape, his back to the curtained doorway. All was in readiness before Hajai brought Rashid to her.

Seated in the embrasure with Rashid on her lap, Livia spread open on the table a bestiary—a volume illuminated with colorful pictures. As she turned the pages, she pointed to each animal and said its name. Now, at almost eight months, Rashid sat erect, grinning and gurgling in delight, his curious fingers playing over her lips. When she had done with the bestiary, she rocked Rashid in her arms and crooned Spanish lullabies in a loving voice.

Livia did not know low long she had been sitting there with Rashid when she heard the scrape of the curtains parting. Gently, she kissed Rashid's cheek and prepared to give him over to Hajai. At a slight sound, as of a clearing of the throat, she glanced up and her heart missed a beat. In the archway, watching her, was Tariq. For an instant she glimpsed a warm expression in his dark eyes, which, as they flicked over Rashid, turned hard as stone. A sudden wild hope that his first sight of his child, who so resembled himself, would convince him that he was indeed Rashid's sire, died within her.

"I finished my duties early and decided to come at once," he said harshly. "We may as well have done with our discussion as soon as possible."

Livia stammered, "I . . . I've no wish to speak, to start a discussion, one that is sure to erupt into an argument before Rashid. I do not want him upset." She nodded toward the cushion on the other side of the table. "Be seated. Hajai, Rashid's amah, will be along shortly to take him away."

The corners of Tariq's mouth turned down in annoy-

ance as he seated himself across from her and stared
fixedly past Rashid out the window at the distant
mountain peaks glowing gold in the sunset.

Intrigued by the newcomer, Rashid wriggled from
Livia's lap and crawled to Tariq. He clutched Tariq's
tunic, rose to his knees and grinned up into his face as
though entranced by a new toy. Tariq scowled and Livia
leaped up and grasped Rashid, who promptly let out an
enraged howl.

Without thinking, Livia blurted, "Like his father, the
child displays a fiery temper." Tariq's eyes met hers
with a questioning glance before he quickly looked
away. As she lifted Rashid in her arms, he broke into
earsplitting shrieks. Tariq raised a hand to restrain her.

"Do not let the child scream," he commanded. "Put
him down!"

Unquestioningly, she set Rashid down on the soft
carpet then drew the curtains across the doorway to
keep him from crawling from the confines of the
embrasure. Instantly, Rashid scrambled into Tariq's
lap. Tariq held out his arms in a surprised, helpless
gesture. Rashid gripped a fold of his tunic, pulled
himself up on a level with Tariq's shoulders, entwined
his fingers in his father's soft full beard and tugged on
it, laughing with delight. Livia smothered a grin as
Tariq gently disengaged the baby hands. Rashid's eager
fingers explored Tariq's face, touched his beetling
brows, trailed down his nose, back to his beard. Rashid
grinned and suddenly began to bounce up and down, as
though riding a horse. Tariq's strong arms went around
him, clasping him tightly against his chest. A mist
blurred Livia's vision, and her lips curved in a wistful
smile. Tariq, clearly unaware that he did so, smiled in
response to Rashid's obvious approval. She heard the
muezzin's call. Hajai would soon appear.

What a misfortune, she thought ruefully that now—
the first time Tariq was showing an interest in his
son—Hajai would come and take him away. At the

same moment, she was nearly frantic with worry that the girl would not come to take him in time. But there was still a half hour, at least, before Julian was to appear.

Minutes flew by. Tariq laughed at Rashid and bounced him on his knee. Hajai did not come. Taut as a bowstring with the strain of waiting, Livia took up the decanter and poured glasses of wine for Tariq and herself, hoping the strong liquid would settle her nerves. Just when she thought she could not endure to wait one minute longer, a movement of the drapery at Tariq's back caught her eye.

Thank God, she thought, letting out a long breath of relief. Hajai had come at last! She glanced up and her eyes widened in horror. Between the folds of the curtain appeared a gleaming eye and a masculine fist clenched about a dagger whose sharp blade gleamed in the light of the setting sun. All at once the curtain parted, the fist shot upward. Livia leaped to her feet, lunged past the table and flung her body between Tariq's broad back and his assailant. Her warning scream ripped through the tranquility. Tariq, clutching Rashid close to his chest, jumped to his feet and collided with the table. Decanter and glasses crashed to the floor, and wine flowed over the table and dripped upon the silken carpet.

Tariq let out an oath and lurched toward the curtain. Livia, weak-kneed and shaking, clung to the drapes, blocking his way. In the moment before Tariq's arm shot out and swept her aside, she cast a terrified glance into the sitting room. It was deserted. She could have wept with relief.

White-lipped, Tariq exploded, "The assassin has fled!" Rashid, gripped tightly in his arms, burst into a terrified wailing. Awkwardly, Tariq patted his back and in controlled, soothing tones murmured, "All is well, all is well."

The baby quieted. Livia gathered up the decanter

and broken glasses, set them on the table and sank down on a cushion as the enormity of what she had done sank into her mind.

Tariq bent down, set Rashid in her lap then stood, feet spread, arms folded across his chest, gazing down at her. His eyes held an expression she could not fathom. Gratitude that she had saved his life? Remorse for the love that they would never know? She shrank inside as his gaze seemed to pierce the innermost recesses of her soul. What did he read there? Guilt? Fear? A tremor of dread shook her as she sat, as though awaiting the stroke of his sword.

When he spoke at last, his voice was low, with an incredible tenderness she had never heard before. "I owe you my life. A debt that can never be repaid, but I shall spend the rest of my life in an effort to honor it."

To Livia's annoyance, instead of the haughty tone she had intended, her words came out in a hoarse whisper. "Please do not trouble yourself."

His eyes clung to hers, holding them in his stare. "Why did you do it? Why did you rush to my defense?"

For a moment she was silent and something stretched between them—an invisible bond, not of their own making. At last she tore her gaze from his and looked down at Rashid snuggled in her arms, sucking contently on a finger. "I . . . I would have done the same for anyone."

The brightness in his face died and his expression took on the closed look she knew so well. He made a small courtly bow. "Then please accept my gratitude." He swung about and was gone.

Numb with shock, Livia cradled Rashid, rocking back and forth until at last he slept. She had no idea how long she had been sitting there when she was roused by the gentle hands of Hajai lifting Rashid from her arms.

"Where have you been?" asked Livia, trying to curb her annoyance. "Why did you not come for Rashid at the usual time?"

Hajai's face brightened with a knowing smile. "I came, but then I heard Tariq Ibn Ziyah playing with him. I knew he would not wish to be interrupted, so I waited until he had gone."

Livia nodded and said no more. She felt drained from the encounter. Julian would think she had taken leave of her senses. And perhaps she had. Why had she flown to Tariq's defense? There was one consolation, thought Livia smiling wryly to herself. She had sworn to make the infidel rue the day he had taken her. For that reason and for that alone, she told herself, she was glad he lived.

When Hajai had gone, she set about mopping up the wine soaking into the carpet, then halted abruptly. Julian was standing in the doorway, hands on his hips, his mouth compressed in exasperated line. His eyes conveyed the expression of a man who had been betrayed.

"Madre de Dios, Livia!" he burst out. "What is the matter with you?"

Livia flung out her arms in a helpless gesture and said contritely, "Julian, I'm sorry—truly I am! I don't know what came over me. It seemed that I could not help myself, that my mind ceased to function—it just happened!"

"You lost your nerve—that's what happened," he said in disgust. "I thought you had more courage, that you were made of tougher fiber—"

"I do not lack courage! It was"—she paused, struggling to fathom her actions—"I think it was because of Rashid. Tariq was holding the child. I did not wish Rashid to see his own father murdered—it could leave a mark upon him."

"Diablo!" spat Julian. "An infant knows not what he sees! You are as weak as a poppy, bending whichever way the wind blows!"

"No!" cried Livia incensed. "I . . . I could not let you do away with Tariq because"—again she paused, searching for the right words—"because, after all is said and done, Tariq *is* the father of my son. Please understand. For the first time, he displayed a spark of affection for the boy. I could not countenance Rashid's father being put to the sword."

Julian's shoulders slumped and he threw up his hands in defeat. "Have it your way, then, but do not ask me again to avenge your faithless husband." He stalked away.

Julian's words—*faithless husband*—echoed in Livia's ears like a death knell. For a few brief moments, while she had watched Tariq holding Rashid, she had forgotten her hatred of the Moor. And what was Tariq thinking? In his self-assured way, she knew he would think that having saved his life meant that she truly loved him. She had still to settle that score with him.

Chapter 20

The next day, Livia discovered to her chagrin that she would have to delay further confrontation with Tariq. The wavering monarch Boabdil had at last decided to take action. The town was a hive of activity, and the palace resounded with the din of armorers and black-smiths.

On a golden morning, the day of the army's depar-ture, Livia donned pale pink trousers and a tunic encrusted with pearls. Now she was seated before the mirror in her bedchamber brushing her long black hair, and daydreaming of Aguilar, wondering if he would find this flowing filmy raiment pleasing, as opposed to the tight bodices and full, heavy skirts worn by Spanish ladies of fashion. Her pleasant reverie was interrupted by her servant who admitted a robust black slave who announced that Tariq Ibn Ziyah had sent him to escort her to his presence at once. The man's firm tone and manner left no doubt that should she refuse to obey, Tariq himself would come to fetch her.

Vexed, she accompanied him to Tariq's apartment. With each step, her ire rose. She determined to take Tariq to task for this high-handed action, and to make clear to him that although she had saved his life, nothing had changed between them. By the time she reached his chambers she had worked herself into a fine temper. She burst through the doorway and stopped short in surprise. The sitting room was deserted. Her angry glance took in Tariq's scarlet and blue figured tunic, his suit of chain mail and cuirass laid out on one end of the divan. Through a slit between the hangings of his bedchamber, she glimpsed a tub on the floor and surmised that he had just finished his bath. Her lips compressed in a grim line and she squared her shoulders, strengthening her resolve to face him down.

The slave announced her presense and departed. The next moment, Tariq emerged clad only in stark white trousers that set off the coppery sheen of his skin and his broad, well-muscled shoulders and chest. Droplets of water glistened in his still-damp hair and beard. His ebony eyes swept her with approval, and a sardonic smile curved his lips as he strode toward her. Before she could utter a word of protest or recrimination, his arms were around her, as sure and hard as on the road to Granada so long ago.

She felt again the rush of helplessness, the sinking yielding, the surging tide of warmth that left her limp. And the devoted face of Don Alonzo Aguilar blurred and faded to nothingness. He took her hands in his, led her to the divan and pulled her down beside him.

She sat stiffly and drew a deep breath in an effort to recover her composure. "What is the meaning of this summons?" she asked coldly.

He regarded her solemnly for a moment. "I wish to bid you good-bye." Without waiting for her reply, he curved his hand around her waist and bent back her head across his arm and kissed her, softly at first, then with a swift graduation of intensity that made her cling to him as the only solid thing in a dizzy, swaying world. His insistent mouth was parting her trembling lips, sending wild tremors along her nerves, evoking from her sensations she knew she was powerless to control. And before a swirling giddiness spun her round and round, she was kissing him with an ardor that matched his own.

She raised her hands slowly, put them behind his head, her fingers widespread and moving gently through his thick black hair. She could smell the faint

fragrance of soap on his clean skin mingling with the
sweet breeze from the gardens as she buried her face
against his throat and chest.

"Livia, Livia," he murmured into her silken hair,
"I've never seen another woman, who can compare to
you."

She opened her eyes to look up into his face and in
the golden brilliance of the morning sunlight, she
thought she had never seen eyes so dark, so tender with
longing, nor a face so virile.

She deliberately mistook his meaning and said sar-
castically, "Then you approve of my attire?"

"Your attire is most becoming"—an amused smile
tugged at the corners of his mouth—" but hardly
necessary." She lay as though mesmerized, as with
swift, gentle hands he removed the pink gossamer tunic
and trousers, then removed his own trousers and took
her once again in his arms.

"I have never wanted a woman as I want you now!"

Suddenly it seemed to Livia that the sunshine
streaming into the room lighted the scene with a
blinding clarity, sharpening her senses, her perceptions
to a breathtaking awareness—almost to the point of
pain. Her lips parted in a quick intake of breath then
mingled with Tariq's. She felt as though her slender
form were melting in an undulent bonelessness. She
thought only of the here and now. The need in her
overruled the insistent promptings of her mind and a
sweet wild ecstacy filled her, carrying her away on the
wings of morning.

At last they lay still, their passions once more fully
sated, the silence disturbed only by the coursing of their
blood, the quieter rhythm of their breathing. Livia lay
in the curve of Tariq's arm, sleep nearly upon her.

"I don't want you to forget me," he murmured. She
made no reply, but smiled to herself, thinking, how
could she ever forget him now, with his love imprinted
upon her . . . embedded in her marrow, the essence of

flame, of red wine, of lute music, of figs bursting ripe, that mouth that always had the taste of them. She lay silent, eyes closed, as he rose from the sofa and donned his battle array. He bent down, kissed her gently on the brow and was gone.

At length Livia roused herself, hurriedly put on her cast-off garments, then hastened to join Ayxa to watch the army depart from the city.

She found Ayxa seated on a balcony that overlooked the courtyard. Morayma, Boabdil's gentle and affectionate first wife, sat by her side, a mournful expression upon her usually placid countenance. With a forlorn shake of her head, Morayma wailed, "I do not see why Boabdil must go to fight when peace reigns over the city."

The sultana threw up her bejeweled hands impatiently. "I should think it would be obvious. The defeat of the Christians near Malaga, and the success of Muley Hassan along the coast has furthered the favorable fortunes of the old monarch. The inconstant populace was shouting his name in the streets and sneering at the inactivity of Boabdil. It is rumored that he prefers the repose of the Alhambra to the danger of hard encampments in the mountains. Boabdil must strike some signal blow to counterbalance the recent triumph of his father."

"Alas," Morayma exclaimed sorrowfully, "it is my own father, Ali Atar, *alcayde* of Loxa, who urges Boabdil to take action. He claims that Andalusia is stripped of the prime of her men, that the spirit of the country is broken—that all the frontier of Cordoba lies open to inroad—and especially open to attack is the town of Lucena, which supplies Loxa with food." Livia watched Boabdil's proud army beginning to wend its way northwest in a vast cavalcade across the plain.

Ayxa's eyes glittered with pride. "Boabdil has assembled a force of nine thousand men. Most of them are his own supporters, but many are partisans of his father.

To their credit, however they may fight among themselves, both factions will unite in any expedition against the Christians."

In the courtyard, many of the most illustrious of the Moorish nobility were assembled round Boabdil's standard. Livia's gaze lingered upon Tariq, seated upon his black stallion, more regal than the king himself. She smiled inwardly, remembering how he had embraced her one more time before he obeyed Boabdil's order.

"The soldiers look more ready for a festival than for war," Livia said skeptically.

Ayxa smiled in satisfaction, "I myself armed Boabdil and gave him my benediction as I girded his scimitar to his side," She gave her daughter-in-law a disapproving glance, "while Morayma hung about his neck."

Where was Khadija, Livia wondered. But then Khadija was doubtless glad to see Boabdil depart.

Tears formed in Morayma's eyes, and she dabbed at them with the hem of her sleeve.

"Why do you weep, daughter of Ali Atar?" asked Ayxa bending a stern eye upon her. "These tears do not become the daughter of a warrior, nor the wife of a king."

"I . . . I am thinking of all the evils that might befall him," Morayma stammered through her tears.

"Believe me," Ayxa said sharply, "there lurks more danger for a monarch within the walls of a palace than within the curtains of a tent. It is by perils in the field that your husband must purchase security on his throne."

Morayma made no reply, but watched the army as it marched in shining order northward along the road to Loxa, and every burst of warlike melody that came swelling on the breeze was answered by a gush of sorrow.

As Boabdil left the palace and passed through the streets of Granada, the people gaily greeted their youthful sovereign, anticipating deeds of prowess that

would wither the laurels of his father. A shout went up
from the crowd, and Livia rose to her feet to peer
across the rooftops of the town to see what caused the
commotion.

In passing through the Elvira gate, Boabdil had
accidentally broken his lance against the arch. Now it
appeared that certain of his nobles were entreating him
to turn back, doubtless regarding it as an evil omen.
She saw Tariq offer his own spear, but Boabdil shook
his head. Refusing to take another spear, he drew his
scimitar and led the way from the city in what seemed
to Livia an arrogant style, as though he would defy both
heaven and earth.

The sentinels looked out from the watchtowers of
Granada along the valley of the Xenil River. They
watched for the king's triumphal return. No less avidly,
Livia, Ayxa and Morayma watched from the Tower of
Comares. Each heart trembled for a different reason:
Ayxa hungering for power; Morayma frantic for Boab-
dil's safety; Livia fearing that a Moorish victory would
further delay her rescue.

Just before dusk on April 21, they observed a single
rider urging his faltering horse across the *vega*. As he
drew near, they perceived by the flash of arms that he
was a warrior; and on nearer approach, by the richness
of his armor and the caparison of his steed, they knew
him to be an officer. As he entered the city the soldiers
at the gate gathered round him, eager for news. He cast
his hand mournfully toward the land of the Christians
and bowed his head, shaking it hopelessly.

Livia's heart contracted.

Then the cavalier urged his mount up the steep
avenue that led to the Alhambra, not stopping until he
arrived before the Gate of Justice.

Swiftly, Ayxa went to meet him, Livia, Morayma,
Khadija, and others of the court following in her wake.
The rider, covered with dust and blood, appeared near
exhaustion, and his dark-skinned face was lined with

despair. Turning to face the warrior, Ayxa demanded, "How fares it with the king and the army?"

Once again the rider cast his hand toward the northwest. "There they lie!" he exclaimed. "The heavens have fallen upon them. All are lost! All dead!"

A cold trembling shook Livia from head to toe and she drew nearer to Ayxa's side. Livia cried out involuntarily, "What of Tariq Ibn Ziyah?"

A pained expression crossed the officer's face. "I saw his horse smeared with blood and galloping without his rider."

Stunned, Livia could only stare at him incredulously. Her mind denied the words she had heard with her own ears.

A shrill scream sliced through the tumult. Livia spun about to face Khadija, who stood apart from the courtiers, her hand clasped over her mouth, tears shimmering in her stricken eyes. Their gaze locked and held.

"Boabdil!" shouted Ayxa. "What of my son Boabdil?"

"Your son fought by my side. We were surrounded by the enemy and driven into the river. I heard him cry out to Allah, but when I reached the other bank he was no longer by my side."

At this news, a gleam of what Livia could interpret only as satisfaction flickered in Khadija's eyes. Abruptly, with a toss of her head, she stamped back inside the palace.

Morayma let out an anguished cry and clung to Livia's arm for support. Livia glanced at Ayxa. The sultana said nothing, but stood transfixed. The man turned his pitying gaze upon Morayma.

"The Christians were joined by cavaliers from Antiquera, led by Don Alonzo de Aguilar. Your father fought hand-to-hand with him, but it was Ali Atar who was wounded. Don Alonzo would have spared his life, but your father did not give up and Aguilar had to kill him."

For a moment Livia thought she would have fallen had Morayma not clung to her side. Aguilar! Her beloved Aguilar had narrowly escaped death from the hands of the Moor—and Tariq lost in battle!

A deep sigh burst forth from Ayxa. She raised her eyes to heaven. "It is the will of Allah!" She stiffened her shoulders and set her jaw in a visible effort to repress the agonies she felt. At that, Morayma threw herself on the ground, hysterically mourning her husband and father.

Ayxa rebuked her sternly. "Control these dramatics, my daughter. Remember, magnanimity should be the attribute of princes; it becomes them not to give way to clamorous sorrow like common and vulgar minds."

Livia gave a hopeless shake of her head. How Ayxa could expect the Morayma to display nobility of mind in such circumstances, Livia could not fathom.

Livia raised Morayma to her feet and led her away to her chamber, where she bathed the tender girl's face. After Morayma quieted down, Livia fled through the silent halls to her own room. She wished to be alone, finding it hard to cope with her own tangled emotions. She should feel relieved, filled with joy to be free of the arrogant infidel who had claimed her body and soul against her will. Strangely, she had felt nothing but shock at the news that Tariq was dead. Now, as the reality of his death forced itself upon her mind, an overwhelming sense of loss possessed her. No more would she feel his strong arms about her, sweeping her up in his powerful embrace. Never again would she thrill to the warmth of his touch or know the rapture of submitting to a passion she was helpless to resist. Never again would she see Tariq, smiling unaware, as he bounced his son upon his knee. For the first time, she uttered a silent prayer of thanksgiving that Rashid was left to her.

And Aguilar! She exulted that his life had been spared, but she could not help but wish that it had not been he who had put Morayma's father to the sword.

Chapter 21

Two days later, to escape the melancholy atmosphere of the palace, Livia strolled down to the square of the Vivarrambla. She breathed deeply of the fragrant aromas that drifted from shops selling ready-cooked dishes, roasted meats and confectionery and ambled past a public oven on the corner into the *Alcaiceria*, the market for fine fabrics and jewelry. Among the maze of tiny alleys and arcades, she paused at a shop to take up a length of fine blue brocade shot with gold when she heard excited shouts and looked up to see a scout pounding through the gates on a sweating horse. "Boabdil lives!"

Livia, mouth agape, disbelieved her ears. The fabric fell from her nerveless fingers as the cry was taken up by the townspeople. "Boadbil lives!"

The news quickly spread that Boabdil had been captured, but had concealed his identity, claiming to be a cavalier of a royal household. However, other Moslem soldiers, not knowing of his pose, had revealed the secret. Several officers, including Tariq Ibn Ziyah, were being held prisoner along with their monarch.

Dazed, Livia stood unmoving in the bright April sunlight, unmindful of the excited throng milling about the market. As the realization of Tariq's resurrection from the dead bore into her, her heart beat violently and a feeling of great joy coursed through her. Why she should feel such happiness that he lived? It seemed that his not having been slain, was a boon, rather than a misfortune. Gradually, she became aware of the mut-

177

terings of the people around her; clustered in groups, they decried Boabdil's talents as a commander and his courage as a soldier. They reviled him for not having dared to die on the field rather than surrender to the enemy.

She noticed the black-robed leaders of the mosque, mingling with the populace, fomenting discontent. They claimed the prediction had finally come true and called for the restoration of Muley.

The longer Boabdil's captivity continued, the greater his father's popularity grew. One city after another renewed allegiance to him. Quick to seize his advantage, the shrewd old king, instantly made preparations to return to the Alhambra.

Warned of his approach, the Sultana Ayxa gathered together her son's family, and treasures to take up quarters in *Albaycin*—the rival quarter of the city where the inhabitants remained loyal to Boabdil.

"If you are wise," Ayxa told Livia sternly, "you and Rashid and his amah will come with us."

Livia paced her chamber in a frenzy of indecision. Although Tariq had been loyal to Muley, he had remained steadfast in his duty to protect the capital city of Granada and thus had cast his lot with Boabdil. How would Tariq's wife and child be regarded? Would Muley now see them as enemies? Would the vengeful monarch draw his scimitar and behead them, as he had been known to do with others he thought disloyal? They would be safe under Ayxa's protection, so long as Ayxa could hold her adherents about her. Livia took a deep breath and squared her shoulders. She and Rashid would cast their lot with Ayxa.

Fortifying herself in the *Alcazaba*—the fortress of the *Albaycin*—Ayxa held the semblance of a court in the name of her son, and sat back to wait. Day after day she occupied herself with her inevitable pack of cards, as though by playing them well, she could control her destiny.

"Won't Muley attack this rebellious quarter of the capital?" Livia asked anxiously.

Ayxa looked up as she shuffled the cards expertly. Rings sparkled on her fingers, and a complacent smile spread over her face. "He dares not exploit his new and uncertain popularity." Her smile broadened. "Many of the nobles detest Muley for his past cruelty, and a large portion of the army and many of his own party as well respect the virtues of Ayxa la Horra and pity the misfortunes of Boabdil."

Livia tried to take comfort in this thought, but the spectacle of two sovereigns within the same city unnerved her. Then she smiled wryly to herself, thinking: Had not Spain been disunited for hundreds of years because of her own warring factions? But now, with Isabella's determination to unite the country in one faith and Ferdinand's resolve to unite all the territories, all Spain would soon be theirs and Livia would no longer have to worry whether Boabdil or Muley reigned over Granada. She sighed deeply. Till then, all she could do was wait, and hope that Aguilar would rescue her and her son.

Unexpectedly, it was Julian who worried Livia most. To her disappointment and chagrin, he had refused to leave the palace with Ayxa and her court. When Livia had pleaded with him, he answered, "Have you forgotten, Livia? I am a prisoner here. And here I will remain to restore the delicate walls of the palace. I have already enhanced the inscriptions upon the walls." He grinned. "Come, I wish you to see the evidence of my great talent."

Taking her by the arm, he had led her through the marbled halls to the Court of Myrtles. He had raised his arm in a sweeping gesture toward an alcove. Livia gasped. Among tongues of flame, jasmine blossoms and snowflakes, geometric stars and roses, she saw the carved scallop shell of Santiago, patron saint of Spain. "Julian! This is heresy! You will be killed!"

Julian had laughed. "But just think! I will be

recognized for my work before my death!" Before Livia
could protest he had said, "Come, there is more!"
Gleefully, he had dragged her back through the halls
into a chamber off the Court of the Lions. "Look!" he
had said proudly.

She had been paralyzed in horror. There on the wall
tapestry of arabesques and geometric designs, he had
carved the Star of David. At her appalled expression,
he had let out a shout of laughter that echoed from the
walls. Then, with a sly wink he had said softly, "I may
be of more use to us both here in the enemy camp.
Don't fret, Livia. I can take care of myself."

Of that she had no doubt; he had always managed to
extricate himself from scrapes. But it was Julian's
everlasting venturesomeness—his eye for the main
chance—that plagued her. She had sighed deeply and
said no more.

"Don't fret," he had said, grinning. "I'll keep in
touch."

She had not long to wait. Two days later, Julian
appeared at the Alcazaba. His dark eyes gleamed with
excitement, and the news he brought set her pulses
racing.

"Muley Hassan has found support for Boabdil still
formidable in Granada and wants to get his hands on
him. The king sent an embassy to Ferdinand and
Isabella offering a fortune for ransom or purchase of
his son and his commanders and promised the release
of ten of Muley's most distinguished captives; and to
enter into a treaty of confederacy with our sovereigns
as well."

Livia let out a long, slow breath. "If Ferdinand
accepts these terms, Tariq will be freed! Much as I
detest the Moor, I do not like to think of him
languishing in a Spanish prison—or worse, executed by
our own people."

Julian raised a hand to silence her. "Wait, there is
more. Muley made plain that he doesn't care whether

his son is delivered alive or dead, just so he is delivered."

The color drained from Livia's face. "Surely he would not dare to—"

Smiling, Julian shook his head. "Our humane Isabella was revolted at the idea. She refused and informed Muley that the Castilian monarchs would listen to no peace proposals until Muley lays down his arms.

A sense of urgency took hold of Livia. Without stopping to question why, she rose to her feet. "Julian, we must speak with Ayxa, at once!"

Acting upon Julian's news, Ayxa, with the consent of Boabdil's adherents, made overtures in a different spirit. She proposed that Boabdil should offer to exchange prisoners and hostages, then align with the Spanish.

In a torment of anxiety, Livia waited while Ayxa's embassy carried this proposition to Cordoba. Her anxiety was quickly overridden by anger and impatience when it was learned that Queen Isabella was absent from the court. King Ferdinand, fearing to act too hastily, made no reply to Ayxa's emissaries. Instead, he ordered that the captive monarch be brought to Cordoba.

To Livia's astonishment, she found herself worrying day and night over Tariq's safety. It's only because he's Rashid's father, she told herself. Had Tariq, too, been taken to Cordoba? Irrationally, she longed for his return to Granada. If only he were here, she thought, near despair, things would not have come to such a pass. Though she would not admit it even to herself, he was her strength, her life in this alien land. He's quick enough to exercise his privileges as a husband, she told herself. Now he could protect her and his son as well, if only he were here! That she could not permit Julian to kill him still confounded her. She knew only that she did not regret having rushed to his defense.

In the meantime, while Granada was distracted with dissension, and before he had concluded any treaty with Boabdil, Ferdinand made an ostentatious inroad into the very heart of the kingdom. It was reported that he sacked and destroyed towns and castles that had offered no resistance. And when he extended his ravages to the very gates of Granada, Livia accosted Ayxa, bristling with indignation.

"Why does King Muley permit the devastation of the *vega?* Does he prefer to surrender to Ferdinand rather than to his own son?

Ayxa's lips curved in a knowing smile. "Muley doesn't dare oppose Ferdinand. Granada is filled with troops, but my husband is uncertain of their loyalty and is afraid that if he leaves, the gates will be closed against him."

It seemed Ayxa's statements were right, for Muley did nothing and Ferdinand returned to Cordoba laden with spoils.

One evening Livia joined Ayxa in a game of cards. As she faced the sultana across the playing table, Ayxa said bitterly, "Now maybe Ferdinand can come to a decision about Boabdil."

Livia looked up from the cards spread before her. "What chance is there that he will accept your proposal?"

Ayxa inclined her head and stared thoughtfully at the ceiling, as if envisioning Ferdinand's council. "He will gather his advisers about him. Some will demand the utter expulsion of Moors from Spain. They will be against setting Boabdil at liberty. Others will speak for the release of Boabdil. That will keep up the civil war in Granada, thereby working for the interests of Spain without her expense."

Ayxa smiled wryly. Livia could almost see her quick, clever mind at work. "As you know, Isabella, whose word weighs heavily with the king, is a pious woman, zealous for the promotion of her faith, but not for the extermination of our people. I think she will be for liberating Boabdil if he will become a vassal to the crown. By this means she will effect the deliverance of many Christians now in Moorish chains."

Livia was not surprised when Ayxa's prediction proved correct. King Ferdinand adopted the magnanimous measure.

Chapter 22

On an early September morning, Ayxa's scouts galloped from the mountain passes, wreathed in mist, to bring word of Boabdil. He would be accompanied by a honor guard to the border. Ayxa lost no time in dispatching the principal nobles and cavaliers of his court to escort him to the capital.

Livia observed these measures with more than a little trepidation; though Boabdil returned to his kingdom, it was no longer the loyal one he had left. Julian had warned her of that. Only yesterday he had paid her a surprise visit.

Boabdil had been represented by his father as a traitor to his country, a *renegado* to his faith, in league with the enemy. Most of the nobility now thronged round the throne of Muley.

To Livia, it appeared difficult and dangerous for Boabdil to make his way back to the capital and regain the little court which still remained faithful to him. To make matters worse, the old tiger Muley lay crouched within the Alhambra, and the walls and gates of the city were strongly guarded by his troops. But one did not offer opinions to Ayxa. She kept silent and impatiently paced the damp gloomy halls of the Alcazaba.

Shortly thereafter, on a moonless night, Livia was awaked by sounds in the courtyard. Fogged with sleep, she thought she heard the clink of armor and the thud of horses hooves. She rose up on her elbows, listening. The stealthy noises continued. A sense of something

ominous happening in the fortress assailed her. If
Muley had come to take them, he would not find Livia
waiting in bed. She flung a cloak about her shoulders
and ran along a dimly lit corridor, and down the stairs
to the great hall. In the flickering light of the oil lamps,
she saw Boabdil caught up in the embrace of his
mother, surrounded by his retinue of gaunt, hollow-
eyed cavaliers.

Swiftly, she scanned the weary faces. Tariq was not
among them. Terror flared within her as she searched
desperately about the hall. And then she saw him
standing motionless in the doorway, staring at her with
a level gaze, a question in his eyes. Her heart contracted at his appearance. His ragged tunic hung loosely
from his broad shoulders; he had lost much weight. His
usually ruddy complexion was ashen, and his black hair
and beard were unkempt. She was at once troubled by
his haggard face and shocked to see dark bruises
beneath one eye and across a cheek. Yet, he still carried
himself with an air of authority.

With no thought but that now all would be well, she
ran toward him, into his outstretched arms. All her
fears for the safety of Rashid and Boabdil's dwindling
court left her. His arms tightened around her and he
buried his face in the fragrant luxuriance of her hair.

"Tariq, Tariq," she murmured, her lips brushing his
rough cheek, "I thought never to see you again."

He grasped her shoulders and held her at arm's
length, smiling down at her, a light burning in his dark
eyes.

"You must know that nothing—no enemy on
earth—could keep me from returning to my wife." He
bent his head close to her ear and whispered, "I feel the
need of a soft bed."

Wordlessly, she took up a candle and led him away to
her chamber. As they left, Livia caught sight of
Khadija, who was staring at her with undisguised
venom. Tonight, however, Livia was concerned only
about Tariq.

When he drew her down beside him on her bed of furs, she made no protest. He kissed her brow tenderly.

Then reason asserted itself. She must set matters straight, and quickly.

Livia looked earnestly into his face and in firm tones said, "Tariq, I am thankful that you have returned safely. That is *all* I wished." Her voice rose with the strength of her resolve. "But as for bedding with you, that is the last thing I will do!"

Ignoring her, he nibbled one earlobe. She drew back and declared heatedly, "That I saved you from an assassin does not give you the right!"

His lips brushed her eyelids, the tip of her nose.

Her eyes flashed fire. "I will never give myself to you. You must understand!"

His lips silenced her protests, lingered on her mouth, then traveled down her slender throat seeking the honeyed softness of her breasts.

"Tariq," she said breathlessly, "our bed is for sleeping!"

When he made no reply, she placed her hands on his shoulders to push him away. His powerful muscles tightened under her touch and without volition her hands clasped him closer, caressing the long, lean length of his back. Her body arched, thrusting forward in a primitive response to the demands of his embrace. Gently, his hands stroked her hips, her thighs, and trailed down her body. Weakness overcame her so that she was helpless to stem the passion that engulfed her like the waves of the sea. He flung her cloak aside and with swift, sure fingers, drew her gown upward. She writhed in his arms, shrugging off the constricting folds, wishing he would hurry. Then all thought fled from her mind. She knew only her need of him.

She was not aware that he had discarded his own garments until his hard frame pressed against hers. Driven by his own need, tenderness vanished. Savage, demanding, he drew her close. His mouth found hers in the searching hunger of a kiss that seemed never to end. Touching, holding each other in an ecstacy of well-remembered rapture, there was no need for words to express their joy in each other. She clung to him, reveling in his embrace as he claimed her body for his own, as if with the fulfillment of their desire they could defy even death. It was not until the first light of dawn tinged the snow-crested mountain peaks with crimson that, desire spent, passions sated, they slept in each others arms.

The next morning Tariq told her of his return to Granada. His dark features were drawn into a scowl, and his voice was heavy with censure. "Boabdil approached the capital by stealth in the night prowling about its walls like an enemy rather than a monarch." He sighed deeply. "At length we galloped through the streets and before the populace were aroused from their sleep, gained the fortress of the Alcazaba."

When they descended to the hall, they discovered that the Sultana Ayxa had taken prompt and vigorous measures to strengthen her party. Boabdil's return was proclaimed throughout the streets and large sums of money were distributed among the inhabitants. The nobles assembled in the Alcazaba were promised rewards by Boabdil as soon as he should be seated firmly on the throne.

By daybreak, all of the motley populace was in arms.

On hearing this, Tariq buckled on his cuirass and scimitar and dashed from the Alcazaba. Livia hurried to the crenelated ramparts where she and the courtiers watched with bated breaths. Livia's heart quailed at the sight.

All Granada was in chaos. Drums and trumpets resounded throughout the city. Shops were shut, their doors barricaded. Armed bands paraded the streets, some shouting for Boabdil, others for Muley Abul Hassan. When they encountered each other, they fought without mercy. Every public square became a battle scene. Although the majority was for Boabdil, it was a mass without discipline. Many citizens were armed with daggers and swords, but the greater number had gone out with makeshift weapons.

Livia's heart sank. They were no match for the troops of the old king. Muley's warriors put down the rabble and soon drove them from the squares. Undaunted, they threw up barricades and fortified themselves in the streets. When the barricades were surmounted, they made fortresses of their houses.

It was impossible that such violent strife should last long and after a while an armistice was achieved. Boabdil was persuaded that there was no dependence upon the inconstant favor of the multitude and was prevailed upon to quit a capital where he could only maintain a precarious position. Livia stood at Ayxa's side in the great hall, scanning the faces of the crowd for Tariq, when Boabdil raised an arm commanding silence. When the babble of voices ceased, Boabdil announced in stentorian tones: "I am fixing my court at the city of Almeria, which is entirely devoted to me!"

A shocked silence fell over the throng. Ayxa's features hardened and she glowered at Boabdil.

Fingering his prayer beads, he added hastily, "It vies with Granada in splendor and importance."

Ayxa's chin rose and defiance glittered from her eyes. "I do not approve your compromise of grandeur for tranquility. Granada is the only legitimate capital. You are not worthy of being called a monarch!"

For a moment Boabdil stared at her, his features breaking up as if torn by indecision: on the one hand, not wishing to incur his mother's wrath; on the other, wishing to do what he felt had to be done. His shoulders slumped in defeat. When he spoke his voice was low, almost apologetic. "Prepare to depart for Almeria."

Livia had long since resolved never to leave Granada, for she wished to remain where Aguilar could find her. Now she had little choice. The prospect filled her with fury. Tariq, having returned bloodied and exhausted, ordered her to pack her belongings for the journey.

Silent and tight-lipped, she thrust her possessions into a carpetbag. Tiring of her ill-humor, Tariq said sharply, "I like this no more than you do. But there is nothing else to be done, so you may as well put a good face on it!"

Livia turned her back to him and made no reply. Inwardly, she seethed with anger. Not only did Tariq expect her to depart with a cheerful mien, but he had made no mention of taking Rashid with them. She would not humble herself to ask his permission.

When at length the procession set out at a brisk pace for Almeria, Rashid, seated before Hajai astride a chestnut gelding, was among the retinue.

Tariq eyed them with a forbidding gaze. "I see that you have brought Malik's child," he said sourly. "I'm surprised that you have not brought Malik as well!"

A flush stained Livia's cheeks. "You wrong me, Tariq. There is nothing that makes me happier than to leave Malik behind." She half-expected him to remind her that Malik had cast his lot with Muley and would not have accompanied them in any case.

Instead, Tariq regarded her with an impenetrable gaze and said nothing. But when they arrived at Almeria, he gave orders that Rashid was to live with his amah in her chamber and to be kept from his sight.

The ancient stone fortress at Almeria was more splendid than Livia had imagined. Once a stronghold of the Phoenicians, the Moors had adorned the walls with silken tapestries and strewn the floors with richly hued carpets. The chambers were furnished with divans and cushions covered in elegant brocades and velvets, hanging lamps, colorful lusterware and low tables of carved wood inlaid with ivory. Dominating a rocky slope, the stronghold overlooked the town, a twisting maze of streets that wound past clusters of square white

houses which clung to terraced hillsides. Beyond the
town, the shining turquoise Mediterranean lapped
against the sandy shore. Blue morning glories, pink
geraniums and purple bougainvillea bloomed in gay
abandon, and groves of oranges and palms were
scattered about. Over all, endless sunshine shed a
golden ambiance.

Despite Tariq's attitude toward Rashid, a time of
happiness passed for Livia. Often, just after sunrise, or
at sunset, she and Tariq would ride down to the shore to
canter along the water's edge, then tie their horses to a
palm tree and climb a path to perch upon a smooth
sandstone cliff where they would watch the water swirl
about gleaming rocks below.

One afternoon at sunset, a flock of flamingos circled
overhead, then following their leader in V-formation,
skimmed low over the surface of the water. In concert,
they soared upward, leaned into the wind, their long
necks stretched forward, legs stretched stiff behind
them, their pink bodies held aloft by wings silhouetted
black against a pale blue sky, as they veered west
toward Gibraltar. Livia felt her heart soar with them.
Tariq put an arm about her shoulders and when she
looked up into his face, he was smiling deeply into her
eyes, as though he shared her elation.

They often ambled among the gardens where roses
clung to the vestiges of summer. The fragrant scent of
rosemary and thyme hung on the air, and all around
them were the chime of goat bells, the chirping of
crickets and the songs of cicadas and nightingales.

Tariq taught her to play chess, and without their
being aware of it, the game became symbolic of their
own tense truce. Still, she steeled herself against
succumbing to the magnetic charm of this brooding
man, and would turn her thoughts to Aguilar. Despite
her Moslem marriage, she considered herself betrothed
to a Christian knight, not to be dazzled by this infidel.

When he grew restless, Tariq would insist that she
play the lute and sing for him. They spent long, languid

afternoons lolling under the shade of a palm tree where
Tariq would read aloud to her from a volume of poems
penned by a twelfth-century poet. Now his deep, mel-
lifluous voice sent a tingling sensation through her.

I swear by the love of her who spurns me—
The night of a man consumed by love has no
end;
Frozen is the dawn—will it never come?
Ah, night—methinks you know no morrow.
Is it true, o night, that you are eternal?
Or have the wings of the eagle been clipped,
So that the stars of heaven no longer wander?

Livia's delicate brows rose in inquiry as she gazed
into his face. Had he chosen the poem at random, or
had he meant to speak of the eagle Aguilar?

"In an Arab poem," Tariq said, smiling into her
eyes, "it is not so much what is said, as how it is said."
His voice was like honey flowing into the secret recesses
of her heart. An intimacy stretched between them, and
she felt color rush into her face. In his eyes was a flash
of longing mixed with sadness that quickly vanished.
She managed a tremulous smile and quickly lowered
her gaze to her hands clutching the stem of the rose that
lay shredded in her lap.

They sat for some moments in silence. With an
effort, she gained a measure of her composure, until
once again Tariq read aloud:

'Twas as if we had not passed the night
With love for our companion,
While fortune closed the lids of those who envied
us.
Like two secrets in the heart of discreet darkness,
Until the tongue of morning all but gave us away.

Fearful that he would see how deeply his words had
stirred her, Livia refused to meet his eyes. Color

burned her cheeks as she recalled the nights she had lain in his arms, submitting to his caresses, her senses roused to heights she was helpless to control, all the while telling herself that it was futile to resist him; that her resistance served only to further inflame his passions.

When she was not with Tariq, she spent most of her time with Rashid. A stocky, rosy-cheeked one-year-old with straight shiny black hair and snapping black eyes, he trudged about on sturdy legs spouting a small fountain of Arabic words. He took delight in the world about him, his pleasure all the greater when he could show Livia his discoveries. Gleefully, he would point to a dew drop clinging to a rose petal, a kestrel swooping down on some unsuspecting quarry, diamonds winking on the surface of the sea gilded with sunlight.

Livia had hoped that Tariq would change toward the child. He had not. If anything, as the mellow fall days drifted past, Tariq appeared to rue his momentary show of affection and bent over backward to avoid him. Upon perceiving this, Livia's heart hardened against Tariq. If he were going to be so hostile, she would spend all her time with Rashid.

But Tariq was a demanding husband. He insisted she be at his side every minute he was not drilling soldiers or attending to the king's business. Had she not known better, she would think he felt incomplete without her. Instinctively, she knew that it was his knowledge that he could never win her that intrigued him. With a wry smile, she thought: What the wooer desires is freedom to adore; what he craves and thirsts for is the assurance of being loved in return. He was bent on conquering her heart as well as her body, and this he could never do.

One night, feeling the need to strengthen her resolve, after they had retired and he turned to take her in his arms, she drew away from him and rolled to the edge of their bed.

"No, Tariq. I'm not in the mood to satisfy your lust. Can you never leave me alone? Do you never tire of taking a woman who doesn't want you?"

Tariq jerked as though she had slapped him and lay on his back, his arms folded under his head. An ominous silence stretched between them. Livia cast a sidelong glance at him over her shoulder. Nude as a newborn, Livia thought wrathfully. The man doesn't waste a moment.

His gruff voice shredded the silence. "Is there nothing you like about me?"

"Nothing!"

"In time, it is possible you will learn to love me."

"Nothing is possible with us!"

"I will show you what is!" He lunged across the bed and caught her shoulder in a vise-like grip. With a violent twist, she wrenched away from him. At the same time there was a loud ripping sound as the fabric of her thin gown parted and she flung herself off the bed. Tariq's hand shot out and clutched a fistful of white chiffon. Livia, whose legs became entangled in the folds, tripped and fell on the soft carpet. Tariq sprang from the bed and knelt before her on the floor. He peered into her face and in his eyes she read concern mingled with a hint of laughter.

"Are you hurt, my Zahareña?"

She rose to her knees to face him, hands on her hips, anger sparkling from her eyes, her breast swelling, unaware that the September moonlight slanting through the window gave her skin the sheen of alabaster. Tariq let out a burst of laughter and his arms went around her waist, molding her kneeling form to his. When she cried out in protest, he brought his mouth down on hers and slowly, relentlessly, forced her downward and spread her body the length of his upon the thick carpet. He rose up on one elbow and gazed down at her jubilantly.

She stared at the dark figure poised above her,

silhouetted against a brilliant shaft of moonlight. He's trapped me! she thought furiously. Here I lie, naked as a statue . . . and as cold and lifeless as marble I will be!

His lips left hers and trailed down the curve of her neck seeking the fullness of her breast. His hands, warm and sure, stroked the long, lithe curves of her body and she squeezed her eyes shut, determined to resist his tender caresses. Gooseflesh rose on her skin. In too brief a time to measure, the alabaster statue became like clay in his hands.

Chapter 23

As the days wore on, despite her resolve, Livia found herself enjoying, even looking forward to the hours she spent with Tariq. As she realized that she was truly happy, an overwhelming sense of guilt assailed her. Feeling disloyal to Aguilar, she rebuked herself sternly and called to mind the days that she and Aguilar had shared in Seville so long ago. She thought how fine and noble an officer Aguilar was, how dedicated to the cause of the holy war, how brave in defending the faith. How could she possibly imagine that she enjoyed the company of Tariq Ibn Ziyah, a barbarian who refused to recognize his own son!

She had been blinded by the beauty of their surroundings at the Alahambra, and now at Almeria. What woman would not be dazzled by days spent in luxury after the hand-to-mouth existence she had endured in Zahara?

What woman would not be captivated by a strong, fearless warrior who wooed her with poetry and masterly seduction, a man whose passions she could rouse to the heights of rapture? No, she assured herself firmly, it was not Tariq who had brought her happiness. She would have felt the same toward any man in such surroundings. It was only the circumstance of her idyllic existence that had tricked her into this false euphoria.

If Livia needed further armor against Tariq Ibn Ziyah, it was not long in coming. One evening, just at sunset, when Livia felt she could not endure the loneliness of the fortress a moment longer, she flung a bright blue shawl about her shoulders, leaped astride her mount and raced down to the curving shore. She dismounted, tethered the horse to a palm tree and turned westward, faced the sun, a red-gold blaze so brilliant that she could not look into it without squinting. Quickly, she glanced away toward the sea. The flat gray-green expanse, stippled with silver, rushed upon the shore and receded, leaving a mass of tangled seaweed in its wake. She bent down to pluck a scallop shell from the damp sand and walked on, enjoying the tranquillity of the early evening. The wind rose and she drew her shawl more tightly about her shoulders. On the terraced hillside to her right, smoke from charcoal cooking fires curled upward, lights flickered on and dogs barked. She strolled toward the huge outcropping of rocks where she and Tariq had often climbed the narrow path between the boulders to watch the ever-changing moods of the sea. As she drew near the base of the great buff boulders, she saw two heads silhouetted against the setting sun. Disappointment surged through her. Others had preceded her and now occupied her perch upon the cliff.

She continued onward. She would stroll farther along the shore. Perhaps on her return the usurpers would have gone. She ambled on, picking her way among jagged rocks that tumbled into the water and as she rounded the base of the cliff above, she heard the low murmur of voices. She stopped short, not wanting to believe the evidence of her own ears. Yes, it *was* Tariq's voice, low and urgent. She could not distinguish his words. And then came Khadija's high-pitched, strident cry.

"I will demand that Boabdil divorce me! He is a most inadequate husband. He does not treat me as an equal with his other wife as the law requires—not to mention his want of decision, his lack of interest in his kingdom. He desires nothing but to hunt and hawk and joust, or to sit in the garden and entertain scholars from Africa and Persia, or to read poetry and discuss philosophy. I may as well be a scimitar hung upon the wall never to be unsheathed!" Her tone turned petulant. "He prefers Morayma because she has given him a son, Prince Aben. He makes no secret of it!"

"Is that why you wish to leave him?" came Tariq's harsh voice. "Because you've discovered he prefers Morayma—and now, suddenly, you recognize the virtue of marriage to a man who loves you?"

"Of course not!" Khadija snapped. "I made a mistake to marry Boabdil in the first place." Her voice sounded contrite and pleading. "But I thought you were dead. It is you I truly love, have always loved." A long, helpless sigh escaped her. "But one cannot refuse the hand of a prince."

Tariq's laugh, filled with bitterness, drifted down to Livia standing on the rocks below. "And one does not demand a divorce from a monarch."

Livia waited to hear no more, but whirled about and ran, retracing her steps along the hard-packed sand. Her heart pounded in her ears. Tariq had betrayed her.

How could she have been so simpleminded as to believe that his tender words, his loving gaze, his ardent love-making signified his love for her? Her first judgment of him had been right after all. He was using her as a woman of the night to satisfy his lustful desires, to fulfill his needs, to feed his insatiable ego, taking delight in bending his Christian captive to his will, reveling in his victory over her.

She tried to whip up a rage to replace hurt with anger, telling herself she should have expected no better at the hands of an infidel. And when anger failed her, she assured herself it was not that Tariq did not care for her that so distressed her, but that he preferred Khadija. How could he be taken in by a woman who, according to both Ayxa and Amina, was a vain and shallow creature! How dare he flaunt his paramour before her very eyes! As suddenly as it had come, her outrage dissolved like mist, leaving her with an overwhelming sense of melancholy, as though someone dear was forever lost to her.

Once inside the stone walls of the fortress, she rushed up the narrow stairs to the apartment she shared with Tariq, gathered up her belongings and retired to a spare room in one of the towers. Here she barricaded herself behind a stout cedar door fortified with lock and key, safely beyond Tariq's reach. She should be grateful to him, she told herself venomously. She had been in grave danger of succumbing to his mysterious charm. The knowledge that he still longed for Khadija brought Livia back to reality with a jolt. She would have nothing further to do with him. She would lock her mind and her heart away from him as irrevocably as she locked her door against him.

Darkness had fallen. Livia had lighted the brass lamps and had just settled down to read when she was startled by a pounding on the door.

"Livia!" Tariq commanded, "Open the door at once!"

She sat unmoving, glaring at the door.

"Livia! Do you hear me? Open this door!"

She made no reply. Frowning, she turned back to her book and read the same paragraph once more. The violence of the pounding increased, the iron door handle rattled.

For a moment Livia froze. Then satisfied that the lock would hold fast, she rose swiftly to her feet and crossed to the door. She stood waiting, her heart hammering with each blow upon the door. When Tariq's pounding momentarily ceased, as though he were listening for her response, she shouted, "Be gone! Go to Khadija!"

A heavy silence pervaded the room and her heart seemed to stop. Would he batter down the door, stride into the room and take her with the savage abandon he had shown at other times when, goaded by desire, his passions raged out of control?

She waited, tense, every nerve on fire. Then she heard the resounding thud of his boots striking the stone floor as his footsteps receded down the corridor.

She turned from the door, marched back to the divan and took up her book. A long sigh escaped her—a sigh of relief, she told herself sternly. It was certainly not one of disappointment, she thought, rereading the paragraph for the third time.

During the days that followed, Tariq did not come near her. Though she spent much time with Rashid, loneliness weighed her down. Suddenly the elegant surroundings depressed her, and the thought of Tariq spending his days and nights with Khadija did nothing to restore her cheerful humor.

On a crisp green-golden day near the end of September 1483, news was brought by Boabdil's *adalides* that Muley had decided to reinforce his position with his people by making an incursion into Spanish-held land. He had been surprised and suffered devastating losses.

It was from Ayxa that Livia learned this, and also that Tariq had left Almeria to join Muley's forces. Livia bit her lip in an effort to keep from crying out, "And what of Tariq?" She cared nothing for the fate of Tariq Ibn Ziyah!

The news of the defeat was eclipsed at the end of October, when the Spanish regained Zahara. Muley retaliated by barricading the former Moorish town of Alhama. The Christians could not move past the gates.

As the bleak October days wore on and Tariq did not return to Almeria, Livia concluded he had been taken prisoner again or—she shivered to think of it—he was dead. Much as she detested the man, she could not wish Rashid's father dead. Maybe tomorrow he would gallop up the narrow road to the Alcazaba on his great black stallion . . . to Khadija's arms.

Though Livia was careful to keep her distance from Khadija, when she happened to see her on the arm of

Boabdil, Livia could not fail to note that the woman's spirits were not dimmed by Tariq's prolonged absence. She was as carefree as any of the nobles who were relieved to be away from the strife that plagued Muley's followers.

One night after dinner, the courtiers gathered in the great hall to enjoy an entertainment. Livia sat cross-legged on a cushion watching with cool detachment as Khadija danced. It was not proper for a prince's wife to perform in public, but then, Khadija was not above flouting custom to spite Boabdil. As she whirled about in a cloud of green chiffon that glittered with precious gems, her gestures, the twist of her hips, the seductive manner in which she flaunted her body, all seemed calculated to entice Boabdil and infuriate Morayma.

When at last Khadija had done, she crossed the great hall to Livia. Small golden bells circling her wrists and ankles jingled as she sank down on a cushion beside Livia. Khadija's almond-shaped eyes gleamed like coal as she said slyly, "Why such a sour face, Livia? Surely you should be happy that you are free from Tariq."

"I have learned to find happiness whatever the circumstances." As though to dismiss Khadija, she leaned forward and plucked a fig from the tray at her feet.

"Then how relieved you must be that Tariq is in charge of the troops at Alhama."

Livia's hand paused in midair. How had Khadija known of Tariq's whereabouts when she herself had not heard from him? She swallowed hard and returned Khadija's glittering gaze. "I shall await Tariq's return with great anticipation."

Khadija rose lazily to her feet and smiled down upon her. "So shall I, Livia. So shall I!"

Chapter 24

October faded like smoke into November and December, and the land took on a barren, forsaken look. The fortress was cold and damp, and the bleak winter days passed slowly.

Livia busied herself with winding silk, copying pages from the Koran and dreaming of her future with Aguilar. Aguilar who had given her that priceless sense of being treasured which now sustained her. As the days passed, she anxiously waited for Tariq, only to settle matters between them. She had convinced herself that Khadija would wheedle a divorce from Boabdil. Doubtless, Tariq would marry her at the end of three months on the day it became final.

A melancholy sigh escaped her. Was this not the very thing she herself desired most? To be free of Tariq to marry Aguilar? She suffered no qualms that her gallant and pious Aquilar would love Rashid as he loved her. Her son was an extension of herself. With effort, she swallowed the bitterness in her heart and found pleasure in the hours she spent with Rashid. Now he chattered Arabic better than she, and she spent time each day teaching him to speak Spanish. She looked with pride upon her dark-eyed son. He had Tariq's wide shoulders, determined mouth, aquiline nose and thick brows. A quiet child, he spent hours scrawling pictures upon sheets of paper provided by Ayxa and occasionally played with Prince Aben. She had the same feeling with Rashid as with Tariq; there was much going on inside his head that she would never know.

With the advent of spring 1484, came news that set
the Almeria abuzz with excitement. Boabdil's scouts
galloped to the fortress to tell of a massive buildup in
Spanish forces at Antiquere, but no one knew where
they would strike.

Ferdinand's army entered the Moorish territory by
the way of Alora, destroying all the cornfields, vineyards and orchards and plantations of olives surrounding the city. It marched through the rich valleys and
fertile uplands of Coin, Cazarabonela, Almexia and
Cartama; in ten days all those fertile regions were a
smoking desert. It pursued its slow and destructive
course to the *vega* of Malaga, laying waste the groves of
olives and almonds and the fields of grain, destroying
every living thing. Then, satisfied with the havoc it had
wreaked in the *vega,* the army turned its back on
Malaga and again entered the mountains. They passed
through the regions of Allazayna, Gatero and
Alhaurin, all of which they devastated. In this way they
made the circuit of a chain of rich green valleys. For
forty days they continued like a consuming fire, leaving
a howling waste to mark their course. Then the army
returned in triumph to the meadows of Antiquera.

On a gray afternoon in April, Livia stood gazing out
the window of her chamber watching the rain slanting
down like fine needles. It seldom rained in Almeria,
and when it did, it came down with a vengeance. She
clutched her shawl more tightly about her as wind
buffeted the fortress and dashed the blossoms from the
almond trees, leaving them to lie limp and tattered on
the sodden hillside.

Dusk had fallen and she started to turn from the
window when her attention was caught by a group of
horsemen. They wore burnooses whose hoods shielded
their faces from the weather. Their leader, bent
forward against the wind, bore a standard aloft. Livia
strained to make out the insignia, but could not, for the
drenched silk whipped about the stave. She spun about

and dashed from her chamber, down the stairs, into the great hall.

Moments later, the door burst open and the riders stamped inside, shaking the rain from their heads and shoulders and flinging off their cloaks. Livia stopped short at the sight of their ragged garments, their scraggly beards, and hair plastered to their heads. She recognized none of them. Their leader jerked his head back, flinging off his burnoose. As Livia glanced up into his ravaged face, his eyes held hers.

"Tariq!" Livia cried, and rushed forward to greet him.

He stood motionless, his arms hanging at his sides, staring at her with an unreadable expression.

Stunned, Livia stood speechless before him, gazing up into his face. His dark brows furrowed. Suddenly it seemed as though everyone in the fortress swarmed about the small troop. Tariq swept past Livia and strode forward to meet Boabdil.

Livia whirled about, staring after Tariq. Willing to let the past bury itself, willing to hand him his freedom, she had run to him. In return she had met with a rebuff. The next instant, Khadija, clad in a crimson gauze tunic and trousers, darted through the throng like a flame and threw her arms about Tariq's neck, exclaiming over shoulder, "Boabdil, our commander-in-chief has returned! How fortunate we are!"

Tears stung Livia's eyes. She threaded her way through the crowded hall swiftly and fled to her room, where she flung herself down upon the sofa.

After a short while, she sat up and dabbed angrily at her eyes with the hem of her tunic. "This sniveling will avail you nothing!" she told herself sternly. "Cease this infantile wailing and come to your senses!"

She rose and lighted the lamps from the taper that burned on her writing table. Then she bathed her face, smoothed her hair and began pacing the floor. She must think of how to cope with this turn of events.

"What did you expect?" she muttered between

clenched teeth. "You knew full well he was coming back to Khadija. What ails you? Did you expect him to enfold you in his arms in a husbandly embrace and tell you all was forgiven?"

The memory of their last encounter rose to her mind and her face flamed. The chamber seemed to echo with the sound of Tariq pounding on her door demanding admittance and her own strident cry, "Go to Khadija!" That she had brought his censure on herself only served to increase her ire. Perversely, she thought, "I will not stand for such treatment! I will not be shut up in this fortress, forced to watch my husband make a fool of me! I will not—"

Her dark thoughts were interrupted by footsteps in the corridor. She swung about and her hand flew to her mouth, smothering a cry, as the door was flung open and Tariq entered. He glowered at her, feet astride, hands on his hips, formidable in his rage despite his ragged garments and the exhaustion etched on his face.

Livia drew herself erect to hide her anxiety. Silence stretched between them.

When he finally spoke, his voice was tight. "I trust you are well pleased!" A wintry smile touched his lips. "It was your chivalrous knight—Don Alonzo de Aguilar—who led this expedition against us, pillaging, ravishing the countryside and its inhabitants, destroying everything in his path!" He inclined his head and added disparagingly, "Not with the noble aim of conquest, but merely in a mad desire for revenge!"

Livia threw out her hands helplessly. "And what would you expect when your own army sacks Christian towns, killing, raping, taking citizens prisoner to work your fields and vineyards and mines, to slave in your palaces so you may enjoy your sybaritic lives of luxury? Do you expect to be greeted with outstretched arms and invited to a feast, to—"

"Enough!" Tariq cried, and in a blind, unreasoning fury he went on, his words flowing over her like hot lava. He seemed to blame her for Aguilar's actions.

When Tariq finally paused to take a breath, she stepped toward him, her eyes flashing fire.

"How dare you take me to task, hold me responsible for the actions of a commander who does nothing but his duty? Aguilar fights in the defense of his country under orders from his sovereigns! You had best look at yourself before you condemn others, Tariq Ibn Ziyah!"

For a moment he was speechless, and pinpoints of light shining in the depths of his eyes bored into hers.

She could almost see him searching his mind to discover the reason for her onslaught. Sensing that she had thrown him off balance, she pushed her advantage.

"Do not insult me further by feigning innocence, Tariq!" Her wrath made her voice harsh and rasping. "It is Khadija who holds your heart! Khadija you yearn for!"

A steely glint came into his eyes. "That is not true, Livia. I once thought I loved her, but that is over and done. You have been misinformed."

"Misinformed, am I?" Livia hissed. "Are you asking me to doubt the evidence of my own eyes and ears? Do you think I've not seen you and Khadija arm-in-arm in solitary strolls in the gardens, or enjoying secret trysts upon the cliff on the shore? Do you think I do not know that Khadija intends to persuade Boabdil to seek a divorce?"

An expression of surprise crossed Tariq's face, but before he could speak, Livia rushed on. "Don't trouble to deny it. Doubtless you, too, wish a divorce. So proceed with your case. I'll be only too happy to comply. And the sooner the better!"

As Tariq stood gazing at her, the color drained from his face and a look of defeat shone in his eyes. His jaw set in a determined line, matching the resolute set of his mouth. Without another word, he swung about and stalked from the chamber, closing the door firmly behind him.

"Infidel!" Livia shouted at the top of her voice.

Any glimmer of affection she might ever have felt for

him drained away and a consuming hatred possessed
her. She did not know it was possible to hate so much.
She crossed to her writing table and began to write the
letter she had written in her mind again and again.
When she had done, she sprinkled sand across the
sheets, blew on the fine grains, then sealed the missive
with wax from a taper. Shortly thereafter, she gave it to
a messenger who would ride to Malaga and deliver it to
Nizam.

Each day dragged interminably until she received a
reply. With trembling fingers, she tore open the letter
and her eyes raced down the page to the paragraph that
was of such importance to her.

> I regret to say, Livia dear, that much as I wish
> to offer you asylum, it would not be wise for you
> and Rashid to stay with me here in Malaga. Every
> day we fear for our lives. In June King Ferdinand
> increased his forces around Malaga and added
> several lombards of a new design and other heavy
> siege artillery. They are manned by engineers
> from France and Germany. With these, the
> Marquez of Cadiz has assured the king he will
> soon reduce the Moorish fortresses.
>
> Raduan tells me that our fortresses are calculat-
> ed only for defense against the engines anciently
> used in warfare: The stone and iron balls thun-
> dered from these new lombards will soon tumble
> the walls in ruins upon our heads.

Livia finished reading the letter with a mixture of
anticipation and dread; feeling sorrow for Nizam that
she must live in peril and, at the same time, thinking
that these new machines must bring the war to an early
end. Her hopes soared. Soon the Christians would
conquer the land: But she must resign herself to wait,
to bide her time until she could return to Granada
where one day Aguilar would claim her for his own. It

was this thought that sustained her through the hot, dry days of summer.

With the end of summer came a letter from Julian. Her eyes misted as she conjured up a vision of Julian, her irrepressible brother, laughing in the face of fortune, making friends with fate against the heaviest odds.

The news was not good. The Christians were engaged in the last foray of the year, before the autumn rains and the onset of winter. They had made an inroad into the *vega,* burned two villages near Granada and destroyed the mills near the gates of the city.

> Old Muley, is overwhelmed at the desolation which has raged year-long throughout his territories and has now reached the very walls of his capital. He shambles about with his head sunk on his chest, speaking little. His spirit is broken. He sent our sovereign an offer to purchase peace and to hold his crown as a tributary vassal, but Ferdinand would not listen. Muley does not understand that the absolute conquest of Granada is the great object of this war. Ferdinand and Isabella will never rest content without its complete fulfillment. What old Muley does not know, which I have heard by diligent listening to apostate Moors, is that Ferdinand, having supplied and strengthened garrisons of places taken in the heart of Moorish territories, has enjoined their commanders to render every assistance to Boabdil in the civil war against his father.

Smiling to herself, Livia folded Julian's letter and tucked it away under the garments in her chest along with the one from Nizam.

The fortunes of the Spanish sovereigns were looking up; and with their armies devoting all their energies to the capture of Granada, her own fortunes as well.

Chapter 25

During the weeks that followed, Livia kept fairly much to herself. Only occasionally did she venture to join the court in the great hall. At those times, she took care to keep her distance from Tariq. If he saw her, he seemed to deliberately ignore her presence. He gave off that same air of authority and arrogance that always vexed her.

Livia quickly perceived that tensions were mounting among the nobles of Boabdil's Court. More than once she had heard Ayxa admonish her son, cautioning him not to be taken in by the friendly overtures of the Castilian sovereigns. But the irresolute Boabdil did nothing, trusting that with shifting events, his popularity might once more be restored and he would again be placed on the throne of the Alhambra.

One mild autumn evening Livia sat quietly listening as the high-spirited Ayxa exhorted Boabdil in an effort to rouse him from his passive state, to strike a blow against his enemies before the onset of winter. Her intense eyes were fixed on him, as though compelling him to heed her warning.

"It is a feeble mind that waits for the turn of fortune's wheel. The brave man seizes opportunity and turns it to his purpose. By a bold enterprise, you may regain your splendid throne in Granada; by passivity, you will forfeit even this miserable one in Almeria!"

The air was charged with silence while everyone waited with indrawn breath for Boabdil's reply to

Ayxa's advice. He reached for a handful of melon seeds, cracked one between his teeth, spit out the shell and dropped it into a silver bowl.

In a fury of impatience, Ayxa burst out, "Do you not wish to regain the Alhambra?"

Boabdil's hand rose to his chest, fingering his prayer beads. *"Inshallah,* if Allah wills," he murmured.

Livia glanced quickly at Tariq. Once again she was struck by his intelligent eyes, intent, as he regarded Boabdil with stern disapproval. He said nothing. Privately, she admired his loyalty to Boabdil, but she could not help but think that the longer Boabdil dawdled, the sooner Ferdinand's armies would conquer the kingdom.

Winter passed uneventfully, one day seeming much like the next. Then one morning early in February, Livia was summoned by a servant who told her she had a visitor. Who the visitor was the servant could not say, but Livia could tell from his shrug and suspicious expression that it was someone out of the ordinary.

Upon descending to the great hall, Livia's eyes widened in astonishment as she saw a grizzled bent old man in a patched burnoose, surrounded by the ladies of the court. They were accustomed to visits of the kind from *renegado* Moors who roamed the country as spies and *adalides,* but the countenance of this man was quite unknown to her. He had a box strapped to his shoulders containing diverse articles of trade and appeared to be an itinerant peddler. He had insisted upon seeing Livia face to face, claiming that he bore a gift from her brother which he must place directly into her own hands. He then withdrew a rolled parchment tied with a red ribbon. With a bow and a flourish, he pressed it into her hands.

"Oh, Livia!" exclaimed one of the ladies poring over his wares. "Do let us see!"

Livia gave her an uncertain smile and with shaking

fingers slid the ribbon off and unrolled the parchment, followed by chorus of "ohs" and "ahs."

In glowing reds, blues, greens and golds, Julian had portrayed two unicorns tilting against a floral background.

Once back in her room, Livia ran to the window to study the picture in the light. Well knowing Julian's flair for the dramatic gesture, she surmised there was more to the painting than met the eye. He would not send her a painting and not a letter as well. But why send it secretly when he had sent the last one so openly? Unless he feared it would be intercepted and read by the wrong eyes. She scrutinized the painting carefully, but could make out no message woven into the design. She ran her hands over the face of the picture, then turned over the stiff parchment. Gently, she tugged at one corner and gradually peeled off the backing. Concealed between the layers lay a thin tissue covered with Julian's flowing script. She scanned the page eagerly.

Muley is failing fast. He has nearly lost his sight and is completely bedridden. His brother El Zagal—The Valiant—has taken over. He is zealous in encouraging Muley's quarrel with Boabdil.

El Zagal diligently foments dissatisfaction with Boabdil through special agents. And now, El Zagal and Malik are conspiring at Boabdil's destruction. They plan a surprise attack on the Alcazaba at Almeria.

A sudden shiver shook her as she realized the reason for Julian's hiding the letter. If El Zagal's ubiquitous spies in the Alhambra had learned its contents, Julian would have met with a swift end.

If you can devise a way in which you and Rashid can flee the fortress, do so at once, for your lives are in imminent peril.

Livia's hands dropped into her lap and fear leaped into her heart—more for the safety of Rashid than for herself. She would leave on foot, if need be, with Rashid. But if she should be taken on the road by *renegados,* what would become of her son? Yet it was unthinkable to desert him, to leave him to Hajai to defend or to leave him to the protection of a father who denied him. Her fingers curled around Julian's letter. Here was her chance to even the score with Tariq. She could keep silent and let El Zagal take the fortress by surprise. No one would suspect that she had known of the planned attack and failed to give warning. Zagal wanted only to do away with Boabdil and his followers; he would not trouble himself with the women and children. With an effort, she tried to think clearly, but her mind refused to function. She only knew that she could not allow Tariq to be caught like a rabbit in a trap. Though she didn't know the day of the threatened attack, forewarned was forearmed. She set her lips in a determined line and made her way swiftly through the halls to Ayxa's apartment.

When Ayxa finished reading Julian's letter and handed it back to Livia, her obsidian eyes gleamed with the light of revenge rather than fear, and her response bore out Livia's opinion.

"Do not trouble yourself with needless fears and imaginings," said the intrepid sultana. "You, Rashid and the courtiers are in no danger. It is only Boabdil, his commander-in-chief and his followers they wish to execute. Furthermore, the soldiers assigned to permanent duty here at the Alcazaba are loyal to Boabdil and will defend them."

"But they should flee now, at once!"

Ayxa shook her head and grimaced. "The height of folly. A sovereign who flees when no man pursues would be a laughingstock. Further, your brother's warning could be but a well-placed rumor intended to reach Boabdil's ears and thereby drive him from the protection of the fortress."

Livia returned to her chamber knowing she should feel reassured by Ayxa's promise of safety; but deep inside, doubts persisted to plague her.

Day after day, Livia kept a sharp watch upon the approaches, as did the sentries in the lookouts positioned along the walls of the garrison.

It was on a cold sunny afternoon in February 1485 that she saw El Zagal riding at the head of a troop of horses along the coastal road that wound about the foot of the citadel. As he drew near, her eyes widened and she let out a startled cry. The *alfaquis* flew from the fortress like crows into the courtyard and threw open the gates. Her gaze darted to the sentries mounted upon the walls. They made no outcry. Still, Livia angrily thought, knowing the vacillating nature of the Moors, she should not have been surprised that they were in league with El Zagal.

She remained paralyzed with fear as El Zagal and his band galloped up the steep road into the courtyard and slid from their mounts. The next instant a short plump scout rushed out and drew his scimitar to offer resistance, but the traitorous garrison soldiers killed him and greeted El Zagal, shouting his name. Zagal had prepared his way even better than she had surmised.

Livia dashed to Rashid's apartment and through the sitting room where Hajai dozed, into the bedchamber to wake her child from his nap. His bed was empty. She ran back to Hajai and roughly shook her by the shoulders.

"Rashid?" Livia gasped. "Where is Rashid?"

Hajai stared up at her, blinking her eyes, uncomprehending. Again Livia shook her violently. "Where is my son?"

Hajai jerked from Livia's grasp and stifled a yawn. "Do not upset yourself. He is in good hands. He plays with Prince Aben in the antechamber with the Sultana Ayxa and her attendants."

Livia sped from the room, down the endless dusky

corridors, shutting her ears to the hue that arose as El
Zagal and his men rushed through the royal apartments
in search of Boabdil. Gasping for breath, she gained
the antechamber. Her gaze swept the room, taking in
Ayxa and her attendants seated at a low table gambling
at cards, the round brazier glowing warm with charcoal
and Rashid tumbling on the floor with Prince Aben.

"Zagal descends upon us!" Livia shrieked.

"Calm yourself," Ayxa said harshly as she dealt out
the cards. "It avails nothing for us to fly about like
chickens, for he will depart when he does not find those
whom he seeks."

Despite Ayxa's confident assurance that they were
safe, Livia, driven by maternal instinct, swept down on
Rashid, scooped him up in her arms and took refuge
behind the window hangings. After all, Ayxa had been
wrong in thinking the soldiers would defend them.

The next moment, El Zagal and two of his men burst
into the room shouting, "Where is the traitor Boabdil?"

Peering around the edge of the curtain, Livia
watched with bated breath as Ayxa's attendants leaped
to their feet, drew their daggers and surrounded Ayxa.

"I know no traitor more perfidious than you!"
exclaimed the intrepid sultana. She bent a basilisk stare
on El Zagal. "We were informed of your treacherous
design long since, and since that day my son and his
followers have held themselves in readiness to fly at a
moment's notice. You see, even your own supporters
betray you!"

Livia winced at the audacity of the old lioness, even
as she admired Ayxa's spirit. Rashid squirmed in
Livia's tight grasp and she quickly covered his mouth
with her hand, warning him not to cry out.

Ayxa went on in a haughty voice. "By now I trust my
son has reached safety, to take vengeance on your
treason!"

In a towering fury, El Zagal let out a stream of
invectives. Terrified, Livia flattened her back against

the wall, and prayed that no one would search the
chamber; that El Zagal would dash from the fortress to
track down his quarry. Earsplitting shrieks turned her
blood to ice. As she had feared, Ayxa had not fully
reckoned with Zagal's wrath. Livia parted the edge of
the drapery a fraction of an inch, then drew back,
choking down a cry of horror. El Zagal had slain Prince
Aben, and his followers had massacred the attendants.

Sickened by the sight, she clapped a hand over
Rashid's eyes and shut her own against the scene.
Without warning, the wall hangings were thrust aside
and one of Zagal's men ordered her to step forward.
Livia thought she could not move, but a quick, stabbing
gesture of the dagger in his hand roused her to action.
Before she knew what was happening, Livia and
Rashid were borne away, prisoners, along with the
Sultana Ayxa and other important personages, to be
taken to Granada.

The journey was a nightmare of hard riding, with few
stops for food and rest. As Livia held the sleeping
Rashid in her arms, she smiled ruefully to herself. Was
this not the very thing for which she had prayed? To
return to the Alhambra where Aguilar could find her?
A chill of fear prickled her spine; she had no wish for
Aguilar to find her moldering in the prison beneath the
palace.

To Livia's amazement, the noble prisoners were not
cast into the dungeon, but were locked in the Comares
Tower to await Muley's decision on their fate. Ayxa
claimed that he dared not risk the ire of the populace by
putting them to the sword, and Livia took comfort in
this.

Less than three days passed before Ayxa reestab-
lished her network of spies which reported what had
happened to Boabdil. Accompanied by Tariq and forty
men, Boabdil had escaped during the confusion. Several of El Zagal's horsemen had pursued him but their
horses were exhausted and could not keep up. Not

knowing if any Moors could be trusted to take him in,
he had no alternative but to seek refuge among the
Christians at Cordoba. Ayxa shook her head mournfully. "It is a humiliating state—a fugitive from his throne,
an outcast from his nation, a king without a kingdom."
Her face brightened as she regarded Livia with an
approving eye. "However, I'm told that the Spaniards
received him with great distinction and the utmost
courtesy. He was honorably entertained by the civil
and military commanders of Cordoba."

Livia bent an amused smile upon Ayxa. "I am
gratified that my countrymen treated your sovereign
with the proper deference and respect."

Ayxa's brows rose. "You should be more gratified
that El Zagal has never discovered it was you who
warned us of his attack. Had he known, your own head
and that of your son would be rolling in the dust!"

The following morning Livia was seated at the
window of her chamber drying her hair, when she
heard footsteps on the rush mats scattered about the
floor. She spun about and her breath caught in her
throat. Malik came striding toward her like a panther
stalking his prey. He wore a black turban and robe that
accentuated his sallow skin, and his thin lips parted in a
twisted smile. As he raised his hand in greeting, the
diamond on his finger sparkled in the sunlight.

Livia turned away and continued to fluff her silken
black hair. She paid little heed to his idle chatter until
her attention was caught by the name Khadija.

"Did you know," Malik was saying, "that Khadija
has long been a favorite of Muley? Ever since El Zagal
brought her back from Almeria, she has had the run of
the palace."

Livia listened to Malik's words in spite of herself, and
fear surged through her as their import penetrated her
mind.

"So you see," Malik went on smoothly, "I've a
witness to your infamy." He stepped to her side and

took up a thick strand of her hair, letting it run through
his fingers. Livia sat rigidly, desperately trying to think.
He bent down and kissed the creamy nape of her neck,
and the smell of his wine-sour breath stifled her.
"However," he continued, "I could be persuaded not
to tell El Zagal who betrayed his plans . . . if you share
your bed with me."

This time Livia knew that ordering Malik to be gone
and threatening to cry out for help would be useless; he
had doubtless bribed her guards. She jerked her head
away, sweeping her long mane of hair from his grasp.
With an arch smile, she said, "I know that the plot to
kill Boabdil was not only El Zagal's, but yours as well.
Two can play at blackmail, Malik. If you leave me
alone, when Tariq returns with Boabdil, as he will, I
will not reveal that you were in league with El Zagal."

Malik crossed his arms over his chest and rocked
back on his heels. "Do not deceive yourself, my
innocent. If Boabdil returns to Granada, it will be for
his own funeral, along with Tariq's."

Livia took a deep breath. "If you tell El Zagal it was
I who betrayed him, he will have me executed. Then
you will certainly not have me."

"Nor will Tariq," Malik replied quietly.

Livia sprang up and confronted him, defiance
shinning in her eyes. "So be it, Malik. Go at once, and
tell El Zagal. And before you have done, I will tell him
it was Khadija who warned Boabdil of his treachery!"

Malik let out a burst of laughter. "Surely you do not
expect him to believe *you,* the wife of one of Boabdil's
commanders?"

With much more confidence than she felt, Livia
laughed. "Do you not think El Zagal would believe
that Boabdil's wife—the woman who pretends to love
him, who stands to gain the power, wealth and position
she has always coveted—would not be the first to save
Boabdil's neck? Not to mention that she has the ear of
many cavaliers in Zagal's own court and could easily
have learned his intention?"

Malik could only stare at her. Anger suffused his face; his eyes narrowed and his lips parted in an ugly sneer. "*I* would not believe such a foolish tale, but I've no doubt that you could convince Zagal of its truth." He clenched his fists at his sides, as though exercising all his control to keep from strangling her. "This time you win, but I will have you one day—and on my terms. That I promise you!" Furiously, he stalked from the room.

Livia sighed and sank weakly down upon her cushion by the window. She had won a respite, but how long could she hold Malik at bay? Oh, she thought, if only Tariq would return! No, no! She corrected her thinking quickly. If only Aguilar would come!

Life went on at its draggingly slow pace. El Zagal put a new *alcayde* over Almeria to govern in the name of his brother. Then, having strongly garrisoned the place, he repaired to Malaga, and a new worry rose to plague Livia. With the young monarch being driven from the land, and the old monarch blind and bedridden, El Zagal was the virtual sovereign of Granada.

Chapter 26

Several weeks later information was brought that Ferdinand had begun his campaign of 1485. He took the field on April 5 and marched toward the seaport of Malaga, on which Granada depended for foreign aid and supplies. The news put Granada in a state of consternation and shock as he sacked various towns and fortresses along his route.

El Zagal hastened to the defense of Malaga on the very day that Ferdinand appeared before the city. A sharp skirmish took place among the gardens and olive trees near the city, which Ferdinand lost. However, he soon took another city, followed by others. No less than seventy-two towns and cities capitulated to the Christians.

One sultry Tuesday afternoon, Livia and Ayxa were drawn to the belvedere by the sound of a great din. A tumultous assemblage was gathered in one of the public squares where a crafty *alfaqui*, harangued them for swaying back and forth between Muley and Boabdil, and called upon the people to legitimize El Zagal as the new king.

Ayxa paled and her trembling fingers clutched the balustrade for support as the crowd shouted its approval. Eventually, a deputation was appointed to go to El Zagal at Malaga to invite him to Granada to receive the crown.

Livia's heart went out to the sultana in her agony

over this ominous turn of events; much as Livia loathed Muley, she loathed his unscrupulous brother more. To her astonishment, she found her sympathies lay with the unfortunate Boabdil.

Quite early the next morning Livia was awakened by a stir of activity in the courtyard. Muley Abul Hassan, no longer able to buffet the storms of his times, was leaving the Alhambra. Not waiting for the arrival of El Zagal, he was going to seek asylum in the little city of Almuñecar in one of the deep valleys along the Mediterranean coast. There he was taking refuge and had ordered Sultana Zoraya and their two sons to follow him.

It seemed to Livia that Muley and his family had scarcely cleared the walls of the town when word came that El Zagal was on his way to Granada, leaving Raduan Venegas in command of Malaga.

As El Zagal pursued his journey toward the capital, he passed by Alhama, making a successful surprise attack against a small troop of Christians. Fame of his exploit preceded him, intoxicating Granada.

With a feeling of foreboding she could not quell, Livia watched from her window as he drew rein and waited expectantly before the gate of Elvira. Her brows drew together in a perplexed frown. What was causing the delay? Perhaps the fickle populace had once again changed its loyalty. And then, before her eyes, El Zagal was proclaimed king.

The new sovereign entered Granada in triumph.

Autumn gave way to winter and day after day bleak skies cast a pall over the brown stubble of the *vega* and the snow-laden slopes of the sierras.

One Thursday morning, when the sun parted the clouds and shone with a glistening light over the city, Julian appeared on the threshold of Livia's chamber. As on previous occasions, he had swept past the guard, artisan's tools in hand, on the pretext of repairing the tracery of leaves and vines adorning the walls. He grinned jubilantly at her.

"Recent losses have checked the tide of El Zagal's popularity. In fact, some have begun to wonder whether they have not been rather precipitate in deposing his brother."

"Surely the fiery heart of the old king must be almost burned out, and all his powers of doing either harm or good at an end," said Livia.

Julian cocked an eyebrow. "Muley is also uppermost in the mind of El Zagal, for he has suddenly shown a great anxiety about his brother's health. He has had Muley removed to Salobreña."

Livia knew Salobreña, a small town encircled on three sides by mountains and opening on the fourth to the Mediterranean. "It's famous for its salubrious air, is it not?"

"Oh, indeed! And the town is deemed impregnable so has often been used by the Moorish kings as a place to deposit their treasures."

Livia laughed. "I would hardly consider Muley a treasure."

"It depends on how you look at it." He regarded her speculatively. "The sultans also use it as a residence for royalty who might endanger the security of their reign."

Livia thought no more about Julian's idle speculations until several weeks later. On a cold starless night in January, she was awakened from a deep sleep by a commotion that seemed to be coming from the apartment overhead. She slipped on a sleeveless robe and sped into the hall. There she was brought up short by a strange sight. Servants bearing carpetbags and wooden chests were trudging up the stairs. She heard a child whine, then a hushing voice. Moments later a woman came into view, leading a child by each hand.

"Zoraya!" Livia cried, running to greet her.

Zoraya halted on the landing. Livia stifled a gasp.

Zoraya's face bore a waxen pallor, her eyes deeply shadowed. The children regarded Livia with fear on their tear-streaked faces. Wordlessly, Zoraya's features were taut with shock.

Livia gazed at her in incredulous disbelief. "Has Muley returned to claim his throne?"

"Muley is dead!" cried Zoraya in a voice near hysteria. "His body has been brought to Granada!" She choked down a sob and rushed on. "Not in state, becoming a once-powerful sovereign, but transported on a mule, like the body of the poorest peasant! My children and I are to be lodged here in the Comares Tower like prisoners! And the usurper Zagal has taken possession of all of Muley's treasure and left us without a dirhem!"

At that moment guards appeared on the stair behind Zoraya and ordered her to proceed.

Livia's heart went out to the sorrowing woman. Poor Zoraya, she thought—all those ambitious schemes for herself and her children, all for naught.

Not surprisingly, Ayxa took the news of Muley's death with her usual composure. Though she had donned the white garb of mourning, Livia thought she saw a smile touch Ayxa's lips as she shrugged and said, "There was nothing extraordinary in his death. For some time past, he might rather have been numbered with the dead than with the living!"

Livia nodded and said nothing. Ayxa's casual acceptance of Muley's death did nothing to allay Livia's suspicions. A cold fear clutched at her heart, seeming to creep through her body. El Zagal was a foe to be reckoned with—one not easily to be vanquished by Ferdinand's armies.

To Livia's relief, she soon discovered that her fears for Granada under the rule of El Zagal were shared by the inhabitants. The populace was fond of seeing things from a sinister point of view, and there were many dark theories about the cause of Muley's death.

Ayxa regarded the gossip with quiet satisfaction. "The public needs someone to like as well as to hate, and already they are inquiring after their fugitive king."

"Boabdil is still at Cordoba, is he not?" asked Livia, and the image of Tariq's inscrutable face rose unbidden to her mind.

Ayxa nodded. The watchful ebony eyes sparkled with malice, and her power was palpable. "I have taken steps to remedy that situation."

Ayxa's strategems were not long in revealing themselves. Her secret overtures to Ferdinand had once more aroused the sympathies of the Christian sovereigns, who had furnished Boabdil the means to set up his standard at Velez el Blanco just within the borders of Granada.

Livia grew increasingly bored and frustrated, her feelings made all the worse by the nagging torment seething deep within her. She had heard nothing from Tariq. True, he could send no message while at Cordoba, but now, surely he could have sent word.

Each time she heard the clatter of horses hooves in the courtyard, she rushed to the window hoping that a messenger had brought word from him. He could not still hold Aguilar's inroads on the vega against her! And if so, she should be vindicated after having warned Boabdil of Zagal's attack on the fortress at Almeria. She told herself that it was not for herself that she longed to hear from Tariq, but that she was concerned only for the safety of Rashid's father.

Livia was on her way to read to Rashid one afternoon when, as she hurried along, preoccupied with her own thoughts, she found her way was blocked by a slender figure swathed in a black cloak. She halted, and stared into the lynx-eyed face of Khadija.

With a semblance of a smile, Khadija said softly, "I was on my way to speak with you."

Livia made no reply, but waited, all her senses alerted.

"I am shortly to depart for Velez el Blanco to see Boabdil," Khadija said, then paused, as though awaiting Livia's reaction.

Livia's heart hammered in her breast, but she continued to regard Khadija steadily and made no reply.

"I'm going on a matter of grave importance to me, and to"—once again she paused—"and to others."

To seek her divorce, no doubt, thought Livia. She felt her face redden as quick anger flared within her. With an effort, she kept her temper in check. She must not let Khadija see that she was upsetting her.

"Go with God," Livia said, her voice a hoarse whisper. She hoped privately that God would mete out a suitable punishment to this woman along the way. Livia took a step forward, as if to brush past Khadija in the narrow passageway.

Khadija quickly raised a hand to detain her, and in the feeble light of the oil lamp hanging upon the wall, her eyes shone maliciously. "Wait!" she commanded, smiling slyly. "Doubtless I will see Tariq. I would be pleased to convey a message to him, if you wish it."

Livia shook her head and once again started forward.

Khadija braced her hand against the wall, barring the way, and her brows rose in astonishment. "But you must wish me to carry a letter, or some other token of your affection to him!"

"Nothing!" said Livia sharply. "And now let me pass. I must make haste, for Tariq's son awaits me!"

An expression akin to hatred flashed across Khadija's features as she glared at Livia.

Her patience at an end, Livia raised her hand as if to strike down Khadija's arm, but in that instant Khadija withdrew it, and Livia struck air. As she hurried down the corridor, she heard Khadija's scornful laughter echoing after her.

Livia was still seething when she settled herself in Rashid's chamber and took him upon her lap to read from a book of animal tales. For once she was thankful that he knew them by heart and would recite the words when she lost her place. Her mind was on Khadija and Tariq, continuing their affair. She chided herself, telling herself that she did not care, but her pride overrode all her resolves, and hatred for Khadija burned within her.

Chapter 27

The spring of 1486 came. Livia's step was light and she hummed to herself as she went about her tasks for it was reported that Ferdinand had assembled a mighty army at Cordoba and even now was on his way to Loxa.

The rival Moorish monarchs agreed to call a truce between themselves and to divide the kingdom.

Ayxa explained the matter to Livia. "It is a clever maneuver, for among the cities granted to Boabdil, they specified Loxa on condition that he immediately take command of it. The coucil hopes that the favor he enjoys with the Castilian monarchs might avert the threatened attack."

El Zagal readily agreed to this arrangement. He had been hastily set upon the throne and might be as hastily cast down again. Now he had been given one-half of a kingdom to which he had no hereditary right. The wily sultan would resort to force or fraud to gain the other half later.

Then Boabdil, however, wrote to Ferdinand, saying that he would hold Loxa and other cities as vassal to the Castilian crown and therefore, entreated the Spanish king to refrain from any attack.

Ayxa's ebony eyes glittered. She added witheringly, "Ferdinand insists that Boabdil has entered into a hostile league with El Zagal, and is now proceeding with his campaign against Loxa."

Livia nodded knowingly. "A kingdom divided against itself cannot stand."

Ayxa's flashing eyes challenged her. "We shall see!"

Livia thought, but did not mention the Castilian proverb in cases of civil war: the conquered conquered, and the conqueror undone.

Loxa, perched in a mountain pass between Granada and Castile, commanded a main entrance to the *vega*. Soon the Spanish legions would overrun the area and the war would end. Each night before she closed her eyes in sleep, she murmured a prayer for Aquilar's safety, but her dreams were invaded by the face of Tariq Ibn Ziyah.

At length word came that Boabdil had made a considerable effort at Loxa until the inhabitants had finally urged him to capitulate. Ferdinand was inexorably closing in on the capital of the kingdom.

By June Ferdinand's army had established its camp in the vicinity of Granada, destroying the grain and fruits of the *vega*, rendering the earthly paradise a dreary desert. Yet, after one indecisive skirmish, Ferdinand retreated to Cordoba, content with having ravaged the crops and kept Zagal shut up in his capital.

Chapter 28

No sooner had the last squadron of Christian cavalry disappeared behind the mountains of Elvira, and the note of its trumpets died away, than the long-suppressed wrath of El Zagal erupted. Livia shuddered at the sounds of shrieks that rose from the halls below and for once she felt thankful to be imprisoned in the Comares Tower and ignored by the court.

Once undisputed monarch of the entire kingdom, El Zagal had trusted to his military skills to retrieve his fortunes and to drive the Christians over the frontier. But they had failed him.

Two days later, Julian, whose daily visits no longer excited the curiosity of the guard, brought Livia astonishing information.

"El Zagal is sending ambassadors to Boabdil. He states that unity is necessary for the salvation of the kingdom and is offering to resign the monarchy to Boabdil if he is given an estate on which he can live in retirement."

Livia sank down onto the divan with a puzzled frown. "It is hard to believe that Zagal would turn over his kingdom so readily."

Julian shrugged. "Perhaps he prefers riches to warfare, fighting a lost cause." He took up his brush, dipped it in vermilion paint and turned to touch up a rosette on the wall.

Deep in thought, Livia was silent for a moment. Finally she asked, "When is the entourage to depart?"

"Tomorrow, they say. Why?"

Livia smiled wryly. "Boabdil is conveniently close to the border. It would not be difficult to slip across, and from there proceed to Cordoba, to—"

"To Aguilar," Julian finished, laughing. "I know you well." He turned from his work and looked at her, his eyes warm with affection, then sighed deeply. "I suppose it's no use telling you how dangerous such a flight would be . . ."

"No more dangerous than remaining here. If Boabdil should return, I warrant he will offer me little more protection than El Zagal."

"And what of your husband? Won't Tariq look after you?"

Livia shook her head. "He still yearns after Khadija." In a harsh voice, she added, "I should have let you do away with him as we planned. Rashid or no." But her tone lacked conviction.

"And what of Rashid? You would not abandon your own child!"

Livia got up and began pacing agitatedly. "I've given a lot of thought to Rashid's safety. Hajai and I have long since planned that if fighting should break out in the Alhambra, she is to take him to her family in the Albaycin. Now I will tell her that once I am in Cordoba, she is to give Rashid to you . . . if you will agree to bring him to me."

Julian nodded. "It can be done. And perhaps you are right. There is no future here for either of you."

Shortly before sunrise the next morning, the artisan who was repairing the fretwork in the Comares Tower appeared before the guard accompanied by a young apprentice in a tattered brown cloak and turban, and was admitted to the tower. Several minutes later, the apprentice reappeared and announced he was going to fetch a tool his master had forgotten. The guard seemed not to notice that the boy was slightly taller than he had appeared at first, and passed him by without question.

Donning the apprentice's turban, ragged brown tunic and boots had been an inspiration, thought Livia, for she could easily pass as a mule boy accompanying the Zagal's ambassadors. She had only one worry. Wishing to doubly ensure Rashid's safety by enlisting Ayxa's vigilance, she had confided her plan to the sultana.

For once the nervous, bejeweled hands turning over the cards at the small table had stilled. After the first shock of hearing Livia's plan, Ayxa's eyes had glowed with approval and admiration. "I must warn you of the dangers of this exploit you propose. If your identity is discovered, it will be assumed you are a spy and you will be killed without question; not to mention the other evils that could befall you once on your own."

Livia felt impatient rather than afraid. "It is worth the risk," she said quietly.

Ayxa nodded and spoke no more of danger. "Since you are determined to go, regardless of my warning, I wish you to deliver a message to Boabdil."

Livia agreed. It was the least she could do in return for Ayxa's promise to keep an eye on Rashid.

"I should explain," Ayxa went on, "that my unfortunate son has three great evils to contend with. The inconstancy of his subjects, the hostility of his uncle, and the friendship of Ferdinand." Undeterred by the look of surprise that crossed Livia's face, she persisted. "The last is by far the most baneful. His fortunes wither under it. He is looked upon as the enemy of his faith and of his country. The critics shut their gates against him; the people curse him; even the scanty band of cavaliers who have so far followed his ill-starred banner have begun to desert him, for he has not the wherewithal to reward—nor even to support them. He must rouse himself to action without delay!" Her fingers drummed on the table for a few seconds then she had reached for pen and paper. "My arguments will be more persuasive if written down for him to ponder. You will give the message directly into his hands."

Once again Livia had nodded assent. Now, con-

cealed under her tunic where it seemed to burn against
the tender flesh beneath her bosom, she carried a letter
for Boabdil from his mother. Livia trembled to think
what would happen should it be discovered, and
quickly put the unpleasant thought from her mind.

Puffed up with the importance of their mission, El
Zagal's ambassadors paid no heed to the slender boy,
one of several bringing up the baggage at the rear of
their train. When the boys looked at Livia curiously and
asked her name, she faced them with a blank stare and
gave the sign of a deaf mute. They shrugged, turned
away and left her to herself.

The mules were slow and plodding, picking their way
cautiously up the steep passes and down ravines of the
barren mountains, and the ambassadors stopped frequently to rest and refresh themselves with wine from
their *betas* and food from their saddlebags. At last they
halted for the night and pitched their tents near the
banks of a stream.

Livia tethered her mule to an umbrella pine behind
the tent of the leader of the expedition, then unloaded
the beast and stretched out on the ground, resting her
head on a carpetbag. Fear and excitement coursed
through her and sleep would not come. How would she
make her way to Cordoba? Would Boabdil lend her a
mount? And how would Tariq receive her? Clearly he
would have no objection to her journeying to Cordoba!

As the camp settled down Livia's thoughts were
distracted by the sound of low voices coming from the
tent nearby. She rolled across the hard-packed earth to
get closer, straining to hear the words. For some
minutes she lay listening. Apparently, the leader of the
expedition was arguing with his comrades. Gooseflesh
rose on her arms and the nape of her neck. That El
Zagal had determined no longer to be half a king,
reigning over a divided kingdom in a divided capital,
came as no surprise to her. But now he had determined
to exterminate his nephew Boabdil and his faction by
any means, fair or foul. The angry voices rose.

"Straddling the border, Boabdil can avail himself of any assistance or protection afforded him by Ferdinand!"

A lower, more resonant voice replied, "But Boabdil's defeat at Loxa has blighted his reviving fortunes. The people consider him inevitably doomed to misfortune."

"Still, while he lives, El Zagal thinks he will be a rallying point and liable at any moment to be elevated to power."

The first voice, deadly and menacing, came clearly to Livia's ears.

"I have pledged my word to Zagal that should we fail to administer secretly the poisoned herbs, we will dispatch Boabdil openly while engaged in conversation."

"Ey-ee!" exclaimed a third voice. "That is a risk I don't care to take!"

"Enough! We have been promised great rewards, and the *alfaquis* have assured me that Boabdil is an apostate whose death will be acceptable to heaven."

Livia waited to hear no more, but rolled back across the rough stubble to conceal herself among the baggage. Her first inclination was to say nothing. Let the infidels kill each other; it was no less than they deserved. But much as she despised the Moors, the wavering Boabdil not the least of them, she caviled at the murder of this ineffectual sovereign. And then there was Ayxa who had befriended her and who had promised to see to Rashid's safety. Livia owed Ayxa a favor. A further thought bore in upon her. If, once again, she saved Boabdil from the hands of his enemies, there would be a better chance that he would offer her safe conduct to Cordoba. She grinned in wry amusement. Allah was smiling upon her, unbeliever though she was!

When they reached Boabdil's encampment, the sun was setting behind the mountains in a blaze of orange light and a voice rang out, calling for evening prayer.

The ambassadors dismounted and knelt on their prayer rugs. Livia strode swiftly toward a tent over which flew the royal standard. Then, remembering just in time that she was posing as a Moslem, she dropped to her knew and bent her head in an attitude of prayer. When their prayers were done, she dashed past an astonished guard into Boabdil's tent. The king, reposing upon a makeshift throne of carpets spread over a mound of cushions, gaped in openmouthed surprise at the ragged mule boy who stood wild-eyed before him. He flung up his arms in a gesture of one shooing away a filthy cur. "Out, out, urchin! You have blundered into the royal tent!"

A paralyzing spasm of panic rendered Livia speechless.

Boabdil leaped to his feet, but before he could shout for his guard, she burst out, "I am Livia, wife of Tariq Ibn Ziyah," then poured out her tale of the treason of El Zagal.

An expression of astonishment and disbelief spread over the king's mild countenance. With swift intuition, she recognized that he was loath to credit her story, for then he would be forced to take action.

"You must believe me!" Livia pleaded.

He gave a vehement shake of his head and his voice rose in indignation. "Zagal would not dare to have me assassinated before my own people!" His doubting eyes assessed Livia, raking over her lopsided turban, her dirt-streaked face and tattered cloak. Then, as if to eliminate the object of his discomfort, he clapped his hands and bellowed, "Begone! Begone from my sight, at once!"

She drew herself erect, raised her chin and regarded him with a stately air. "If you do not heed my warning, you will die before sundown."

Glowering at her, Boabdil replied, "And if you do not obey my command, *you* will die before sundown!" With that, he shouted to the guard posted outside.

At the same moment the guard burst through the

tent flap, Livia whipped off her turban and her silken black hair cascaded about her shoulders. Boabdil was taken aback, but having shouted for help, he would not be dissuaded.

"Away with this troublemaker!" he roared. "See that he does not trouble me again!"

The guard gripped her arm and turned toward the doorway.

"Tariq!" Livia cried out in desperation. "I tell you I am his wife!" With a lightning motion, she wrenched free of the guard. He moved behind her swiftly and his arms closed around her chest. An expression of shock lighted his swarthy face.

"He is a *female*, sire! It is possible that he—she speaks the truth."

Boabdil frowned in annoyance, clearly disliking the turn of events. He let out an exasperated sigh and sank down on his carpeted throne. "Summon my commander-in-chief!"

Moments later, Tariq strode through the doorway of the royal tent. At the sight of Livia, his face broke into an astonished smile. "Livia!"

He stepped forward, folded her in his arms and pressed her to his chest in a fond embrace. A tremor seized her and his grip tightened. She felt his strong blunt fingers encircling her slender waist, and every part of her was tormented with longing for him. For a moment they stood locked in each other's arms while Boabdil glared at them from his throne. Common sense asserted itself, and color suffused Livia's face as she stepped back from Tariq's embrace.

If Boabdil had at first doubted her identity, all doubt was removed. Exploding in sudden fury, he leaped to his feet shouting to the guard, "Summon my council to assemble at once!"

As the soldier rushed from the tent, another dashed inside. "Sire," he said breathlessly, "Ambassadors have arrived on a mission of peace, bearing gifts from El Zagal."

With a roar heard throughout the camp, he bellowed, "I do not grant an audience to the ambassadors! Nor will I accept gifts from the murderer of my father, the usurper of my throne!" His pale complexion turned choleric and he shook his fist at the heavens. "Nor shall I relent in enmity to him until I place his head on the walls of the Alhambra!"

The ambassadors, hearing the commotion, took to their heels. Though Boabdil sent his men in swift pursuit, they escaped among the mountain ravines under cover of the fast falling darkness.

In Tariq's tent, where he had told her to wait for him, Livia sank down on a bed of animal skins in an agony of apprehension. His greeting had baffled her. His smile, the warm expression in his eyes and his ardent embrace all bespoke his joy in seeing her. Doubtless, in his arrogant way, he thought she had journeyed here for the sole purpose of being reunited with him.

Livia was even more dismayed at herself, at the thrill of happiness that had swept through her when he folded her in his arms, and at her spontaneous response to his muscular body pressed to hers. She must flee now, while she had the chance. She knew only too well that she would be helpless to resist him when he returned. She could almost imagine she was in love with the Moor; but she loved Aguilar, had always loved Aguilar, would always love Aguilar! What she felt for Tariq was—she blushed furiously at the thought—was a physical longing. Her body had betrayed her into thinking that this could be love. She would feel the same longing and affection—and more—for Aguilar when she lay in his arms as his wife. She would not let this virile Moor play upon her emotions.

She started to rise from Tariq's bed when a further thought brought her up short. She could not flee now, not yet, for she had forgotten to deliver Ayza's letter. And she must prevail upon Boabdil to provide her with an escort.

The pulling aside of the tent flap roused her from her

musings. She looked up and gasped. Khadija was in the doorway, her eyes incredulous, no less startled than Livia. Although the cool night breezes had dispelled the warmth of the day, Khadija was wearing filmy white clothes through which her flesh was clearly visible, and the diaphanous fabric clung to her body, leaving little to the imagination. In her long, flowing black hair were entwined ropes of pearls. Her eyes were made luminous with kohl and her full lips enhanced with color. Gold bracelets that dangled from her wrists and ankles tinkled like bells as she stepped inside the tent. Her dark eyes had a malicious sparkle as she looked at Livia.

Livia sat bolt upright. She felt a surge of anger so intense that she could only stare, speechless, at the intruder.

Khadija gave her an insolent glance then her eyes made a quick sweep about the tent. When her gaze returned to Livia, she spoke with the air she would accord a servant.

"Where is Tariq? He is usually here this time of evening."

Khadija's presence was a nightly occurrence! Eyes blazing, her breast swelling with indignation, Livia leaped to her feet. "Tariq attends the king!" cried Livia, barely controlling an impulse to strike her. "And when he returns, *I* will be here to greet him. *You* may go!"

"Go!" shrieked Khadija. "Who are you to order me about? No more than a captive slave, booty from one of Tariq's forays!" Her face contorted in an ugly mask, and her eyes glittered with hatred.

With all the dignity she could muster, Livia replied, "I am Tariq's wife! Leave my presence at once!"

"Wife!" spat Khadija. "You are no more Tariq's wife than one of old Muley's concubines. Are you so witless that you do not know that Tariq married you only to avenge me? He married you only because I did not wait for him, because I thought him to be lying dead in some forsaken fortress in the mountains, and in my grief I turned to Boabdil."

Livia, having regained a measure of her composure faced Khadija with cool contempt. "Your grief was not for Tariq, but for yourself!"

Khadija took a step toward her and raised her clenched fists in fury. "Do not pretend to me that you care for Tariq, you Spanish bitch," she shouted. "You care nothing for Tariq, yet you want no one else to have him!"

Biting back the hot denials that rose to her lips, Livia's dark eyes narrowed and she moved toward Khadija with a measured tread, a murderous expression on her face. "Out, *puta!* Out of my sight!"

The color drained from Khadija's face, leaving her pale and white-lipped as Livia proceeded menacingly toward her, relentlessly driving her backward.

Khadija gave ground until at last she was brought to a halt by the entrance. Clutching at the flap behind her, she screamed, "And your own lover Aguilar has taken a wife!" She whirled about and plunged into the darkness.

Chapter 29

Weak with shock and rage, Livia staggered backward and sank down on Tariq's bed of pelts, covered with a rabbit fur spread. With an effort, she forced herself to be calm. Khadija is lying, Livia told herself. She must be lying. How would *she* know that Aguilar had taken a wife? And yet, she could know, thought Livia miserably. She had spent several months here in the camp on the border. Many Christians went over to the side of the Moors to save their own skin, or their lands, and every shred of gossip about the Christians, particularly their commanders, was reported to the infidels. Livia clenched her jaw, choking down the sob that rose in her throat. She could not—*would* not believe it! Another of Khadija's barbs struck her with the force of a blow: that she wanted no one else to have Tariq—all the more infuriating because deep in her heart, Livia knew it was true!

"What has you so upset, my Zahareña?"

Startled, Livia looked up to see Tariq walking toward her. He reached out and placed his fingers under her chin, tilting her face up to his. She shrank back and glared up at him, her eyes flashing fire. "Don't touch me, you barbarian! Don't even come near me!"

Tariq gave an amused laugh and dropped down on the bed beside her. "Thorny as always, my rose laurel." He gently smoothed a wisp of hair back from her brow and let his fingers trail down the curve of her neck.

Quickly she rolled to the far side of the thick pile of

pelts. He caught her shoulder in a firm grasp and rolled her back to face him then, gripped her upper arms pinioning Livia to the furs, bent his head to hers and smiled into her eyes. "After our long separation, I'd think you'd have recovered your good humor!"

"*My* good humor!" cried Livia, bristling. "It was *you* who held me to blame for Aguilar's maneuvers against Granada!"

"Aguilar has long since passed from my consideration. Let us not speak of him." Tariq's smile widened. "Come, let us rejoice."

In reply, Livia tried to wrench free, but his strong hands held her fast. He laughed softly, bent his head and kissed her brow.

She stared up at him through narrowed lids, loathing shining from her eyes. "If Aguilar has passed from your consideration, Khadija certainly has not!"

Tariq's thick brows rose in astonishment. "Khadija! The woman means nothing to me!"

"Nothing!" shrieked Livia, outraged. "I suppose her nightly visits to your tent, bedecked like the favored houri in the king's harem, are merely to keep watch over you!"

Tariq's black eyes bored into hers. "If she chose to come here, it was not at my invitation. I have given you my word that Khadija means nothing to me. That should suffice." Abruptly, his solemn expression changed to one of amusement. "If you need further proof, I will show you that I mean what I say." He held Livia fast with one hand, while with the other he stripped off his tunic and flung it across the tent.

"No!"

Smiling as though she had not spoken, he slid an arm about her waist and drew her to him. She arched her back, straining away from him, struggling to escape the prison of his arms. His other arm slipped around her back, and he entwined his fingers in her soft, thick hair, drawing her closer so that she felt his hard chest pressing against her breasts. He breathed deeply of the fragrance of her hair and murmured her name again and again.

Her breath was coming in short gasps and she cried out, "No, Tariq, no!"

His mouth covered hers, but this time Livia was determined not to let him succeed in silencing her protests as he had always done before. With a sudden, violent motion, she brought both her hands upward, braced them against his shoulders and with every ounce of strength she could muster, shoved him away. At the same moment she twisted her body in an effort to free her legs and gain her feet.

Unexpectedly, Tariq released his hold on her. Thrown off balance, she collapsed onto the furs. He let out a shout of laughter and before she could rise up, he was upon her. The tattered cloak was wrenched from her shoulders and cast aside, followed by her rough cotton trousers and tunic. Swiftly, Tariq discarded the rest of his garments then molded Livia's gleaming white body to his, pressing her down onto the bed. She kicked out savagely, shouting, "No, no, no!"

He chuckled softly. "Quiet, you'll wake the birds!" He covered her mouth with a huge hand and she sank her teeth into the fleshy heel of his thumb. His hand flew from her mouth. Watching him through a haze of indignation, Livia saw a flash of anger kindle in his eyes and vanish quickly.

"You wish to be free?" Tariq asked, laughing. "Then go!" He rolled onto his back, watching her, a smile of admiration and pleasure curving his full lips. She rose to her hands and knees. In the instant before she sprang from the bed, he grasped her firmly about the waist then lifted her up and set her astride his hips, locking his hands at the small of her back.

"Let me go!" cried Livia furiously, pummeling his chest with her fists.

"In good time, my love," he murmured, his deep voice tinged with amusement. "I've something to prove to you first."

Her eyelids stung with tears of frustration. She clenched her teeth and glared into his eyes shining with excitement and anticipation in his handsome brown face, knowing it was useless to struggle against his caresses, that he would mock her with his great animal strength. *No!* She would not give in to him. Had she nothing left of the courage that had once been second nature?

Abruptly she arched her back and flung out her hands to brace herself on the bed, but before she could leap up from the furs, she felt Tariq's warm hands slide up her back in a caress that made her flesh tingle. He clasped her slender neck and drew her face to his. She felt his eyelashes flutter like the wings of a moth and heard his quick intake of breath. His free arm, firm on her back, was bending her to his will. His mouth sought hers, savage and demanding. She twisted her head this way and that, until he placed the palm of his hand on the back of her head and held her firmly, forcing her lips to meet his. He stroked her back in a gentle soothing caress. His kiss grew more ardent. His hands roamed her body, arousing sensations she was helpless to deny.

Every nerve in her body caught fire where his flesh touched hers. A sob rose in her throat as he pressed her closer, straining her to him convulsively, raining kisses on her shining hair. Holding her slender, quivering form with tender strength, he pressed her head against him, his cheek on her thick black hair. She felt the warm curve of his arm around her and the steady beat of his heart under her cheek, and she seemed unable to check the emotions that overwhelmed her.

Tariq's low voice came to her through the darkness. "Livia, Livia, do not cry. If only you could understand how much you mean to me, how much I want you! You need have no fear. I will care for you always. I will never let you go!"

She lay inert against him and gradually her sobs

subsided. Confused and upset, she was too tired to
unravel the strange conflicting emotions within her.
Livia did not understand them; she did not try.

His arm tightened around her and he rolled over,
carrying her with him so that she lay supine on the soft
furs. Kneeling above her, Tariq turned her face up to
his. Her eyes were closed and the wet lashes lay black
against her pale cheeks. His lips touched them, brushed
her lips, her breasts. With quickening heartbeat, she
felt herself responding with a growing intensity, and
ardor that swiftly culminated in a wild abandon.

As their bodies fused, a warm velvet darkness
seemed to envelop her and she felt as though she were
floating free, soaring above and beyond their bed of
rabbit furs into a world unbound by time and place.

The next morning she awoke with a feeling of
languor, a sense of well-being she had never known.
She stretched in contentment and turned to look at
Tariq, who lay sleeping at her side. In repose, his face
lost its harsh, brooding, forbidding expression and gave
an impression of quiet strength and depths she had yet
to know. It was this thought that he was withholding
something that disturbed her and spurred her to
penetrate his reserve. As she watched him, Livia could
not help but admire the breadth of his shoulders, the
strong body that had so possessed her the night before.

Still, she told herself sternly, he had taken her
against her will. She did not belong to this man of
unbridled passions and swiftly changing moods. She
belonged to Aguilar. She must escape this seducer of
women, and quickly, before he could bed her again.

Quietly, she slipped from their bed, donned her
rumpled garments and hurried to the royal tent where
she was challenged by a burly guard who barred her
way.

"The king sleeps, and does not wish to be awakened
until the sun is high over the mountains."

Livia assumed a regal air and with an imperious tone,

said, "I must see him at once on a matter of great importance. If you refuse me an audience, he will have your head!"

Moments later, she presented the scowling sovereign with the letter from his mother.

As his eyes traveled down the page, Livia watched his face carefully for a reaction. She well knew what it said, for Ayxa had made no secret of her position and her admonishments to Boabdil, which she had set forth in her letter.

> For shame, to linger timorously about the borders of your kingdom when a usurper is seated in your capital. Why look abroad for perfidious aid when you have loyal hearts in Granada? The Albaycin is ready to throw open its gates to receive you. Strike home vigorously. A sudden blow may mend all, or make an end. A throne or a grave! For a king there is no honorable compromise!

He read the letter through twice, then gazed through the doorway to the distant mountain peaks. As if immersed in a dream in which he beheld a vision of Granada, he murmured:

"Granada, beautiful Granada with its stately Alhambra, its delicious gardens, its fountains sparkling among groves of orange, citron and myrtle." His slender fingers clutched his prayer beads. "What have I done that I should be an exile from this paradise of my forefathers, a wanderer and fugitive in my own kingdom, while a murderer sits upon my throne? Surely Allah will befriend the righteous cause. One blow, and all may be my own!"

Watching him, Livia recalled what Ayxa had told her on the eve of her departure from Granada.

And then as though suddenly aware of Livia watching him, Boabdil waved a hand in airy dismissal. "You may go."

Livia drew herself up to her full height, took a deep breath to bolster her courage and looked him straight in the eye. "I wish to speak with you about a personal matter."

His face broke into a smile of understanding. "Ah yes, it was you who warned me of Zagal's plot against my person. Now you wish to claim your just reward." He paused, as though embarrassed, then cleared his throat and went on. "And a fitting reward you shall have, but we must wait until I return to the Alhambra, for I have not enough silver or gold in this encampment with which to reward you."

Livia shook her head vehemently. "I wish no reward, sire." She suppressed a smile at the expression of relief that crossed his face at her refusal and it gave her courage to go on. Blushing furiously, she said, "I do request a favor."

He waved his hand in a sweeping gesture. "Anything you wish!"

Fixing him with a steady gaze, she said, "I wish you to give me safe conduct to Ferdinand's court in Cordoba."

Boabdil's eyes widened and he gaped at her in surprise. His nervous hands, fingering the prayer beads, stilled. "But what is this? The wife of my commander, Tariq Ibn Ziyah, wishes to flee our kingdom?"

Livia stiffened. "I am the wife of Tariq in name only. He much prefers—" she caught herself just in time— "another."

"That I doubt," Boabdil said dryly.

"It is the truth!"

Boabdil shook his head stubbornly and rose from his throne, as if to end the interview. "Tariq is my most valued commander. I cannot afford to affront him. He is a proud and gallant warrior. I know him well. He would not take kindly to my aiding you in your folly." He smiled benignly down upon her. "Legions of Christian women have wed Moors and learned to love them, to lead happy and peaceful lives. I suggest that you do the same."

Livia threw out her hands in entreaty. "But I tell you, Tariq would not care if I were gone. He would not even notice my absence—"

"Enough!" interrupted Boabdil. "You do not understand the Moor. It may be as you say, that he loves another; but to the Moor, his wife is a most treasured possession, inviolate. Aside from that, Tariq has only one wife. The Koran countenances four. If he desires another, he is free to marry her. You need not leave him!"

Livia stared at him aghast.

Seeing her shocked expression, he abandoned that course and said, "If I let you go, Tariq would never forgive me. I can ill afford to lose even one loyal follower, let alone my commander-in-chief!" He sank down again upon his throne. "In any case, there is no use discussing the matter. Ferdinand and I are no longer on amicable terms, and I cannot risk our tenuous footing by putting a fly in the ointment.

"But I am betrothed to one of his captains!"

Boabdil eyed her sternly. "You are *married* to Tariq Ibn Ziyah!"

Desperately, Livia searched her mind for an adequate reply, but she found none.

Boabdil sighed, took up Ayxa's letter and turned it over thoughtfully in his hands. "Now I must set my own house in order. You will accompany me and my squadron back to Granada."

Overwhelmed with disappointment, Livia stood motionless, tears welling in her eyes.

"Begone!" cried Boabdil, clapping his hands for the guard.

Livia's shoulders sagged in despair as she turned from him and strode from the royal tent.

Good as his word, Boabdil called together his scanty band of cavaliers. Livia watched morosely as they gathered before him on the barren slope.

"Who is ready to follow his monarch unto the death?" shouted Boabdil. Every one laid his hand upon his scimitar. "Let each man arm himself and prepare his steed for an enterprise of toil and peril. If we succeed, our reward is empire!"

Livia cast a speculative gaze over their handsome Arabian horses, and pressed her lips together in a determined line. Soon she would mount one and fly—not to Granada, but to Cordoba!

Chapter 30

Shortly before dawn, Livia stole from Tariq's tent and made her way to the corral on the outskirts of the encampment. She held her breath as she crept in a wide circle around a guard who sat cross-legged on the ground, dozing. She drew near the band of horses and in the light of the rosy dawn that enameled the slate-gray sky, she chose one that looked particularly handsome and well-muscled. She entwined her fingers in his mane, led him a short distance from the others and leaped lightly up his back. Still clutching his mane, she leaned forward, gripped his body with her knees and dug in her heels.

Suddenly, the animal let out a loud neigh and reared up, as if to toss her from his back. At the same instant, a voice behind her said sharply, "So eager to depart, my Zahareña?"

Livia gasped, her head snapped around and she saw Tariq, one hand on the horse's rump, the other holding onto his tail with an iron grip.

"Tariq!" she cried, feeling her heart skip a beat. His dark eyes were rimmed with white, his features contorted with anger.

In a menacing voice, he said, "You have chosen a fine stallion. Boabdil's!" He placed his hands firmly about her waist and lifted her down. "I will find you a more suitable mount."

Now she sat stiff and silent before Tariq on his own mount as they rode with Boabdil through the high rugged mountains between the border and Granada. An advance guard galloped swiftly through the valleys and paused to look out cautiously from the summit of every height while the squadron followed warily at a distance.

Livia uttered a fervent prayer that the entourage would meet no one in the fastness of the mountains, for the richness of their armor and attire showed them to be warriors of noble rank, and their leader rode with a lofty demeanor which left no doubt as to their identity.

For two nights and a day they pursued their arduous journey, avoiding all populated parts of the country and choosing the most solitary passes. Often the roads were mere mule paths over which they straggled amid rocks and along the brink of precipices. They clambered up craggy heights and descended into frightful chasms with narrow and uncertain footholds. Despite her aversion to the Moors, Livia accorded them a grudging respect, for though they suffered severe hardships and fatigue, they endured them without complaint. Her own bottom was bruised and numb, but she would die before she would admit it, or admit that riding with Tariq's arms securely about her was not altogether unpleasant. Her gaze fell on Khadija, who rode saucily at Boabdil's side. Now and again Khadija would cast a sidelong glance at Tariq, and when her flirtatious looks were intercepted by Livia's angry glare, she would avert her eyes quickly. If Tariq noted the clash of glances, he showed no sign of it.

Shortly after midnight, they descended from the mountains and galloped across the plain to the city of Granada. All was dark and silent. They passed along quietly under the shadow of its walls until they arrived near the gate of the Albaycin. Here Boabdil drew up his mount and ordered his followers to halt and remain concealed. He gestured to two warriors in his band.

"You!" Boabdil jerked his head toward the gate, "this way." They resolutely spurred their horses to the gate, and Boabdil knocked sharply on it with the hilt of his scimitar.

Livia shivered in the cool night air. Tariq's arms drew closer around her. She heard the low rumble of voices as the strangers were challenged and asked who sought to enter at that unseasonable hour.

"Your king!" Boabdil exclaimed. "Open the gate and admit him!"

The guards swung their lanterns high, and on recognizing their youthful monarch in the golden aura of light, they drew back, their faces betraying their awe. They threw open the gates and Boabdil and his followers entered unmolested. They spread swiftly through the town. Tariq and the other cavaliers galloped to the homes of the principal inhabitants of the Albaycin, thundered at their portals and summoned them to rise and take arms for their rightful sovereign. Livia, breathless with fear and excitement, clung to the charger's mane and prayed they would not be struck down by Zagal's men before Boabdil's forces could be marshaled.

The call was obeyed instantly. Trumpets resounded through the streets. The gleam of torches and the flash of arms revealed people hurrying to their gathering places. After a while, Tariq turned his mount toward the Alcazaba, where he retired with Livia to fall into a fitful sleep. With grim foreboding, Livia made note of the exits from the fortress. As soon as it was light, she would seek out Rashid and Hajai—if only Zagal would keep to the Alhambra.

By daybreak, the whole force of the Albaycin was rallied under the standard of Boabdil. As Livia had feared, tidings of their arrival roused El Zagal from his slumber. Tumult in the streets brought Livia and Tariq to their feet. Peering out a window, Livia's heart lurched at the sight of the fiery warrior, accompanied by his guard making his way, sword in hand, through the streets of the Albaycin. Tariq buckled on his cuirass and took up his scimitar.

"The old wolf hopes to take Boabdil by surprise! But it is he who will be surprised!" He kissed Livia hastily on the lips and was gone.

Livia flew from their chamber down the passageways and outside to join the crowd on the ramparts of the fortress. Her heart pounded and she covered her ears against the clash of swords and shrieks. Boabdil and his men appeared as if sprung from the walls and were fighting vigorously, driving El Zagal and his guard back into the quarter of the Alhambra.

The combatants halted before the Great Mosque and the throng drew back forming a circle. In the clearing stood Boabdil and El Zagal, fighting hand to hand with implacable fury.

Suddenly a familiar figure leaped into the foray, brandishing his scimitar. "Tariq!" Livia breathed. As she leaned forward between the stone merlons to see, others joined the fray in an attempt to separate the figures. Abruptly, the throng re-formed itself, the clearing was alive with men engaged in deadly combat. With bated breath, Livia clung to the merlon until at last she saw that Boabdil and his defenders were succeeding in driving El Zagal from the square.

The battle raged on and on in the streets and squares of the city until cramped within such narrow limits, both parties went into the fields and fought until evening. Many fell on both sides. At night each party withdrew into its quarter until the morning gave them light to renew the conflict.

With the morning, Livia, beside herself with worry over Rashid's safety, resolved to go herself to the house of Hajai. Surely Hajai's family would have news of her and Rashid. Livia put on her ragged brown cloak and had crossed the hall toward the portal when she was detained by a servant who pressed a message from Hajai into her hand. A long, tremulous sigh escaped her. The amah had fled the Alhambra and taken refuge with her family. Rashid was with her. Her first impulse was to hurry to Rashid and bring him back to the fortress, but she immediately thought better of it. The child would be safer with Hajai in an obscure court of the Albaycin than here in the fortress which could be taken at any moment. Livia let out a wistful sigh and with heavy steps returned to her room.

For several days the two divisions of the city remained arrayed against each other. The defenders of the Alhambra, greater in number, contained most of the nobility and chivalry; but Boabdil's supporters were men strengthened by labor and habitually skilled in the exercise of arms.

Each night Tariq would return to their chamber only to fall into an exhausted sleep until morning, when he would again lead his squadron into the foray. Livia, lying sleepless at his side, tense and on edge, would tell herself that she would know no peace until this carnage ended. Inwardly, she knew a deeper yearning that made her toss and turn night after night. She would not admit, even to herself, that she longed for the comfort of Tariq's arms about her, the urgency and excitement of his embrace, the contentment she always felt after the passionate union of their bodies.

In the days that followed, the Albaycin underwent a siege by the forces of El Zagal. They effected breaches in the walls and made repeated attempts to carry it sword in hand, but were as often repulsed. In retaliation, the troops of Boabdil made frequent sallies; and in the conflicts which took place, the hatred of the combatants arose to such a pitch that no quarter was given on either side.

One evening, after a particularly long and bloody day of skirmishing, Tariq returned to their chamber and sank down on the divan, dour and silent. Weary with battle, his face was lined with fatigue, his eyes hollow in their sockets. Livia's heart went out to him. Suddenly, she felt an overwhelming sympathy for this soldier who fought so valiantly for a cause that was long since lost. She started forward, wanting to kneel beside him and put her arms about him, to cradle his head on her breast and whisper soothing words of comfort. Then thinking better of it, she turned to the window and stared out at the Alhambra on the opposite hill. "Is the fighting done at last?" she murmured.

Tariq let out a deep sigh. "Boabdil has finally recognized the inferiority of his force. He dreads also that his supporters, being for the most part tradesmen and artisans, will become impatient at this interruption of their work and disheartened by these continual skirmishes. He has sent missives to Don Fadrique de Toledo who commands the Christian forces on the frontier, begging for his assistance."

What a blow it must be to Tariq's pride that his sovereign had stooped to enlisting the aid of the Christians. Knowing what it must have cost him to make such an admission to her, Livia said nothing. At last she said, "Surely Don Fadrique will not come to Boabdil's aid."

"Do not be deceived," said Tariq harshly. "Ferdinand is an astute politician. He has instructed his commander to aid Boabdil in all his contests with his uncle."

Tariq was right. Several days later the Christians wound around the base of Mount Elvira. In due course, the challenge to battle was offered to Zagal, which the old king declined. Shortly thereafter, an envoy from Zagal was seen to enter the tent of Don Fadrique.

That afternoon Livia rushed forward to greet Tariq at the door. "What does this signify?" she asked eagerly. "Is the kingdom of Granada to surrender to the Spaniards at last?"

Tariq's face darkened with scorn as he thrust her aside and strode into the room. "Cease your foolish prattle, woman," he said sharply. "Granada will never surrender, and you would do well to remember it!"

Bristling, Livia said with haughty contempt, "Infidels can never stand against a holy war fought by the true believers, and you would do well to heed my warning!"

"Holy war, indeed!" Tariq scoffed. "Even now,

Ferdinand's captain listens to the proposals of El Zagal, who is doubtless offering to enter into an alliance on terms still more advantageous than those of Boabdil!"

Arms folded across his chest, Tariq paced the floor, silent and scowling, until Livia was tempted to provoke an argument with him if only to end the unbearable silence that rose like a wall between them. It seemed to her that he seethed with hatred for all Christians.

Tariq's fears were not realized. Don Fadrique broke off negotiations with Zagal and went back to the border, leaving the Moorish kings to continue fighting until an uneasy truce developed out of exhaustion.

Chapter 31

The decision by Turkey and Egypt to jointly come to Granada's aid was an unexpected development in the spring of 1487. The news bolstered Tariq, but worried Livia who was totally unprepared for this turn of events, which was sure to prolong the war. A war, that with each conflict, increased the possibility of death for both Aquilar and her son's father.

On a blustery day later in the season, Julian risked slipping from the Alhambra to visit his sister in the rival quarter of the city.

"Ferdinand is going to take Malaga," he said with excitement. "Its seaport is vital to the Moors, and Ferdinand doesn't want to take the chance that it will be refortified by the Egyptians and Turks who plan to take the town."

Livia's smooth brow furrowed in a frown. She was thinking not of Malaga's value to her sovereigns, but of the danger to Nizam and Raduan.

On the eve of Palm Sunday, Tariq told her, in a voice heavy with irony, that the Catholic monarch, along with Don Alonzo de Aguilar, had started toward Malaga.

Livia refused to discuss the matter. Inwardly, she hoped Malaga would fall quickly with a minimum of bloodshed. She was concerned for her sister-in-law and for Aguilar. The horror of this war was that Livia loved people on both sides.

The following Monday, after visiting with Rashid, she hurried through the crowded streets of the

Albaycin toward the Alcazaba. The people were in ferment and it seemed El Zagal's name was on every tongue. He had left Granada at the head of a large force to relieve the territory near Malaga, currently under enemy attack.

Hard on the heels of his departure, Ayxa escaped her prison in the Tower of Comares and went to the Alcazaba, where she kept a vigilant eye on Boabdil.

It was while strolling along the parapet of the fortress two weeks later that Livia and Ayxa caught sight of scattered puffs of dust rising from the *vega*. As they watched, men appeared out of the clouds, spurring their horses toward the city.

"It is the news we've waited for!" cried Ayxa. "Victory!"

They hurried down to the courtyard to discover the men were not scouts, but fugitives from the Moorish army who brought the first incoherent account of its defeat. Ayxa paled and clutched Livia's arm as if she were too weak to stand.

Each of the soldiers who attempted to tell the tale spoke of unaccountable panic and dispersion. None knew how or why it came to pass.

Hour after hour the arrival of other fugitives confirmed the story of ruin. The disgrace ignited widespread dissatisfaction with Zagal and popular acclaim for Boabdil to be reinstated in the Alhambra.

That evening, shortly after sunset, Livia and Tariq made their way to the Hall of the Ambassadors where the court had assembled to celebrate Boabdil's ascendancy to the throne. The hall rang with music and laughter as brass trays laden with roast stuffed lamb, figs, raisins, pomegranates, almonds, candies and pastries were brought before the courtiers who lounged upon silken floor cushions. Young female slaves danced with abandon to the music of lute, tambourine and flute.

With a wry smile, Livia turned to Tariq. "Much as I fear and detest Moors, I must confess I'm relieved to see Boabdil restored to power. He, at least, appears to wish only peace."

Scowling, Tariq shook his head. "Do not be deceived, my innocent. Boabdil puts no great faith in the duration of the loyalty of the multitude. He knows he is surrounded by hollow hearts and that most of the courtiers of the Alhambra are secretly devoted to his uncle."

Livia's dark eyes widened in surprise. "Has he not ordered the beheading of some principal nobles who zealously supported his uncle?"

Tariq shrugged. "Executions of the kind are matters of course during any change in government. It does not mean that—"

Livia's attention was distracted by a dancer who appeared to materialize from the curling smoke of the gleaming braziers. She was garbed in sheer chiffon, layers of crimson, gold and orange, that accentuated the volumptuous curves of her figure. Diamonds and sapphires sparkled from her sleek black hair, catching the light from the wall sconces. Gold-hooked earrings, bracelets and anklets jingled as she moved. She seemed to reflect a moment with closed eyes. The rhythm of the music quickened and as she looked up, her ebony eyes shone with fire. She glided forward like a cobra, fluttering her palms together while she leaned her head as though listening to an incantation. Then, wending her way through the crowd, she paused before Tariq.

Khadija! Livia felt as though the blood had ceased flowing through her veins.

The throbbing music continued and Khadija's hips writhed sensuously. Her arms reached out beckoning, as she clicked her fingers in a tantalizing invitation to Tariq. She whirled about, her sinuous body revolving before them. As the music rose, swelling to a full pitch she sank to her knees, her head thrown back, her full breasts thrust toward Tariq, luring him to possess her. Regaining her feet, she undulated before them. Arms outstretched, her fluttering fingers caressed the air in an eloquent message as she gazed into Tariq's face through half-lidded eyes, smiling seductively.

Livia's gaze flew to Tariq. He betrayed no expression as he sat motionless, watching the woman before him in sober silence. As Khadija danced on, as though one with the swelling melody, Livia had a terrible feeling of loneliness. It was as if she stood in a solitary corner at a gathering where she was the only stranger. She bit her lip savagely to keep from shrieking at the woman to be gone, and gripped the sides of the cushion beneath her to keep from leaping to her feet and running from the hall. At length, Tariq bowed his head in a solemn nod to Khadija. Whether in approval of her performance, in dismissal, or in silent acknowledgment of their commitment to one another, Livia could not tell. She only knew that for the first time in her life, she felt an overwhelming desire to plunge a dagger into the heart of another human being.

Khadija moved on, her graceful figure swaying about the room, not pausing before any other men present, Livia noted ruefully. She sat stiffly erect, not trusting herself to speak.

After they returned to their chamber and had retired to their bed, Livia lay silent beside Tariq, her long slender form as rigid as a rapier. When Tariq turned to her and reached out to draw her closer, she rolled on her side, presenting her back to him.

"What is this foolish behavior?" asked Tariq in a baffled tone. He rose up on his elbow and peered down into her face, her stricken expression revealed by the moonlight. "Can't we continue the merrymaking begun earlier this evening?"

"If the celebration was well begun, it was for you and Khadija," said Livia over the strangling sensation in her throat.

Tariq let out an exasperated sigh. "So it is Khadija once again who troubles you." He sank down onto his back. "I know of no other way to prove what should be accepted as truth simply because I say it is so. Think what you like."

Moments later, his deep even breathing assured Livia that he was asleep. Tears of frustration formed in the corners of her eyes and rolled down her cheeks. She would not admit, even to herself, the depth of her disappointment that he had not taken her in his arms to reassure her.

Chapter 32

As the days slipped away, the populace extolled Boabdil to the skies and the name of El Zagal became a byword of scorn. Zagal and the handful of followers made a gloomy retreat toward Granada only to find the gates of the city closed to them. The deposed monarch turned for a city within a few leagues of Granada. Here he remained to rally his forces and avail himself of any sudden change in the fluctuating policies.

Livia settled into the rhythm of life at the Alhambra once again. She spent pleasant sunny afternoons playing with Rashid, visiting with Ayxa, or strolling in the gardens. Even though Tariq had forced her to share his chamber, to her astonishment, she felt content and her cheerful demeanor was no longer feigned. And of course there was Julian, whose ebullient air never failed to lighten her spirits.

One rainy morning late in March, Julian appeared unexpectedly on the threshold of Livia's room garbed in a white turban, green and white striped cloak and sturdy boots. His eyes were alight and his lips curved in a secretive smile.

"I've come to bid you good-bye, *niña*. Soon I depart from Alhambra."

"Julian, no!" Livia cried out in protest. "You cannot leave me!"

Julian patted her shoulder comfortingly. "Do not ruffle your feathers. I will return." He laughed with charming arrogance, threw out his chest and gave her a mock salute. "I go on a mission for the king."

"You!" exclaimed Livia. "I cannot believe it!" Suddenly, she had the oppressive feeling that the last grains of his good sense were running like sand from an hourglass, and with it, most of his caution. The streak of recklessness in him—his craving for excitement—would not be denied.

Julian grinned and dropped down on the divan, his expression serious. "Nonetheless, it is true. Boabdil wishes to send letters to the Christian sovereigns announcing the revolution of Granada in his favor. He solicits their protection for all who have returned to their allegiance and for those of all other places which should renounce support of his uncle. By this means, the whole kingdom of Granada will soon be forced to acknowledge Boabdil's sway and will be held by him as a vassal of the Castilian crown."

Livia smiled in amusement. "Boabdil is more clever than we gave him credit for, though I suspect Ayxa's fine hand is directing him. But why do you carry the message?"

"Boabdil doesn't know whom he can trust. He wisely chose a courier, half-Christian, half-Jew, who has nothing to lose and much to gain by carrying out his mission." Julian threw out his arms in a jubilant gesture. "Me!" At the sight of the stricken expression on Livia's face, he went on. "There is no danger. If I am apprehended, I will claim to be an apostate Moor, Jew or Christian, whatever the occasion demands."

Livia smiled at him fondly and let out a resigned sigh. "I see the wisdom of Boabdil's choice. Go with God."

After Julian left, Livia's apprehensions grew. Thoughts of a thousand pitfalls plagued her. She would not rest easy until he returned to Granada.

Her fears mounted when, ten days later, a messenger arrived at the Alhambra bearing letters from the Catholic sovereigns. She dashed down to the hall to meet him, but when she asked for news of Julian, the courier shrugged. He knew nothing of Julian Larreta. Fraught with worry, Livia waited in a fever of impatience until the next morning when Boabdil held court, listening to petitions. Her turn finally came. Resolutely she approached him, presented her case and asked that he send someone to seek out Julian. Boabdil, clearly elated by the news from the Catholic sovereigns who had complied with his request, and caring nothing for Julian's welfare, dismissed her summarily, denying her request. Choking down tears of vexation and despair, Livia fled from the hall.

As the days dragged past and Julian did not return, her nerves were frayed beyond endurance and she grew cross. She longed to ask Tariq to help her to find Julian, but she would not, for since she had repulsed him on the night of Khadija's seductive dance, they had carried on a tense truce, speaking only when necessary. He had not attempted to make love to her again and this, too, had put her in a fine temper. Still, she must do something about Julian.

In desperation, she penned a letter to Nizam. Surely Nizam could prevail upon Raduan to find Julian. Optimism flared within Livia as she hurried into town to the Corral del Carbon where she found a grizzled one-eyed peddler loading an ancient pack-mule. Livia showed him the handful of dinar she had snatched up from the pouch in her marriage chest, and he agreed to take her message to Malaga.

She dropped several coins into his clawlike hand. "Half now, half when you return."

The man scowled and stroked his matted gray beard. "I cannot say when I'll be back. I must sell my wares along the way, purchase new goods in Malaga, travel the seacoast, then north to Granada."

Livia looked skeptically at the broken-down mule. "Please. I will pay double if you ride straight to Malaga and return at once."

The old Moor's one good eye stared balefully at Livia. "I must follow my route," he said relentlessly. "My customers expect me."

Biting her lip in vexation, Livia pressed the letter into his hand and turned away. There was nothing to do but wait. That same afternoon, on May 7, 1487, Ferdinand marched directly for Malaga.

After a week had dragged past, Livia began to pay daily visits to the caravansary, hoping to find the peddler. On the day when she had almost despaired of ever seeing him again, she spied him slumped in a corner of the courtyard, deep in his cups. She bore down on him and shook him by the shoulder.

"What of my message?" she demanded in an urgent whisper. "Have you brought a reply?"

He raised his head, and the one red-veined eye stared at her, uncomprehending.

With an effort, she held onto her temper. "My letter, I gave you a letter two weeks ago. Did you deliver it?"

The Moor nodded, but when she shook him again, pressing him for Nizam's answer, he shook off her hand and muttered, "No message. There was no message for you." His head lolled and dropped to his chest in a drunken stupor.

As the hot days of summer wore on, all the news from Malaga was bleak. Having surrounded the town by land and sea, the Christians attacked. The fire from the Spanish batteries was incessant and frightful damage was made by the seven great lombards. The Christians took the suburbs. Then, Queen Isabella swept into camp and insisted that offers of peace be made. Yet the Moorish commander refused to acknowledge this message. He insisted the offer was made in despair and now counted on the autumn rains to defeat the Spaniards.

Livia pursued her tasks in morose silence, convinced that her message had never been taken to Malaga. Then one sunny morning an *adalide* who brought intelligence for Boabdil also brought a letter from Nizam. Hope soared within Livia as she ran to the small

private garden of Daraxa, where she could be alone to
read it. As her eyes traveled down the page of fine
script, her bosom swelled in consternation.

I could not write at once because I didn't know
about Julian then. Now he is with us, safe for the
time being, so set your mind at rest.

Livia frowned, not liking the tone of Nizam's words.
She read on:

The Spaniards make preparations to storm the
city. Towers of wood have been built to move on
wheels, each capable of holding a hundred men.
They are furnished with ladders to be thrown to
the tops of the walls, for the descent of the troops
into Malaga.

We now face possibility of famine. All the grain
in the city has been ordered to be gathered and
stored for the sole use of those who fight. Even
this is dealt out sparingly.

Everyone who wants peace, mourned over the
resistance which destroys their homes and their
families. It was decided to make private terms
with the Christians before it is too late. Thinking
that Julian would be well received by Ferdinand,
your brother was prevailed upon to take the
proposition to the Christian camp.

Julian was successful with his mission—the
Spanish sovereigns gave a written promise to
grant the conditions. But when Julian returned to
the walls of Malaga, he was apprehended as a spy
by our own soldiers. He managed to escape, but
was wounded in the process. Although a shaft
pierced him between the shoulders, he kept
running and finally reached our house. Julian has
no wish to fight against Ferdinand's forces. He
wishes only to return to the Alhambra.

Livia's lips curved wryly. Even wounded, Julian had not lost his penchant for keeping an eye out for the main chance. Her gaze dropped to the end of the letter.

Though Julian's wound is healing, he remains in constant danger. If he is discovered, he will be executed.

Surely Nizam would keep him safe. A wave of gratitude swept through Livia. How strange fate is, she thought: her fragile sister-in-law who had once been her enemy now proved her most trusted friend and ally.

Chapter 33

Despite constant Spanish reinforcements and fresh summons for the Malaga to surrender with a promise of life, liberty and property in case of immediate compliance, the Moorish commander remained obstinate. He told his officers that the mighty Spanish fleet would be scattered by the winds of heaven and he would attack and utterly defeat the Christians.

"Utter nonsense!" Tariq raged, striding the length of their chamber and shaking his clenched fists over his head. He's a fool—and worse than a fool—to believe he'll win."

Another letter from Nizam came soon after. Livia tore it open eagerly, hoping that some means had been found by which Julian could make his way back to Granada. The news left her weak and shaking.

> Famine has come and is getting worse. The soldiers range about the city, taking by force whatever they find edible. We no longer have bread to eat. Many perish of starvation or of the unwholesome food with which they try to relieve it. It is only because Raduan serves with the army that we have any food at all.
>
> Julian continues to progress, but is weak. He would regain his health more rapidly if only we had nourishing food. Meanwhile, Raduan protests at harboring a fugitive in our house and I do

not know how much longer I can hold out against him. I will do all in my power to keep Julian here, but how long he will be safe, I cannot promise. He dares not go over to the Spanish camp, for they regard him as a *renegado,* an apostate Moor.

For several moments Livia sat staring at the letter, then folded it away and tightly clasped her hands in her lap to still their trembling. But she could not still the fear that gripped her heart.

Tariq's prophecy proved accurate. Early one morning when the soldiers of Malaga descended from their stronghold to assault the Christians, they were rushed on all quarters. The Spaniards opened fire from their bulwarks and the Moors fled in confusion.

Ferdinand refused any terms except unconditional surrender when the starving inhabitants finally treated with him, insisting that they must accept the fate of the vanquished. The Spaniards took possession of the city and the standards of the cross and of Saint James and of the Catholic sovereigns were raised.

It was midafternoon while Livia and Ayxa were engaged in a game of chess in the sultana's apartment that a servant brought Livia a letter written in Julian's flamboyant hand.

At a gasp from Livia, Ayxa's head jerked up from pondering her next move, her brows raised in question.

"Julian writes that King Ferdinand and Queen Isabella have agreed to allow the great mass of Moors to ransom themselves by an amount paid within a certain time."

"Most generous!" Ayxa snorted. "If Ferdinand holds out a prospect of hopeless captivity, the people of Malaga will throw all their gold and jewels into wells and pits and he will lose the greater part of the spoil; but if he fixes a general rate of ransom and takes their riches in part payment, nothing will be destroyed."

As though she had not spoken, Livia read aloud:

All their valuables should be received immediately in part payment of the amount and that the remainder should be paid within eight months—

Ayxa shook her head, clucking, "And if it is not, they will all be considered slaves."

Livia's gaze traveled swiftly to the end of the letter:

Livia, I have no money, nor have Nizam and Raduan. Please find a way to send us the means for our ransom.

A cold fear and crushing disappointment was growing in her. Without reading the rest aloud, she folded the letter and clutched it tightly in her hand. It would not be wise to let Ayxa hear Julian's desperate plea, for the shrewd woman would quickly divine Livia's intention and put a stop to it. Her hands grew damp, and she drew a deep breath to compose herself. Thank God she had the money. At this moment her tooled leather pouch was safely fastened about her waist under the folds of her tunic.

"Your move, Livia," came Ayxa's impatient voice.

Livia absently slid an ivory rook forward. Whom could she trust to take the money to Julian? She could count on no help from Tariq, for he had banished Nizam from his life on the day she had fled from Granada; and Livia would not humble her pride to ask him to help Julian. There had to be another way.

"Checkmate!" cried Ayxa triumphantly.

Livia smiled and with a slight bow of her head acknowledged Ayxa's victory, thinking: the game has just begun.

That night before retiring Livia donned a sheer white gown then sat on a floor cushion before the table which held her silver filagree mirror and brushed her long shining black hair, abstractedly. Usually she entertained Tariq with tidbits of gossip gleaned from Ayxa or details of the day, but tonight Livia's mind was in turmoil. The silence weighed heavily on the warm night air.

In the mirror reflection she saw that Tariq, seated on the divan, was watching her, carefully. The stark whiteness of his robe and turban accentuated his dark skin and the breadth of his shoulders. Her eyes met his fully for the first time since the night of Khadija's seductive dance. A smile twisted his lips.

"Why so pensive, Livia? I'd think you would rejoice in the Christian victory at Malaga."

She gazed stonily into the mirror. "I am more concerned about Julian. He has never returned from Malaga."

Tariq rose from the divan and she watched in the mirror the springing lithe power of his body as he walked on the soft carpet. He stood behind her and placed his hands gently on her shoulders. "You need not worry about Julian. He can take care of himself, and the Spaniards will hardly harm their own." He bent his head to bury his face in the luxuriance of her hair, nuzzling the thick strands aside, exploring the softness of her neck, kissing her earlobe, her temple.

She wanted to turn to him and fling herself into his arms, to blurt out Julian's misadvantures and his taking refuge with Nizam; but any mention of Nizam brought fire to Tariq's eyes and vengeful words to his lips. She sighed deeply, got up and crossed to their sleeping alcove. Wearily, she sank down on the bed and closed her eyes.

Moments later she felt his weight on the mattress as he lay down beside her. He rose on one elbow and in the pale gleam of the new moon and stars Livia saw him looking at her lovingly. He smoothed her tousled hair away from her face and his fingers trailed down her cheeks, her throat, tracing a path between her breasts. With his free arm, Tariq gathered her to him, his lips hard and warm and searching. She lay passive, submitting to his caresses as one under the influence of opium, her heart and mind distracted with thoughts of Julian and Nizam. She desired only to be sheltered in Tariq's arms, to hear his heart steady beneath her ear as she rested her head on his shoulder.

As though sensing her distress, Tariq made love to her with an urgency, as if to dispel it by demanding her response. He possessed her with a tenderness she would not have believed possible. Still, she lay remote and listless in his arms.

His comforting voice came softly to her ears. "Though we lie as one, you are far from me tonight, my Zahareña."

For one wild moment Livia was tempted to pore out all that tormented her, but reason reasserted itself and she checked the impulse. Not only would Tariq refuse to help her, but worse, he might well decide to prevent her from aiding Julian and Nizam. She made no reply.

Vexed, Tariq turned from her, muttering, "Women!" Shortly thereafter, he fell asleep.

Livia remained awake far into the night, her mind seething, taking up one plan then discarding it for another. She could hide the money and jewels in clothing, or in the sheath of a sword, or in her lute and send it by an *adalide*. Yet, if she were fortunate enough to find one she could trust, how could she be certain he would reach Julian? How could she be sure that the Christians would not capture the messenger and confiscate her valuables? There was Julian's friend, the man her brother had sent to her in Almeria, but how could she find the peddler? Tomorrow she would go into town and seek him out. And if not the peddler, one of the black-robed *alfaquis* who watched the intrigues and machinations of ambitious politicians and looked to their own factions as well. Perhaps she could find a priest enroute to Malaga who would take pity on her brother. There must be a way to send money and tomorrow she would find it. She smiled ruefully, thinking how ironic it was that Julian must be ransomed from his own countrymen.

Chapter 34

Livia lay just on the verge of coming fully awake. Slowly, her arm slid over the empty bed and a vague sense of disquiet assailed her. Then, like a stormcloud, the problem of ransom. Suddenly the solution came to her. She leaped out of bed. In her bridal chest she found the bundle of ragged garments she had worn on her journey to the border, for it would not be safe to appear well-to-do. She dressed quickly, donning the brown tunic and cloak, secured the pouch containing her dowry to her belt, snatched up some dried fruit and meat from a brass tray and stuffed them into a carpetbag.

Livia hastened along the dimly lit corridors to Rashid's room and after securing Hajai's promise to take good care of her son, kissed him good-bye and made her way through the busy halls of the Alhambra and outside to the royal stables.

Summoning a confident smile for the stable-boy, Livia ordered him to saddle her mount. On occassion she had ridden out with Tariq and if the boy now wondered at her riding out alone so early in the morning, the silver dirhem she pressed into his grubby palm satisfied his curiosity. She leaped astride the horse and with hands that seemed frozen to the reins, kept the animal at a slow walk. Afraid that she would be stopped and questioned, Livia did not breath freely until she had passed through the gate of the city. She spurred her mount to a canter as she turned his head south toward Malaga.

On the afternoon of the third day, when the molten sun burned high overhead, Livia drew rein on a low rise at the foot of the mountains. Before her, in a wide valley rose the walls and towers of Malaga, and beyond, the *vega* white with tents of the Christian encampment, their pennons fluttering victoriously in the breeze. She murmured a silent prayer that Nizam still resided at the same address she had named in a letter.

Livia's journey had been agonizing for she had had to remain ever alert for roving fugitives, not daring to trust anyone until she was safe in Nizam's house. At every sound of horsemen approaching or hunters thrashing through the underbrush, she would fly for cover. She was grateful for her journeys with Tariq from Zahara and the border in Boabdil's entourage, for she had learned how to find shelter for the night, when to rest her mount and where to seek water. Nothing is ever lost, no experience without benefit, she thought. Ironically, it was Tariq's tutelege that enabled her to make good her flight from her alabaster prison.

She urged her horse into a brisk trot. As Livia drew near the gate of the city, every nerve in her body was taut, her stomach in a knot. Here she would face the greatest danger.

A hawk-nosed guard stepped forward to bar the way with his lance. When he demanded her papers, Livia said imperiously, "I am the Contessa de Silva, wife of the Count Enrico de Silva of Seville."

The guard eyed her suspiciously. "You speak with the tongue of a Sevillana, but your clothing is not one of a noblewoman."

"Naturally not!" Livia retorted. "Do you think we announce to all the roving bands in the countryside that we are persons of wealth and position? The Count de Silva and I journey to Malaga for the purpose of purchasing Moorish slaves."

The soldier cocked his head and surveyed her through narrowed lids. "And where is your husband? And, where are your attendants?"

Livia sniffed and cast down her eyes. "Alas, his horse stumbled on a mountain precipice. He lost his balance and fell down a steep slope. Even now our servants have gone to rescue him." There was no need to feign agitation, since her waxen pallor lent truth to the lie. "You must let me pass at once. I must find a physician to help him."

She saw doubt clouding the guard's eyes and before he could voice the unpleasant thought that her husband would not likely survive such an accident, she swallowed hard and blinked back tears of desperation.

"I beg you, allow me to pass!"

He gave a hopeless shake of his head. "The doctors are all busy with the wounded and dying—"

"Oh, please!" Tears coursed down her cheeks.

With a resigned shrug, the guard stepped back and Livia urged her mount inside the city.

Devastation met her eyes everywhere. Livia pulled her cloak up across her face, covering her nose and mouth, but she could not hide the sight of the walking dead, and emaciated bodies lying unburied, those who would have buried them perished as well. Her stomach lurched at the stench of decaying flesh which lay over Malaga.

What would become of the old people and children? She could have wept with pity for the once-happy families now scattered, never again to be united. Rashid rose to her mind. The heart-wrenching thought of being separated from her son was not to be borne.

She forced her tired steed forward and at length turned down a narrow cobbled street lined with white-washed houses. Small wire cages adorned the walls, but no bird lived to warble a song, nor did a single flower bloom in the once-colorful windowboxes. She dismounted, looped the horse's reins to a post and pounded upon the scarred green wooden door of Nizam's house. Livia's wildly beating heart seemed to echo the sound. When after several moments no one answered, she thumped on the door again then peered up at a window. She saw a white curtain flutter then fall back into place.

In a little while the door was flung open and Livia was pulled inside a dim candlelit room. The door slammed shut behind her and all at once sinewy arms caught her up in a fervent embrace.

"Livia!" Julian murmured against her hair, *"Madre de Dios!* What are you doing here? I had not intended for you to come to this place of death!"

Livia stepped back and surveyed him critically. She would not have recognized him had they met on the street, he was so thin and pallid; though his eyes sunken in sockets above hollowed cheeks still shone. At last she managed to speak. "It was the only way."

Footsteps sounded from the rear of the house and Nizam appeared in the doorway, her face taut with alarm. Her black hair, dull and lifeless, was skewered into a knot atop her head. Her thin gray tunic matched her careworn expression and her shoulders were hunched. Lines etched around her eyes made her appear ten years older than when Livia had last seen her. The soft curve of her chin had become sharp.

"Livia!" she shrieked, and rushed forward to fold Livia in her embrace.

Together they sat down on the threadbare sofa and Nizam poured everyone glasses of a brew concocted from leaves of a plant whose origin Livia could not imagine. After imparting the news of Granada, Livia drew forth her gold-tooled leather pouch.

"I have brought your ransom." She poured out the contents, spilling silver dirhem, gold dinar, rubies, sapphires and emeralds upon the small wooden table. "It is yours."

"No, no!" protested Nizam. "Raduan will look after us."

Julian glanced quickly at Nizam then looked away, but not before Livia saw a flash of astonishment in his eyes that quickly disappeared.

Livia placed a hand on his arm beseechingly. "I

insist. Besides, with me here, you will have another
mouth to feed."

Julian's eyes widened in incredulous disbelief. "You
cannot be serious!"

Livia regarded him steadily and made no reply.

His voice rose in agitation. "You must go, Livia, and
at once. You are not safe here."

"Nonsense. I am a Spaniard—a Castilian. Ferdinand's soldiers will not dare to touch me!"

Relentlessly, Julian shook his head. "You are wrong,
niña. You, just as I, will be considered an apostate
Moor, deserving of a worse fate than the Moors
themselves. The king's soldiers do not pause to ask
your lineage before they arrest you."

Nizam spoke up, her tone urgent and pleading. "Go,
Livia, I beg you. All those who were strangers in the
city and have entered either to take refuge here or to
defend it, were immediately considered slaves."

"But the Christians will not know I am here!"

"They will know," Nizam insisted. "We were numbered by houses and families, and our names taken
down. Our most precious effects were made up into
parcels and sealed and inscribed with our names.
Moors were obliged to leave their houses one by one.
All their money, necklaces, gold bracelets, pearl, coral
and gems were taken from them at the threshold. They
were so rigorously searched that nothing could be
concealed. It is only because of Raduan's promise of
payment of full ransom within the week that we have
been spared. In any case, when Raduan returns, I fear
he will not permit you to stay."

"Since you entered the city without mishap, let us
hope you can depart as easily," Julian said as if to end
their visit. "Pray that the guard has not changed and
that you can convince him that you could not find
anyone to treat your stricken husband. But hurry—
before it is too late." He scooped up her money and
jewels and dropped them into the drawstring pouch.
"And take your dowry with you!"

Reluctantly, she rose to her feet and let out a resigned sigh. "Very well. I will go, but only if you agree to keep my dowry." Tears misted her eyes as she gazed fondly at Julian and Nizam. "If you find no use for it, keep it against your return to Granada."

"Yes, yes!" said Julian, fraught with anxiety. He dumped the contents of the pouch on the table, leaving her with two dinar, and thrust it into her hands then led her to the door. "Now go, before you are discovered."

Livia blinked back the tears that stung her eyelids and took a deep breath to bolster her courage. To leave them now was the hardest thing she had ever done. She clutched her brown cloak about her. Under the lowering sun Livia mounted her horse and turned him toward the city gate.

As the animal clattered across the main square, his hooves striking sparks on the cobbles, Livia saw two of Ferdinand's soldiers emerge from the Great Mosque. She dug in her heels, spurring her mount, but as she passed the men one grabbed the reins, jerking the animal to a halt. He was ungainly tall, with long arms and legs and a wide mouth that stretched in an insolent grin.

"A fine piece of Arab horseflesh," he sneered.

"And a finer piece of female flesh," crowed his leering companion. "Both look good enough to eat!"

Livia's contemptuous gaze traveled over his stiff matted hair and beard, down his bandy legs that reminded her of a rooster.

"Not on your life!" growled the lanky soldier. "The animal will serve me well as my mount."

"And I will mount the maid!" gloated his friend. "She will serve me better!"

He reached up, clasped Livia about the waist and pulled her off the charger. Her hand flashed out, striking him violently on the cheek.

Snarling, the man twisted her arm behind her back. Her cloak dropped to the ground.

"Unhand me, you *renegado!*" she shrieked, struggling to wrench from his grasp. The man gaped at her in astonishment.

"Here, here, what's this?" questioned the tall man with an insolent grin. "A Moorish maiden who speaks like a Castilian and dresses like a goatherd!"

"Caramba!" exclaimed the other. "It is a trick, you oaf. Don't you see? The wench is Spaniard, gone over to the enemy to save her skin!" His hands encircled her waist and found the pouch. "And to save her fortune, which she carries with her as she flees the town." He let out a burst of laughter that sent a chill down Livia's spine. "We shall have the fortune and then the maid!"

He reached out a filthy hand, snatched her belt and pouch from her waist then caught the neck of her rough cotton tunic, ripped it from her shoulders and flung it aside. She stood quaking, clad only in her thin white undertunic.

The tall soldier smiled slyly. "Let's search her to see what other treasures she has." His long arms reached out for her. Livia let out an earsplitting scream and kicked viciously. He slapped her across the cheek. She bit back a cry and stood rigid while the man's hands explored every inch of her body, lingering over her full young breasts, flattening his palms against the slender curve of her hips, then closing hard around her buttocks.

"She doesn't have anything else," said her tormenter, scowling in disgust. He thrust her toward his companion. "Take her. Perhaps you can find something!"

Livia squeezed her eyes shut and clenched her jaw, suffering in silence while the bandy-legged soldier searched her body, his long, thin fingers pinching her flesh here and there, relishing his search. "No gold, but a greater treasure awaits!"

The tall soldier stood regarding her with a calculating stare. At last he snarled, *"Estupido!* You think only of the moment at hand. The wench speaks with aristocratic accents and, carries herself like a lady. There could well be a greater reward for us if we turn her over to Queen Isabella."

"No!" snapped his companion. His steel grip closed more tightly about her arm. "She is mine and I will have her!"

The other Spaniard caught Livia's free arm and like dogs fighting over a bone they continued to argue over her fate. As their quarrel grew more heated, their shouts drowned out the clatter of hooves as a rider drew abreast of them. Sunlight glanced off his gilt helmet and his raiment indicated he was a captain in Ferdinand's army. Beady black eyes looked out from under brows that met over a long nose, and a wispy moustache drooped over the corners of his mouth.

"Captain, captain!" shrieked Livia. "I beg you! Deliver me from these *renegados*. I am a Castilian, daughter of an aristocratic family of Seville!"

The captain frowned down at her. "You are fomenting discontent among my men!" Before her astonished captors could utter a word, he leaned down and with one swift motion swept her up before him on his black charger and cantered down the crowded street, leaving his men agape, their faces dark with anger.

Livia turned to face her rescuer, tears of gratitude brimming on her eyelids. "I don't know how to thank you! Those vile men did not believe me when I told them I am a countess from Castile!"

The captain's eyes met hers. "I don't either!"

"But you must believe me!"

The officer stared straight ahead as he guided his mount around a corner and pelted down a narrow street. When he spoke, his tone was uncompromising. "Then you need not worry, for you must have the means to pay your ransom."

"No, I have not!" Livia cried. "I have given away everything . . ." her voice trailed off as she realized how ridiculous her words must sound. She lifted her chin in seeming confidence and said, "Take me to Queen Isabella—at once. She will judge me rightly!"

A grim smile spread across the captain's face, and the ends of his moustache drooped further. "You will see our good queen in due course."

"Where are you taking me?" asked Livia, sudden terror constricted her heart.

"To the Alcazaba, where we shut up our prisoners," he replied in flat harsh tones.

"But you cannot!" she exclaimed. She begged, threatened and pleaded with the captain, all to no avail and shortly he herded her into the courtyard of the Alcazaba, with the throng of unhappy captives like a sheep in a fold. She approached an elderly stoop-shouldered Moor who squatted in a corner, his head bent over a battered copy of the Koran. She sank down on the hard-packed ground beside him. "What's to become of us?"

The old man raised rheumy eyes to hers and in a feeble voice replied. "They will send us to Seville, where we will be distributed. Each Christian family will have at least one of us to feed and maintain as servants until the term expires for the final payment of the ransom."

Livia leaned back against the warm wall and closed her eyes. If that were her fate, no family of Spain would dare use her so.

The feeble voice at her side continued. "Some captives have obtained permission to go about among the Moorish towns of the kingdom to collect contributions to aid in the purchase of their liberties."

Livia brightened. "That prospect has possibilities."

"You had best get down on your knees and pray to Allah," said the old Moor, "for that fate will avail you nothing. All our towns are too much impoverished by the war and engrossed with their own problems to help. Listen to me well. All the fifteen thousand captives of Malaga will become slaves!"

Chapter 35

As the blazing sun set over the walls and towers of Malaga, it came to Livia that she missed the swelling notes of the muezzin. Instead, Christian bells rang out over the devastated city sounding the angelus. The inconsistency of her thoughts struck her and she put them from her mind. Still, they were a measure of how much she had changed since her imprisonment in the Alhambra five years ago. She felt a hundred years old.

Gradually, she became aware of the babble of the prisoners in the corrale and as she listened to the rumors flying she gathered that the queen had taken up residence in the Alcazaba, where she had a view of the entire city, and the king had established his quarters in the warrior castle of Gibralfaro.

A commotion at the gate caught her attention and she stood motionless, holding her breath as a squad of soldiers charged inside the enclosure. Livia shrank back in the corner as the eyes of the men combed the mass of citizens, then with threatening thrusts of their lances singled out the most delicate and lovely of the Moorish girls. Her eyes met those of the cocky bandy-legged soldier whose clutches she had escaped outside the mosque. A quick stab of fear went through her and she turned her back, hoping he would have forgotten their earlier altercation. She gave a startled cry as she felt the sharp point of a lance pressing between her shoulder blades. As she turned around, the lance came to rest upon her left breast. The man glowered at her, and a vengeful grin spread across his florid face.

"Move, wench. You are to have an audience with the queen!"

A surge of hope flared within Livia then quickly died. The soldier's sly smile warned her that this was not to be the audience she craved. Her suspicions were borne out when she perceived that the men were counting heads. When they had rounded up eighty young Moorish women, the soldier prodded her again. Her eyes blazing defiance, Livia moved forward.

The captives were driven through the dark corridors of the Alcazaba into the great hall. At the far end of the chamber, the pudgy, jowled Isabella was seated upon a canopied throne flanked by several of her cavaliers. Livia strained to see, but she could not distinguish the knights, for the torches burning high on the walls cast their faces in shadow.

A staff was pounded on the floor commanding silence. Isabella stood and calmly scanned the Moorish women huddled together. An attendant ordered them to form a line and Isabella passed before them, appraising them as though judging prize hunters to be purchased for the royal stables. When she was finished, a benign smile curved her lips. "I see that my men have chosen well. You maidens are privileged indeed, for fifty of you are to be sent to Queen Joanna of Naples, sister to King Ferdinand, and thirty to the queen of Portugal. You will prepare yourselves for the journey immediately."

As Isabella turned away, a mournful protest rose from the crowd of women. Livia darted after Isabella. If only she could speak to the queen, she could convince her monarch that she was a true and faithful subject; and if that failed, she might at least persuade her sovereign to allow her to remain in Spain.

A sharp pain at the back of her head brought her up short as a rough hand clutched a handful of her hair and held fast. She let out a startled cry and her head was snapped about to meet the leering gaze of the long-limbed soldier who had accosted her before the mosque.

"This way, wench!" Keeping a tight hold of her hair, he twisted her about and led her away with the other women.

"Spanish dog!" hissed Livia through lips white with rage. The man gave a jerk on her mane of hair that brought stinging tears to her eyes. She clenched her fists at her sides in an effort to control her temper, knowing it was useless to resist him now. The women were herded into a large room with high slitted windows, lighted by flaring torches in wall sconces. Colorful gowns were piled on the furniture, and tubs were scattered about the room. Apparently, Isabella wished her gifts to present a comely appearance before being sent abroad, thought Livia bitterly.

They were ordered to disrobe. Kettles of steaming water were brought to fill the tubs. Oval cakes of fine castile soap were handed out and under the appreciative eyes of the guards, the young women were made to bathe. Livia stepped into a tub and slid the soap over her body trying to ignore the curious stares of the men who gawked at her ivory skin gleaming in the glow of the torches so unlike that of her olive-skinned sisters. She sank down and closed her eyes, to block everything from her mind for the moment, to revel in the soothing comfort of the water enveloping her body. Suddenly she felt a rough hand trail down the curve of her neck. Her eyes flew open. The leering Spanish soldier knelt beside the tub. He reached for the soap in her hand. "I'll help you—"

Before he could finish speaking, Livia's hand shot out and she swept the slippery soap hard across his eyes.

He shouted an oath and leaped to his feet as Livia's shrieks pierced the air.

Two guards rushed to her side, shouting, "Hold! No one defiles the queen's property! Off with you!" At lance point, they hustled the furious soldier from the chamber.

Livia stepped from the tub and rubbed her skin briskly with a linen towel. From the corner of her eye she saw the guards watching her. Blushing furiously, she put on a long white shift tossed to her by one of the men.

She crossed to a sofa and snatched up a gown made of ivory silk strewn with gold and green flowers, a scoop neck edged with lace, fitted bodice, long sleeves and full skirt. Despite her anxiety, Livia grinned to herself, for the skirt was fitted with a framework of rigid hoops designed to stand away from the figure; a style introduced years ago by Queen Juana of Portugal to hide a pregnancy that could not be attributed to her husband. Though it was still in fashion, Livia surmised that all the gowns were castoffs donated by Isabella's ladies-in-waiting. She donned the gown and was fluffing out her shining black hair when she saw a robust florid-faced soldier enter the room. Her heart beat nervously as he marched straight toward her. She stiffened and faced him with a stony stare as he stopped before her.

In an authoritative tone he said, "One of the queen's men has taken a fancy to the light-skinned Moor." He took her arm and propelled her toward the door. "This way."

As the soldier's intent bore in upon her, Livia's initial fear turned to anger. A knight who enjoyed the queen's favor had singled her out and now she was to be given to him like chattel! When he had satisfied his lust she would be cast aside to be put aboard a ship for Naples—or worse—passed around among his comrades throughout the night! Suddenly the life drained out of her. She felt as though she were dying and feared she would not. Her steps lagged and she stumbled to her knees. The soldier gripped her elbow and dragged her through the halls of the dismal stone fortress.

In the courtyard he swung her up on the back of his horse, leaped up behind her then cantered through the streets, through the gate to the encampment of Isabella's legions. Under the starlit sky, Livia saw row upon row of white tents whose pennons fluttered in the June breeze. Music from stringed instruments and bursts of laughter came to her ears. The soldier drew rein before one of the larger tents, swung off his steed then handed Livia down. He muttered a few words to a guard at the entrance and the man pushed the flap aside and thrust her roughly inside.

Livia stumbled, then regained her balance. In the soft aureole of light shed by an oil lamp, she realized the tent was deserted. It must be the quarters of an important person, she decided, for the walls were hung with woven tapestries, and a rich red and blue Oriental carpet graced the ground. A heavily carved teakwood chest stood in one corner and a bed covered with gold brocade and strewn with colorful pillows occupied the far wall. She sank down on a cushion and sat waiting, her hands clasped tightly in her lap, refusing to succumb to the apprehension which threatened to overwhelm her. Livia squared her shoulders, bracing herself to face this new ordeal.

She had regained a little of her composure when the tent flap was thrust aside and a tall figure wearing the garb of a Spanish captain burst through the doorway. He smiled at her as though she were the only woman in the world, and she was his.

Stunned speechless, Livia could only stare at him. In three strides he crossed the room. His arms went about her waist, and raising her to her feet, he pressed her close to his chest. "Livia, Livia, *mi amor*," he murmured. "I feared you were lost to me forever!"

A sob rose in her throat and in a voice choked with emotion she whispered, "I would wait forever for you, Aguilar."

His lips sought hers, and she clung to him, wishing this moment would never end. At last he drew her down on his bed, adoration shining in his fine brown eyes. Placing his palms on her cheeks, he turned Livia's face toward the soft radiance of the lamp and gazed at her fondly, devouring every feature as though starved for the sight of her.

"You are even more lovely than I remembered," he said softly.

A surge of happiness flowed through her. Aguilar's face was not as she remembered it. It was lean and hard, as though his features had been honed down by years of battle. Like a mantle, he bore the air of one who was a leader of men. His eyes were the same velvety brown with a golden spark in them, and though his mouth was set in a firm line, there was a gentleness about his lips.

"I had resigned myself to waiting until you conquered Granada before seeing you again, Aguilar. I cannot believe my good fortune that you found me here."

"You sparkled among Isabella's Moorish maidens like a diamond among worthless baubles, *mi amor.*"

Livia smiled in amusement, thinking it was more likely her stature and pale skin that set her apart from her honey-toned companions. "Then you must have been among the knights attending the queen in the hall. I could not distinguish one from another," she said, grinning. "And it is just as well, for I'd have rushed forward and flung myself at you and our good queen's guards would have spitted me upon a lance like a chicken."

Aguilar laughed and stroked her hair. "How come you to reside at Malaga?"

Livia let out a long sigh and settled back into the curve of his arm. Though she was loath to do it, she must tell Aguilar about Tariq.

"It began with the Moors laying waste Zahara."

Tears formed in her eyes as she told him of the death of her parents, and of her abduction. She swallowed hard and, choosing her words carefully, told him of her forced marriage, dreading to see his reaction. To her great relief, Aguilar took the news calmly, regarding her with grave attention and making no comment. She went on to tell of her futile attempts to escape, the birth of Rashid, Julian's arrival, and of the game of kings played by the populace, ending with her flight to Malaga to free Julian and Nizam.

When she had done, he looked at her for a time in thoughtful silence. When he spoke at last, it was with a finality that made her uneasy.

"Then Julian can pay his ransom and that of Nizam and Raduan as well. There is nothing more to be done." He gazed deeply into her eyes. "And you must remain with me." He sighed and took her hands in his. "I wish to God these everlasting campaigns were at an end, that we could fly away together to begin our lives anew, but the time is not ripe. However, Queen Isabella travels with her armies and is well protected. You will join her retinue. There you will be safe from harm."

Slowly, Livia shook her head, her eyes full of regret. "I cannot do that, Aguilar. I cannot desert my son." She smiled ruefully. "Though it is no marriage at all, I am wed by Koranic law to Tariq Ibn Ziyah."

Aguilar's sharply chiseled features contorted in a frown, and anger made his voice harsh. "I recognize no marriage with an infidel!"

"Alas, the marriage is a fact in the eyes of the world. But all is not lost, for Tariq—" the words *loves another* caught in her throat and she went on—"may be persuaded to grant me a divorce."

Aguilar stared at her incredulously. "Are you certain this is possible?"

She nodded mutely.

"Then it must be done, and done quickly. Tomorrow

I will arrange for you to proceed to Granada under guard, and upon your arrival you must . . ."

The rest of his words were lost to her, for the question that had tormented her all these long months rose to the surface. She could wait no longer for the answer. When Aguilar had finished, she smiled up into his face and in as casual a manner as she could manage, she said lightly, "A rumor came to my ears that you have a wife."

Once again Aguilar's face darkened. The lines in his cheeks deepened, and his mouth turned down at the corners in a grimace of pain. He sat up straight and held Livia's arm tightly. A look of pleading shone in his eyes.

"Please understand, Livia. I was told you had died at Zahara, that your entire family had been killed. For almost three years I was disconsolate. I refused to believe that you were gone. I nourished a dream of finding you, hoping that somehow you had escaped and hidden from the Moors. Then our army retook Zahara and after days of searching for you, I had to accept that you were not there. I also obtained the list of prisoners taken to Granada, and your name was not among them. Now, of course, I realize you did not march with the other prisoners . . ."

Livia felt a chill prickle the back of her neck. Aguilar was explaining too much, rambling on too long, and as he continued, she knew with deadly certainty that the gossip Khadija had flung at her on that long-ago night in Tariq's tent was true. Livia lowered her eyes. She could not bear to see Aguilar's tortured expression, could not endure listening to his explanations, but she could not drown out his voice.

"One cannot mourn forever," he said softly. "Life must go on. Two years ago I married a gentle young woman of an aristrocratic family." He paused and she glanced up at him quickly. A mist formed in his eyes that tore at her heart. "She was a fine and devoted wife . . ." Again he paused, as though it were difficult for him to go on. At last he said, "Her vigor was as fragile as her beauty. A year ago she gave birth to a daughter. Neither she nor the infant survived."

A pang of sympathy swept through Livia, "I'm sorry, Aguilar," she said.

He took her hands in his comforting grasp. "I loved her truly, but never with the same depth as for you, *querida*. I have never ceased loving you." He let out a long sigh. "In the past, fortune was against us, but our time will come. Soon the Moors will be driven from the land." He smiled down at her. "Even Allah blesses our union. Soon we will be together always. I wish I could delude myself with the pretense that my wife-to-be is my wife of this moment." He shook his head regretfully. "But the prize is sweeter for the waiting." He bent his head to hers, his lips brushed her brow in a parting kiss. "I bid you goodnight."

An overwhelming sense of disappointment surged through Livia. For the first time she wished that Aguilar were not so much the chivalrous, gallant and pious knight. She yearned for him now as she had never yearned for any man, longing to be possessed, wrapped in the safety of his love. Her arms crept upward about his neck and her body, taut with desire, molded to his. She felt his lips, warm and responsive on her own. His hands slid up her back, his fingers moving through her hair. She heard his sharp intake of breath as he pulled her down among the pillows, straining her to him, raining kisses on her brow, her cheeks, her lips.

"Livia, *mi amor*," he whispered, "my love, my true love, I will love you always." Abruptly, he thrust her from him and rose to his feet. "Now I must go before it is too late, before my passion flies in the face of honor."

She smoothed the folds of her flowered silk gown and managed a semblance of a smile, thinking how incongruous it was that Tariq, the man she hated, had possessed her wildly, forcing her to submit to him against her will, and now the man she loved was leaving her as a gesture of honor. She too stood up and ran her fingers through her hair in a careless gesture in an effort to hide her agitation.

"Of course you must go," she said quietly.

As he started toward the door he flung an arm about her shoulders. At the doorway, she turned within the circle of his arm and standing on tiptoe, kissed him lightly on the cheek. "Good night, my love." Aguilar's eyes lingered on the gentle swell of her breast rising above the lace ruffle of her low-necked gown. She trembled, her lips parted.

They stood in a sort of frozen silence. She saw a bereft expression fill his face with a desperate longing. The restraint he had shown thus far now vanished and they were clinging to each other. Livia was hardly aware that they were walking back to the bed. When they were seated, Livia stared up into his face. His deep brown eyes reflected the lamplight and in them she read the naked desire.

"Aguilar," she murmured.

Swiftly, he pushed her back upon the bed and his lips curved in a tender smile as he lay beside her. She felt the hard thrust of his chest against her breasts, the pressure of his thighs, his hunger, as she yielded to the strength of him in a caress that she knew could end only in the ultimate embrace. A vision of Tariq's brooding face rose unbidden to her mind, and resentment surged through her. He had taken her by force, married her against her will and now cast her aside and wanted another. She banished the vision of Tariq and pressed closer to Aguilar, her passion matching his, savoring the sweetness of his embrace. She wished the night might never end.

And yet, when the storm was spent, a slight sense of disappointment crept through her, for the rapture she had expected to feel in the consummation of their love, had escaped her. Aguilar lay with his head on her breast, his face still and peaceful, content. Livia lay wide-eyed and wakeful, her hands resting lightly on his shoulders. For some reason she could not fathom, her desire was unfulfilled.

Chapter 36

Livia was awakened the next morning by the sound of horses snorting and stamping and the clink of their trappings outside the tent. She glanced at the bed beside her. Aguilar had gone. She ran to the doorway, drew back the flap and peered out. The stars were already fading into the cobalt dome of the sky.

She whirled about and, with her back to the doorway, donned her lawn shift and gown. The tent flap parted, the sound of approaching footsteps deadened by the carpet. She felt strong arms encircle her waist. Startled, she spun about and looked up into the adoring eyes of Aguilar. He held her close in an ardent embrace, his mouth lingering on her own. At length he drew back and regarded her solemnly.

"It is time, *muy amada mia*. Parting from you once again is the most difficult task I've ever had to do. But all the sooner you can arrange for your freedom from the Moor so we can be together always."

Wordlessly, she laid her head against his chest and holding onto him with desperate strength, loath to face the moment of departure. Aguilar gently placed a finger under her chin and tilted her face up to his. He bent his head, his mouth seeking hers in a searing kiss to be etched in her memory until they would meet again.

Aguilar led her outside where her steed waited, flanked by chargers bearing two of Aguilar's burly men armed head to toe. Livia mounted her horse and took up the reins. She squared her shoulders, summoned a smile for Aguilar and spurred her mount into a canter. She must look forward, she thought resolutely, always forward. She did not look back.

As they galloped eastward through the opalescent dawn, she noticed that the mountain peaks were veiled in mist. Gradually, the pearl-gray sky was streaked with salmon, and her spirits rose with the sun. With the capture of the seaport of Malaga, the western part of the kingdom of Granada had now been conquered by her Catholic sovereigns.

Throughout the arduous journey to Granada, the night she had spent with Aguilar burned in her memory, and with each long stride of her mount that brought her nearer to the Alhambra, the forbidding image of Tariq's unyielding countenance invaded her mind. A feeling of remorse assailed her that she could not dispel. Tariq's barbaric treatment certainly justified her succumbing to Aguilar, she told herself sternly. There was no reason why she should feel guilty, yet for reasons she could not understand, she now felt she had betrayed Tariq. She had not spent the night in Aguilar's arms to get even with Tariq. That was not the way she would choose to penetrate his granite heart. She had stayed with Aguilar only because she loved him.

The disquieting thought came back to her that even having spent the night in Aguilar's bed, she had felt unsatisfied. Perhaps it had been a mistake to encourage him, but she had so craved his touch, to feel his mouth once more. In a future that looked so bleakly empty, she had to have some fresh memories of Aguilar. Everything would be different once they were married, she reassured herself. She wished she could be as confident as Aguilar that the day of total Christian victory would be soon, but she understood far better than he the determination of the Moors to hold their earthly paradise until the last drop of blood was shed.

It was midafternoon when Aguilar's Spanish cavaliers took leave of Livia at the far boundary of the *vega*.

The soldiers were in no hurry to return to the siege of Malaga. As Livia had done, they spent two nights enroute bedded down in caves in the fastness of the mountains. The crenelated towers of the Alhambra glowed vermilion in the burning June sunshine, and to her astonishment, Livia looked forward to her return with more joy and anticipation than she would have believed possible. "I'm only eager to see Rashid," she told herself firmly.

She entered the Court of Myrtles adorned with a profusion of star-flowered jasmine and deep pink oleander and hurried down the length of the mirrorlike pool breathing in the sweet fragrance of jasmine. She ignored the courtiers who gaped in astonishment at the sight of a disheveled girl in a flowered gown, long black hair streaming out behind her as she hastened through the splendid halls to Rashid's apartment.

She burst through the hangings in the doorway and stopped short, struck by the deathly stillness of the empty sitting room. "This means nothing," she assured herself. "Rashid is resting—that's all." Swiftly she crossed to his bedroom. On the threshold her hand flew to her mouth stifling a gasp. Rashid's bed was neatly made up, and Hajai's mattress and pillow were laid away. This room, too, was deserted.

She tried to still the wild beating of her heart. Hajai must have taken Rashid for a stroll, or into town and had been delayed. Livia rushed to the window, hoping to see them plodding across the courtyard. It was occupied only by the usual beggars and idle passers-by. There was no sign of the amah and her small, sturdy charge trudging at her side. With an effort, Livia fought down panic and drew a cushion over to the window where she forced herself to sit quietly and wait. They would be back soon. She must be patient.

As time dragged on and Rashid and Hajai did not return, she grew increasingly nervous. When at last she could endure waiting no longer, she jumped to her feet and fled from the room. Her heart hammered in her ears as she raced to Ayxa's apartment and burst inside.

Ayxa, in a bejeweled saffron tunic sat before a small table, cards spread before her, her brow furrowed in concentration. Her head snapped up, and her small bright eyes widened in astonishment at the sight of Livia.

"Livia!" she exlaimed with a cry of pleasure. "We thought you had left us!"

"No, no," said Livia bending down and bestowing a perfunctory kiss on her brow. "I was . . . detained in Malaga. We will speak of that later. Where is Rashid?"

Ayxa cocked her head to one side. "Rashid?" she repeated, her voice dry and flat. "Why, I assume he is with his amah."

"Yes, yes," said Livia impatiently, "but where? I did not find him in his chambers as I'd expected."

Ayxa's thin brows rose. "No? Then I would think she has taken him somewhere." Calmly, she turned over a card and placed it face up on the table.

"Of course!" Livia cried. "But where?"

"How would I know, my dear? Rashid's amah does not apprise me of her whereabouts." Ayxa continued to turn over the cards.

With an effort, Livia restrained an impulse to sweep the cards off the table. "I know she does not tell you her plans, but it is almost sundown. She should have been here long since. I thought perhaps she had been summoned to her home in the Albaycin. If she had taken Rashid to stay with her, she would have left word with you, wouldn't she?"

Ayxa shrugged and scowled down at the Queen of spades in her hand. "Perhaps, perhaps not, if it was necessary for her to leave in great haste. Perhaps she left the child with Tariq . . ."

Livia stared at Ayxa, doubt clouding her face, racking her mind to think of someone with whom Hajai may have left a message. After a moment, she said doubtfully, "It is possible he is with Tariq."

She left, hurried along the maddeningly zigzagging corridors to Tariq's apartment.

"Tariq?" she called sharply. "Tariq!" An ominous silence closed in around her. Tears of frustration and worry sprang to her eyes. She brushed them away impatiently with the back of her hand. Quickly, she searched Rashid's chambers. There were no clothes, no toys, no evidence of Rashid's presence there. Livia could think of but one thing to do. Once again she flew through the marbled halls, across the Court of Myrtles, unmindful of sudden shouts and footsteps pounding after her until a hand grasped her arm in a tight grip bringing her to an abrupt halt.

Furiously she whirled about. "Malik!"

His teeth gleamed white beneath his thin moustache as a benign smile spread over his features seared by disillusion and cynicism. "I've missed you, my pigeon. Where have you been?"

"Let me go!" Livia screeched.

His mouth turned down at the corners. "In a moment. Where are you bound in such a hurry?"

"I'm searching for Rashid! Now let me go!" She tried to jerk away, but he held her in a cruel grip.

As though she had not spoken, he went on, smiling. "In the town? Surely you jest. Doubtless he is here in the palace." A look of cunning and malignant satisfaction crept into his eyes. Have you looked in the gardens? He may have drowned in one of the pools."

For a moment a paralyzing fear choked Livia so she could not speak. Then reason reasserted itself. "If he had drowned, the entire court would be buzzing with the news!" she said savagely.

Malik emitted a harsh laugh that made her want to scream. "I was teasing you!" He tugged on her arm. "Come, I will help you find him."

"No! If you wish to help me, search the palace. I will look in the town. If you should find him, sound the bells on the tower of the Alcazaba."

With a violent wrench, she freed herself from his grasp and ran heedlessly across the Square of the Cisterns, through the Gate of Justice, headlong down the hill into the Albaycin quarter. Though she had visited Rashid at the home of Hajai many times during the days when she had taken refuge with Boabdil's court in the fortress of the Albaycin, today she had entered the area from a different direction, and the narrow crooked streets were strange to her.

She turned right, ran down the length of the street and at the corner sighted the familiar stall of a carpet vendor. But when she drew abreast of the shop, it was not the one she knew. She rounded another corner and found herself in the smelly roofed-in streets of the bazaar. The jostling wrangling crowd of shopkeepers crying their wares vied with the louts and mannerless street urchins who darted about. Frantically, Livia dashed down one street then another. She was lost. Darkness had fallen and now nothing was recognizable. The houses were shuttered against the night. Only beggars and derelicts roamed the streets. A ragged urchin racing down the street collided with her. She caught him by the shoulders. "Hold, child!" she commanded. "Tell me where—" she stopped abruptly as he kicked out at her and struck at her face with his hand. She dodged the blow and hung on to the wriggling boy.

"Let me go!" he howled.

She shook him hard and his head wobbled on his scrawny neck. "Be quiet, rascal. Tell me, where is the Street of the Infantas?"

He pointed a grimy finger over his shoulder and babbled words she could not understand. She started to loosen her hold on him, then thought better of it. Clutching him tightly by the collar, she started forward. "You will show me the—"

"No!" he shouted, wild-eyed with fright. "Let me go!"

Livia bent down and hissed in his ear. "Enough! When we find the house I'm looking for, you shall have a reward."

"Now!" the child shrieked. "Give it to me now!"

"When we get there," said Livia flatly. "Not before."

"Show me the money!"

With a start, she realized she had not a dirhem to her name. She made no reply. With firm and rapid strides she hurried along the street, pulling the half-walking, half-running child beside her.

Once they found the right street, Livia had no difficulty finding Hajai's house. She rapped smartly on the door. She could have wept with relief when it flew open and she saw Hajai standing in the lighted square of the doorway. She begged a coin from the astonished amah to pay the suspicious urchin, then stepped inside, closed the door and leaned her back against it.

Hajai, in a red and yellow striped tunic and trousers, stood regarding her in amazement. When Livia had caught her breath, she managed a tremulous smile and said apologetically, "I'm sure you have given me up for lost, Hajai, but you see, I've returned, none the worse for wear. Now I will take Rashid home with me."

Hajai's mouth fell open and she stood as though thunderstruck, gaping at Livia.

"Where is Rashid?" Livia demanded. "I've come to take him home."

The little amah's usually lively countenance grew solemn and she ran her tongue over her lips. "Rashid . . . he is not here!"

"Not here!" echoed Livia incredulously. "But he must be here! What have you done with him?"

Hajai's face paled. "I've done nothing with him. They told me I was no longer needed."

Dread began to constrict Livia's throat and her voice rose. "They? Who are they? Who told you you were no longer needed?"

Hajai shook her head dumbly. "I know not who—

one of the servants whom I did not know came soon after you left. He told me that Rashid was to be taken to his mother and that I should leave . . ." her voice trailed away.

Livia could only stare at her, disbelief paralyzing her powers of speech. Rashid had been missing almost a week! Fear flooded through her. When at last she spoke, her voice was a harsh whisper. "Hajai, this cannot be true. No one but you knew where I had gone!"

Hajai dropped her gaze and gave a stubborn shake of her head. "Rashid told others you had gone. The servant told me you had sent for Rashid, that he was to be taken to you. He did not say where."

"What did he look like, this servant?"

Hajai raised her eyes and studied a crack in the ceiling overhead. "He was taller than I, dark-skinned, dark of eye . . . and he wore a full beard," she finished, smiling her satisfaction at her ability to remember.

Her description could fit any one of a thousand Moors, thought Livia, seething with impatience. She managed to hold onto her composure and pressed Hajai further. "Was he frail, heavy, thin, old, young, a soldier, a noble, what?"

"I don't know," Hajai replied shaking her head, for he wore a black albornoz. The mantle hid his figure and his calling."

Livia let out a long, hopeless sigh. "I must go—"

Hajai, overwhelmed with worry and guilt, put a restraining hand on her arm. "Wait, I'll go with you." Moments later Hajai's brother escorted them through the darkened streets to the Alhambra.

Chapter 37

Once in the halls of the palace, Livia ordered Hajai to scour the place high and low for the servant who had spirited away Rashid. Livia rushed to Tariq's apartment where she found him seated cross-legged on the floor polishing the hilt of his scimitar. It's precious gems seemed to mock her in the soft glow of the lamplight. The carpet muffled the sound of her footsteps as she crossed the room and came to a halt before him.

"Tariq!"

He did not look up. "Ayxa informed me of your departure for Malaga," he said coldly. "And Malik told me of your return. If you could not tell me yourself, you could have done me the courtesy of leaving a message in your fine script."

"I had neither the time nor the inclination to write anyone letters," snapped Livia. "And I am not here now to plead for your welcome and forgiveness as the prodigal wife!"

"Then why have you come?" he asked, dipping a cloth into the dish of paste with which he was shining his scimitar.

"Will you put that weapon down and listen to me!"

At her tone, bordering on hysteria, Tariq's head jerked up and his eyes met hers in startled inquiry.

"Rashid is gone," she said in a tremulous voice. "Ayxa doesn't know of his whereabouts, nor does Hajai." Her eyes narrowed speculatively as a new thought struck her. "What do *you* know of his disappearance?"

Tariq shrugged. "I thought he was with you."

She shot him an indignant glance. "Why would you think that? Your reason should tell you I would not risk our child's safety by taking him into a beleaguered city!"

"I was told you had taken him with you."

Hot anger suffused her face with color. "And you believed it! Who told you such a ridiculous tale?"

Tariq shrugged again. "I cannot recall. It may have been one of the servants or one of the nobles. You know how rampant rumors are." He held his scimitar up to the light and rubbed the hilt vigorously.

His casual acceptance of Rashid's disappearance infuriated Livia. She bent down swiftly and snatched the gleaming sword from his grasp and in a voice hysterical with fear shouted, "You—you barbarian—you have done away with Rashid!" Her eyes blazed as she clutched the sword in both hands and lifted it high over her head.

In the moment before she swung it down in a murderous arc on Tariq's head, he leaped to his feet and wrested the weapon from her grasp, shouting, "Have you taken leave of your sense, woman?"

Her breath left her body in a rush. Livia covered her face with both hands and sank to her knees, her body shaking with convulsive sobs. The next morning she felt strong arms about her as Tariq gathered her to him, pressing her cheek against his chest, stroking her hair, murmuring words meant to calm her fears.

"No one has done away with the child. There is no reason. *He* has not attempted to seize the throne, or declared his allegiance to El Zagal, or plotted Boabdil's demise. I will order the city to be searched, and I myself will help search for him. Doubtless he wandered off in a moment when Hajai was not looking and became lost in the city. Naturally Hajai will not admit to being negligent."

"She is not negligent!" Livia burst out. "And Rashid knows where he lives. He has a tongue in his head. If he were lost, he would ask to be taken back to the Alhambra." Despite her efforts to hold them back, tears flowed down her cheeks.

"Of course, but the boy has a vivid imagination and an insatiable curiosity. I warrant he thought what a fine opportunity it was to explore the world while his mama was conveniently gone. I'm sure he thought to enjoy an exciting adventure, no more. A child gives no thought to the worry he may cause others." Tariq took up a clean bit of cloth and gently wiped the tears from her face and kissed her brow. "Don't worry, my Zahareña, we'll find him."

He left her then for a short while. When he returned he told Livia he had reported Rashid's absence to the king's stewards and ordered the royal guard, and his own men as well, to begin the search. "I told them to bring to me at once anyone who has seen Rashid or has news of him. If my men do not find him tonight, tomorrow we will search every part of the city. Rashid will be found."

Livia nodded mutely, knowing there was nothing more to be done at this hour of the night but wait for Tariq's men to report to him. Tariq lifted her gently in his arms and carried her into the bedchamber. Her stomach churned with fear. Her hands were moist and her mouth dry. She lay quietly while he removed her garments then discarded his own and lay down beside her. She made no protest when he took her in his arms; she was only thankful for his comforting presence. But even his tenderness could not dispel her anguish. She lay awake far into the night. Just before she drifted off to sleep, she realized that since her return to Granada, she had not given a thought to a divorce, or to Aguilar.

The days dragged past, and the palace guard, Tariq's men and Livia and Tariq as well, combed the palace and the fortress without success. Tariq divided the city into sectors and ordered his men to scour the city. They searched house-to-house in every street and alley, all to no avail. At the end of each day, Tariq would try to console her, telling her that surely the next day they would find him. And when they did not, Livia grew increasingly discouraged and depressed. If they did not find him, it could mean only one thing. Rashid was dead—buried deep in the earth in a place where he was meant never to be found.

When at last there was nowhere else to explore, Livia and Tariq returned to their rooms exhausted and defeated. Livia felt as though her heart and mind had shattered and a suspicion that had preyed upon her now hardened into certainty. One day she whirled upon Tariq in a mindless fury.

"If you don't know what has become of Rashid, I do! Or, I should say, Khadija knows!"

Anger kindled in his eyes. "Khadija cares nothing for Rashid and has no interest in him."

"Exactly!" said Livia, her wrath mounting. "But she knows very well that *I* care for him! That woman is consumed by hatred of me and she has taken this way of wreaking her vengeance upon me. She has done away with our child!"

Tariq began to pace the floor, his hands clasped behind his back. "That is utter nonsense. Khadija could never do such a thing!"

"She could and would!" said Livia enraged. "That—that *puta* is capable of anything, even murder!"

Tariq halted his pacing and looked her directly in the eyes, fists clenched as though barely controling his outrage. His voice was like granite. "I know you dislike her, and she you, but your accusations are not only ridiculous, but unjust!"

His defense of the woman inflamed Livia beyond all reason. "You deny you love her, yet you dare to defend her in such treachery!"

Through whitened lips, he spoke in an ominously quiet tone, "I am merely asking you to think rationally."

"I am! It is you who refuse to see the truth shining like a beacon under your very nose!"

A bitter smile curved Tariq's lips. "If you insist upon finding a culprit, it is more likely to be the child's father who has made off with him. Why don't you ask Malik if he knows where his son is?"

Livia reeled backward, recoiling from his words as though he had struck her. Stunned, she stared at Tariq, her breath coming in short gasps. Let him think what he would, she thought miserably.

"Malik, cruel and cunning as he may be, would not steal his own child," she retorted. "Do not judge others by your own want of principal." Before he could reply, she fled from the chamber.

Blinded by her anguish, she ran heedlessly down the winding passageways, not thinking or caring where she was going. At length she paused before a doorway at the end of an unfamiliar corridor. As though something apart from her conscious thought had driven her, she knew this was where she had to come here.

A young slave girl stepped forward and barred her way. In an imperious tone, Livia said, "You are wanted at once by the king's steward. I will look after your mistress." A frightened expression crossed the girl's face and she hurried down the corridor. Livia strode into Khadija's apartment.

Khadija, dressed in a purple tunic, her long dark hair caught at the nape of her neck in a circlet of pearls, was seated in the window embrasure in the sunlight, painting her nails with henna. At the sight of Livia, her face flushed with emotion. Khadija drew herself erect and regarded Livia malevolently.

Livia drew a deep breath. "What have you done with Rashid?"

Khadija's gasp of astonishment seemed genuine, and for a brief moment, a pang of doubt assailed Livia, but then, she told herself, Khadija's surprise could be due to having been confronted with an accusation she had never expected to face.

Recovering her poise, Khadija said, "I don't know what you're talking about."

"Yes, you do!" insisted Livia. "And you best tell me, and quickly."

Khadija's eyes glittered. "Why would I know anything of your brat?"

For a moment Khadija's calm composure unnerved Livia, but her certainty as to the woman's guilt spurred her on. "Do not play with me!" Livia took a step nearer. "I know you had Hajai dismissed and have taken Rashid. What have you done with him?"

Her dark eyes had a hard, malicious sparkle as she looked at Livia. "Your anxiety over the child has unhinged your reason. Get out!"

Livia noted that the hand painting Khadija's nails trembled. Livia summoned all her willpower to control the rage boiling within her and in a tight voice she demanded, "Where is Rashid? Tell me, at once!"

Khadija's head jerked up. "I tell you, I do not know!" she snarled. "Now go away!"

Livia's hand flashed out, sinking deep into the mass of Khadija's thick hair and with a violent upward motion, she yanked the woman to her feet. The pot of henna flew from her grasp and overturned, streaking Khadija's purple gown with red. At the same instant, Khadija's hands flew upward, clawing at Livia's wrists in an effort to free herself. She yelled frantically for her slave.

"Leave off your shouting," cried Livia. "It will do you no good, for I have told her she is not needed." Holding fast to the silken skein, Livia wound it around the flat of her hand. Khadija let out a shriek and her face contorted with pain. She reached out her arms, groping for her assailant, but Livia darted behind her and gave a vicious tug, pulling Khadija's head back so that her eyes bulged toward the ceiling. Livia raised one knee and pressed down hard against the small of Khadija's back. The woman's screams were choked off by the manner in which Livia had inclined her head and, unable to face her attacker, Khadija's arms flailed the air in futile gestures.

"Where is Rashid?" shouted Livia, giving another savage tug on Khadija's hair. Khadija's groping hands found Livia's wrists, scratching the ivory skin and digging into the flesh. Livia, intent on wringing the truth from her adversary, felt the scratches as no more than pinpricks.

"Malik!" sputtered Khadija. "Ask Malik!"

"Malik!" Was this the way Malik had chosen to avenge her rejection of him?

"Maybe Malik knows where he is," rasped Khadija.

Momentarily put off by the mention of Malik, Livia relaxed her hold on Khadija's long mane. Khadija whirled about, placed her hands against Livia's shoulders and shoved her backward. Livia's hand flew up and smote Khadija a stinging blow across the face. Stunned, the woman reeled backward. Instantly, Livia was upon her. Thankful for her height and strength that gave her an advantage over the smaller weaker woman, Livia gripped Khadija's upper arms and forced her toward the open window.

"If Malik knows where Rashid is, *you* know too. And you will tell me. Now!"

Khadija's mouth clamped shut. Livia pushed harder, driving Khadija closer to the window. As though sensing her purpose, Khadija screamed in terror. Unmindful of her shrieks, Livia drove her on until they were stopped by the pilaster dividing the double arched window. Khadija braced her back against the pillar, her breasts heaving, her eyes wild with fright. Livia's gaze traveled over her shoulder, taking in the valley where the Darro flowed a thousand feet below.

Through clenched teeth Livia hissed, "Tell me this instant where I can find Rashid or I will hurl you to your death!"

Livia felt the woman's arms encircle her waist in a

viselike grip, and Khadija's full lips curled in a sneer. "Dog of a dog! You cannot kill me without losing your own life as well. I will take you with me!"

"Do you think I wish to live without ever seeing my son again?" shouted Livia. "Do you think I wish to share the rest of my days and nights with the infidel, with your lover?" With that she lurched sideways, wrenching Khadija from her post of safety, bending her backward over the low sill.

Khadija's mouth fell open and Livia saw the naked terror shining from her eyes. With a visible effort Khadija gasped, "The maristan!"

The maristan meant nothing to Livia and she pressed forward, straining against Khadija, forcing her still further backward like an archer's bow.

With a desperate cry, Khadija blurted, "Rashid is in the maristan, but I did not put him there!"

Livia clutched Khadija's shoulders and jerked her upright. "The maristan—where is it?"

Khadija's mouth opened, but no sound came out. Livia shook her so that her head wobbled on her neck. In a hoarse whisper she said, "It is on the Street of the Great Mosque. Rashid is there."

Livia's eyes narrowed. "I will go to the maristan. If Rashid is not there, I will kill you. That I promise!"

She flung the woman from her with a violent motion that sent Khadija sprawling across the floor and dashed from the chamber. As she raced down the stone stairs, a sudden thought brought her up short. Khadija may have given her the wrong directions. And if she found the place, they might not let her in. She swung about, dashed through the halls to Tariq's apartment.

He was seated before a brass tray heaped with food. At the sight of her, his hand holding a vine leaf stuffed with meat and rice paused in mid-air. As though they had never quarreled, she rushed to his side.

"Tariq! Rashid is in the maristan! Quickly, you must come with me!"

He dropped the food and sprang to his feet. "Rashid, in the maristan? You cannot be serious! The maristan is for lunatics!"

She clutched his sleeve, tugging on his arm. "It is true! Khadija told me. Oh, hurry, I beg you!"

Chapter 38

It seemed to take forever to make the steep descent to town shoving their way through the crowded streets. At last they came in sight of a long gray two-storied building whose forbidding facade was broken only by two tiny windows on the lower level and four windows high on the upper level.

Tariq muttered a few words to the guard and they hurried through a stout wooden door in the center of the building and emerged onto a broad inner courtyard dominated by a gurgling fountain and encircled by a gallery which opened onto the rooms of the second floor.

Bewildered, Livia looked about her, as if hoping to catch sight of Rashid, but the courtyard was deserted. She was startled by the howls of inmates who, having caught sight of the visitors, clung to the grillwork across the doors of their cells. Tariq had approached the overseer, a fat oily-faced man in a soiled striped tunic who was now shaking his head doubtfully. Livia felt as though her heart were being squeezed by a giant hand and the strangling fear which she had not allowed to surface rose within her: The fear that Rashid was dead.

Tariq bent his solemn gaze upon her and in a sympathetic voice said, "The overseer has no record of a five-year-old child being admitted to the place. He says that during the uprising many derelicts and homeless sought refuge here and Rashid may be among them, but he does not think so."

Livia fixed the man with a stern eye. "There *are* children here, are there not?"

In a whiny voice he replied, "Several children have been brought in, but . . ." He shrugged helplessly.

"Where are they?" demanded Livia. "I wish to see them."

The overseer averted his eyes. "I will look, and send word to you if I should find your son."

"No, no, we must look for ourselves!" insisted Livia feverishly. "I'll not leave until I have searched the place."

He threw up his hands in a helpless gesture, but Tariq intervened, commanding him to allow them to look in the small chambers housing the inmates. The greasy man cast a nasty glare at Livia and unlocked the door to the first room with a key from a ring tied to his belt.

As he opened the door, Livia recoiled from the stench. She pulled her mantle up over her nose and mouth and stepped over the threshold, choking down her horror. In the light that filtered in from the doorway, she saw nearly a dozen derelicts crammed into the tiny room. Several vulturelike figures rushed toward them, wailing and clamoring to be released. Other bodies lay like ragged bundles on the earthen floor. One man sat wide-eyed and grinning, leaning against the wall.

Livia stepped up to him and in a quavering voice, asked if he had seen a little boy. When he made no reply, Tariq prodded his arm and his stiff, lifeless form fell sideways to the floor. Livia's hand flew to her mouth. Somehow she forced herself to examine every ragged creature, then stepped outside, squinting against the blinding sunshine. As they continued their search, viewing room after room of human flotsam and jetsam, Livia's hopes plummeted. Either Khadija had lied, or Rashid had not survived captivity in this appalling place.

They proceeded to the second story and, starting at the far end of the building, Livia strode resolutely inside a cell and glanced about her. She stifled a scream as a rat scuttled across the floor. In one corner a toothless hag squatted protectively before a bundle wrapped in a badly torn cloak, as though to shield it from sight. When Livia drew near, she flung out her arms, as if to prevent Livia from robbing her. Her eyes kindled with a frantic light and in a high-pitched, cracked voice, she shrieked, "Go away!"

Livia smiled and bent down, thinking to reassure the crone, when her gaze strayed over the woman's shoulder and locked with a pair of dark burning eyes buried in the depths of the tattered cloak. With a cry, Livia sprang forward, eluding the old woman's outstretched arms, and snatched the cloak away. A small, emanciated form clad in filthy rags lay hidden inside its folds.

"Rashid!" screamed Livia dropping to her knees beside him. As she gathered the child in her arms, the old crone descended upon her, beating on her back, clawing at her mantle, cursing. Swiftly, Tariq pulled her away from Livia and the woman cried out piteously, "My child! You cannot take my baby!" and dissolved in a paroxysm of weeping.

Livia held Rashid close to her breast, cradeling him in her arms, rocking back and forth. The boy lay inert, pale as death, a glazed expression in his eyes. In a broken voice, Livia cried out, "He is near starvation!"

At that, the crone shook a gnarled fist and screeched, "I gave him my own bread! Every crust and crumb!"

Tariq thrust the poor demented creature into the arms of the sour-faced overseer. Then he bent down and scooped Rashid up in his arms. Frowning, he said, "The child is nothing but skin and bones, but we'll soon fatten him up!" He held Rashid in the curve of one arm and drew Livia to her feet. Tears of joy ran down Livia's cheeks and she thought she saw a tender light in Tariq's eyes.

"At least he's alive," breathed Livia, uttering a silent prayer of thanksgiving. The woman wailed louder and the obese man clapped a hand across her mouth. A pang of sorrow went through Livia as she realized they were taking away the only thing in life the woman had to love. Livia placed a detaining hand on Tariq's arm. "Wait, Tariq. I wish to leave some money for this woman's care. I am certain it is only because of her that Rashid's life has been spared."

Tariq shook his head and bent down to whisper in her ear. "If I leave money, she'll never reap the benefit." He glared at the Moor. "We're taking the woman with us as well. I will send someone to get her."

A crafty look came into the man's beady eyes. "You can take the boy, for he is one of your family, but the crazy hag stays."

"You are foolish," Livia exclaimed. "Think! If we take her, you will have one less mouth to feed."

The man shook his head stubbornly.

A sardonic smile crossed Tariq's face. "How much do you want for her?"

The overseer named his price and Livia gasped. To her amazement, instead of haggling, as the Moors were inclined to do, Tariq promised to send the money with his servant to be handed over when he fetched the woman. He placed an arm about Livia's shoulders and led her out the door, down through the courtyard, away from the hellhole she hoped never to see again. Whether it was Khadija or Malik who had put Rashid there, she would probably never know. But Livia was so relieved to have found him that she put it from her mind.

Heads turned to stare as they strode rapidly through the town, the ragged urchin in the arms of the powerful man, the lithe woman striding at his side.

If any good could come of Rashid's ordeal, thought Livia ruefully it was that Tariq, despite his doubts as to Rashid's father, appeared to share her joy at finding him.

Hajai once again took up her duties to Rashid and together, she and Livia nursed him back to health.

Livia begged Tariq for a guard, and to her great relief, he complied. Whether it was to humor her, or because he truly felt the child's life was in danger, she had no way of knowing.

The pitiful woman they had rescued was installed in the servants' quarters and, in time, regained her health and her senses although Tariq insisted she would never be more than a half-wit. She was never seen garbed in anything but a cast-off black mantle which she clutched about her like armor against the world. To Livia's amusement and Hajai's annoyance, the woman steadfastly refused to keep to her quarters, but would crouch outside Rashid's chambers night and day waiting for him to appear; and when he and Hajai ventured forth, she would follow them about like a shadow. Livia smiled and shrugged off Hajai's indignant complaints, for secretly she felt that the woman was more protective than the guard whom Tariq had found for them. And eventually Hajai grew accustomed to the crone's presence and paid her no heed.

As the blazing heat of summer beating down on the vega gave way to the lazy, warm days of fall, Aguilar seemed very distant and there never seemed to be a proper time to mention Tariq's divorce. Livia, Tariq and Rashid would stroll among the gardens of the Generalife, or sing together while Livia played her lute. Sometimes they would amble along the riverbank to watch the *noria*. Rashid never tired of watching the great wheel, tall as a house, scoop up water in compartments and dump it into raised channels to be carried to the fields and gardens. Often, after Rashid had gone to bed, Livia and Tariq would play chess.

One rainy night after Tariq had won in only four moves of his ebony chessmen, he lifted his brows and smiled wickedly across the board at Livia. "Did you know that the expression *checkmate* comes from the Persian-Arabic *ash-shah mat,* which means 'the king is dead'?"

"I know that *shah* is a Persian word for king," Livia said briskly, "and that the game of chess which the Arabs took over from the Persians and passed on through all of Europe, is the king's game."

Tariq nodded and raised a finger to stroke his beard. "It not only centers around the figure of the king, but the whole game concerns the art of kingship. It shows the connection between freedom of action and the inevitability of fate."

Livia raised one delicately arched eyebrow. "And is it this inevitability that makes you entirely without fear?"

Tariq threw back his head and laughed. "Ours is not the fatalism as Europeans think of it. We followers of the Prophet do not see life as predestined and therefore inescapable. We are simply confident that what happens is best. We still have to make choices." He looked directly into her eyes. "You must learn to curb your passions . . . in chess."

Livia thought she saw a twinkle in the depths of his black eyes, and her cheeks burned with color as he went on. "It appears that you have unlimited possibilities open to you before a move—unless, of course, you're in a corner. But you must take care, for any false choice will gradually reduce your ability to maneuver. This is a law of the world."

Livia smiled inwardly, thinking Tariq's choices may be right at the game of chess, but his choosing to take her captive had been a mistake. In the end, she would win her own game. Still, to her own amazement, she found she was happy when she was with him. It is gratitude I feel for him, she told herself. Gratitude for his kindness to me and to Rashid. No more. Somehow he gave her the priceless sense of being treasured that gave her the confidence to face the future. The next morning after Tariq's talk about kingship, Boabdil sent him on a reconnaissance mission and she missed him more than she would admit.

Ever since Rashid's rescue, Livia had never mentioned the maristan to him, for she did not wish to reawaken the horror of his ordeal. But one evening at bedtime, after she had read to him the tale of "Ali Baba and the Forty Thieves" from the *Arabian Nights*, he gazed up at her with a puzzled expression and asked, "Mama, why did you let them put me in that place?"

Stunned, Livia stammered, "The maristan?"

Rashid nodded. "Why did you leave me there?"

"I did not know you were there, *niño,* or I would have come for you at once."

Rashid's straight dark brows drew together in a frown. "But they told me you sent me—that they were taking me to you."

"Who?" demanded Livia, feeling anger boiling up inside her. "Who told you this?"

"Malik and Khadija told me," Rashid said, his eyes on her face as though searching for an explanation of his mother's betrayal.

Both of them! thought Livia. Khadija and Malik both wreaking their vengeance on her. Livia's knuckles whitened on the book. "And was it they who took you to the maristan?"

Rashid nodded.

Her mind reeled. The overseer knew who had placed Rashid there. If for a price he had kept silent, for a price he could be made to talk.

"And did they speak with the overseer?"

"Not Malik and Khadija. We walked to town and looked around the courtyard at the Corral del Carbon. They said we were looking for you. When we didn't find you, they began talking to an old beggar—"

"Yes," said Livia eagerly. "What did they say?"

Rashid shrugged. "I couldn't hear."

Livia suppressed a sigh. "Go on. What happened then? Tell me!"

Rashid cocked his head, as though digging deep into the recesses of his memory.

"All I remember is, we walked down the street with

the beggar. Then they told me to go with him inside
that big building. They said they would watch while he
took me to you, and wait for me to come out. We went
across the street and I looked over my shoulder to see if
Malik and Khadija were still there, but it was crowded
and I couldn't see.

"Go on," Livia said, seething with anger.

"We went inside. The beggar gave the fat man some
money. He counted out the coins and told me he would
take me to you. The beggar left and the fat man took
me to a room . . ." His eyes filled with tears, and his
face seemed to crumple before her eyes. "It was dark
and smelly and filled with people, and you weren't
there—" His voice broke and he buried his head in her
lap.

"There, there," she said soothingly, hugging his
small, quivering body close to her breast. "They lied to
you, Malik and Khadija. You are too young to understand why, but all that is over and done. Past. You will
never go there again. Now we are together and we will
be happy. But you must promise never to go anywhere
with Malik or Khadija—or with any stranger." She put
a hand under his chin and lifted his tear-streaked face
to hers. "Promise?"

Rashid nodded mutely. She dried his tears and
tucked him into bed then crooned a Spanish lullaby
until he slept.

Livia's first inclination was to go directly to Khadija,
then Malik, and accuse them of having abducted
Rashid and left him to die in the maristan. She
controlled the impulse, for that would avail her nothing. She wished she knew when Tariq would return
from the mission on which Boabdil had sent him.
Boabdil! Perhaps he would see justice done!

The following morning when Boabdil held court in
the Hall of Justice, Livia waited impatiently for her
turn. At last Boabdil gazed down at her, a smile of
pleasure on his placid countenance.

"You are Livia, wife of Tariq. What is it you wish?"

Livia took a deep breath and plunged into the story. Gradually, the monarch's face lost its smile. His nervous fingers fiddled with his prayer beads and his bland features settled into a scowl of disapproval.

"You accuse one of my most trusted viziers and my beloved second wife of this infamous deed. I find it hard to believe that either of them would be guilty of such heinous actions. To me, it appears the beggar kidnapped the child and meant to conceal him in the maristan until you should ransom him. But when he discovered that you had gone to Malaga, he had nothing to do but leave the child to his fate."

Livia felt hot color creep up her neck into her face. "That is not the way of it at all!" she cried. "I have told you the truth!"

Boabdil eyed her coldly. "The child has been restored to you unharmed. What is it you ask of me?"

"Justice!" cried Livia distraught. "I wish Malik and Khadija brought to justice!"

Boabdil's hands dropped from his prayer beads and placing them upon his knees, he leaned toward her. "You have no proof of their treachery. It would be your word against theirs."

His tone left no doubt in Livia's mind as to whose word would be believed. Doggedly, she continued. "We have the word of the overseer. He will speak in Rashid's behalf. I know he will!"

Boabdil's brows rose, his mouth curved in an infuriating smile. Slowly he shook his head. "If I heard you correctly, the man treated only with the beggar. He had nothing to do with Malik and Khadija."

With a sinking heart, Livia realized that her plea was in vain. She stiffened her spine and gazed straight into Boabdil's eyes. "It is my opinion that if you wish to rule, if you wish your people to be content and support you, you must see that the villains in your court are punished, rather than severing the heads of all who oppose you."

An angry flush spread across Boabdil's flaccid features and a dangerous light came into his eyes. His chin lifted and with lofty condescension he replied, "I have long since learned that if you wait, other will fight your battles for you. You should do the same." He raised a hand in dismissal and motioned the next petitioner forward.

Chapter 39

Tariq did not return to the Alhambra until well after midnight the following Tuesday. When he slid into bed, Livia struggled upward through layers of sleep to find herself enfolded in his arms. She was tempted to pour out all the rage at Khadija and Malik, and now Boabdil, which she had bottled up inside herself. Now, thinking better of it, she curbed her impulses. She knew the way his mind worked. Instead, she determined to please him.

She felt his mouth on hers, his kiss deep and ravaging, and she responded with an ardor that surprised herself. His hand found the round swell of her breast, brushing aside her gown to expose its creamy contour to the pale white gleam of moonlight sifting through the window. His lips left hers to travel down her throat, seeking the honeyed sweetness of her breasts. Slowly, she let her arms creep around his neck and her fingers stroked his thick black hair.

His hands slid down her abdomen, her thighs, down the slender length of her legs to the hem of her gown. She drew in her breath sharply as with a smooth swift movement he slipped the filmy chiffon over her head, and cast it aside. With tender urgency, his sure hands caressed her trembling body, leaving no part untouched, setting all her senses aflame with desire. Her legs entwined with his and his broad chest pressed against her breasts. A velvet warmth closed around them, and she suddenly felt soft and wild and free.

She had meant to yield to him only to gain his favor

and now she found she had to summon all her willpower to deny the tormented urging of her heart. Though her body was yielding, inside she forced herself to be hard against him. The next moment she felt torn asunder, for while defying him in her mind, she gave herself to him with abandon. Her blood pounded in her ears and her heart beat wildly as he joined his body to hers. A feeling of exultation swept through her, as though she had ascended a towering mountain of the sierras and had attained the peak in a glorious burst of triumph.

After a while their passions were sated, their breathing quieted, and Livia lay curled at Tariq's side, her head resting upon his shoulder.

"Tariq," she whispered, "I wish something of you."

His sleepy voice murmured close to her ear, "Anything, my poppy. You have only to ask."

"I wish you to avenge a wrong."

She felt his muscles tense and as she looked into his face revealed in the shaft of moonlight she saw his alert questioning gaze. With an effort she kept her voice calm while she repeated the tale of Malik's and Khadija's villany and her failure to obtain justice from Boabdil. When she had done, a long hollow silence lay between them. She held her breath, waiting.

There was an ominous tightness about Tariq's mouth and his eyes kindled with annoyance. At last he said, "You know I would deny you nothing within reason, but this is not reasonable."

Livia bit her lip in vexation. "Surely you would not allow such treachery to go unpunished!"

She heard Tariq's weary sigh slice through the darkness. "There is no proof—"

"Either Malik or Khadija, or both, must have arranged beforehand with the overseer to take Rashid in. Money talks. The man can be persuaded to tell who it was who—"

"No!" Tariq exploded. "It will not serve. Any judge would see through your ruse at once."

Livia's voice rose in agitation. "But it would not be a ruse. It is the truth!"

Tariq shook his head vehemently. "No one would believe it."

Livia rose up on one elbow and stared down into Tariq's bearded face. His eyes were closed, his jaw set in the stubborn line she knew so well. "And you? Do you not believe what I tell you?" He was silent for so long, she wanted to strike him.

He let out a defeated sigh. "I believe you."

Reassured, she plunged on. "Besides, there is Rashid's word."

"No one will take the word of a child seriously," he said scornfully. "Everyone knows they invent more stories than truth, particularly an imaginative child like Rashid."

Livia bridled. "He knows what happened to him and who is responsible."

"That may be so, but his word will avail you nothing in a court of justice."

"Then we will have to take matters into our own hands," determined Livia. "You granted me any wish within reason. Is it not reasonable to expect an eye for an eye and a tooth for a tooth?"

Tariq's eyes flew open and he grinned at her in amusement. "Is that what you wish of me? To extract an eye and a tooth from each of your enemies?"

"Do not make light of a matter which is of the greatest importance to me, a matter in which Rashid's life hung in the balance."

Now thoroughly roused, Tariq sat up. She knew she had roused his fierce temper to the point of danger, but this was what she had wanted, she told herself; to make him angry enough to do her bidding.

"What is it you want of me? Am I to seek out Khadija and Malik and cut them down in cold blood?"

"It would not be the first time you have done such a thing! And no doubt it will not be the last!"

"I cut down the enemies of our country!"

"Khadija and Malik are *my* enemies! I do not ask that you put them to the sword, but you can threaten as much, and at the very least, you can drive them out of Granada!"

"No!" shouted Tariq, slamming his fists down on the bed. "Your son is alive and well. I have set a guard on him. Let that be the end of it. I cannot do as you ask."

"You would avenge this wrong if anyone else were guilty!" Livia shrieked. "It is because it is that *puta* Khadija that you refuse me!"

"Your thinking is clouded," snarled Tariq. "Think well. If I drive away Khadija, I must drive away your own lover as well. Or have you forsaken Malik in favor of Aguilar, who is in Malaga? The fact is, you should never have gone to Malaga!"

Livia rose to her knees, facing Tariq in the moonlight. "My reason for going there had nothing to do with Aguilar! And for the last time I tell you Malik is not and never has been my lover, which is more than you can say for Khadija!"

In a deadly calm voice he replied, "I had no affair. I've tried to tell you that, but you will not believe it!"

The jealousy that swept through her was as painful as on that faraway evening when she had looked across the Partal garden and Tariq's head bent to kiss Khadija, who was looking up at him and laughing.

"May you both burn in perdition!" She leaped from the bed, snatched up her robe and stormed from the room.

During the days that followed, Livia remained sequestered in Rashid's apartment. If she and Tariq happened to meet, they passed like strangers, avoiding each other's eyes. Livia had decided to put him from her mind, to have nothing further to do with him, ever. She kept to her resolve for almost three weeks. Then, on a rainy afternoon late in September, Nizam returned to the Alhambra.

Everyone rushed to the Court of Myrtles to welcome

her. Even Tariq seemed to have relented, as though time had softened his heart against the sister who had defied him and run away with the scoundrel Raduan Venegas.

When the first excitement of the greetings subsided, Livia brought Rashid forward to meet her. He looked up at Nizam with great dark eyes and smiled shyly. Nizam knelt down, put her arms around him and kissed his brow. She released Rashid and glanced up into Tariq's face, as though comparing the two. Smiling, she said, "I would not need to be told that he is your son, Tariq."

Tariq only scowled. Nizam turned to Livia and murmured, "I often think how different our lives would have been if you had departed with me from Granada—"

"Yes," Tariq said bitterly. "Rashid would never have been born!"

Nizam's brows rose in surprise. "Do not be ridiculous, Tariq. Of course he would have been born. The world does not stop spinning outside the Alhambra. He would simply have been born in Malaga rather than Granada. Livia stayed behind only because she was carrying your child."

Tariq was thunderstruck. Speechless, he stared at Nizam. Livia could almost hear the swift processes of his mind as he figured out the truth: Malik had freed her from the Comares Tower after Tariq had dragged her from the caravansary. If she were with child before that day, the child must be his. His face brightened and pure joy shone from his eyes. He stepped forward and caught Livia's arm. Before he could speak, she jerked away and threw him a look of reproach more devastating than if she had slapped him. It was too late. Too late for love and understanding.

She turned to watch Nizam, noting now with a little stab of shock how much she had changed. She was no longer the happy, gentle girl Livia had once known. Her step was no longer quick and light; rather, she walked as though she bore a heavy burden upon her frail shoulders. She had lost the bloom of former days. Her face was gaunt, her features sharp and angular. In her eyes there was a lingering sadness Livia had not seen before. She supposed Nizam's melancholy mien was because she had been forced to leave Raduan behind.

Now Nizam regarded her with solemn eyes. "You will be pleased to know that your dowry paid our ransom, Livia dear, and I was set free, but Raduan—"

At these words, Tariq's head whipped around toward Livia. "*You* paid Nizam's ransom!" Clearly the reason for her trip to Malaga had struck him like a streak of lightning.

"Yes," said Nizam, "and Raduan's and Julian's as well. She gave us everything. The Spaniards took the dowry and then," her words choked in her throat, "they refused to set Raduan free. Because he was a commander, they considered him dangerous." With a wry smile she added, "They consider a woman no threat to their security."

"And Julian," asked Livia anxiously. "What of Julian?"

Livia's eyes clouded over and she shook her head slowly from side to side. "The Catholic sovereigns had to devise new ways and means to replenish their exhausted coffers. As this is a holy war, the clergy contributed vast sums of money and large bodies of troops. A fund was also produced from the first fruits of the Inquisition."

Livia squirmed with impatience, wishing Nizam would get to the point and tell her of Julian's whereabouts. With talk of the Inquisition, Livia had already surmised that he had once again fled for his life. Now Nizam avoided her gaze and, in true Arab fashion talked all around the subject at hand.

"It appears there are many families of wealth and dignity in the surrounding kingdoms whose forefathers had been Jews, but had been converted to Christianity

It was suspected that many of them had a secret longing for Judaism. It was even whispered that some of them practiced Jewish rites in private. The Catholic monarch ordered an investigation of the conduct of these pseudo-Christians by the Inquisitors."

A chill ran down Livia's spine. Surely Julian had not been taken by the agents of the Inquisition!

Nizam swallowed hard and went on. "Many families were convicted of apostasy from the Christian faith. Some who reformed in time were again received into the Christian fold after being severely fined and condemned to heavy penance; others were burnt at the *autos da fé* and their property confiscated. As these Hebrews were of great wealth and had an hereditary passion for jewelry, there was found in their possession abundant store of gold and silver, of rings and necklaces and strings of pearls and coral and precious stones—"

"Nizam!" Livia burst out. "Where is Julian?"

Tears welled in Nizam's eyes. "Dear Livia, I'm telling you what happened. Queen Isabella discovered that many outrages had been committed under the color of religious zeal and many innocent persons accused by false witnesses of apostasy. She held a strict investigation into the proceedings, many of which were reversed and offenders punished. I'm sorry to say that her good offices came to late to save your brother."

"Julian!" Livia screamed. "Julian burned at the stake!"

Nizam lowered her gaze and dabbed at the tears trickling down her cheeks.

"He cannot be dead!" shrieked Livia. She shook Nizam's arm. "Tell me he is not dead!"

But Nizam could not.

Livia covered her face with her hands, and her slender shoulders shook with sobs that racked her body. Tariq quickly put an arm about her and led her from the courtyard.

Once in their chambers, he seated her upon the divan and poured a small goblet of wine. He held it to her lips and said softly, "Here, drink this. It will help to calm you."

Wordlessly, she sipped the wine, her hand on Tariq's as he held the goblet. She began to feel numb, her senses deadening against the disaster that had taken Julian's life. At the realization, anger coursed through her. Tariq was drugging her senses so that she felt nothing, so that she was ignoring Julian's death, passing it off as though it were nothing. She struck the goblet from Tariq's hand.

"Do you imagine I wish to ignore Julian's death! Go! Leave me alone, you infidel! It is you who are the unbeliever!" As Tariq placed his hands lightly upon her shoulders and gazed directly into her face, she thought she had never seen such misery in anyone's eyes.

"Livia, I'm truly sorry I misjudged you. Knowing how much you despised me, and knowing Malik's intent to wreak his vengeance upon me, I *did* believe he had sired Rashid. You will never know how deeply I regret misjudging you."

"But it was not until Nizam spoke for me that you accepted the truth!" Livia said savagely. "You never believed me!"

"I have never trusted anyone but myself. It is my nature." He sighed regretfully. "I know now that I can believe in you. I love you very much, Livia."

Livia turned tear-dimmed eyes to him. "I no longer care what you think, or what you feel. It is too late!" She sprang up and ran into their bedroom and flung herself on the bed. She sobbed convulsively, hating Tariq with all her being. She felt a weight settle upon the bed. Strong arms enfolded her and she collapsed against Tariq, pressing her cheek against his broad chest, weeping into his shoulder.

Chapter 40

Life went on at its draggingly slow pace, and as fall wore into winter, Livia could not shake off her melancholy over the loss of Julian. She withdrew into a cocoon of grief, and try as he would, Tariq could not console her. She could not think of a future without Julian. Late one cold gray afternoon, Tariq, frustrated and at the end of his patience, brought things to a head.

"You were right!" he shouted. "It is too late for us. Whatever I have felt for you—or you for me—is over. I wish nothing more to do with you!" With that, he strode from their chamber and was gone.

The long winter with its floods and rains set in, and the armies ceased their campaigns for the winter. But with the coming of spring, El Zagal felt it was necessary to do something to quicken his popularity with the people and that nothing was more effectual than a successful inroad.

"The Moors love the stirring call to arms and a wild foray among the mountains and delight more in a hasty spoil wrested with hard fighting from the Christians than in all the steady and certain gains secured by peaceful trade," Livia said bitterly to Hajai one day.

"Who are the Christians, Mama?" asked Rashid, his innocent eyes upon her.

The question brought Livia up short. What did one tell a child of war and death?

"The Christians are the enemies of the Moors," Hajai said firmly.

With a slight sense of shock, it came to Livia that the

infant she had suckled at her bosom was growing up to be a Moor. Distraught, she resolved to explain the matter of Moors and Christians to Rashid, but at present he was far too young to understand. She had just begun to understand herself; without Tariq to lean upon, she had been forced to accept Julian's death.

During that winter of 1488, El Zagal raged with sanguinary fury about the whole frontier of the kingdom of Granada. He attacked convoys, slaying, wounding and taking prisoners, surprising the Christians whenever they were off their guard, carrying on a continual war of forage and depredation. The stormy winter passed, and the spring of 1489 was advancing, yet the heavy rains had broken up the roads, the mountain brooks were swollen to torrents and the formerly shallow and peaceful rivers were deep and turbulent.

One afternoon late in May, Livia was seated beside the fountain in the garden of Daxara admiring the parchment blossoms on a almond tree when she heard brisk footsteps crossing the courtyard behind her. Tariq stood before her garbed in a red, gold and black striped tunic and carrying his gleaming helmet and cuirass. He gave her a twisted smile.

"I've come to bid you good-bye, Livia. Ferdinand's army has assembled for an invasion of Baza. It is the key to our remaining possessions, and El Zagal has called upon all true Moslems to meet there to make a stand. I go to join them."

Livia rose to her feet and glared at him with contempt. "Boabdil is a vassal of King Ferdinand and Queen Isabella. You cannot betray your allegiance."

"I, and many other brave soldiers of Granada who spurn the quiet and security of Christian vassalage, will leave the city in secret to join our countrymen. I wish to go with your blessing, Livia." He reached out to take her in his arms.

She stepped back swiftly, out of his grasp. She

longed to beg him not to leave, but all the old torments and wounds rose to her mind, stirring her ire anew. This man had been the cause of all her misery!

"You go with my blessing, Tariq," she said venomously. "Every day and every night of my life, I will thank God that you are gone!"

The look of hurt that came into his eyes tore at her heart. She would have given anything to be able to take back her searing words, yet she could not help saying them. His arms dropped to his sides and an unyielding expression spread over his rugged features.

"So be it. I'm sure it would please you most should Allah decree that I never return. Perhaps you should pray for that!" He made her a stiff bow and strode from the garden.

Livia sank down on the stone bench and buried her face in her hands, wishing she could cut out her tongue.

Several days later, word came that a brutal battle had taken place at Baza. Livia was beside herself with worry over Aguilar. Where was he now? Did he think of her when he rode out on his great charger to slay the Moor? Or was he, too, dead? She lived in torment as month after month passed away and the fighting continued. At last word arrived that Ferdinand had surrounded the city and cut off the water supply, and on December 4, 1489, after a siege of six months and twenty days, the city of Baza surrendered. Livia allowed herself a small ironic smile, for the surrender came upon the feast of Santa Barbara, the patroness of thunder and lightning, fire and gunpowder.

The Christian victory did not allay her fears for Aguilar, for she had no way of knowing whether he had survived. She had to be content with the news that the surrender of Baza was followed by that of other strongholds. El Zagal buried himself in his castle until scarcely a territory remained to him. It came as no surprise to Livia that on December 21, El Zagal surrendered to the Christians. In return he was given the title of king of Andarax with two thousand conquered Moors for subjects to hold as vassal of the Castilian crown.

There was no news of Tariq. Was he alive? she wondered. Time had cooled her anger toward him, and now the thought that he might have perished disturbed her more than she would have thought possible.

One gray December afternoon, as she entered her chambers after having visited Rashid, she stopped short in surprise. The lamps had been lighted, and a scarlet cloak, a gleaming cuirass and shining golden helm were strewn about the divan and a tub of water stood near the glowing brazier. She dipped her fingers in the water and found it cool. At a sound from the bedroom, her eyes flew to the curtained doorway.

Abruptly, the curtains were flung apart and her hand covered her mouth, stifling a cry of surprise. Tariq, clad only in a towel draped about his waist, stood unmoving, unsmiling in the doorway. He regarded her with a question in his eyes.

"Tariq!" cried Livia. Without thinking, their old quarrel forgotten, she rushed forward and flung herself against him. Tariq's strong arms closed around her, crushing her to him. Her arms went around his neck and as he pressed her close, she strained against him, enjoying the sensation of his powerful body molded to her own. His full, soft beard brushed her cheek, and his mouth found hers in a desperate, searching kiss as though he had found a long-lost treasure.

He parted her lips with his own. Livia was dimly aware of his hands stroking her back, slipping around her waist and caressing her breasts under the soft woolen folds of her tunic. She stood motionless, hardly daring to breathe, lest she break the spell. After a little while, he drew her down with him onto the thick carpet and when she felt his hands easing off her garments, in mounting desire, her hands guided his, slipping off the restricting tunic and trousers.

Through lowered lids, she watched him kneeling above her, his skin glowing bronze in the red glow of the brazier, and smiled to herself, thinking he resembled a devil rising from the fires of hell from whom she should leap up and flee for her life. Instead, she raised her arms in a languorous stretch, reveling in the passion of his caresses.

His lips, close to her ear, whispered, "You are like the poppy, my scarlet Zahareña, and you have drugged my senses. Though I had sworn to part from you forever, I cannot!"

His admission struck her like a blow. She had conquered the granite heart of the Moor! With a sense of wonder it came to her that her triumph was not won through an act of revenge, but of giving of herself. As his kisses trailed down her throat, lingering on each breast, circling her abdomen, all her senses seemed on fire with her longing for him and when at last they came together, she was transported, as though floating, disembodied, soaring with a rapture that mounted to dizzying heights, as though only she and Tariq existed in the world. And the world belonged to them alone.

She was not aware of the moment when the rosy glow in the charcoal brazier flickered and died. Nor did she feel the chill that pervaded the room.

The next morning when Livia awoke, Tariq was already up and dressed in a rich blue tunic trimmed in gold, for shortly they were to ride down to the town in a glorious procession with King Boabdil. Livia sprang from the bed and threw open her marriage chest. "I'd best hurry and dress—I doubt that Boabdil will wait for me."

Tariq lifted the flap of his saddlebag lying in one corner of the room and withdrew what appeared to be a folded length of fabric. As though embarrassed, he thrust it into her hands. "I brought this for you."

Eagerly she unfolded the material, a tunic of fine black silk brocade on which was woven a design of gold and red peacocks. The wide flowing sleeves were adorned with bands of gold script. Livia threw her arms about his neck and placed a kiss upon his cheek while thanking him profusely. Tariq scowled and turned away. But when she stood before him in her finery, the admiration shining in his eyes brought a blush to her cheeks. She had coiled her gleaming black hair high upon her head in which she had entwined a circlet of rubies and pearls that Ayxa had given her. Her face glowed and her dark eyes, fringed with thick lashes were clear and sparkling.

At eleven o'clock Boabdil summoned his retinue to gather in the courtyard. Livia, riding at Tariq's side, kept her own counsel, for her thoughts were in dire opposition to the celebration at hand. She was wary, for Boabdil's optimism frightened her. Yesterday when El Zagal's capitulation had been announced, Boabdil had shouted, "I am sole monarch of Granada, my throne fortified by the friendship and alliance of the Castilian monarchs. From now on no man can call me The Unlucky!"

Tariq had tried to deter him, cautioning him that although the tempest had ceased from one point of the heavens, it may begin to rage from another. Nevertheless, Boabdil had insisted upon riding into town to receive the acclamations of the populace.

As they proceeded through the streets toward the Great Mosque, crowds began to gather. Livia heard mutterings and ominous growls, and to her horror, instead of rejoicing, a violent agitation rose from the throng. In a ferment of grief and indignation, shouts went up extolling El Zagal, who had fought to the last for the salvation of his country and had scorned to compromise the dignity of his crown.

Boabdil, on the contrary, had looked on exulting at the hopeless yet heroic struggle of his uncle, and had aided in the downfall of the empire. Now as they saw him riding in gorgeous state on what they considered a day of humiliation for all true Moslems, they could not contain their rage. As Boabdil rode through the mass of people amid the clamor that met their ears, Livia heard his name coupled with epithets of traitor.

The smile faded from Boabdil's lips; his face drained of color. Shocked, he wheeled about in the square and turned his horse back up the hill toward the Alhambra. Once safely inside the walls of his palace, he shut himself inside and vowed to remain there until the inhabitants came to their senses.

Chapter 41

On the heels of Boabdil's rejection by his people, there came a further blow in the form of a letter from Ferdinand. The shrewd monarch called upon Boabdil to deliver up the city in accordance with their treaty made at Loxa. Once again Livia's hope soared. Surely Boabdil would see the wisdom of surrender—a disastrous battle would be avoided, no lives lost, the city saved. Boabdil swiftly summoned his council and commanders and Livia waited in a frenzy of impatience for Tariq's return.

When at last he strode through the doorway, Livia tensed in anticipation, for judging by the expression on his face, she surmised that surrender must be in the offing.

He stood looking out the window, his hands clasped behind his back, rigid with disapproval. At last he said, "Boabdil is trying to put Ferdinand off, promising Ferdinand that when he gains full sway over his capital he will rule over them as vassal to the Castilian crown."

Disappointment surged through her. "How typical of Boabdil to try such a delaying action, but this strategy will not succeed with Ferdinand."

Tariq faced her, scowling. "Even if Boabdil possessed the will, he has not the power to comply with Ferdinand's demand. He is shut up here in the Alhambra while a tempest rages outside!"

"Nevertheless," Livia went on, determined to have the last word, "Ferdinand will not stand by idly and allow Boabdil to roost on his throne like a hen on a nest!"

Tariq's jaw stiffened and he cast her a hard look. "There is nothing Ferdinand can do about it short of storming the city, and he is wise enough to know he cannot take Granada by force!"

Seething, Livia made no reply.

On the following Friday afternoon Livia was seated on the divan mending Tariq's scarlet cloak, which she uneasily surmised had been rent by the thrust of a Toledo blade, when Tariq burst through the doorway.

"You must have had an ear to the walls of the Spanish monarch's council chambers," he said heatedly. "Ferdinand has borne out your prediction."

"Oh?" Livia said, not looking up, but her flashing needle paused in the fabric, waiting, as Tariq began pacing the floor in agitation.

"He has denounced Boabdil as a faithless ally and has discarded him from his friendship. To make matters worse, the Catholic king has sent a second letter, not to Boabdil, but to the commanders and council of the city demanding a complete surrender. If we comply, he promises generous terms. If not, we are to suffer the fate of Malaga!"

Livia felt the hair on the nape of her neck raise.

"You would not believe the commotion going on in town! The tradesmen who wish to preserve their businesses are all for capitulation. Others with wives and children dread, by resistance, to bring upon them the horrors of slavery—"

"Surely you cannot blame them!"

Tariq ceased his pacing and threw up his arms in exasperation. "You do not understand. The city is crowded with refugees ruined by the war, vexed by their sufferings and eager only for revenge; and with others reared amidst hostilities who have lived by the sword to whom a return of peace would leave without home or hope. Besides these, there are our valiant and haughty cavaliers of the old chivalrous families who have inherited a deadly hatred for the Christians. To them the idea is worse than death that Granada, for ages the seat of Moorish grandeur, should fall to the unbelievers."

Mounting anger turned Livia's face scarlet. "And you count yourself among them, I warrant, thirsting for Spanish blood!"

"It is not that I thirst for blood," Tariq said wrathfully, "but that I wish to preserve the kingdom for which Moors have fought and died for seven centuries—which we have nourished and tended until it is a paradise on earth. Do you fault me for wishing to keep it?"

"I fault you not for that, but for refusing to bow to the inevitable. It is foolish to give up all these lives, to allow a kingdom to be destroyed for a cause that was lost from the start!"

"It is not lost!" he bellowed, his eyes flashing. "Does Ferdinand think that we are old men? We will let him know that a Moor is born to fight. If the Christian king desires our arms, let him come and win them—but let him win them dearly! For my part, sweeter were a grave beneath the walls of Granada or the spot I had died to defend, than the richest couch within her palaces, earned by submission!"

Furiously, he strode from the chamber, leaving Livia pale and shaken. She had never seen him so on fire. She shuddered to think what would happen now. If Tariq spoke with the same fury to others, they would be roused to defend the city till the last man, woman and child met their death.

She did not have long to wait. The commanders and council dispatched a reply to the Christian sovereigns declaring that they would suffer death rather than surrender their city.

Chapter 42

In that same month of December 1489, word came that Ferdinand was preparing for hostilities; but because the winter season did not permit an immediate campaign, he contented himself with placing garrisons into all his towns and fortresses around Granada.

Granada resounded with the stir of war. Each day Livia watched from the rampart as Tariq drilled his men in the square. For the first time, she saw him as he must appear to the Moors: a man of noble lineage, of a proud and generous nature, and a figure of strength and valor. She could not help but admire him. He commanded the cavalry which he disciplined with uncommon skill. None could excel him in the management of the horse and dextrous use of all kinds of weapons; Livia was well aware that he had long complained of Boabdil's timid policy, and now he sought to counteract its enervating effects, to keep alive the martial spirit of Granada.

He promoted jousts and other public war games. He also tried to inculcate into his companions those high sentiments which lead to magnanimous deeds. Clearly, he had been successful. He was the idol of the youthful cavaliers who regarded him as a mirror of chivalry and endeavored to imitate his lofty and heroic virtues. They had caught his enthusiasm and panted for the field, while the common soldiers, devoted to him, were ready to follow him in the most desperate enterprises. To Livia's chagrin, he did not allow their courage to cool for want of action.

The gates of Granada once more poured out legions of light cavalry which galloped swiftly up to the very gates of the Christian fortresses, sweeping up sheep and cattle. The name of Tariq became formidable throughout the frontier.

The winter passed away, the spring advanced, yet Ferdinand did not take the field. "Why does he delay so?" Livia asked Tariq. "If he is going to attack, why not have done with it?"

Tariq smiled wryly. "He knows the city is too strong to be taken by assault, and too well provisioned to be speedily reduced by siege. The man is shrewd and he counts heavily on perseverance, thinking that by ravaging the country this year, he can produce a scarcity the next, and the city may be surrounded with success."

Livia nodded and, suppressing a deep sigh, said nothing; but she was plunged into gloom. If Tariq were right, another year would pass before the war was finally over.

During the interval of peace that followed, the warm sunshine, gentle rains and fertile soil had restored the *vega* to all its luxuriance and beauty. On a bright morning, Livia and Tariq rode out to enjoy a picnic in the gardens. Their mood was exuberant as they cantered along the banks of the Xenil past a *noria* dripping bright strands of water.

Tariq smiled, and with a sweep of his hand said, "Look! The watermill! An invention of the Moors which enables the farmer to grind his corn as well as water his gardens."

"Not so!" shouted Livia, laughing. "We irrigated our lands long before the advent of the Moor!"

"But it was by our industry and toil that you succeeded," Tariq persisted. "And we brought you sugarcane and rice and—"

An amused grin curved her lips and she threw up a hand in mock surrender. "I bow to your infinite superiority and wisdom!"

Tariq let out a shout of laughter. "I am glad to hear it! My wife willingly submits at last!"

Her black eyes sparkled with challenge. "Never!"

They drew rein under the shade of a silver-green leafed olive tree and dismounted. Grinning, Tariq bent down and plucked a poppy from a clump at his feet and tucked it behind her ear. He made her a mock bow. "A flower for my queen!"

Sharing his ebullient mood, Livia made a slight curtsy and murmured, "Thank you, my sovereign."

Tariq spread his cloak on the ground and with a jubilant air, drew from his saddlebag a small parcel of food and a leather bottle of wine. Livia's gay mood matched his, and soon they had finished a repast of meat and rice folded in unleavened bread; dates and almonds; and drained the last drop of wine from the bottle.

The bright sunlight, the soft breeze and the wine all combined to make Livia feel a delicious languor. She stretched out on her back, her arms behind her head, and closed her eyes. And when she felt Tariq's lips touch lightly upon hers, she smiled and made no protest. As their pressure increased she tried to summon the strength to resist him, but her willpower dissolved in the delightful sense of euphoria that overcame her. She felt the weight of his body sliding down upon hers, and without volition her arms went around his shoulders, clasping him. His mouth bruised hers in hungry passion, and her hands locked behind his head. She was filled with a sweet excitement as he murmured words of love. His firm, gentle hands stroked her hair, her cheeks, and moved lower over the soft roundness of her body, loosening her garments. A glow of warmth and well-being flowed through her. With a small sound deep in her throat, she moved against him. She clung to his shoulders, wanting, needing to be closer and closer still. When at last their bodies joined, she reveled in their union under a

cloudless blue sky. The heat of their bodies blended
with the warmth of the sun and a vagrant breeze
caressed them, as though blessing them.

Sated, they rested on Tariq's cloak, entwined in each
others arms. At length she raised up on one arm and
smiled down at Tariq who lay, eyes closed, as though at
peace with the world. Once again it came to her that at
this moment, she was happy. And with a slight sense of
shock, she realized that she had not thought of Aguilar
for some time.

She enjoyed the way Aguilar treated her, like
precious porcelain, but just occasionally a strange hot
longing rose in her to be handled roughly and passionately. She banished the thought.

Her gaze traveled beyond Tariq's bare shoulders,
lingering upon the scene that lay before her. The green
pastures on the borders of the Xenil were dotted with
flocks of sheep; the blooming orchards gave promise of
abundant fruit; and the open plain was waving with
ripening corn. It is time to reap the golden harvest, she
thought. Staring at the farthest edge of the fields where
they came to an abrupt end at the foot of the
mountains, her brows drew together in a frown. She
shaded her eyes with her hand to see more clearly the
movement which had caught her attention.

"Tariq!" she whispered, tugging at his arm. "Look!"
She gestured over his shoulder. "It looks like a column
of ants is coming down the mountain passes!"

Tariq braced his elbows on the ground beneath him
and stared at the slow-moving line. Livia watched, her
breath coming in shallow gasps, as the column drew
nearer. What had appeared to be ants now enlarged
into riders mounted on horses and heavily-laden pack
mules.

"Ferdinand!" shouted Tariq.

And Aguilar, thought Livia, her heart pounding
against her ribs.

Tariq sprang to his feet and flung on his clothes while
Livia quickly donned her tunic and trousers. They

leaped astride their mounts and galloped toward the Alhambra, whose red towers shone resplendent with the standard of Mohammed waving defiance at the Christian army.

Pandemonium reigned in the palace. The word had spread like wildfire that Ferdinand had come sweeping out of the mountain. Tariq left Livia to find Boabdil, and she ran to her chamber. The name "Aguilar" seemed to echo with her footsteps down the passage-way and she thought, he has come for me at last!

Shortly, Tariq burst through the doorway, snatched up his scimitar and buckled on his leather shield. "Ferdinand has thundered across the *vega,* halting under the very walls of Granada. He has detached parties in every direction to lay waste the country. Every man in Granada has risen to the call of arms!"

Livia, along with the entire court, stood on the walls of the tower, watching the holocaust below. Though they were horrified, they could not drag their eyes away from the awesome sight. Villages were sacked and burned, and the lovely *vega* was once more destroyed. The ravage was carried so close to Granada that the city was wrapped in smoke. Choking, Livia thought she would never banish the evil odor from her lungs or her memory.

Boabdil still remained cloistered in the palace. And despite Livia's eagerness for the Christians to take over the city, her heart went out to the hapless monarch. He dared not even show himself among the populace, for they cursed him as the cause of the miseries once more brought to their doors.

That night, when Tariq returned to snatch an hour's rest, his dark eyes flashed and his jaw was set in determination. "I will see to it that we do not allow the Spaniards to carry on their ravages unmolested, as in former years!"

Good as his word, Tariq incited the Christians to incessant sallies. He divided his cavalry into small

squadrons, each led by a daring commander. They
would hover round the Christian camp to harass it from
every direction, cutting off convoys and straggling
detachments; or waylay the army on its expeditions,
lurking among the rocks and passes of the mountains or
in hollows and thickets of the plain; or draw the enemy
out into ambushes carrying havoc and confusion into
the midst of their forces.

After almost two weeks had passed, Tariq returned
to their chambers, his eyes sunken, his face gray with
fatique, but the fire of battle burned in his eyes. His
features were contorted angrily as he flung himself
down on the divan.

"I fear your clever sovereign has caught on to our
strategy. He has realized that we seldom provoke a
battle without having the advantage of the ground.
Though the Christians generally appear to have the
victory, they suffer the greatest loss. He has discovered
that our retreat is only strategic: We draw our pursuers
and then attack them violently."

Livia felt the color drain from her face. She was not
thinking of Ferdinand, but of Aguilar taken in ambush.

Tariq's mouth turned down in a grim smile. "Ferdinand has commanded his captains to decline all chal-
lenges to skirmish and pursue a safe course of destruction."

"I see," said Livia, and let out a long, silent sigh of
relief.

El Zagal grew impatient with the inaction of his
mock kingdom and, assembling his men, had joined the
Christian camp so that he might see Granada wrested
from the sway of his nephew. Zagal's action only
served to reawaken Boabdil's popularity.

For thirty days the *vega* had been overrun by the
Christian forces. Now the destroying army, having
accomplished its task, wound up into the mountains on
the way to Cordoba. With a heavy heart, Livia watched

them go, her eyes searching eagerly for the sight of
Aguilar's pennons. She felt torn apart by conflicting
emotions. On the one hand appalled by the devastation
wrought by her own countrymen, and on the other,
wishing they would attack to emerge victorious to end
this interminable war.

It was on a windy day in June that Boabdil buckled
on his armor and prepared to take to the field. The
great square of the Vivarambla shone with legions of
cavalry decked with the colors of the most ancient
Moorish families. At their head rode Tariq, wearing
one of Livia's scarves as a talisman. She had bid him
good-bye with some misgiving; though she was loyal to
Aguilar, she was loath to see this proud soldier lose his
life.

Chapter 43

Tariq survived. The war went well for the Moors that summer, so Boabdil ordered further forays during the bleak winter of 1490. These were repulsed, but considerable booty was gained. Shortly thereafter, Ferdinand made a second terrible siege around the walls of Granada that lasted fifteen days. Scarcely a plant or animal was left on the face of the land. But the most astonishing event concerned El Zagal. The half-crazed monarch, deserted by his adherents after appearing under the Christian banner, left for Africa.

As the spring of 1491 advanced, melancholy reigned in the marble halls of the Alhambra. Tariq was restless and out-of-sorts, impatient with waiting to engage the Spanish again. Knowing the time was near when she would leave him forever, remorse assailed Livia, and she did her best to divert him, playing her lute and singing, reading the poems in which he had once taken delight, or playing chess with him. But nothing she did seemed to please Tariq. Whenever they sat across the chessboard in silent contemplation, the game once again became a symbol of their private struggle. His only pleasure seemed to be in coming out the victor, time and time again.

Even their love-making took on a strange new aspect. Night after night he took her. The tenderness that had once tempered his strength was replaced by an unbridled passion that frightened and challenged Livia at the same time. It seemed as though he assuaged his need to battle, to conquer the enemy, by subduing her in their bed, and that his insatiable lust was a way of affirming life and holding back death.

One soft spring night after he had done with her, Tariq thrust Livia from him with an exclamation of frustration and annoyance.

"Why do you continue to deny me?"

She shot him a sharp glance. "I do not deny you! Have I not shared your bed whenever you demanded?"

"Yes, when I demanded—insisted—but you have never once submitted to me of your own volition."

"I do not submit to anyone, Tariq," she replied proudly.

"Well I know that. And I know as well that your body alone has responded to my love-making. You have never given yourself to me with your heart."

She drew a deep breath in an effort to keep her voice level. "I told you once, Tariq. We spring from different worlds, you and I."

"And as I once told you, it is the union of opposites which together make a complete entity. A violin must have a bow; a lock must have a key; a servant a master, to be himself."

"I will never be a Moor."

"So be it. But I shall never let you go. Never!"

Livia made no reply, but at the same time she thought, you shall have very little to say about the matter.

On April 23, just when Livia thought that neither she nor Tariq could endure the waiting much longer, they saw the Christian horsemen glistening through clouds of dust as they poured across the *vega*.

Boabdil quickly assembled his council. When Tariq returned from the gathering, his brows drawn in a scowl, Livia quailed beneath his fearsomeness.

He threw up his hands and paced the room. "Many of the members—even several of the bravest—terrified with the horrors hanging over their families, advised

Boabdil to throw himself upon the generosity of the Christian monarch!"

Livia bit back the words that rose to her lips: that this was surely the wisest course.

"The vizier of the city reports there are sufficient provisions for only a few months. Already he has given up!" Tariq said disgustedly. "He asks of what avail is a supply for a few months against the sieges of the Castilian monarch, which are interminable?"

Yes, thought Livia, of what avail?

"And worse, he agrees that the number of men capable of bearing arms is great, but then asks what can we expect from mere citizen-soldiers who can be menacing in time of safety, but when soldiers are at the gates, hide themselves in terror!"

Livia regarded Tariq with a steady gaze. "And did you speak upon the matter?"

"Of course!" he roared. "I asked them what reason we have to despair. The blood of the Moors who conquered all of Spain still flows in our veins. Let us be true to ourselves, and fortune will again be with us. We have a veteran force, well seasoned in war. As to our citizens, why should we doubt their valor? There are twenty thousand young men who will rival the most experienced veterans. Do we want for provisions? To a soldier, there is no morsel so sweet as that wrested with hard fighting from the foe!"

"And Boabdil?" asked Livia quietly, thinking surely that the indecisive king would temporize, as always.

Tariq's lips stretched in a twisted smile. "Boabdil told his commanders to do what is necessary."

Livia's mouth compressed into a thin line. Boabdil had evaded the issue, as she had surmised he would; but in so doing, he had left the fate of Granada in the hands of the army. Such a course could have but one outcome. She let out a long, tremulous sigh. It had come to this, after all. What she had most feared: a battle to the death.

Nothing now was heard but the bustle of preparation. Wherever Livia went, she observed that the
excited populace considered the power of the Christians as nothing. Tariq infused his own zeal into the
troops. The new recruits rallied round him as their
model; the veterans regarded him with admiration; the
commoners followed him with shouts and old men and
women hailed him with blessings as their protector.

His horsemen were always completely armed and
ready to mount at a moment's warning. On the least
approach of the enemy, a troop gathered inside the
gate ready to launch outside like lightning. Tariq was no
empty braggart. He executed daring exploits beyond
even the boasts of his admirers.

As each day passed, Livia's trepidation mounted.
Although Granada was nearly cut off from all aid, its
mighty castles and massive bulwarks seemed to set all
attack at bay. She began to despair that not even
Ferdinand's army could wrest it from them.

Night after night, Tariq would enter their room
consumed with rage because the Castilian king refused
to engage in battle. Instead, Ferdinand's armies forged
into the valleys and sacked the farms upon which the
city depended for its supplies. Scouting parties ranged
the mountains behind Granada and captured every
convoy of provisions.

As their situation became more hopeless, the Moors
became more daring. Like a man possessed, Tariq
harassed the borders of the Spanish camp and even
invaded the interior, leaving his course to be traced by
the slain and wounded.

Then, in the heat of early summer, Queen Isabella
arrived in state with all her court and the prince and
princesses. Livia knew her monarch's presence was
intended to demoralize the Moslems by showing her
determination to reside in the camp until Granada
surrendered. Now Livia realized how much she had
missed the pageantry reinforcing the might of the

Castilian kingdom . . . and most of all, how much she
missed Aguilar. Her longing for him returned tenfold.

Nothing was heard from morning until night but
shouts and bursts of martial music, so that it appeared
to the Moors as if a continual festival reigned in the
Christian camp.

But the arrival of the queen had no effect in damping
the fire of the Moorish chivalry. Tariq inspired the
youthful warriors with heroism. "We have nothing left
to fight for but the ground we stand on!" Tariq exhorted
them. "When this is lost, we cease to have a country
and a name!"

One brilliant June morning, Tariq sought a brief
respite from his duties by taking Livia to bathe with him
in a secluded pool sheltered by a thick hedge of yews.
In a rare, playful mood, he scooped up handfuls of
water and splashed it over her head. Livia dived into
the clear water, her gleaming white skin rippling the
mirror surface like a slender dolphin.

Tariq threw back his head and laughed. "I see the
fishing is good in these waters." He plunged in after her
and catching her feet, upended her. In an instant, Livia
bobbed to the surface, laughing, gasping, shaking the
water from her long black hair. Swiftly, she flung water
at Tariq's furred chest, then dived into the cool depths.

Tariq let out a burst of laughter and again lunged
after her. He gripped her about the waist and gaining
his feet, lifted her upward in his powerful arms. He
held her high above the surface of the water and stood
grinning at her while she shrieked and kicked and
flailed her arms to no avail. Abruptly her hands flashed
downward, her fingers sunk into his thick black hair
and tugged his head to and fro.

"Vixen!" he howled in mock pain. He released his
hold on her and as she dropped downward he caught
her to his chest and pressed his face between her full
breasts. Livia writhed in his arms, struggling against
him and all at once her slippery body slid from his
grasp. She swam to the side of the pool and clambered

up over the edge. Breathless, laughing at Tariq, she sank down on her white robe spread on the grass.

Tariq followed Livia and dropped down beside her, capturing her in his arms. "You won't escape me so easily, my Zahareña!" He buried his face in the hollow between her ear and shoulder, nuzzling her slender neck.

"Stop, oh, stop!" Livia shrieked, laughing "Your beard tickles!"

His mouth moved to her lips and he drew her into his lap. As she tried to wriggle from his grasp, his mouth traveled downward in a swift arc to her navel, and she let out a gasp. "Tariq, no!"

As though she had not spoken, he laughed, flung an arm across her thighs, imprisoning her long legs, stilling their churning, and bestowed quick kisses on her lips.

"No, Tariq!" she shrieked again, knowing what his seemingly harmless caresses could lead to.

The next moment, a burst of martial music split the still air. Spilling Livia from his lap, Tariq leaped to his feet and strode through an opening in the hedge to the stone parapet overlooking the *vega*. Quickly, Livia gathered her robe about her and ran to stand at his side. Thunderstruck, they stared at the scene before them.

A magnificent train was issuing from the Christian camp. The advanced guard, composed of legions of heavily armed cavalry, looked like moving masses of polished steel. Livia's breath caught in her throat as her gaze locked on the green and gold pennon of Aguilar flying proudly before him. Then came the king and queen with the prince and princesses and the ladies of the court, surrounded by the royal bodyguard sumptuously arrayed, whom Livia recognized as the sons of the most illustrious houses of Spain. After these rode the rear guard, a powerful force of horse and foot. The glorious pageant moved along in radiant lines across the *vega* to the melodious rhythm of music while banners, plumes, silk scarves and rich brocades gave a gorgeous relief to the grim visage of iron war that lurked beneath.

The army moved toward the hamlet of Zubia built on the skirts of the mountain to the left of Granada, commanding a view of the Alhambra. As they approached the hamlet, Livia felt as though the blood would stop flowing in her veins. Her palms grew moist and her pulse beat in her throat. Aguilar and his comrades-in-arms presented a living barrier between the sovereigns and the city.

"They offer battle!" bellowed Tariq. "They shall see we do not hesitate to accept it!"

Chapter 44

Livia hurried through the garden to join the courtiers who were flocking to the rampart to view the battle that was about to erupt. Halfway there, she stopped short, thinking of the terrible scene of bloodshed she was rushing to see, the killing, maiming, the cries of the wounded and dying. She thought of Aguilar . . . and Tariq. And she knew she could not bear to watch.

Dusk was creeping over the landscape when at last an ominous quiet settled over the palace, signifying that the fighting was done. Livia paced the floor in a frenzy, waiting for Tariq to return. But he did not come. A suffocating dread assailed her. He had not come because he had died. She felt the sweat of panic, fear clutching at her heart. "No!"

Summoning all her courage, against hearing what she did not want to hear, she marched to Ayxa's chamber to learn the outcome of the battle.

The indomitable sultana wore an expression of brooding gravity. For once her pack of cards was set aside and her voice was harsh as she recounted the events of the afternoon.

"The cavalry poured into the *vega*, but strangely, the Christians remained motionless with fixed swords. Though the Spanish were repeatedly challenged, they remained immovable.

"Finally, a Moor rode before Isabella. Tied to the tail of his horse, and dragging through the dust, was a parchment bearing the inscription *Ave Maria*. Naturally, the Christians could not let such an insult pass. Combat ensued between the Moor and a Spanish soldier in which the Moor was killed. Tariq led the charge upon the Spaniards advance guard."

Livia uttered a choked cry. Aguilar was with the advanced guard.

A look of quick impatience crossed Ayxa's face, and her brow furrowed in annoyance as she continued.

"In the midst of the fighting, panic seized our foot soldiers. They took flight. In vain, Tariq tried to rally them. Some took refuge in the mountains, but the greater part fled to Granada in such confusion that they trampled upon each other. The Christians pursued them to the very gates."

"And Tariq?" asked Livia in a voice barely above a whisper.

"Tariq survives. But upwards of two thousand Moors were either injured or taken prisoner. To make matters worse," Ayxa said in obvious disgust, "we've since learned that Queen Isabella and her retinue have approached the city. It's only to gratify her desire to get a better look at our city whose beauty is renowned throughout the world, and they have entertained no thought of inviting battle."

Livia returned to her chamber to wait for Tariq. She braced herself to face him, knowing he would rage against his troops who had thoroughly humiliated him.

The sun disappeared behind the distant mountain peaks and darkness settled over the restless city, but still Tariq did not appear. Restlessly, Livia moved about their apartment, straightening a wall hanging, rearranging the books in the niches, dusting the brass and lusterware. At last she sank down on the sofa and took up her mending, but her mind was in a turmoil. She told herself that Tariq was probably rounding up his men and haranguing them.

As the night wore on, her anxiety rose. Surely he would have done with his men by now. Why had he not come to her? Was his humiliation at the hands of her countrymen so great that he was loath to face her? This she found hard to believe, but if it were true, where would he go? An unpleasant suspicion crossed her mind, and though she tried to put it down, it persisted, nagging at the back of her mind. No one was more loyal to Tariq and his cause than Khadija. He must have gone to her, Livia thought bitterly. And the vision of Tariq seeking solace in Khadija's arms filled Livia with anguish. Suddenly, she felt abandoned. How this accursed infidel had the power to make her feel so wretched, she could not fathom. Disconsolate, she cast her mending aside, turned down the lamps and climbed into bed. She lay tossing and turning, watching the bright moon. Sleep was a long time in coming.

Shortly before dawn, Livia awoke with a start. Tariq was easing under the bedclothes.

"Tariq!" Though she hated herself for sounding like a shrew, she could not stop the words that burst from her lips. "Where in the world have you been?"

"Armilla!" he muttered.

"Armilla! Why, Armilla?"

In a voice hoarse with exhaustion, he mumbled, "Burying our dead. Aguilar was waiting in ambush with fifty men."

The vision of Tariq trying to bury his comrades under attack from his enemies brought a lump to Livia's throat. She frowned and pursed her lips thoughtfully. To attack the buriers of the dead was not the same thing as engaging a foe on the field of battle or attacking the defenders of a fortress. Not the act of the chivalrous knight she had always thought Aguilar to be.

"Go on," Livia urged softly.

"Surrounded them . . . those not cut down were drowned . . . few escaped . . . avenged the disgrace of the morning . . ." his voice faded into a weary sigh.

Livia lay tense. Her relief that Tariq had not spent the night with Khadija or been killed was superceded by another worry. Softly, she asked, "What of Aguilar?"

Tariq, deep in exhausted sleep, snored softly. She dared not press him further. Suddenly, she felt a terrible weariness, as if she were very old. A vision of Aguilar lying dead or dying upon the rocky ground possessed her, and as she watched the rosy light of dawn creep into the room, Livia resolved that if Tariq had killed Aguilar, she would run the blade of his own scimitar into Tariq's heart.

The ravages of war had, so far, spared a small portion of the *vega* of Granada. A green girth of gardens and orchards still flourished round the city along the banks of the Xenil and the Darro. They had been the solace and delight of the inhabitants in their happier days and provided food in this time of scarcity. Shortly, Boabdil was informed by his spies of Ferdinand's intention: to make a final extermination to the very walls of the city so that there should not remain a single living thing for the sustenance of man or beast. The day appointed for this act of desolation was July 8, 1491.

On that morning, the air was oppressive, even in the early morning hour, hot with the scorching promise of a day of glaring blue sky and pitiless bronze sun. Tariq had already bathed, and now perfumed himself, as Moors of high rank were accustomed to do when they prepared to endanger their lives. Livia rose hastily and donned the red, gold and black peacock brocade tunic that Tariq had given her, and got ready to descend to the hall to see him off to battle. Tariq put on his shining chain mail, and in dismal silence they went to join Boabdil and his men in the antechamber of the Tower of Comares. Hajai had brought Rashid to bid his father goodbye and now, as they stood at Tariq's side, a chill fell on Livia's spirit.

Ayxa la Horra, with her usual dignity, blessed Boabdil and gave him her hand to kiss. His son and his daughter clung to him with sobs. Tariq looked solemnly down at Rashid. "I place your mother's care in your hands. Look after her well." Tariq patted his head and turned to Livia. The moment had come. He took Livia's long slender hands in his and raised them to his lips. He looked at her long and desperately, as if he wanted to carry away with him every detail of her face and figure. "Wait for me, my poppy."

Livia managed a semblance of a smile. Thinking he was going out of her life, perhaps forever, she said softly, "Go with God," and was struck with the fact that she truly meant her benediction. Her eyes misted as she watched him mount his charger and lead his squadrons out of the courtyard.

Though Livia had not meant to watch the battle, Nizam grasped her arm, dragging her through the crowd. When she protested, Nizam cast her a reproachful glance.

"But Livia, you must. You owe it to Tariq! What use is there for him to perform bravely if you are not there to see him and lend him your support?"

Livia's head rose, her shoulders went back and, drawing a deep breath to bolster her courage, she moved forward.

All Granada had crowded on towers and battlements to watch the outcome of this fateful day. Livia stood between Nizam and Ayxa, her hands white-knuckled with dread, clutching the sides of the merlon as the battle erupted. Like a terrifying travesty of a colorful pageant accompanied by blare of trumpet and pounding of drum, the action revolved in a dizzying blur.

She could not discern Aguilar's green and gold silk pennon among the forest of standards flowing across the *vega,* and the paralyzing fear that he had perished at Armilla swept through her with the suddenness of a summer storm.

The Christian army approached close to the city and were laying waste the gardens and orchards when Boabdil sallied forth surrounded by all that was left of the flower and chivalry of Granada.

Ayxa said through tight lips, "This is one place where

even the coward becomes brave—that sacred spot called home!"

As Livia watched the carnage before her, she perceived that every inch of ground was violently disputed.

Tariq's cavalry was in every part of the field, and the Moorish soldiers, fainting with heat, fatigue and wounds, were roused to new life at his approach. But the Moors, scattered in various actions, were severely pressed, and once again in the heat of the battle, panic seized them. They retreated, leaving Boabdil dangerously exposed to an overwhelming force. Then, when he was on the point of falling into the hands of the Christians, he galloped away to take refuge within the city walls.

Tariq threw himself before the infantry, shouting at them to fight for their homes, their families, for all that was sacred and dear to them. Totally broken and dismayed, they ignored him. Reluctantly, Tariq retreated toward the city of Granada. As Livia's gaze followed his proud figure astride his great charger, her vision clouded with tears of anger and her heart ached for him.

Livia sat on the divan and tried to compose herself. Uneasily, she wondered how Tariq, who could never accept defeat, would react to the desertion of his men. Where now was the Moors' noble aim to die in the course of a "holy war" and thus gain admission to paradise? After awhile he strode through the doorway, his tunic spattered with blood and dust, his gaunt face set and haggard. Wordlessly, he threw off his suit of chain mail and dropped down onto the sofa.

Moved and shaken by the sight of this fearless warrior brought low through no fault of his own, Livia wished only to comfort him.

"Surely no one has ever fought with more prowess, dexterity and daring than you," she said softly.

His bosom swelled with indignation, his voice was

swift and rough. "Nevermore will I sally forth with foot soldiers to the field!"

Startled, she looked up to meet ebony eyes that were bitter and full of tired futility. She felt a stirring of compassion and reached out to him, her arms going around his waist. "Come, Tariq, let me help you bathe. Then you must rest. Tomorrow you will have a more favorable outlook."

"Do you imagine that a bath and the cajoling of a Castilian wench will change anything? Will soothe a commander who can't control his men?"

Livia only half-heard his harsh words, for her attention was distracted by the feel of something warm and sticky on his thigh. Swiftly, she drew back from him, gazing at her hand splotched with blood.

"Tariq! You've been hurt!"

"One expects to be wounded in battle." His mouth twisted. "A misdirected thrust of a lance. Don't concern yourself. It has stopped bleeding. It is nothing."

Livia rose to her feet. "Nevertheless, it must be tended to, at once."

She ordered steaming kettles of water brought and shortly Tariq took off his garments and stepped into the tub. Ignoring his frowns and dour mien, Livia gently washed him clean then held up a huge linen towel. Impatiently, he snatched it from her hands and briskly rubbed down his bronzed skin.

"Over here." Livia motioned him to the divan. "I will tend your wound."

He looked at her tense face. His own dark face was inscrutable. Something flickered in his eyes, but he said nothing. Then, apparently deciding that she would not be deterred, he stretched out on the couch while she spread an evilsmelling salve over his injury. She fetched a shift from her clothes chest, ripped it into strips and bandaged his thigh with the soft linen. If he noticed the crimson that flooded her neck and cheeks, he gave no sign of it.

"The wound appears clean," she murmured. "Let us hope it has not gone too deep."

"It has not," he assured her testily. "Do not fuss over me, Livia. I wish only to chase the Spaniards from the *vega*."

"It is of no use, Tariq. While you led your men back into the city, King Ferdinand called off his troops and returned to his camp. In any case, King Boabdil will now see that it is the better part of valor to surrender the city."

"Never! We will never surrender the city!"

Livia sat next to him and gazed at Tariq, her eyes earnest and pleading. "Do not let your ardor muddle your thinking. For nearly ten years the war has endured with one disaster after another to the Moors. All your towns have been taken and their citizens slain or led into captivity. And now, when your capital is cut off from all relief and a whole nation is thundering at your gates, you still maintain defense as if you hope for some miracle to save you."

Through clenched teeth, he retorted, "We'll never draw back while we have hands to fight or fortune to befriend us!"

"But you cannot win!" she cried. "Why can't you accept defeat!"

"Enough! Do you think I do not see through your concern for the welfare of Granada? You wish this war to end only to insure the safety of your beloved Aguilar!"

Livia stared at him, speechless. Aguilar, *safe!* Not cut down at Armilla, as she had feared! Her mind no longer tangled with their argument over surrender. She felt only overwhelming relief and gratitude that Aguilar lived. She felt tears pricking her lids and gazed down at her hands. She realized with startling clarity that both Spaniards and Moslems, both of whom claimed to be driven by religious zeal to fight a "holy war," believed in one God; and though one fought under the banner of Christ, and the other under the standard of Allah's prophet Mohammed, both knew God to be on their side. Bitter irony twisted her heart. Oh, God, she thought in fervent silent prayer, if this be so, if you are on the side of Moselm and Christian alike, let the fighting stop. Let there be peace. She looked up into Tariq's face and murmured, "I wish everyone's safety, Tariq. Is that so unreasonable?"

"Not unreasonable," he replied harshly. "Impossible!"

Chapter 45

The Moors now shut themselves up gloomily within their walls and to Livia's intense relief, there were no longer any daring sallies from their gates. The entire palace was sunk in despondency. She herself felt at the mercy of a two-edged sword. Her heart ached for the Moors who faced the loss of their kingdom and for Tariq, whose valor never flagged in the face of defeat; yet she waited in an agony of impatience for the day that Ferdinand's army would storm the fortress and she would be reunited with Aguilar.

At sunset, two days after the disastrous battle of the *vega*, Livia found herself strolling along the battlements with Rashid. She smiled at him as he ran before her, laughing as he captured vagrant fireflies and popped them into a glass bottle. Her gaze wandered beyond the walls where the sun shone splendidly upon the Christian camp. The various tents of the royal family and nobles were adorned with rich hangings, forming a glorious city of silk and brocade. The pavilions of various gay colors, surmounted with waving standards and fluttering pennons, vied with the domes and minarets of the capital city they were besieging. Livia scanned the gaudy city for the sight of Aguilar's gold and green pennon, but did not see it. Perhaps it was hidden behind Isabella's lofty tent which rose in the center like a stately oriental pavilion.

A gusty wind swept down from the mountains that

blew her hair about her face and molded her tunic to her body.

"Come, Rashid. It is time we went inside."

"A moment more, Mama," he pleaded. "I want to catch one more firefly."

Livia grinned at him. "One more, and then we must—" She broke off abruptly, her attention caught by a sudden glare of light and wreaths of smoke rising from the queen's pavilion. In an instant, the entire tent was ablaze. The high wind whipped across the *vega*, whirling the fire from tent to tent. All at once, the whole camp was enveloped in flames. The soldiers' lean-tos of dry branches crackled and blazed, adding to the rapidly burning fires.

Livia was mesmerized with horror and clutched Rashid's hand. The splendid camp was now a scene of wild confusion. The ladies of the court fled, shrieking and half-clad, from their tents. An alarm rent the night, and distraught men half-armed, milled about the camp.

The flames filled the air with sparks, cinders and columns of smoke. It seemed to Livia that the entire sky was lighted with a bright red glare. She saw turbaned heads gazing from every roof, and armor gleamed along the walls, yet not a single warrior sallied from the gates.

"Is this a trick of the Christians, Mama?" asked Rashid looking up at her worriedly.

Livia shook her head. "I think not, *niño*. But the Moors must suspect some strategem, for they are keeping quietly within our walls. Have no fear. They guard us well."

They stood watching in awesome silence until the flames gradually subsided and the city faded from sight and all again became dark and quiet.

Just before dawn the next morning, Livia slipped from her bed, threw her mantle about her shoulders and made her way back to the ramparts. Her heart sank at the devastation. Nothing remained of the stately pavilions but heaps of smoldering rubbish with arms and masses of melted gold and silver glittering among the ashes.

At the sound of a step behind her, she spun about. Tariq strode to her side. The ghost of a wintry smile touched his lips. "It's said that a careless servant in the queen's tent placed a candle too near the hangings."

"It appears that the entire camp is in ruins."

Tariq nodded in agreement. "We hope the catastrophe will discourage them; that as in former years, their invasion will end with the summer and they'll withdraw before the autumn rains."

They stood together, watching the sun rise over the city and, as if to put the lie to Tariq's words, drums and trumpets sounded the call to arms and the Christian army marched forth from among the dark ruins in shining squadrons with flaunting banners and bursts of martial music as though the preceding night had been a time of high festivity instead of terror.

Livia turned to Tariq with an expression of cool contempt. "I have told you before, if you would but heed me, Ferdinand will depart only after you surrender!"

Upon the heels of the fire, an event took place which was meant to dash all hopes of the Moors. So rapidly it seemed like a miracle, a formidable city arose with solid buildings and powerful walls and mighty towers where lately had been nothing but tents and light pavilions. The city was shaped like a cross and named Santa Fé. Every day long trains of mules entered and departed from its gates. The streets were crowded with shops filled with all kinds of costly and luxurious merchandise. It appeared a scene of bustling commerce, while unhappy Granada remained desolate.

The besieged city now began to suffer the distress of famine. Livia herself ate little and gave most of her small portion of barley bread and rice to Rashid, as did the ancient crone who had come to live at the Alhambra. Livia was especially grateful to her, for the woman could little afford to do without.

One bright September afternoon Livia had washed her hair and was drying in the sun at her window when she saw a cavalcade of sheep, and mules laden with provisions, coming out of the mountains to relieve Granada. To her astonishment, as it grew closer, she saw that it had been taken by the Spaniards who now led it in triumph to their camp. Sickened to see the food so desperately needed lost to the enemy, she started to turn away when her attention was caught by the sight of Rashid running across the garden toward the pool.

In one hand he clutched a carved wooden boat and in the other, a small chunk of bread she had given him for his noon meal. Smiling fondly at him, she watched as he knelt and sailed the boat along the mirror surface of the water, at the same time munching on the crust of bread. She let out a nostalgic sigh. He would be nine years old this month, no longer a little boy. To her consternation, he had insisted he was too old to have his amah following him about, and his guard had long since departed to fight the Christians. Now she noticed that someone had followed him into the garden. She stiffened and a stab of dislike swept through her. She could not mistake the sensuous stride, the full-blown figure of Khadija.

The woman glided toward Rashid who was engrossed with his boat, her footsteps silent on the soft grass. She came up behind him and with a lightning movement, leaned over his shoulder and snatched the food from his hand. Her laughter trilled across the garden as she spun away. Livia let out an outraged cry. Rashid ran shrieking from the garden, clutching his boat as if fearing that it would be taken as well.

In the next instant, a thin, dark form swiftly detached itself from behind the high yew hedge. Through some trick of sunlight and shadow, it resembled a vulture whose head glowed pink in the reddish glow of the sun. Arms spread, flapping like wings, the creature swooped down the path in pursuit of Khadija. A hand flashed out from beneath a black mantle. Sunlight glinted on steel and a piercing scream rent the air, ending in a gurgle in Khadija's throat as she crumpled to the ground.

Paralyzed with horror, Livia watched as the vulture bent over its prey. Clawlike fingers curled round the woman's arm, dragged her across the grass in a scuttling, crablike movements, and up the stone steps to the rampart. With a mighty shove, the creature thrust Khadija upward between the merlons. One final push, and the limp body toppled over the edge of the battlement and hurtled to rocky chasm a thousand feet below. Khadija's attacker spun about, scurried down the steps and across the grass to disappear beyond the yew hedge as swiftly and silently as she had come.

Livia could not believe the evidence of her own eyes. It had all happened so fast and was so incredible—like a mirage in the desert, seen and not seen. Khadija here one moment, and in the next moment gone from this life forever. Livia clenched her hands together to still their shaking. There was nothing she could do for Khadija, and *she* was not the one to tell Tariq of her death. She sat there at the window for some time, trying to regain her composure and at length the thought came to her that Boabdil's prophecy had come to pass: her battle had been fought for her by the crone from the maristan.

If Tariq mourned Khadija's passing, he gave no outward sign. His dour expression and taciturn air were not unusual these days. He was cold and indifferent toward Livia, perpetuating the tense truce which lay between them. Gradually, she became aware that deep within her burned a desperate need to know whether or not Tariq grieved for Khadija—a need that lay much deeper than mere curiosity, almost as if her future happiness depended upon knowing—though she assured herself it did not. Then one morning just before Tariq left their chamber, the words she had no intention of speaking burst forth from her lips.

"Tariq, I am sorry for your loss."

He paused in the doorway, his thick, straight brows lifted in question.

Lest he misunderstand and think her hypocritical, she rushed on. "Though I disliked Khadija, I do feel compassion for you in having lost someone dear to your heart."

"Do not waste your sympathy," he said coldly. "The death of my comrades in battle causes me more grief than hers."

"Tariq, you don't need to spare my feelings. I know how much you loved her, how much it hurt you that she married Boabdil."

He came to Livia then and took her slender hands in his. He gazed directly into her eyes and when he spoke his tone was solemn. "It is true that we were betrothed, and that I was angry that she married in my absence. But not for the reason you think. I was taken with her at the time, and, as is our custom, it was incumbent upon me to take a wife." He permitted himself a wry smile. "I needed no woman, but I knew I could no longer indulge myself by prolonging my search for the perfect wife. I had to marry, to take a mate to bear my sons. That the woman I had chosen proved perfidious and had married another when my back was turned was insupportable. As you know, I do not accept defeat. Despite the fact that she was willing to cuckold Boabdil, I was finished with her."

Livia gave a doubtful shake of her head. "She still held sway over you, Tariq. That was all too clear when I saw you together—"

"The times you saw us together were the *only* times we were together, and every meeting was engineered by Khadija."

"But what of her divorce from Boabdil? With my

own ears I heard you lament that one does not ask a prince for a divorce."

His lips turned down in a grimace of a smile. "You forget, the Moor is ever chivalrous. I was but telling her in a subtle manner that there was no hope of a divorce. I did not think it necessary to add that should she succeed, I would never divorce my Zahareña."

Livia drew in her breath sharply. "But what of the nights you spent together at the border?"

Tariq let out a burst of laughter. "Ah, Livia, what an innocent you are. Did you not see that it was only because you had come to our camp that Khadija invaded my tent? She had come before, yes, on one pretext or another, but had never gained admittance. Even if I had wanted to bed her, do you think I'd be foolish enough to do it right under Boabdil's nose?"

Livia felt the color drain from her face. Her wild imaginings had led her astray. He had kept his affair with Khadija a well-kept secret because he had nothing to hide!

Tariq gave a hopeless shake of his head. "Khadija only wanted to upset you. And how well she succeeded!"

Livia's head swam with what he was saying. Custom had required him to take a wife, and because of time and circumstance, he had chosen Khadija. His sense of completeness—of possessing everything within himself—had been his answer to his inability to find a woman he could love. She felt a strange light-headedness, as though she had drunk too much wine.

"Until I met you," Tariq said, "I had always taken great satisfaction in my self-sufficiency, in being impervious to the isolation of our encampments, to the months away on expeditions to drive out the enemy." His impenetrable mask of cold indifference settled upon his features once again. "I will continue to do so."

He wheeled about and strode from the room, leaving Livia pale and shaken.

Autumn arrived, but the harvests had been swept from the face of the country. Now the rigors of winter were appraoching and Granada was almost destitute of provisions. The people were depressed and called to mind all that had been predicted by astrologers at the birth of their ill-starred sovereign, all that had been foretold of the fate of Granada at the time of the capture of Zahara.

Livia drew on all her courage to face the days ahead. The thought sustained her that each day that passed brought them one day nearer to the time when the Christian army would descend upon the city and free the inhabitants from their self-imposed imprisonment within the walls; one day nearer to the time when Aguilar would come to claim her. Meanwhile, she fastened her belt more tightly about her small waist, accepted the scraps of food distributed among the court and gave the larger share to Rashid.

The child worried her, for he was shooting up like a fig tree and needed more food on which to subsist. His dark hair was flat and lifeless, his eyes lackluster, his complexion pallid. He appeared to be fading away before her very eyes. Even now he lay abed, unmoving, brought down by hunger or some malady she would not diagnose. His soft brown eyes followed her every movement, large, round as dinar, a childish bewilderment in them as though her own fears had been communicated to him. At her wits' end, Livia took to boiling rose hips from the bushes in the garden, thinking that the broth might give him extra strength.

One mellow afternoon early in November, in desperation, she was in the garden stripping the last roses of their blossoms when a shadow fell upon her. Startled, she looked up into the malevolent face of Malik. His eyes gleamed ferally and his jaw had the sharpness of a jackal. His cynical half-smile twisted one side of his mouth.

"What frivolous pastimes you engage in, my love, plucking roses while the people starve. Do you hope to grace your table with flowers, though there is no food upon your plate?"

She turned from him and bent to her task. "You mistake me, as always, Malik. It is my intention to make a broth for Rashid. His health wanes, I fear."

"Broth!" Malik let out a burst of laughter. "Broth will not assuage Rashid's hunger."

"It is better than nothing!"

"Nothing, is it?" His voice took on a calculating tone. "Suppose I were to tell you that I know where there is food."

Livia straightened and turned to face him. "Do you know where I can find food, Malik?"

He nodded, studying her appraisingly. "I am provident, you see. I look to the future. I've set aside a small store of smoked fish and dried fruits . . ."

Livia's mouth watered at the very mention of these luxuries they had not enjoyed since so long ago, she could not remember when.

He smiled ingratiatingly, all scorn gone from his face. "They can be had, for a price."

Livia's shoulders sagged. "I've no money, Malik, nor jewels. I've parted with all my possessions long since."

"Not all . . . you've yet to give of yourself."

"You have no food, Malik," she said scathingly. "This is but a cruel ruse to entice me into your room."

Feigning unconcern, Malik shrugged. "Think what you wish. But if you will accompany me to my apartment, I'll show you the provisions: meat, fruit, nuts, I have locked away there."

Livia's tongue slid nervously over her lips. If Malik were lying, she could escape him. If the food were there . . . No! She could not give herself to this heathen even for Rashid. Rashid! A vision of her son lying weak and helpless upon his bed rose to her mind and she compressed her lips in a thin line. She would see how much food Malik had hidden away. If he had enough to help Rashid—well, perhaps she could strike some other bargain with him. A plan began to form in her mind, one she was confident would serve her well. She took a deep breath to bolster her courage.

"Then let us go quickly, Malik."

Chapter 46

Once in Malik's apartment, she stood stiffly in the center of the sitting room and watched him approach a stout oaken chest studded with brass nails. Taking a key from a ring fastened to the belt at his waist, he unlocked the chest and threw back the lid with a flourish.

Livia stepped forward and caught her breath in astonishment. True to his word, Malik had a hoard of meats, fruits and nuts. He picked up several dried figs and handed them to her. Eagerly, she bit into one; then, thinking of Rashid, clenched it in her hand.

Malik laughed and took up a small dried codfish, wrapped in grape leaves. "You see?"

She stared down at the fish as though it were an apparition.

"I will share with you, Livia. Half of all I possess can be yours . . . if you are willing to share with me . . ."

Livia's chin rose and she stared at him with contempt. "I should think you'd be ashamed to blackmail me into submitting to you, Malik, an action hardly becoming the Moors who pride themselves on their chivalry."

"On the contrary." His mouth formed a superior smile. "We are expert bargainers."

Livia forced a smile in return. "I'm glad to hear it. I will strike a bargain with you, Malik. In return for half your store of provisions, I promise to intercede on your behalf when the Christian army descends upon the Alhambra. I will prevail upon Don Alonzo Aguilar, my betrothed and a captain in King Ferdinand's army, to let you go free—" Her words died on her lips as a wide grin spread across his sharp features.

"I do not fear Ferdinand's army," Malik said condescendingly. "Has it not occurred to you to wonder where I got this food? You, of all people, must know there is none to be had in the city."

Livia's eyes widened in amazement as the truth struck her. "You've stolen it!" she exclaimed. "Stolen it from the Christain camp!"

Slowly Malik shook his head. "Not stolen it, my pigeon, it was a gift. A gift from a grateful commander in King Ferdinand's army, for favors rendered."

She drew in her breath sharply. She had made a grave mistake to think she could bargain with Malik! "You are abominable! A traitor to your own king and country!"

"Come now, Livia. I am merely provident, for which you should be most grateful. And now it is time for you to show me how grateful you are." He heaved himself away from the wall against which he had been leaning, grasped her elbow and propelled her toward his bedroom.

She jerked away. "Unhand me, you loathesome creature! I wish nothing to do with you!"

He shrugged and his dark brows rose in surprise. "You wish no food for your dying child?"

Livia stared at him in torment, feeling the color drain from her face. In desperation she threw out her hands beseechingly and cried out, "Give me the food, Malik. You cannot want to take me against my will!"

An evil light came into his eyes. "But you see, I do not take you against your will." He bent down, gathered up a handful of fish, fruit and nuts and thrust them into her arms. "You may take these with you when you depart."

"You said half, Malik," she burst out. "This is far from half."

A cunning smile twisted his lips. "Tomorrow, when

you return, there will be more. Every day there will be more. And when this is gone, I can easily replenish my supply."

Livia lowered her gaze to the life-giving food clutched in her slender hands. She felt suddenly sick and discouraged.

"Come, Livia." He caught her arm and led her toward his bedchamber.

"No! I'll not share your bed!" Choking on the words, she stammered, "The . . . the divan."

Malik smiled, as though savoring his triumph.

Hating herself, Livia let him lead her across the room. She placed the food on a brass tray and sank wearily down on the sofa. A feeling of revulsion, so strong she thought she was going to be ill, swept through her.

Malik dropped down beside her. Lightly, he said, "I think the supply of food I give you shall be in proportion to the enthusiasm you display, my pigeon." With that he unfastened her belt and his hands reached up under her tunic and curved possessively around her firm breasts. She squeezed her eyes shut and clung to the edge of the divan to keep from running away.

His mouth came down on hers, hard and bruising, forcing her head back against the cushions. She felt as though she were drowning in a bottomless well from which she would never rise, never again see the light of day. A loathing such as she had never felt in her entire life overwhelmed her, and suddenly her arms and legs were flailing the air desperately, striking out at Malik. She jerked her head free from his hot moist lips and screamed with every bit of strength she could muster. Malik swore viciously and drew back, looming over her, his face murderous with rage. His eyes were wild, his teeth bared in fury. Livia's hysterical screams echoed in her ears.

His arm arched through the air, striking her so violently on the side of the head that she was sent sprawling to the floor. In a moment he was upon her, ripping her tunic from her shoulders. Livia beat at his head with her fists and then, above her wild screaming, she heard a bellow of rage like that of a wounded bull issue from deep in Malik's throat. Abruptly, she felt the weight of his body lift from her own.

Strong arms slid under her knees and back, lifting her up, holding her close, and a deep gentle voice called her name. She stopped screaming and forced herself to open her eyes. She gazed into Tariq's face, full of anger and concern. Numbly, she glanced down at the floor. Malik lay still. The hilt of Tariq's dagger protruded from his back and a dark red stain spread upon the colorful carpet. Livia envisioned another day, another time when she had watched a red stain spread over a carpet—when Julian had tried to kill Tariq—but then it was wine. Now it was not. She buried her face in Tariq's shoulder. Sobs shook her and her voice quavered. "He promised me food for Rashid, but I could not . . . could not . . ."

"Malik will trouble you no more, my Zahareña," said Tariq in a rasping voice. "Moslem justice is swift and sure. He has forfeited his life, and his provisions as well."

With rapid strides he carried her to their chambers and placed her gently upon the divan. "Tariq," she murmured, "I do not know what possessed me. I . . . I'm sorry, I . . ."

He took her hands in his and gazed deeply into her eyes. "Calm yourself. The past is done. We must look to the future. I will take care of you, always."

One cold gray morning early in December, Boabdil, alarmed by the gathering dangers from without, and by the clamors of his starving people, summoned his council to assemble in the great hall. When Tariq returned from the meeting, despair shone from his eyes.

"Boabdil demanded of us what was to be done," he told Livia in a tight voice, "and their answer was: 'Surrender!'"

Her heart lurched violently and she held her breath, waiting for him to go on.

He sat down, crossed his long legs and rubbed a finger across his beard. In a dry voice he said, "Our granaries are nearly exhausted, and no further supplies are to be expected. The grain for the war-horses is required as sustenance for the soldiers; the very horses themselves are killed for food. Of seven thousand animals which once could be sent into the field, only three hundred remain. Our city contains two hundred thousand inhabitants, each with a mouth that calls piteously for bread.

"The leading citizens declared that the people can no longer endure the defense of the city."

"And what had Boabdil to say?"

Tariq gave a hopeless shake of his head. "He kept a gloomy silence. He had cherished some faint hope of relief from the soldan of Egypt or the Barbary powers, but it is now at an end. Even if such assistance were to be sent, we no longer have a seaport to use. The counselors, seeing that the resolution of the king was shaken, united in urging him to capitulate!"

Tariq's voice rose in anger against the council and his dark eyes blazed with the zeal of his convictions. "I alone spoke in opposition. I told them it is too early to talk of surrender. Our means are not exhausted. We have yet one source of strength remaining, terrible in its effects, which often has achieved the greatest victories: our despair. I exhorted them to rouse the mass of the people, to put weapons in their hands and urge them to fight the enemy to the very utmost, until we rush upon the points of their lances!"

Livia stared at him bleakly, shaking her head.

Ignoring her silent disagreement, he said furiously, "I am ready to lead the way into the thickest of their

squadrons. I would much rather be numbered among
those who fell in the defense of Granada than of those
who survived to capitulate!"

A stab of fear went through Livia, for she knew how
persuasive Tariq could be. "And did the council heed
your words?"

Tariq shook his head. "No! My words were without
effect, for they were addressed to broken-spirited and
rabbit-hearted men!"

Livia said gently, "Older and wiser, perhaps. As you
once told me, one must learn to bridle his passions in
the game of kings. Courage and bravery are all very
well, but they do not withstand starvation."

"You are as blind as Boabdil!"

For a long moment she regarded him with a steady
gaze. She would not quarrel with him over something
that could not be changed, but must be endured. At last
she said quietly, "And did your protests sway Boabdil?"

"Boabdil yielded to the general voice." Tariq
slammed his fist into his hand in frustration. "They will
capitulate to the Christian sovereigns."

Capitulate! The word rang in her ears like a bell
tolling victory. Her heart soared and it took all the will
power she could summon not to leap up from her seat
and shout for joy. Then, just as quickly, her elation
faded, replaced by an aching sadness. What would it do
to her proud, unconquerable Tariq to be taken by the
Spaniards?

Ferdinand and Isabella granted a truce of sixty days
during which time they formulated the terms of surrender that had to be ratified by the Moorish king.

Boabdil immediately assembled his council in the
Hall of the Ambassadors. Eager to hear what transpired, Livia hastened to the doorway of the great hall
and mingled with the courtiers who crowded the
doorway.

With a dejected countenance, Boabdil laid before his
council the articles of capitulation. A heavy silence fell.
Livia held her breath.

Now that the dreaded moment had arrived when
they were to blot themselves out as a nation, all control
deserted them and many burst into tears. Tariq alone
remained impervious, his features unyielding, as
though chiseled in stone.

He leaped to his feet. "Leave this idle lamentation to
helpless women and children!" he shouted. "We are
men! We have hearts not to shed tender tears, but
drops of blood. I see the spirit of the people so cast
down that it is impossible to save the kingdom. Yet
there still remains an alternative! A glorious death! Let
us die defending our liberty. Our mother earth will
receive her children into her bosom safe from the
chains of oppression. Allah forbid it should be said the
nobles of Granada feared to die in her defense!"

Tariq ceased to speak, and a dead silence reigned in
the assembly. Livia rose on tiptoe, straining to see over
the heads of the throng. Boabdil fingered his prayer
beads and looked anxiously around the hall, scanning every face. All bore the anxiety of careworn
men who had grown callous to Tariq's impassioned
appeals.

"Allah Akbar!" Boabdil exclaimed. "There is no
God but God, and Mohammed is his Prophet! We no
longer have the strength to resist our powerful enemy.
It is in vain to struggle against the will of heaven. It was
written in the book of fate that I should be unfortunate
and the kingdom expire under my rule."

"Allah Akbar!" echoed the viziers and *alfaquis*.
"The will of God be done!" An excited clamor of voices
rose in the hall. All agreed that these evils were
preordained; that it was hopelese to contend with
them; and that the terms offered by the Castilian
monarchs were as favorable as could be expected.

Once again Tariq rose in violent indignation, his face
dark, his eyes flashing fire. "Do not deceive your-

selves," he shouted, raising his clenched fists to heaven, "nor think the Spaniards will be faithful to their promise, or their king as magnanimous in conquest as he has been victorious in war. Death is the least we have to fear. It is the plundering of our city, the profanation of our mosques, the ruin of our homes, the violation of our wives and daughters, bigoted intolerance, the dungeon, the fagot and the stake—such are the miseries and indignities we shall see and suffer. At least those groveling souls will see and suffer them who now shrink from an honorable death. For my part, by Allah, I will never witness them!"

Shaking with fury, Tariq strode from the council chamber. The courtiers, awed by his terrible rage, fell back as he swept through the doorway and stamped down the marbled halls.

Livia's first thought was to run after him, but she quickly curbed the impulse. In his present mood, she knew she would only inflame him further. She forced herself to turn back to the doorway and watched, her heart hammering against her ribs, while the capitulation for the surrender of Granada was signed.

When it was done, she hurried back to their apartment, anxious to offer Tariq whatever solace she could. Upon entering their chambers, she halted in midstride. Tariq's scimitar and dagger were gone from their place on the wall, as were his cuirass and lance. She dashed outside to the stables where she found Tariq's stocky young attendant. At her approach, he turned away, as if to evade her, but she caught at his sleeve.

"Where is Tariq Ibn Ziyah?" Livia demanded. "Tell me at once!"

The youth regarded her with a sorrowful expression. "He has armed himself, mounted his favorite war-horse and left. I don't know where he has gone, nor if he will return."

Livia studied the man's solemn face for a long moment. Deciding he spoke the truth, she walked slowly back to her room. A feeling of sorrow and loss such as she had never known surged through her. Sternly she reminded herself that this was what she had prayed for. It was done, over. Her bondage to Tariq was ended at last. Still, she could not shake off the desolation that filled her heart.

Chapter 47

The signing of the capitulation on November 25 produced a sudden cessation of those hostilities which had raged for so many years. To Livia's dismay, she saw Christian and Moor mingling courteously on the banks of the Xenil and Darro, where to have met a few days previously would have produced a scene of bloody contest.

Ferdinand, fearing the Moors might be suddenly roused to defense if within the alloted term of sixty days, succor should arrive from abroad, and certain that the Moors were at all times a rash inflammable people, maintained a vigilant watch upon Granada and permitted no supplies of any kind to enter.

December had nearly passed away and Tariq had not returned. To Livia, it seemed as though he had died unexpectedly, leaving her bereft. She moved through the beautiful, deadened halls of the Alhambra as one in a nightmare. Her only solace was Rashid, whose health was improving thanks to the food Tariq had given her following Malik's death. On the day of Tariq's departure, Rashid had gazed up at her with enormous trusting eyes and asked, "Where is my father?"

Over the quick, stabbing pain in her heart, she said quietly, "He has gone away to fight the great holy war which rages within him."

"When will he come back?"

Livia suppressed a sigh and said only, "I know not,

niño.'' She had not been willing to admit to herself—
much less to Rashid—that she feared his father had
gone forever.

Nizam went about with a long face and abstracted
air, mourning the absence of Raduan, and relied on
Livia to keep up her spirits. Nor was Ayxa of any
comfort. Since the surrender, there was no longer any
softness in the face of this strange powerful woman—
rather, a barely veiled hostility. Or did Livia imagine
that? No matter. She would survive and she would
forget.

The famine became severe, and all in the palace
knew there was no hope of rescue. Boabdil saw that to
hold out to the end of the allotted time would be but to
prolong the miseries of his people. With the consent of
his council, he decided to surrender the city on January
2. Immediately, Livia asked Boabdil's permission to
remain in the Alhambra to await the occupation of the
Christians. To her dismay, he would not hear of it.
"You are the wife of a Moor, and you will depart with
the Moorish court!" he declared.

Though Livia maintained an outward semblance of
calm, now that the time had come to leave, she felt a
pang of regret. Never in her lifetime had she thought to
live in such splendid surroundings. It was not only the
beauty of the palace itself she would miss, but her life
there; for along with the saddest of days here Livia had
also spent her happiest.

On the night preceding the surrender, Livia packed
her belongings, shutting her ears against the doleful
lamentations that echoed throughout the halls of the
Alhambra. The entire household of Boabdil was preparing to take a last farewell of their home. All the
royal treasures and precious belongings were hastily
packed upon mules; the beautiful apartments were
stripped.

In the ghostly predawn light, Livia, with Rashid
seated before her on her mount, rode with the mournful cavalcade through a postern gate of the Alhambra

and departed through one of the most secluded quarters of the city still buried in sleep. If for nothing else, she was thankful that Boabdil had sent them off privately that they might not be exposed to the "eyes of scoffers, or the exultation of the enemy." Beside her rode Nizam, dry-eyed and remote, lost in her own thoughts. Ayxa rode before Livia in silence with a dejected yet dignified demeanor, but Morayma and all the women in Boabdil's household cried profusely as they looked back at the forest of gloomy towers behind them. They were attended by the ancient servants of the household and by a small guard of veteran Moors loyally attached to the fallen monarch who would give their lives in defense of his family.

They proceeded along the banks of the Xenil until they arrived at a hamlet at some distance from the city and there halted to wait to be joined by King Boabdil.

It occurred to Livia now that although Tariq had decried surrender, he had perhaps through some sense of fidelity to his monarch, returned to escort him from the city. Preoccupied with her thoughts, she was staring absently at the golden-pink beams lighting the snowy summits of the Sierra Nevada when three guns boomed heavily from the fortress of the Alhambra. Rashid started in alarm.

"It is the signal that all is ready for the surrender," Ayxa said sourly. "King Ferdinand and Queen Isabella will wait at Armilla until the Grand Cardinal and the soldiery meet with my son on the Hill of Martyrs. Ferdinand will descend to the *vega* where he will meet Boabdil to receive the keys to the kingdom. Then the Grand Cardinal and his cavaliers will enter the Alhambra to take possession."

As they watched, a silver cross slowly rose to the top of the Torre de la Vela, or great watch tower, sparkling in the sunshine. Beside it was planted the pennon of the apostle of Saint James, and a great shout of "Santiago! Santiago!" rose throughout the army raising gooseflesh on Livia's skin. Lastly the royal standard was raised

amid shouts of "Castile! Castile! For King Ferdinand
and Queen Isabella!" The words were echoed by the
entire army in a great roar that resounded across the
plain. Livia thrilled to the sound of their cheers,
imagining that she heard Aguilar's voice among them.

At length the deposed king trotted into view on his
white steed, his shoulders slumped in defeat, at the
head of his slender retinue. Eagerly, Livia scanned the
forlorn faces of his followers but Tariq was not among
them. Resolutely, she put him out of her mind.

After they had ridden almost two leagues, the
cavalcade winding into the skirts of the Alpuxarras,
ascended a high hill which commanded the last view
of Granada. At its summit, the Moors drew rein and
turned to take a farewell look at their beloved city
which in a few strides would be shut from their sight
forever. It seemed to Livia that the sun shone with an
unnatural brilliance, lighting up each tower and minaret while the pedestal of the *vega* spread below
glistened with the silver windings of the Xenil. It tore
into her heart to see the Moorish cavaliers gazing in
silent agony upon the magnificent palace, the scene of
their loves and pleasures. Her own eyes misted and she
brushed away tears with the back of her hand.

A light cloud of smoke burst from the citadel,
followed by a peal of artillery. Ayxa said in a voice of
doom, "The Christians have taken possession of the
city, and the throne of the Moslem kings is lost
forever!"

In grief-stricken tones, Boabdil cried out, "Allah
Akbar! God is great!" Abruptly the words of resignation died upon his lips and he burst into tears.

Livia's gaze swung quickly to Ayxa. Her eyes
watched Boabdil coldly. She looked proud, indestructi-
ble and a little cruel. She said sharply, "You do well to
weep like a woman for what you failed to defend like a
man!" She wheeled about and spurred her horse
forward.

The unhappy monarch's tears continued to flow.

"Allah Akbar!" he exclaimed. "When did such misfortunes ever equal mine?"

Rashid leaned back and whispered in Livia's ear, "What ails King Boabdil, Mama?"

"Nothing, *niño. El ultimo suspiro del Moro*—it is the last sigh of the Moor."

Chapter 48

With each swift stride of her mount Livia grew more distraught. How would Aguilar know she had fled with the king's retinue? And if he discovered she had gone, how would he find her, buried here in the Valley of Purchena? A bitter smile curved her lips. How ironic that now, when Aguilar had at last ridden victorious through the gates of the Alhambra, she should have departed its halls. The fates are conspiring against me, as they have against Boabdil, she thought ruefully. But she was not Boabdil and did not want for decision.

Livia squared her shoulders and sat more erect in the saddle, her mouth set resolutely. She could not remain idle day after day, hoping that Aguilar would find her. There was but one thing to do. She must go to him. Her smooth brow puckered. She could not risk losing herself and Rashid in the fastness of the Alpuxarras Mountains. She must find some travelers bent upon a journey to Granada and arrange for herself and Rashid to accompany them.

Livia, Rashid, Hajai and Nizam were lodged in one of the small whitewashed cottages that lined the dirt road through the village. Livia settled in, then waited impatiently for an entourage to pass through the town. But it soon became apparent that no merchants or travelers were making their way toward Granada.

Ayxa had somehow retained her scouts and spies, however, and word was brought to the exiled court that on January 6, the Day of Kings and Feast of the Epiphany, Ferdinand and Isabella would make their triumphal entry into Granada. Livia's eyes shone and her heart pounded with anticipation. Aguilar would ride into the city. She must be there to greet him.

That evening when she told Nizam of her plan, Nizam cried out in dismay. "No, Livia! I cannot let you go! You court danger. If you are not taken on the road, you will be taken in the city."

Livia waved an airy hand as if to brush all her protests aside. "Did I not ride to Malaga? Don't worry. I can manage."

Nizam's usually soft voice took on a cutting edge. "You are my brother's wife!"

"Wife!" scoffed Livia. "Your brother has deserted me."

Nizam shook her head and let out a long, hopeless sigh. "I grant you are right. But if you've no regard for your own safety, think of Rashid. Leave him here with me. When Granada is settled and we are certain the Moors will offer no further resistance will be time enough for you to take Rashid. Until then, I will care for him."

Livia gazed at her for a long moment, weighing her words. Though she was loath to leave Rashid, the wisdom of Nizam's suggestion could not be denied. She let out a long, reluctant sigh. "So be it."

The following morning Livia stole out to the stables, took a horse and spurred him through the sleeping village, north toward Granada. She leaned forward on the horse's neck, her hair streaming out behind her as she rode at a relentless pace through rocky heights that rose to the clouds, through pleasant valleys past plantations of mulberry trees and groves of orange, figs and pomegranate, and past hillsides covered with withered vineyards. She paused only to water her mount and eat the food she had packed in her saddlebag.

It was shortly before noon when she heard the music and shouts accompanying the grand military parade. She gained the gate of the city and drew rein. Breathless, her eyes shining with excitement, she awaited the approach of the Spanish sovereigns. It was hard to believe that the day she had so longed for had arrived.

A splendid escort of cavaliers in burnished armor appeared first. Then followed Prince Juan, glittering with jewels and diamonds. Flanking him were the Grand Cardinal clothed in purple, the bishop of Airla, and the archbishop elect of Granada. They were followed by Queen Isabella, her eyes downcast with an air of humility, and the king astride a proud and mettlesome stallion.

Then came the army in shining columns, the hardy warriors in tossing plumes and shining steel with flaunting banners. The streets resounded with the tramp of hooves and the inspiring clamor of military music.

Livia's hands grew moist as she leaned forward on her mount to scan the ranks of plumed knights for Aguilar. At length she saw him, and a thrill tingled down her spine. Aguilar, chin lifted, eyes straight ahead, a stern expression on his face, riding proudly at the head of his troops. If he had seen her among the cheering crowd of spectators, he gave no sign.

She saw not one Moor. They had obviously buried themselves in their dwellings, mourning the fallen glory of their race, Livia thought with a pang of remorse.

The royal procession advanced to the Great Mosque which had immediately been consecrated as a cathedral. Livia tethered her horse and went inside to listen as the sovereigns offered prayers. The choir of the royal chapel then chanted the *Te Deum Laudamus*, in which they were joined by all the courtiers and cavaliers so that the anthem resounded within the walls.

Livia's heart beat rapidly and her face was flushed with joy as her gaze fastened upon Aguilar. The moment the service was ended, she tried to thread her way through the throng toward him. But the crush of spectators who streamed from the cathedral pressed around her, blocking her way, and before she could approach him, the court of Isabella and Ferdinand had left the square and ascended to the Alhambra.

Once again Livia mounted and urged the animal into a brisk trot up the hill and across the Square of the Cisterns. She dismounted and entered the Court of Myrtles. In a moment we'll be together, she thought, in a rapture of wonder and delight, hurrying onward.

The halls so lately occupied by turbaned Moslems now rustled with stately dames clad in velvet fur-lined cloaks over their wide silk skirts, and men in short cloaks and bright-colored doublets and hose, who wandered about with eager curiosity admiring the patios and gushing fountains, the halls decorated with elegant arabesques and inscriptions, and the splendor of its gilded and brilliantly painted ceilings. To Livia these people appeared out of place; and a sudden resentment flared within her at their intrusion.

She allowed herself to be swept along with the crowd to the Hall of the Ambassadors, where the Spanish sovereigns had placed their thrones. Here the prinicpal inhabitants of Granada stepped forward to pay them homage and kiss their hands in token of vassalage; they were followed by deputies from all the towns and fortresses of the Alpuxarras which had not previously submitted.

Despairing of ever being able to join Aguilar, Livia cornered a scrawny young page and prevailed upon him to carry a message to her captain.

"Aguilar will reward you well for bringing him word of me," she promised. "Tell him I will await him in the garden of the rose laurel in the Generalife—the garden of the king's summer palace on the hillside which overlooks the Alhambra."

In a fever of excitement and happiness, Livia rushed from the palace, mounted her steed and spurred him along the road past fig trees now bereft of their shining leaves, and clumps of aloe sprouting fans of azure blades, across the ravine of Los Molinos, and trotted swiftly up the narrow track leading to the Generalife.

At the deserted guardhouse, she tethered her horse then walked swiftly up the curving lane between the rows of tall pointed cypresses. Though the trees were still a somber mass of velvety green, the lilies and roses that had flowered at their feet when she and Tariq had strolled these paths last summer had faded and died under the chill of winter. There flashed into her mind the memory of long, pleasant afternoons she had spent here with Tariq, the warm comfort of his encircling arms, her head resting on his shoulder. A pang of nostalgia assailed her. She let out a sigh and resolutely banished those memories from her mind, but in her heart she knew they were past forgetting.

She caught a glimpse of the lower gardens now devoid of their glowing color, and beyond them, the square towers of the Alhambra and the barren stubble of the *vega*. She hurried on.

Instead of the sense of well-being she had felt when she was here with Tariq, melancholy settled upon her dispelling the joy she had felt earlier. She made her way swiftly toward the high windowless walls, past the slender pillars, under the fragile tracery of the galleried portico and through the halls of the miniature palace to the mirador, whose arched portal gave onto the garden of the rose laurel.

In the center of the pond, the enormous laurel which had bloomed like a vast bouquet of delicate pink flowers when she had sat here in those golden, long-ago days with Tariq, was now bare of blossoms, its shiny leaves dulled. The fountain that sprayed it with jets of water now stilled. Fallen leaves floated on the surface of the dark water in the pond beneath.

Livia sat stiff-backed and tense upon a stone bench to wait for Aguilar. Naturally, it would take him some time to disengage himself from the celebration. A chill had begun to settle upon her, despite the warmth of the afternoon sunlight. She shivered and drew her cloak more tightly about her. Soon he would be here, she thought, trembling.

She had no idea how long she had been sitting there when she heard footsteps along the stone floor of the palace behind her. She leaped up and whirled about. Aguilar, resplendent in black velvet cloak and doublet and scarlet hose, strode through the portal, his dark eyes sparkling with happiness. With a cry of joy, Livia flung herself into his arms. His arms closed about her like bands of steel and his mouth upon hers was insistent. "Livia, *querida*," he murmured. "To have you back again, to be my own wife, before God and man, *amada mia!*"

Her heart fluttered and her face was alight with happiness. "Aguilar," she whispered. *"Amado mio!"*

After the first feverish joy of their reunion, he drew back and held her at arms length, his eyes devouring her. Livia's searching gaze met his and a small stab of shock went through her. His features were set, his face lined, as though he had become calloused by the years of battle. The vivacious spirit which had so attracted her was gone. Suddenly he seemed a stranger, like a creature from another world caught up in concerns in which she had no part; remote, detached from their past. She dismissed the thought as being foolish. Aguilar was here, adoration glowing in his eyes. The years had come between them, but soon they would bridge that span, and once again enjoy the love they had known so long ago.

He took her hand in his and drew Livia down beside him on the bench. "Come, we must speak of our future. First of all, where is the child?"

"Rashid is staying at Purchena with—" She stopped short. She had started to say, "with my husband's sister." Instead, she said, "With Nizam." She must stop thinking of Tariq Ibn Ziyah as her husband!

Aguilar nodded, and a smile of satisfaction spread over his features. He lifted one hand and kissed it, and

taking the other, laid it against his cheek for a moment.
"That is well. I did not look forward to having to
contend with the offspring of a Moor."

Livia's eyes widened in astonishment. "But Aguilar,
I had thought to take Rashid with us when we return to
Cordoba."

Aguilar's brows drew together. "I may not return to
Cordoba for some time. Ferdinand wants me to remain
here until we are certain that every Moor is subjugated
to his reign. So you see, it would not be wise to nurture
one of them in our bosom."

Aware of a growing sense of unease, she said, "By
the time Rashid has grown, we will surely be back in
Cordoba. Besides, he will be brought up a Spaniard."

Aguilar smiled condescendingly. "Once a Moor,
always a Moor. It is in the blood. And the bastard of a
commander in the Moorish army could well grow up
with the idea of reclaiming his dominions for the
Moors."

At the word *bastard*, a quick surge of anger swept
through Livia, which she quickly suppressed. She had
hoped that once the war was over, life would resume its
old face. She had hoped that Aguilar's return to her
would bring back some meaning into life. Now both
hopes were fading. She forced a light laugh. "Rashid is
only nine years old, Aguilar. I think you borrow
trouble."

Aguilar frowned and looked down, turning her palm
over in his hands. "What of the child's father? Has he
obtained a divorce?"

Mutely Livia shook her head. It would avail her
nothing to explain that Tariq would never have divorced her. "His paramour was . . . killed. And Tariq
has gone—departed the city in a monstrous rage on the
day Boabdil and his council agreed to the surrender. No
one has seen him since. I doubt he will ever come
back."

"In that you are wrong!" roared a voice from the
doorway. "I have returned to escort my king to his

residence in the Valley of Purchena—too late. And, to claim my wife . . . which I do at once!"

Livia and Aguilar spun about. The formidable, white-turbaned figure of Tariq filled the doorway, his black eyes smoldering with fury, one hand grasping the hilt of his scimitar.

Aguilar leaped to his feet and drew his sword from its sheath. Livia felt as though she were turning to stone as a cold sinking fear gripped her. How long Tariq had been standing there, she had no way of knowing. He strode toward Livia, his face thunderous, his footsteps ringing on the stone path like a death knell. He caught her arm in an iron grip and jerked her to her feet. His words lashed out at her like the crack of a whip.

"Why are you here?" Without waiting for her reply, he bellowed, "I have just ridden from Purchena, where I was told you had been taken for safekeeping, only to find you had flown. Fortunately, Nizam knew where you'd gone. All afternoon I have scoured Granada for you, frantic for your safety, only to find you here consorting with the enemy!"

Thunderstruck, Livia opened her mouth to speak, but no sound came out.

Aguilar caught her elbow and jerked her free of Tariq's grasp. "Your concern is of no importance, infidel. This woman is promised to me. I have taken the city, and now I claim my betrothed. You took her against her will. It is I whom she loves—has always loved!"

"Livia is mine!" Tariq thundered, drawing his scimitar.

"You must accept the inevitable," Aguilar said coldly. "Call it the will of Allah. Livia loves me and has always loved me. Submit to your destiny!"

"It is destiny that brought us together!" rasped Tariq, his face livid.

"You Arabs pride yourselves on your chivalry," Aguilar taunted. "Prove it. Release Livia from her vows. I know that your religion sanctions divorce."

"But your religion does not," Tariq countered smoothly.

Aguilar's lips curved in a superior smile. "Nor does our religion recognize marriage to an infidel! Until now, I have paid you the courtesy of recognizing this marriage. Now I—"

"I did not come here to parley," Tariq interrupted. "Nor do I accept defeat. Livia is mine!" With a lightning motion, he lunged forward and his scimitar flashed upward, the sun glinting on the shining Damascus blade.

Livia screamed, and flinging herself between them, clung to Aguilar's shoulders and buried her head on his chest. Only Tariq's swift reflexes deflected his aim in time.

Aguilar's arms closed protectively around Livia. She could feel his clenched fist braced against the small of her back as he gripped his sword pointed menacingly at Tariq. Her head whipped up. "Aguilar, please!"

As though she had not spoken, he glared at Tariq. "Then let her choose between us."

Tariq erupted in a burst of fury. "There is no choosing to be done! To me, Livia is more precious than any treasure here on earth, or in the heavens above!"

Startled, Livia whirled in Aguilar's arms to stare at Tariq, her eyes wide with wonder. Suddenly, her body seemed to collapse. His dark, piercing gaze locked with hers.

"Livia is my wife, and mine she shall remain until our lives on earth shall end."

Aguilar's face reddened. His arms dropped to his sides. He executed a mock bow and stepped back several paces so that Livia stood alone between the two men who claimed her.

Aguilar's gaze met hers. His lips curved in a semblance of a smile. In a low voice he asked, "What have you to say to that, my love?"

Livia stood in the sunlit garden as though transfixed.

glancing first at Aguilar, then at Tariq. Aguilar, whom she had known since childhood, who had always been a part of her life and the world she had known. Tariq, who had invaded her home, her heart, her body, who had taken her against her will and held her captive in an alien land.

She walked slowly toward Aguilar, smiling tenderly. In a soft voice she said, "I have long cherished a dream of you, Aguilar." She paused, choosing her words carefully. "But now reality has replaced the dream." Again she paused, unable to speak her thoughts. All the feelings that had lain dormant deep within her for longer than she was aware, now crystallized in her mind.

How could she tell him that he was too much the noble knight, too much the gentleman; that she loved—needed—this strong-willed, fierce-eyed Berber of violent moods and passions; that he and he alone could bring her to life? At length she found the words to go on.

"I am bound to Tariq by ties that cannot be broken, though time and distance should part us forever." She held out her hands, beseeching him to understand. "Through the years, Tariq has taught me the nature of love. I no longer doubt his love for me, nor my love for him. I am sorry, Aguilar."

She turned to face Tariq. With a proud lift of her chin, her face radiant, she said, "My future lies with Tariq."

Tariq strode toward her, his expression solemn, but the love shining from the depths of his dark eyes told her all she wanted to know. Smiling up into his face, she stepped within the circle of his arms. "It is the will of Allah."

About the Author

A Pennsylvanian by birth, *Dee Stuart* was reared in Virginia. The early years of her marriage brought Mrs. Stuart back to Philadelphia where her daughter and son were born. Later, her husband's job caused the Stuarts to move to Kansas City, which they truly enjoyed.

Dee Stuart has served as both a social worker and as a teacher. After her children entered school she began to write on a freelance basis. Her articles and short stories have appeared in numerous national magazines. This led to teaching creative writing.

Five years ago, believing she should challenge herself further, Mrs. Stuart plunged into writing novels. Several have been published, including the historical romance *Freedom's Flame*, and a contemporary romance, *Golden Interlude*.

Leisure time pursuits are bridge, scuba diving, all types of music and travel. Trips have been throughout the United States, Europe, Mexico and the Virgin Islands. Now transplanted to Dallas, Dee Stuart and her husband have become converted Texans.

Romance & Adventure

New and exciting romantic fiction—passionate and strong-willed characters with deep feelings making crucial decisions in every situation imaginable—each more thrilling than the last.

Read these dramatic and colorful novels—from Pocket Books/Richard Gallen Publications